ENTREPRENEUR

GEORGE ONSTOT

ENTREPRENEUR

ISBN-13: 978-0-9881571-3-2
ISBN-10: 09881571-3-6

PART ONE

Chapter 1

San Francisco, 1975

Coach Kainer blew his whistle halfway through basketball practice and called it a done deal because the vice-principal had come for Phil Parrish. While Phil went in to get changed, the vice-principal spoke to Kainer. Minutes later, Phil left with the vice-principal, and Kainer explained to the team that Phil's older brother, Jordan, had just been confirmed as killed in Vietnam. Phil had been sent home to be with his family, and Kainer, seeing that the other boys were now too distracted to continue practicing, told them to take off early. Elsewhere on campus, the track, football and baseball guys kept on doing their things. Parrish's loss was not their problem.

Paul Steeves, the team's six-foot point guard, went into the bathroom and took a shower he scarcely needed. He seldom showered at home because there were too many people and only one bathroom. Western Hills High School, built just after World War Two, was a relic from when America ruled the world and San Francisco was flush with cash. The school was big, with roomy showers, many toilets, unlimited hot water, an Olympic-sized swimming pool, a tennis court and gymnasium. But it was getting old and needed renovations, and who knew where they would get the money for that?

Paul said that if the Parrishes had a memorial service, as they surely would, the team should send a flower arrangement; something dignified, nothing pink and faggy. They wanted to impress the dead man's family with their style and class. Decent flowers would cost money, and Paul had often observed that the boys with the bucks were always the stingiest. They got their clothes at Union Square shops and had walking-around money. Paul's clothes came from Eddie's Discount Store and a hippie joint called the Gap.

He put on his button-down shirt and Levi's, then sauntered alone through the school's main entrance doors, not wanting to walk with any of his teammates today. They were still asking, "Why were we in Vietnam, anyway?" and Paul was damned if *he* knew. He really wasn't surprised that Jordan had died out there in the jungle, like the 57,000 others who had been killed by Viet Cong or friendly fire. Paul had scarcely known Jordan Parrish, and didn't especially like Phil, who lived for basketball, surfing, girls and drugs. Paul believed there was more to life than getting high and feeling up cheerleaders. He wanted to get out of school and on with life. To him, school was merely preparation for life, and sometimes not even that. His friends believed that Paul Steeves already had everything figured out.

Occasionally, so did he.

Paul looked up into the sky and smiled. Only a few scudding clouds drifted across the horizon. Whoever said San Francisco was all fog and no sunshine? He headed north, his knapsack slung over his shoulder, a light breeze caressing his face. Climbing a hill, he took a left turn, then a right. He liked to walk home in good weather. The news media kept gushing over chic and sophisticated San Francisco, everyone's friendliest city. Paul thought the travel writers should come to Western Hills and check out the wrought-iron gates that protected you from your friendly neighbors.

At the summit of the modest hill where Tower Street intersected with Diego Avenue, Paul did a slow 360-degree turn and surveyed his turf. People moved here from all over the world, and Paul thought those alienated folks were in for a big disappointment when they discovered how closed and snobbish the city could be, with its astronomical prices and wrought-iron paranoia.

Sometimes, he wished that he could have gone to Vietnam and experienced the excitement of wearing a uniform, flying off to war, maybe even guarding the coastline from a helicopter. War was a guy thing, the adventure many males craved throughout their lives, the thing that made you a man.

His parents, preoccupied with the war from its beginning in 1966, watched TV as Johnson, Nixon, Rusk and McNamara promised an end to the nightmare by 1968, then 1970, then 1972. The end had just come, with the chaotic evacuation of Saigon, in May. Paul Steeves hadn't gone anywhere near Vietnam. He had stayed home, everyone's good boy.

He lived on Tower Street, filled with butcher shops, small markets and specialty stores. Lots of women's fashions, costume jewelry places. Even Western Hills had prospered from Vietnam, tourism and the other economic forces that formed the Bay Area. Rarely did a whitewashed storefront appear, and when someone moved out, someone else moved in soon. He stopped in front of Mel's Sporting Goods, in business for decades, and stared at the expensive tennis racket he coveted. Mel had many things Paul wanted.

He then went into Bud's Good Eats, his family's delicatessen. Behind the counter, his mother, in a dark-green, mustard-smeared apron over her white blouse, stood making a roast beef sandwich.

With unthinking deftness, she finished the sandwich and slipped it into a wax paper bag. Behind the counter were myriad meats, vegetables and condiments. A big refrigerator next to the cash register was packed with cans of Coke, Pepsi, 7-Up and small bottles of fruit juice; Bud had recently stopped selling Miller Lite Beer because the only customers who wanted it were underage.

Paul dashed into the delicatessen's backroom, threw on an apron and sidled up to his mother. Pecking his mother on the cheek, he whispered, "Go home."

The Steeves family lived just upstairs from Bud's Good Eats. "Thank you," she murmured.

With a smile that could have sold oil to the Arabs, he asked the next customer, "May I help you?"

They ate dinner together in their cramped dining room. Bud insisted that their dinners be substantial: meat, vegetables. The apartment had four bedrooms, all on the top floor. Below were a living room and dining room, squeezed into scarcely more than a thousand square feet.

Jamey, the youngest in the family, didn't much care for these meals and these people. If he didn't like what his mother served, he could always eat later on Market Street. His sister Dee, who was always on some kind of diet, mainly picked at her food, even though she was skinny enough already. Paul's mother ate fast, not seeming to taste her food, and she was always the first one done. Bud Steeves, a burly man, devoured his meals.

Dee declined dessert and got ready to leave for Pacific Point Army Hospital, where she volunteered two evenings per week. She also had a nine-to-five clerical position at Grandinetti Chocolate, the confections giant competing with Hershey and Mars for the world's sweet tooth.

"I'm off," she said, pulling on her coat.

"Don't spend too much time around the healthier soldiers," her father admonished. "You'll be getting them all worked up."

After dinner, Jamey took off, too. Nobody asked where he was going. He went off to do his own thing, and he would be back when he felt like it, or he wouldn't.

Bud Steeves sat in his living room recliner and read the *Times* before heading back downstairs to Bud's Good Eats to do his night's work. Paul stayed in the kitchen and helped his mother clean up. Then he went upstairs to do his homework in his tiny bedroom. He wanted more and better than what his father had managed to provide; in modern American culture, that meant hard work, education and ambition. Paul was always on the honor roll and took his studies very seriously. Good grades and discipline would take him wherever he wanted to go.

It might be funny, Bud Steeves thought as he sliced tomatoes in Bud's Good Eats, if I went berserk one day and started slashing all my customers' throats. Just imagine what the papers would say. Mr. Nice Guy finally flips out.

He drank the vodka from a flask. He rarely felt its relaxing effects anymore. He rarely felt anything, period. But he could still smell the vegetables surrounding him all the time. He couldn't escape it. Even in his occasional erotic dreams, his penis had turned into a cucumber, his balls into onions.

When you've been really bad in a previous life, and God wants to punish you, he makes you work in a place like this all day...and he makes you feel grateful for it. He gives you the knife to end your misery, but for some reason you don't kill yourself, you just prolong your agony.

ENTREPRENEUR

He walked over to the window and stared out for a moment, smoothing the green apron stretched across his broad chest. He thought of San Francisco Bay, a couple of miles away, which did not freeze in the winter, unlike Lake Michigan. Maybe that was why he had left Chicago all those years ago. He had grown to hate the Windy City, where in the winter he'd had to step over the bodies of hypothermic homeless men. In Chicago, the major-league sports teams often failed to make the postseason. Al Capone could have changed that; he could have bought the fans a winner or two, just to amuse himself. But Big Al ended up in San Francisco's Alcatraz Prison, psychotic from syphilis. Well, one thing was for sure: Chicago didn't miss Bud Steeves, so why should he miss it?

He shrugged and went back behind the counter to slice more tomatoes.

In his bedroom, Paul was doing homework of a different kind. He had his sketch pad in his lap and closed his eyes, concentrating hard on his mental image of Miss Trinh, his American history teacher. She was naked. He had never seen her undressed, naturally; he needed to use his imagination. But he had scrutinized her body so often that he was confident of having an accurate notion of what her blouses and skirts covered; she never wore slacks, and at times her curvaceous legs distracted him so much that her words flew past him like words spoken in a foreign movie.

He knew the course content nearly as well as she did and always got A's. To him, class time was for ogling Miss Trinh. He knew they would never have a personal relationship of any kind. The only reason she thought highly of him was his meticulous preparation. Still, he enjoyed sketching and fantasizing about her.

He put down his sketch pad and pencil and looked closely at himself in the mirror on his wall. He scrutinized himself daily, wondering what others thought when they looked at his face. His short dark hair was always clean, neat and parted at the side. He was clean-shaven, clear-skinned and fastidiously trim. He was careful never to talk too much, laugh too loudly or goof around. He walked and dressed with attention to how others might perceive him. For exercise, he played tennis and jogged. Around Western Hills High School, Paul Steeves was a Big Man on Campus, smart and together, a winner, someone everybody wanted as a friend. Paul, naturally, thrived on everyone's high opinion of him.

He picked up his sketch pad and looked again at what he had drawn. He had her Vietnamese features perfectly captured: dark, slanted eyes, small narrow nose, fat pink lips, short straight dark hair. She was petite and small-breasted, with narrow hips and a small, tight butt. He imagined her as having tiny brown nipples and a sparse triangle of pubic hair.

He got ready for bed. His mother frequently got after him for not getting enough sleep, and he knew she was right. Once or twice he had gone to school after only four hours' sleep and could barely stay awake. When you were a Big Man on Campus like Paul Steeves, you needed to be careful about showing up for school looking sharp, looking good.

In the musty darkness of the vast Franciscan Theatre, Clint Eastwood, forty feet tall, was giving the bad guys what-for. Jamey Steeves slouched in his back-row seat and chewed on Milk Duds from a jumbo-sized box.

"Got any of those motherfuckers left?" asked Bubba Ozinski, Jamey's best friend. Whenever he tried to sound tough, which was always, Bubba used profanity. His father was an accountant, one of his uncles was a pharmacist and another was a nurse. *A nurse!* Bubba aspired to be the one male in his family who wasn't a wimp. He accepted the box from Jamey and shook out a handful of chocolate-coated caramels. "Thanks, amigo. You steal nothing but the best."

"Don't thank me, thank Woolworth's." Jamey studied the bright yellow box in the darkness. "I shoulda lifted more."

Jamey and Bubba were disappointed that the Franciscan's usual cashier was on her day off. A homely girl with a crush on Jamey, she always let them in after getting a kiss and a smile from Jamey. Unwilling to pay for something they normally got for free, the two boys went to the theater's alleyway exit, tugged open a warped, creaking back door and sneaked into the rusted-out grindhouse.

They sat in the very back row. Jamey squirmed in his seat. *Magnum Force* was too damn confusing. He surveyed the mostly empty theater and pointed to a couple of silhouetted figures down a few rows back from the screen.

"Bubba, do you see what I see?"

"Yeah, I see. Fuckin' jarhead."

A United States Marine, wearing the unmistakable peaked cap. He was smoking a cigar; its tip glowed bright red and its smoke curlicued up from his head as if his cap were a crooked chimney. Next to the Marine sat his petite blonde date.

Bubba laughed. "He's got his little bimbo, too."

"We're looking for a few good men," Jamey said. "Looks like we just found one."

"Damn," said Bubba, "he looks like a big bastard."

Jamey scowled. "Oh, and *I'm* puny?"

"No, but you ain't *his* size."

Jamey let out an exasperated sigh. "Dammit, Bubba! How many times I gotta tell you—"

"Yeah, yeah: 'It's not the size of the man in the fight. It's the size of the fight in the man.'"

Jamey nodded. "Fuckin' A. Let's go to war."

He got up, bounded down the aisle and ran a hand through his shaggy blond hair. Approaching the Marine, he felt exhilarated, as if he were a pugilist entering the ring for a gold-medal bout, an underdog who knew he would win.

Trailing him, Bubba looked up at the screen and wished for a moment that he could climb up into the movie and become part of Dirty Harry's adventure, not crazy Jamey's. Bubba was no Dirty Harry. His real name was Bobby but someone said he looked more like a Bubba, and the nickname stuck. Pudgy and pimply, he had a round, doughy face with freckles sprinkled across his pug nose. His parents made him wear his frizzy hair in a severe cut that emphasized his ungainliness. They sent their son to school every day in brightly colored shirts, pleated slacks and loafers instead of the T-shirts and tennis shoes everyone else wore. Bubba read all his textbooks in the first weeks of school so that he could ditch class whenever Jamey wanted to hang out.

Jamey seemed everything Bubba wanted to be—handsome, virile, dangerous. An indifferent, remedial student, Jamey had given up on adulthood in advance and was free to revel in the power of his youth. In exchange for Bubba's deference and companionship, Jamey promised to confront any school bully who hassled Bubba, so the fat boy could be as obnoxious as he wanted with impunity.

Bubba and Jamey slid in behind the Marine and his girl. The soldier's left hand held a stogie; the other one was busy at work between her legs. Bubba glanced at the man's massive shoulders and mouthed, *No. Way too big.*

Jamey took a hit from an imaginary cigarette. He mouthed back, *Do it.*

Bubba tapped the Marine on the shoulder. "Excuse me, Admiral, but would you mind extinguishing your cigar?"

"I'm in the Marines, not the Navy."

Jamey leaned over and stabbed the Marine with his forefinger. "My friend asked you to put out that cigar. If you refuse, we'll have to get the manager."

The Marine stared straight ahead. "Gotta be a thousand empty seats in this dump. Your friend can sit away from the smoke."

Jamey winked at his best friend.

"I *love* Dirty Harry," Bubba said aloud. "Dude doesn't take shit from *nobody.*"

"Watch your language," the Marine said.

"Just ignore them, Roy," said the blonde.

Bubba tapped on his shoulder again. "Please extinguish your cigar. I have an incurable lung disorder. I need fresh, clean air at all times."

"Then move to Alaska," the man said. His girlfriend giggled. He chuckled.

"Are you laughing at my friend?" asked Jamey, sitting inches behind her. Her blonde hair fell in brassy ringlets and her face was shiny with makeup. She smelled of perfume and cigar smoke. He strained to peer down her blouse. "I don't think it's very nice to make fun of people."

"Especially since Vietnam just ended," Bubba said to the Marine. "Didn't you see enough pain and suffering during the war?"

"Where is your compassion, man?" Jamey demanded, his voice growing louder. "Where is your humanity?"

"Oh, piss off," said the girlfriend.

"Did I hear you right?" Jamey asked in mock outrage. "Nobody speaks to *me* that way!"

They all stayed silent for several moments. Jamey sat back and said, "Maybe this guy is a war hero. Maybe he's got a dozen Purple Hearts. But now he's too shell-shocked to do anything but sit in movie theaters and smoke cigars."

"Shut up!" The soldier snarled. "We're tired of your crap. We just wanna watch this movie."

Jamey grabbed at his crotch. "Same here. We thought this was a porno flick. We came in here to jerk off."

The Marine sprang up. "Get out!"

The boy folded his arms. "Make us."

The Marine looked at Jamey and Bubba. He seemed to falter a bit. He took a deep breath. "I'm gettin' the manager."

The girl touched his arm. "Let's just leave."

"I'll be right back, Tammy." He stuck his cigar back into his mouth and marched up the aisle.

Jamey leaned over and said, "Tammy, his hand's gone. You can cross your legs now."

The Marine came back with the manager, a small Filipino man in a blue serge suit.

"These kids the problem?" the manager asked.

"Please sit down," Bubba said. "Dirty Harry's just about to blow someone's head clean off, and I don't want to miss it."

"This Marine won't put out his cigar," Jamey said.

"We allow smoking in here," the manager explained. "If his cigar bothers you, just find another seat."

"I would get sick from the smoke wherever I sat," replied Bubba. "You see, I have an incurable lung disorder."

"What a shame," said the manager.

Jamey stood up. "I resent this Marine for thinking he can intimidate us. I bet he didn't kill even one single gook. I bet he never even went to 'Nam. He's just a coward."

The Marine nearly shook with rage. "If you don't throw them out, I swear to God—"

The manager nodded. "All right." He turned to Jamey and Bubba. "Here's the deal. If you two boys leave now, I'll refund your money. OK?"

Jamey felt everyone staring at him, even Dirty Harry. A couple of other customers called out to him to shut up and go home to his mother.

"Yeah," he said. "We'll take a refund."

The manager escorted them to his office. He gave them each two dollars without asking for their ticket stubs or even if they were of legal age to see an R-rated triple bill. Jamey, getting something for nothing, grinned as he stuffed the theater's greenbacks into his pocket and filled out a refund slip. In the space that said REASON FOR REFUND, Jamey wrote, "Too many rude people." He signed it Dirty Harry. Bubba scribbled the name Richard Nixon.

On the sidewalk, they hooted and exchanged high fives. "I fuckin' *loved* that," Bubba said. "What's next?"

Jamey rubbed his chin. "Round two. We'll come back when the movie's over."

At the McDonald's across the street, Bubba sucked down a chocolate shake. Jamey sipped on a cup of coffee, staring out the window. This place had a good sound system, so why did they have it tuned to the news station? Some deep-voiced asshole was going on and on about Vietnam-this and Cambodia-that. He wanted to puke. Why didn't they play some rock 'n' roll? Nobody gave a rat's ass about Vietnam—it was *over*, man, so why keep on talking about it? He liked a good fight as much as the next guy, but he always fought to win. In Vietnam, Uncle Sam had fought to lose. Jamey would never join the Army, that was for damn sure. He wouldn't go to the next one, and there would *always* be a next one. Uncle Sam, like Jamey Steeves, just couldn't seem to stay out of trouble.

As an employee walked by, Jamey asked, "Can't you put some music on?"

"Aren't you interested in Vietnam?"

"We're too young to die," Jamey said.

"And I have an incurable lung disorder. Check this out." Bubba forced out a few croaking coughs, and the two boys burst out laughing.

The sky grew black as Jamey and Bubba stood under the Franciscan's huge, grimy marquee, its lurid red letters creeping askew. 3 ACTION HITS. BARGAIN MAT TIL 2.

"Maybe we shouldn't do this," Bubba said, fidgeting. "He's so big. If the pigs come by—"

"Fuck the pigs." Jamey smoothed back his blond locks. Just make sure this guy doesn't get me by the hair. Otherwise I'll be all right."

Business people hustled past the two boys to the underground Bay Area Rapid Transit station at the end of the block. Presently the Franciscan's customers trickled out. Jamey and Bubba stood aside as the soldier and his girl emerged.

"I'm starved," the Marine announced, looping an arm around the blonde. "Let's go get a pizza."

Jamey went up to them and jumped out in front. "Where you goin'?"

The Marine groaned.

"I ain't done with you, soldier."

The blonde girl glowered at Jamey. "What's your *problem,* punk?"

"I'm not a punk and I don't have a problem, Tammy—"

"Don't say her name," said the Marine.

"I'm just a guy who wants some respect," Jamey said.

The Marine shook his head and let out an exasperated sigh. "Kid, just go home." He tried to push the boy aside.

"I'm talkin' to you, warmonger!" Jamey barked, reaching out and plucking one of the gold buttons off the Marine's tunic.

The man looked down, his face red with fury. "My button! Little bastard!"

The blonde's eyes glittered with rage. "Kick his ass, Roy!"

"Little fucker needs to learn some manners." He reared back and threw a right cross that barely missed Jamey's chin. But the boy yelped, staggered backwards and grabbed at his face.

"A big guy like him picking on a smaller kid!" exclaimed a middle-aged man who had stopped to watch. By now about a dozen onlookers had stopped to watch.

"Oh, he just said he would teach the kid some manners," replied a woman enjoying the spectacle.

"Please step back," Bubba told the crowd, even though the Market Street sidewalk was five times broader than it needed to be. The people smiled at Bubba, who, in his rainbow-hued shirt and gabardine slacks, was the unlikeliest character ever to try to referee a downtown street fight.

The Marine came after Jamey and swung as hard as he could. Jamey easily ducked and plowed his fists into the big man's groin. The Marine doubled over, his face contorted in agony. Jamey pounded some more and the soldier fell, silent. He curled up into a fetal ball on the filthy Market Street sidewalk.

"Well, it's nice to see the underdog win once in a while," said the woman bystander.

Jamey looked down and said, "Want some more?" The Marine lay prostrate and did not respond. Jamey glanced at Bubba, who turned to the crowd and said, "Next performance is at nine, folks. Tickets at the Franciscan box office."

Some people laughed as Bubba and Jamey strode past the crowd and rounded the corner.

"You pounded him!" Bubba danced around and pumped chunky fists into the air, his flabby breasts and stomach quivering under his garish sports shirt. "Just fucking *pounded* him!"

"'Kick his ass, Roy!'" Jamey squealed. He shook his head. "Maybe next time we should pick on a Stanford or Cal football player. That Marine was a candyass. No wonder we lost in Vietnam." Then he walked with a curt "Later." Jamey needed to be alone now, to savor his victory. He wandered into the Tenderloin and stood at the front entrance of Juanita's, the nondescript brothel where he had lost his virginity one evening. Jamey loved money and sex; he just never seemed to get enough of either one.

He kept walking and ended up at the Powell Street cable car turntable, a forbidding place at night, but packed most weekends with pickpockets who victimized fat Okie tourists. Jamey wondered why he wasted his time shoplifting Milk Duds and scamming petty cash from a movie theater when his pickpocket friends had offered to teach him their trade. Well, why not? A guy had to take advantage of his opportunities.

He boarded the Muni bus for Western Hills and got lost in his own pleasant thoughts until it reached his stop. Walking down Tower Street, he saw his sister Dee about to enter their home. He stood back and watched as she fumbled at the lock of their wrought-iron gate, as if the boogeyman were chasing her. Jamey didn't want to see or be seen by her. The two of them didn't have much use for each other. She worked sometimes at that hospital in the expensive part of town. He bet she had a real good beside manner.

Jamey watched Dee disappear into their home, then he walked up to their big iron gate and stood for a few minutes looking at the shabby old building in the shabby old neighborhood that had been his home all his life. Him, Buford James Steeves, Junior, the unwanted third child his parents could not afford to bring into the world. Not far away, the lights from Bud's Good Eats continued to burn as his father slaved away. Jamey knew that Western Hills was supposed to be classified as one of those "blighted" neighborhoods like the black ghettoes. The redevelopers wanted to come in and tear down everything and build new things. No big loss if they do, he thought.

Jamey entered their home and climbed up the stairs. He always went in as quickly and quietly as he could. He wanted to get to his own room and crawl into bed without any kind of conversation with Paul. He could picture his brother in his jammies, all tucked in, teeth, asshole and conscience clean, homework all done. Jamey could imagine the conversation they might have at that moment.

"Didn't hear you come in."

"I tried to be quiet, so I would wake anyone."

"Where've you been, Jamey?"

"Went to the movies."

"How was it?"

"I've seen better."

Paul would sniff loudly. "Have you been drinking? You stink." Then, "What's that blood on your sweatshirt? Did you cut yourself?"

If I wasn't such a nice guy, Jamey would want to say, I would kick your ass from here to Timbuktu.

But no such conversation happened. Jamey stripped down to his underwear and crawled into bed, wishing he'd begged, borrowed or stolen enough money to visit Juanita's. He got twice the service for half the price because he had been such a frequent customer and had sent his friends there, too. Yeah, that would have been the perfect way to end a very thrilling evening. He had never told Paul about Juanita's. Paul wouldn't know what to do with a woman if a naked one jumped on him. Paul wasn't interested in Tenderloin whores; he was waiting for Princess Charming or he was a prude or maybe he was just a faggot. Well, that wasn't Jamey's problem. Maybe he would take pity on Paul and take him to Juanita's, just to see the look on the poor bastard's face.

Jamey closed his eyes and fell asleep, smiling. He dreamed of beating up Marines and making love to Tenderloin whores.

Dee had worked that evening at Pacific Point Army Hospital, located in the northwest corner of the city, near the Pacific Heights, one of the city's most affluent neighborhoods. Pac Point was full of recovering soldiers. Dee volunteered two evenings each week, distributing magazines and newspapers to the men and keeping them company. She had started there with a girlfriend, and when her friend grew bored and quit, Dee continued, mainly because she enjoyed helping those who genuinely appreciated her. Also, she now had an excuse to get out of the house a couple of evenings each week to be around others her age. Dee's father demanded that she live at home till age twenty-one.

At Grandinetti Chocolate, she and her coworkers seldom socialized; they simply hurried to process the endless stream of orders. At quitting time, they all went home, exhausted and sick of smelling chocolate.

At the hospital, Dee observed occasional, discreet hanky-panky between the nurses and doctors and less discreet flirting between patients and female volunteers. She, however, affected a polite aloofness that said *Forget it*, and the men complied, especially since she was hardly the only pretty girl in the facility. There were others the guys could grope.

Dee had dated and kissed boys many times. But they had been so tentative and amateurish that she'd nearly laughed. She also failed to see the appeal in the varsity lettermen her girlfriends ogled, especially after meeting the wizened young men in the hospital who made her high school friends look like little brats. Dee honestly didn't know yet what she sought in a man but assumed she would recognize the desired qualities when she met the man who possessed them. Who was in a hurry? Not her. She was young; she could wait.

As she went about in the hospital wearing the immaculate white smock that made many patients mistake her for a nurse, she enjoyed the sense of being needed and valued. She also shared the soldiers' relief at being home, or at least on their way home after that nightmare called Vietnam. Many of them were in San Francisco for the first time and scarcely knew how the city looked beyond the hospital grounds. They were eager to explore the city before returning home. Dee was relieved that her brothers were too young to be drafted.

They had dimmed the lights in the wards and all the patients were given their bedtime medications. As usual, Dee had spent a few minutes saying goodnight to a few of the most critically wounded patients, believing that a few private moments with a pretty blonde girl all in white made their plight somehow a bit more tolerable. Each night she made a point of cleaning up the common area where the men read magazines, played board games and generally visited to get through the days. She hated her family's cramped apartment, and wandering through the spacious rooms of the Army hospital made her feel as if she were the lady of the grandest Pacific Heights mansion.

Dee was finishing up in the common area where the wounded men unthinkingly left everything in disorder when she heard a soft voice. "Hey," murmured Red Tarlane. An Army infantryman, he'd been admitted months earlier, critically wounded. About to be discharged, he still limped from his injuries. He was tall but not handsome, broad shouldered, a bit thick around the middle even though he didn't eat much. Red had small brown eyes, a wide nose and a big, goofy grin. Dee, when first meeting him, had thought him thick-headed; but after being cornered by him for conversations a few times, she sensed his quick intelligence and nihilistic view of life. She knew he was from Florida, had an older brother and had few if any plans for the future.

"Can't sleep?" Dee asked.

He shook his head. "Too much snoring. Thought I would hang out with you for a spell."

"I hate to disappoint you, but my shift is nearly over." She glanced at the clock. The last bus from the Presidio to downtown left at just after midnight. Buses crawled all over the city at all hours, so why did Dee's quit so early? Maybe, she thought, out here in the high-rent district, everyone has a car and no one needs the bus.

"You better hurry up, then. I know you take the bus. Your boyfriend might panic if you're late."

"No boyfriend here," she said. "Still with Mom and Dad and my kid brothers."

"Well, that'll change soon enough." He took out a package of Pall Malls and offered her one.

"No, thanks," she said.

"Good for you." He lit up and stared at the tip of his cigarette. "I'm no draft dodger. I *wanted* to go into the Army, you know. I wanted to join up and see a little bit of the world, even if it meant going to Vietnam. It's a quick road to emotional maturity. Kind of hard to be your own man with your parents and family and such around all the time." His voice lacked bitterness, she thought. He sounded matter-of-fact, adult.

Dee said, sounding dreamy, "I want to travel around a little, too."

"Really? Where?"

"Europe, maybe."

Red grinned. "Good choice. You can forget Southeast Asia, at least for a few years. Not much of it left. I did my part to expedite its destruction."

"Well, I guess that should make us more grateful to be living here, where we're not afraid for our lives."

"That it should." He looked down at his feet. "That it should." Then he looked at her. "So why do you think we're not more grateful?"

"Oh, I suppose we're spoiled."

"Even you?"

She laughed. "Sure. But I should be the queen of humility. After all, I'm nineteen years old and work at a chocolate factory. I come home each night swearing I'll never go back to that place."

"So why don't you quit? Find something more fulfilling?"

"Because I have to bring home a decent paycheck. Otherwise my father would shit."

Red guffawed.

Her face turned red. "I don't usually swear."

"I like a girl who does things she isn't supposed to do. Not afraid to follow her instincts."

"You got a girl back in Florida, Red?" Dee asked.

He shook his head. "No, ma'am. Wouldn't have minded finding one out in 'Nam, but I'm afraid there weren't too many eligible young ladies around. Just lots of snakes, Agent Orange and napalm."

"Maybe you'll find a girl now that you're back."

"Maybe." Red thought a moment. "And maybe I just have, right here, right now." He placed his hand over hers.

Dee felt a bead of sweat trickle down her back. She was acutely aware of him, alone together in the common room. Its walls suddenly closed in around her.

"Tell you what, Dee," he said, his voice quiet but intense. "I've had you on my mind plenty, and I've decided that when I get out of here, which will be tomorrow, I would like for us to spend the day together."

Dee felt the room spinning around. "I think it's unethical, hospital personnel having relationships with wounded guys."

He snorted. "Who cares? I have three thousand dollars in back pay coming to me, and I would just as soon give it to you as to anyone else. We could have fun together and no one would ever have to know."

"No, Red, I gotta go." Her voice sounded loud and strong, as if she would start yelling in a moment.

"I'll be staying for a week or two at a place called the Patricia Hotel, downtown. 'Newly refurbished.' We can go to some Italian place and get take-out and a bottle of wine and have us a real nice time in my room." His eyes bore into hers. "An event to remember. You're lookin' mighty good to me, Dee, and I've been all banged up for months. I'm just starting to feel like a man again, if you know what I mean. I can't remember the last time I—"

Dee wrenched her hand loose from his and started towards the door but he blocked her. "Three thousand dollars in back pay. Think about it, Dee. How long you gotta work at that smelly chocolate factory to make that kind of bread? And after your daddy gets done takin' his share for room and board...well, that doesn't leave much money for you. You want to move out and make a life for yourself, right? Well, three thousand dollars will give a young lady a pretty decent start anywhere. Think about it."

Red went back into the ward. A few more minutes passed before Dee could even think clearly. Presently she found her way out of the common room and into the corridor that led to the changing room and the building's exit. She managed to get back into her own clothes and hurried to the bus stop.

She sat in her bedroom, trying to tell herself that Red didn't exist. She stared at her mirror and tried to decipher the image before her. But she saw nothing, really, saw nothing at all. But she heard was a voice, a soft Southern voice. *I can't remember the last time I—*

She could not go back. That much she knew. She would call the volunteers' supervisor in the morning and give some ludicrous excuse that they would have to accept. She would do it with a clear conscience, too. After all, how much had she given them, and how little had they given her in return?

Dee got up and stood in the room's feeble light. In the mirror she could see her body: her plump, firm breasts with large, round, rosy nipples; her tight belly, muscles well developed; her generous triangle of blonde pubic hair. Her hips were narrow, her thighs sleek and smooth. She had heard, many times, that beauty was a woman's passport to independence. Well, she would find out.

I've got to get out of here, she thought.

Donna Steeves stares out the bay window directly above Bud's Good Eats, which for the moment is enshrouded in fog. She watches as her husband jogs around the block, and she believes he is running from her. Other times, he goes swimming in San Francisco Bay, and she hopes he will drown. Maybe *he* does, too.

In the delicatessen, her husband does the work of two men, checking the supplies or the equipment for the umpteenth time. He will come up whenever he pronounces his day's work done, get a few hours of sleep, then go back to the delicatessen for another marathon workday. He is a workaholic if only out of necessity; he fears that if he doesn't work so hard he may one day lose Bud's Good Eats.

And, of course, he is probably right.

And, Donna finds as time goes on, that she couldn't care less about Bud's Good Eats or Bud Steeves.

She sighs and turns away from the window, from Bud's Good Eats, from Bud. She is dressed in her ancient white bathrobe, which is now somewhat gray. She gave up cigarettes years ago but still gets the cravings. Years earlier, she would never have considered smoking. Her foster parents taught her never to smoke, swear or lie. They took her to church and taught her about the Almighty and salvation. But she has forgotten most of that now, or at least put it all behind her, and now believes that she never did have faith despite being reared in the Bible Belt. No matter; had she believed, it would have resulted in fights with her hateful, atheistic husband from Capone's Chicago.

She had often wondered about her natural parents. The foster homes had provided for her as best they could, but could tell her nothing about her real parents, probably for legal reasons that superseded a little girl's right to know. But she was told, by them or someone else, that her natural mother had, unthinkably and unforgivably, conceived and given birth out of wedlock; Donna, consequently, must always be twice as virtuous to compensate for her wretched, sordid parents. When Dee was born, Donna had wanted to name the child Caroline to honor her home state, but her husband said no, his virginity had been claimed, years earlier, by a girl named Dee and that was that. As a compromise, they agreed to name the girl Deirdre but call her Dee. By the time of their first wedding anniversary, he looked at her with revulsion.

They had met on a westbound Greyhound bus, when Donna, in her early twenties, had been the singer of a quarrelsome jazz quartet which dissolved following a turbulent weeklong gig in Chicago. She had some money; her better judgment told her to head south, to New Orleans, the birthplace of jazz, where she had performed many times. But, impulsively, she went to San Francisco instead, an unknown place in which she assumed she could find a new band. On the two-day trip the bus was seldom more than half full. One of her fellow travelers was a large, quiet young man whom she befriended and sat beside. On his lap sat a battered satchel he gripped with white knuckles. He, too, was going to San Francisco, an unfamiliar destination. She guessed he would welcome her company once they arrived. At the San Francisco bus station, they found the YWCA on the directory, and he escorted her to its front door. Then, to her utter disbelief, he reached into his satchel and took out a hundred dollars for her two weeks' stay. He came by nightly to invite her to dinner.

So, Donna Costello, because years earlier she had left her band over a trivial dispute and taken a westbound bus at a certain hour, was now standing in a cramped living room in a small apartment above a delicatessen in Western Hills. She had given her all to Bud Steeves: her youth, beauty and potential.

Her earliest days with him had been promising, or at least comforting. A gentleman, he spoke with almost childlike enthusiasm about his plans to open a business and be his own man. She asked no questions; she assumed the battered satchel whence her YWCA rent money had come would bring his dreams to fruition. Nor did she inform him that her own plans possibly excluded him. She, a musician, eventually would, ideally, resume performing. The city was full of nightclubs; she found plenty of jazz on the radio. Her kind of music hadn't ceased altogether despite the exhaustion of jazz's innovative energies and the deaths of some of its greatest players.

Proud of her voice, she sang for Steeves, showing off, and at these times repeated her desire to entertain large audiences again. He just smiled, indulgently, as if at a child's foolish dream.

He was hesitant to hold her hand when they courted during those early days, although she guessed that he hadn't lacked sexual experience. She supposed he merely feared alienating her by being too aggressive. He went to work at Sandwich Heaven, and was amazed at its volume of business. He decided that if a man was industrious and lucky, he could open a thriving chain of such places.

A year after their arrival in the city, Bud proposed to Donna. She accepted, having made few friends and saw little improvement for her life on the horizon. Her first week in town, she had looked through the Employment Development Department's job listings. Nobody wanted a jazz singer. She ended up busing tables, at Ann's, a nightclub on Broadway Street. Ann's specialized in live entertainment; the bands played rock 'n' roll, each one indistinguishable from the next, their melodies mindless as rain. She hated it and knew she would never sing it. Each night, Steeves, after making sandwiches all day, came by to walk her home; to employees of Ann's he was known as the big, good-looking brown-haired guy who always arrived for Donna, the good-looking, silent bus girl. He knew she had been raised by foster parents in the South, and told her he was estranged from his people in the Midwest. He had a younger sister who had married an American-born Englishman named Jack and they lived in Sacramento. Bud and his sister lived three hours apart but never saw one another.

Donna made him promise never to cheat on her. He was not to use profanity or mistreat her in any way, and they were to be married in church. He eagerly agreed to her terms, nodding so vigorously that she wondered if he was taking her seriously.

He found a property for lease on Tower Street, in Western Hills, a neighborhood so obscure that he had difficulty finding it on a map. Still, he leased the store and the apartment above it, and shortly before their marriage he and Donna took the bus to see where they would spend the next many years. The building was cream-colored, or perhaps had once been white but was now soiled. A pull-down iron grill covered the entire storefront, and a fixed one over the door of the apartment building where they would live. The street, lined with stores, seemed somehow subdued. She worried that it was too much so; would there be enough customers to keep them afloat?

Donna let her imagination run wild. If she couldn't sing to an appreciative audience, she could at least become the proprietress of the best eatery in town. She imagined being dressed in finery and showing Western Hills' elite, whoever they were, to their tables. They would serve dainty sandwiches and tea and elegant desserts. She would be welcomed, naturally, in all the best homes and she would invite those people to hers.

But the neighborhood wasn't what she had anticipated and the people whose companionship she sought had no interest in her, and those circles that were open to her held little appeal. She learned, over time, that Western Hills was ugly as oatmeal, lumpy and colorless, vulnerable to economic downturns and invasions of clayey fog banks rolling in from the Pacific. The people with money, who could have revitalized the neighborhood, chose other parts of the city, and Western Hills became another beleaguered San Francisco district. The building next to the delicatessen was razed to accommodate a parking lot and many businesses moved in and out of the area. Bud's Good Eats never became the quaint little gathering place Donna had sought. The delicatessen remained viable; it was cheap, filling and humble, and its owners were just stubborn enough to keep it open.

The nightmare began on her wedding night. They married at City Hall, and by then the apartment above Bud's Good Eats was ready for occupancy. He insisted they didn't have the money for the weekend honeymoon in Carmel she wanted. They consummated their marriage in a bloody, grunting ceremony, he above her and much bigger, thrusting into her till he tired and rolled over to snore, she shivering and terrified. She knew it would not improve, and in fact would almost surely get worse.

Within days she planned an escape, and would make repeated attempts during their marriage. She checked Greyhound's schedules and tried, always unsuccessfully, to talk herself into going somewhere, anywhere, away from him. But fear, overcame her, and she remained his prisoner.

ENTREPRENEUR

By all outward appearances, he was the model husband, unfailingly punctual and courteous. He came by Ann's to pick her up after work, took her window shopping all over Union Square and bought jumbo malteds for them to slurp as they sat on benches by the Bay. She could scarcely believe that this was the same man, capable of a Jekyll-and-Hyde personality transformation, who would practically maul her in bed hours later. He did so with an icy savagery, pinning her like a wrestler and grinding into her, ignoring her tearful protests, her desperate squirming.

He wanted the satisfaction of her resentment and hatred, and when he perceived only meek resignation, his behavior in bed became even worse, leaving her welted and bruised. He was no adulterer; he knew other ways of humiliating her. He kept it up for two decades, his sexual exuberance seldom waning. She walked around him absently, having gradually accepted these rapes as a sort of sexual communion. He kept her prisoner in the small, gloomy apartment directly above Bud's Good Eats.

When she learned she was pregnant, she fingered a wire clothes hanger and considered attempting a self-inflicted abortion.

Steeves hoarded money. Donna never learned how much money he'd had in that battered satchel, or how much he made, or how close to insolvency the deli had come. Only after some time did he agree to sign her on to the Bud's Good Eats checking account, and that was only so that she could make purchases for the shop. She had to scream to get a few dollars from him for basic personal necessities. He said she ate too much and food was expensive. When Dee was ready to start kindergarten, Donna spent an hour to persuading her husband to invest in a new set of school clothes for the child. He had been raised during the Great Depression, knew about poverty and hoarded money as if expecting an imminent economic collapse. When his brother-in-law Jack came down from Sacramento and offered to make him a partner in redevelopment plans for the capital city, Bud, realizing that such an investment would involve a bank loan, became indignant and sent him away. Jack, a tall, sturdy man, dressed well, lived comfortably and provided well for his wife and their two children. Jack wasn't averse to borrowing money to make his well-considered plans come to fruition, just as most of America's wealthiest people had done to amass their fortunes.

Dee, like Paul, had been an honor student in high school, but when she graduated, her father dismissed her plans for higher education and instructed her to find a job immediately. She surrendered half her Grandinetti paycheck to her father. Paul was another matter entirely. He wanted to learn music, so Steeves bought him a trumpet, then an electric guitar. He learned to play both well. He was liked by his teachers, admired by his peers and behaved with a quiet dignity at all times.

Donna loves her son Paul. She is ambivalent about her other two children, and by now acknowledges her feelings, if only to herself. If the torment of her entire adult life has any redeeming value, it is Paul. How did he turn out so well in this environment? Better not to ask.

Her youngest child, Buford James, Junior, is hopeless. Blond and angelic-looking, he is immature, irresponsible and universally disrespectful. What can she do to help such a child? she asks herself. Nothing. That is the answer. Nothing at all. Let him alone.

Chapter 2

At Grandinetti Chocolate, Dee always worked as fast and accurately as she could, if only to challenge herself. Her co-workers admired her efficiency. She admired her own efforts at not going insane from boredom.

Today she worked with lightning speed. She had told her boss that she had a dental appointment in the city and would need to leave work early.

Dee was friendless, mostly by choice. At Western Hills High School, she and her three greatest friends—Sheri Rawson, Diane Walker and Janet Burns—had comprised a prominent, smug clique. But only Dee's family lacked college money for her, so she went to work while the three other girls attended Bay Area universities. Although not far away, the girls vanished entirely from Dee's life. She felt relieved; she didn't want them asking about life at the factory.

She had called Pacific Point Army Hospital and told the volunteer coordinator that her daytime work obligations made it impossible for her to continue. The coordinator, accustomed to having young, unpaid workers grow frustrated and quit, accepted the news with a halfhearted "good luck" and hung up the phone. Her family scarcely noticed she was no longer going to the hospital.

With her newly gained free time, Dee pondered her options in life. She ordered her priorities, rehearsed what she would say and went down to see her father in the backroom of Bud's Good Eats after the deli had closed for the night.

Steeves, unpacking lunch-sized bottles of orange juice picked up that afternoon, frowned when he saw his daughter enter through the door connecting to their apartment. But he said nothing.

Dee sat down. "I've got something on my mind, Dad."

"Talk."

"I've got a problem with my job at Grandinetti."

"Laid off? Reduced hours?"

"No."

"Then you don't have a problem."

Dee sighed. "I hate my job."

"Gee, that's too bad. But we need your income." He finished unpacking the orange juice and started on another box.

She took a deep breath and said, "Let me tell you what I think. I believe the best thing for me to do is to go to Los Angeles and get a job down there. With my skills, I could get something much better."

Her father frowned. "How old are you now?"

"Nineteen."

"Then why are we having this conversation?" Steeves asked, straightening up. "I thought I made it clear. No matter what the law says, *I* say my kids aren't adults till age twenty-one. My nineteen-year-old daughter, therefore, is still very much a minor who must obey her father. Next question?"

Dee feared her father too much to antagonize him. If her job had been less awful, she would have simply have endured things till she was twenty-one. She was an adult, regardless of what her old-fashioned father believed, and if she surreptitiously packed up and left one day while he was minding the deli, he would have no recourse. But he would never forgive her and probably disown her, and guilt would torment her for the rest of her life. Fighting back tears, she said, "God, I hate this city."

Steeves looked at her and laughed, mirthless. "Oh, and Los Angeles is the Promised Land? Listen, when you *do* move out, I bet you'll stay close by Western Hills."

In South Bay, not far from the Pacific Ocean, Grandinetti Chocolate sprawled like a miniature city. Sweet black smoke oozed, nonstop, from a half-dozen sources. The company's name crept across the factory's main entrance in huge brown letters, below which a convoy of yellow trucks entered with loads of cocoa beans and other ingredients, while identical vehicles exited with mountains of meticulously wrapped confections. Everywhere, security guards with crackling radios patrolled the grounds all day and night, as if to capture industrial spies who might be creeping about to learn and disseminate the myriad secrets of this company that had proven itself a worthy competitor to Hershey and Mars.

Emerging from one of larger buildings at two in the afternoon, Dee Steeves, who had punched out minutes earlier ostensibly to visit her dentist, hustled across the street to the bus stop as seagulls cawed overhead. Some people were awaiting the next bus into San Francisco: children and their parents who had come down for the Grandinetti Chocolate one-hour tour, plus a dozen or more workers who had just completed their shifts.

ENTREPRENEUR

A small boy gazed at his family-sized, yellow-wrapped, complimentary Grandinetti Milk Chocolate bar that all visitors received at the end of the free tour. Pinching his nose at the cloying odor, he said, "Yuck. Stinks out here." Dee rarely smelled anything anymore. She believed the seabreeze got rid of most of the odor.

She wished she could get on the phone and talk to Paul, who seemed to be the only one who understood her. But of course he was unavailable. Maybe others were seeking him out to solve *their* problems.

The bus arrived presently and she climbed aboard with the others. She eased down onto one of the scarred vinyl double seats and within a minute or so the bus began its brief journey up the coast to downtown San Francisco.

Nobody on the bus knew her, nor did anyone pay her any attention. Young, well-dressed women took the bus to and Grandinetti Chocolate all day. The factory operated every day and night of the year; its hundreds of employees worked various shifts.

The bus lumbered along the freeway. Dee stared out the dirt-flecked windows, at the expensive houses sitting complacently in the distance on one side, then turned her gaze to the Pacific Ocean on the other, calm for the moment. South Bay was growing now, finally. Only a few parcels of undeveloped land remained; for the longest time, South Bay had been little more than Grandinetti Chocolate, People's University and a handful of stately homes where the university's elite lived.

At the front of the bus, the driver, a middle-aged, paunchy black man, sat in a brown Muni uniform wearing a police-style cap. Everywhere, the bus's interior was smeared with swirls of gang graffiti. Had the punks boarded and defaced the bus while it was in service, as the driver, too afraid to object, simply drove on?

She disembarked at the San Francisco Civic Center, where she normally waited for the Western Hills bus. The Civic Center, filled with government buildings, malls and restaurants, always hummed with activity during the day but turned creepy after dark. Many homeless people spent their nights huddled in sleeping bags here, then wandered around the Tenderloin for the rest of the day. Dee entered a Burger King and ordered a chocolate milkshake. She sat by a window, sucked at the milkshake and stared out at Market Street. Cars inched along; horns honked nonstop. Civic Center bureaucrats hustled past; con men awaited their next marks. Crazy San Francisco.

She left Burger King and headed down Market Street. Shoppers scurried into and out of stores; a cable car clanged its bell in the distance. Dee continued, turning north, her heart pounding, her pulse racing. She found the Buddha Hotel, a flophouse recently given a facelift.

Inside, a desk clerk was checking the register. Dee imagined Red Tarlock somewhere upstairs, perhaps leaning against a closed window, watching her with fascination and anticipation.

She did not see the gleaming black Mercedes as it came up from behind and slowed down. Nor did she hear the gentle hum of the power windows being lowered, or the radio's dying blast as it was turned down.

"Deirdre? Deirdre Steeves?"

She turned around, alarmed.

Then, smiling, she ran a hand through her hair. "Mr. Grandinetti?"

"I'm flattered you remember me." He paused. "Mind if I ask why you're in *this* neighborhood?" His voice was full of mirth, as if he were most amused by zipping through the Tenderloin and finding one of his prettiest employees.

"It's such a fine day, so, um, I was going for a walk."

He frowned. "There's no such thing as 'a fine day' in this neighborhood. Especially all by yourself."

"I guess I'm feeling adventurous." He must think I'm an idiot. Or a whore. "I'm on my way back now."

"On your way back where? To home? To work?"

She threw up her arms. "Whichever." She paused. "Isn't this just the dumbest conversation?"

He threw back his head and laughed.

Dee said, "Why are *you* here?"

"Just passing through," he said. "Why don't you climb in? We'll just 'pass through' together."

Dee shrugged, climbed in and Grandinetti raised the windows back up, then raced the powerful German car up a few steep, foggy San Francisco hills. "Had lunch yet?" he asked.

"Lunch?"

"Yes. The meal between breakfast and dinner."

She laughed. "No, I haven't had lunch."

"Well, is Kincaid's all right with you?"

Kincaid's, the four-star restaurant at the top of the St. Jeremy Hotel, was one of the Bay Area's most famous and expensive restaurants.

"This street is too damn busy," he said. "I'll have to take a detour."

Dee wondered what a man like Lido Grandinetti thought of the Tenderloin, this destitute part of a world-famous, wealthy city. Most people made do on very, very little so that others, like him, could own candy factories, live in the Pacific Heights, drive new cars and not have to worry about things like money.

Minutes later, they arrived at the St. Jeremy. Grandinetti gave the keys to the valet. Dee checked herself in the mirror and deemed her appearance satisfactory. She took his proffered arm and they walked into the lobby of the hotel. He was dressed in a perfect blue suit with a white dress shirt and burgundy tie. His short black hair was mildly windblown. His black shoes sparkled. His very businesslike attire, Dee knew, meant little; he rarely showed up at the candy factory, and when he did appear, he mainly visited with his top managers. His indifference seldom mattered; Grandinetti Chocolate thrived because of the world's consistent demand for candy.

They took the elevator up to Kincaid's on the top floor. In the mirror Dee saw Lido Grandinetti taking office clerk Dee Steeves to the most expensive lunch in town after picking her up in the Tenderloin.

What's wrong with this picture? she wondered.

Kincaid's was a vision of stained-oak paneling and plush carpeting. "Mr. Grandinetti, nice to see you," said the smiling maitre d'. "To the bar?"

"No, right to our table," Grandinetti said.

"Yessir."

They were led to a window table displaying a magnificent view of the Bay and Alcatraz. They sat and ordered drinks. "White wine for me," Dee said, having heard a movie heroine say that and figuring it was the right thing to order.

"I'll have a Manhattan, straight up, with bitters," Grandinetti said.

"Yessir," the man repeated and left. Minutes later he returned and set the drinks before them. "To you," Grandinetti said, clinking his glass against hers.

Dee took a sip. The wine was heavenly, like the smoothest, lightest grape juice, very cold as it washed over her dry, tingling throat. Within seconds she took a few more sips and found herself pleasantly lightheaded.

Grandinetti smiled. "You're almost done. Another one, please." He gestured to the waiter.

She watched as Grandinetti took off his blue suit jacket and more or less threw it over his chair's back. He also loosened his tie. She could see a few dark hairs sticking out through his collar. "That's such a beautiful suit," she said.

He smiled. "Glad you like it. Kind of odd, though, isn't it? Dressing like a Wall Street banker so that I can drive out to the chocolate factory and hang around once in a while."

"I guess you don't much like your job."

He laughed. "Do you like yours?"

"Well..."

He laughed again. "You get up first thing in the morning in Western Hills and doll yourself up so you can take the bus down to South Bay and work all day at my candy factory. That doesn't sound like much fun to me."

At some point they ordered and their food arrived. As she ate, Dee thought about what Grandinetti had said. Well, come to think of it, *he* did have reason to dislike his job.

"It would figure, wouldn't it, that I would be stuck with the candy business and not one of my family's more exciting interests?" Grandinetti cut into his filet of sole.

"Your family is world-famous for Grandinetti Chocolate."

"Well, so what? We have other enterprises."

"Then why not do something more fulfilling?"

"My family wouldn't trust me with anything else. They figure even *I* can't destroy the chocolate company. The world's sweet tooth is eternal. Can you remember a time when there *wasn't* Grandinetti Chocolate?"

"I guess that's why you rarely show up at the factory. Because you don't like your job."

He nodded. "Exactly. Plus, I've been here in San Francisco all my life, so my family knows I won't have too much trouble finding my way home at the end of the day." He sat back. "My mind wanders, you know. Ennui makes me dangerous."

She smiled, and he said, "Did I say something funny?"

"No. I was just thinking. You seem to be unhappy even though you have everything."

He reached over and touched her hand. "I don't have *everything*. Not yet."

The sky above Alcatraz Island glowed cobalt, the nearby Golden Gate Bridge sparkled and business at Grandinetti Chocolate hummed along while Lido Grandinetti got Dee Steeves drunk thirty stories above San Francisco. The two coffees—or four?—with baked Alaska did nothing to sober her up or make her less garrulous. She told Lido (he had ceased being Mr. Grandinetti an hour earlier) about her life—about Paul and Jamey and *her* family's business.

"Bud's Good Eats? Sorry, never heard of it," he said. "You say it's a quaint little delicatessen somewhere in Western Hills? Your family *owns* it?"

Dee nodded. "'Bud' is my father. We live in the apartment right above the business."

He smiled. "How nice."

"He and my mother live for that deli."

"And do *you* live for it too?"

She shook her head vigorously. "No. They barely make a living."

ENTREPRENEUR

Just then the waiter arrived with the check and Grandinetti simply scribbled his name on it. He straightened his tie and put on his jacket, as if for business down in South Bay. But of course she knew better.

They left Kincaid's, took the elevator down into the parkade and got back into his Mercedes. Driving out, he said, "You never did answer my question: *why* were you in the Tenderloin when I drove by?"

Still buzzed and talkative, she told him about Red Tarlane at Pacific Point Army Hospital, their conversation, his invitation and offer of money. She didn't mind telling Grandinetti after their wonderful lunch with the view of the Bay and that fine wine.

"This guy, Red, just seemed so friendly and free-spirited. But also somehow sinister. Do you know what I mean? He grinned like an idiot. Maybe it was stupid of me to get into such an intimate conversation with a complete stranger. But he was just one of the Army wounded and I guess I had expected him to be honorable and all that." She did her best to sound indignant, repulsed.

Dee paid no attention to where they were going. She mainly looked into her lap and occasionally at him as she spoke. The car took one smooth turn after another. Then, looking around her, she was shocked to see that they were back in front of the Buddha Hotel.

Grandinetti sneered. "A charming establishment, I'm sure. Is this where your wounded Army boyfriend Red is? Red Tarlane, the Florida hillbilly with the recently rehabilitated penis?" He stared, his eyes cold with contempt. The Buddha now looked dark and forbidding, its glass doors shiny, a sticker on its window confirming its status as an acceptable establishment according to a lodging association. "Better go up and see him,

Deirdre. I think you said he has something for you. A nice long sausage, maybe?" Grandinetti reached across her, unlocked the door and pushed it open. "Loverboy awaits."

Dee, her head spinning, stumbled out of the car and straightened up. She stared for a moment at the Buddha's large glass doors, its dim narrow lobby.

Lurching forward, she vomited, her body convulsing. Wondering, for a mad instant, if Red Tarlock was up there somewhere, watching her, chuckling. Little Miss Purty Dee, all liquored up, nice big blonde boobs filling out her fancy white blouse, puking up a fine expensive meal all over the sidewalk, the guy in the fancy Mercedes staring at her tight little ass. She retched again, and again.

Dee absently wiped her mouth on the sleeve of her blouse. She spat a few times, trying to rid her mouth of the vile taste. Grandinetti got out and came over to her and murmured, "Come, Deirdre, get in the car."

She felt far too ill to resist, although she wanted nothing more to do with him. Once in the car, she closed her eyes and fell into the lightest sleep as she felt the soft San Francisco breeze caress her face and the car rise up one hill and down the next.

He touched her arm. "Open your eyes."

She looked up at a tall wrought-iron fence. Beyond it was a beautifully manicured front lawn. A huge flagpole stood on the lawn, with Old Glory flapping in the wind. Behind it sat a gleaming mansion, like photos she'd seen of the White House.

"Yours?"

"Yes, ma'am," he drawled. "Our fabled home. Better than the Buddha Hotel, don't you think?"

Inside, he led her up to his bedroom and made love to her after she had showered and brushed her teeth. They slept for many hours in each other's arms. Just before dawn, they climbed into his Mercedes and drove through the silent misty streets till they reached Bud's Good Eats. Dee climbed out of the car, unlocked the apartment's front door, then hurried upstairs.

She was wide awake, restless. She undressed and crawled into bed but did not sleep. She did not think about Lido Grandinetti all weekend long. When she went back to work on Monday morning, she found a business envelope in her desk drawer. It contained a cashier's check for three thousand dollars from Lido Grandinetti to Deirdre Steeves with a note saying: "For services rendered."

Chapter 3

The Western Hills Community Center, Jamey Steeves decided, was the most interesting place outside of the Tenderloin. The center had pinball machines, pool tables, a weight room and the cheapest snack bar around. His favorite activity was the forbidden poker game that inevitably got started in one or another of the center's more isolated nooks and crannies. They always played for money; Jamey, a superior player, often won. They normally limited the game to four players and the age limit was sixteen. But Jamey got in on his own terms. He had made his debut by kneeling down with them and saying to Gabe Reeder, "Fuck off, chump. I wanna play."

Reeder, a temperamental Western Hills High senior, had lettered in wrestling. Jamey chose him precisely because he was big and mean.

Reeder's eyes narrowed. He stood up. "You gonna make me?"

"Yeah. Let's go."

Jamey and Gabe marched into the bathroom, where fights usually happened on slow nights because the manager locked himself in his office with a nudie magazine. Gabe knew plenty about varsity wrestling but nothing about the dirty tricks of street fighting. As the other boys watched in horrified fascination, Jamey elbowed and kneed Gabe into a pleading, cowering hulk. Jamey thereafter was always accommodated at the poker games, and everyone spoke to him with respect.

ENTREPRENEUR

Tonight, the only entertainment came from John Synon, a gangly young man showing off the Purple Heart he had earned in Vietnam. He had been in Pacific Point Army Hospital and still looked ill.

Jamey listened as Synon bragged to a small group of guys about how he had saved some fellow soldiers in Khe Sanh. Jamey felt Synon was embellishing his wartime exploits so he would come off looking like Clint Eastwood, but at least Synon had gone and fought, not like thousands of American pussies who ran off to Canada.

Bubba then stole up behind Jamey and clapped him on the back. "Hey, amigo! What's doin'?"

Jamey shushed him. "I wanna listen to this guy."

Synon talked on about how he had saved a number of men and gotten shrapnel in the process. He looked with pride and love at his Purple Heart.

"Like hell," said Bubba, playing his and Jamey's favorite game. "That's not a real Purple Heart. That's just some piece of shit you bought on Market Street."

Synon glowered at him. "Watch it, kid. Nobody talks to *me* that way. I didn't go to Vietnam and almost get killed so I could come back here and get attitude from someone like you."

"Kiss my ass," said Bubba.

"Let's go outside, loser," said Synon, who, sick or not, could take Bubba in ten seconds.

"Right here, right now." Bubba assumed a fighting stance, his flabby belly jiggling. He looked scarcely able to beat up a hamster.

Just then, Jamey spoke up. "You wanna fight my pal? You gotta get past me first."

"OK, whatever," said Synon. "Let's do it."

Another guy grabbed Synon's arm. "No, man. He's a mean son of a bitch. He'll kick your ass."

Synon stared at Jamey's prodigious soldiers and fearless deameanor. As he lost his nerve and slipped away, the others grinned and shook their heads.

Bubba said, "Got some news for you, amigo."

"Yeah?" Jamey asked. "You finally get laid?" The other guys laughed.

Bubba's face went red. "It's about your sister."

"You laid Dee?"

The guys roared. Bubba's face went redder. He wondered why Jamey, after their fun with Synon, would turn on him and humiliate him in front of these guys. But then he shot back, "It ain't me Dee's layin'. But if you don't wanna know—"

"Let's take this outside." On the street, Jamey said, "Talk."

"Dee is at Grandinetti's place." Bubba was breathless. "I hear that Grandinetti's been driving her to his mansion every night."

Jamey shook his head. "My sister? With Lido Grandinetti? I totally fuckin' doubt it." He paused. "See, Bubba, *she's* not his type and *we're* not his type. He wouldn't lower himself to shit on us."

Bubba arched an eyebrow. "You looked at your sister lately, dude? He wouldn't condescend to shit on *you,* but he's a guy and she's a fox. Wanna go check this out? I've got my bike."

"I don't even know where he lives," Jamey said.

Bubba smirked. "Don't you ever read the society pages?"

They got on Bubba's puny Kawasaki and chugged the many blocks to Grandinetti's Pacific Heights estate. Jamey grinned at the fence's elaborate scrollwork that made getting a foothold easy. Why put up a fence so easy to climb?

They quickly scaled it and crept up like spies to the front window. Both boys were tall enough to see inside Lido Grandinetti's living room. The softly lit room appeared empty except for a piano, furniture, tables and a sofa.

"Nice," Bubba murmured. "He gets all the pussy he wants, probably. Even *I* could score if I lived here."

"Nobody's home. Let's forget it." Jamey turned away.

"Just wait. We came all this way."

Jamey glared at Bubba. "I said, let's jam. Nobody home."

"Shit, this guy? He's *always* home. Maybe he's somewhere upstairs. He'll come down soon."

Jamey didn't want Lido Grandinetti to come down. He didn't want anyone to be home, and he didn't want to be here. Looking into his window was probably illegal and definitely stupid. Fuck, what if the cops drove by? In this rich neighborhood, you probably just had to pick up the phone and the heat would show up in ten seconds, sirens screaming and guns blazing. He and Bubba had probably already just broken a dozen laws, like trespassing and invasion of privacy.

Jamey sighed as the famous San Francisco fog was rolling in, as he'd heard it so often did up here in the Pacific Heights. One mansion or fancy-ass apartment building after another. Only the rich bastards could live here, and the working people like Jamey's father had to carry the tax burden for most of these zillionaires. Grandinetti, among the worst of them, lived alone in this mansion. He probably wouldn't last five minutes working at Bud's Good Eats. As for screwing Dee, she was just his flavor of the month.

Where was the justice in life? Jamey Steeves wondered.

He felt Bubba's gentle punch. "Check it out!"

They peered into the living room.

Bubba chuckled. "He just came from upstairs. Told ya we'd see something!"

The two boys watched as Grandinetti passed through the living room, disappeared, returned with two bottles of what Jamey recognized as wine coolers, then walked towards the boys. He stopped at the fireplace and set the bottles on the mantle. He was completely nude.

"So even rich people look ugly without their clothes on," Bubba said.

"Quiet," Jamey muttered.

They watched Grandinetti reach down, pick up a log and toss it into the fireplace. The fire gained brilliance, and combined with the lamplight, he was clearly visible. Messy, short black hair, pencil neck, sunken chest, scrawny arms and legs. Jamey had seen heroin addicts with sexier bodies. His flaccid penis, circumcised, dangled almost to his knees.

Jamey froze as he watched Dee enter the room, also naked. His hands shook with rage and he felt an inexpressible sense of betrayal. She came up behind Grandinetti and slid her arms around him. He smiled and gently turned her around so that she faced the window, her eyes closed and her face radiant, as he grabbed a lock of her golden hair, pulled it back and nuzzled her neck. Jamey and Bubba, a few feet and an inch of glass away, stared with bulging eyes at Dee's heavy, round breasts and creamy thighs.

Jamey, overcome by the need to do *something*, pounded soundlessly on the thick glass. He wanted to kick in the front door and pull those two people apart.

Dee placed her hands at his sides and began kissing his chest. Then, lowering herself, she planted kisses on his stomach. On her knees, she placed her hand on his long, stiff phallus and accepted him into her mouth slowly. Soon his entire penis disappeared into her.

"Jesus, he's hung like Johnny Wadd." Bubba giggled. He loved his father's pornographic magazines.

Jamey closed his eyes, his legs weak. He felt bile rising in his throat. "Let's go."

"Like hell. It's just gettin' good."

Jamey reached over and grabbed Bubba. "Let's go now! And if you *ever* say a word about tonight, I'll fucking kill you. Understand, *amigo?*"

Bubba, snarling, pried himself from Jamey's grip. "What's your fuckin' problem? You don't like her anyway."

They sneaked around to the side of the house, scaled the fence and got back on the motorcycle. "Now I know why everyone thinks you're a head case," Bubba said. "If I wasn't such a nice guy, I'd tell you to get your own fuckin' ride back home."

Dee sat up in the oversized bed, sipping her wine cooler. Grandinetti's bedroom seemed bigger than the entire Steeves home. The mirror on the ceiling showed an identical blonde woman wearing only a lazy, complacent smile. She quite liked being here. If he was an incompetent business administrator, he did have other skills. His staff kept his home immaculate and he ravished Dee. They were all alone to do what they did best and liked most. She chuckled about how she had just met him downstairs, caught him by surprise and given him a surprise.

The bedside clock said eleven fifty-five. Not far away, the young men at Pacific Point Army Hospital would be asleep or restless in bed, perhaps wondering what Dee was doing.

They didn't need to know. She was back as a volunteer, once per week. She lied to her family when she told them she went to the hospital every night. She also noticed how little she minded being a liar.

These evenings were her favorite things in life. If, because of them, she showed up late for work, as she occasionally did, she paid little attention to her supervisor's reproachful looks. If Grandinetti had to play little mind games with her, as he did with the three thousand dollars that now sat in her savings account...well, those little mind games were one of his kinks. If he wanted to pay her for sex, fine.

They said nothing about the money. She would need it, probably soon. The day after she got the cashier's check, she left work for the day and saw him in his Mercedes by the main gate. He took her to Nob Hill for dinner. Then they went back to his place for more lovemaking. He drove her to Western Hills and she got out half a block from Bud's Good Eats.

He took her to his doctor downtown for the right birth control pills and bought her a white-silk dress at Boccasio of Union Square.

Dee liked Grandinetti, although she certainly did not love him. At times she disliked his scrawny body even when he was dressed in his finery. He was spoiled and smug, cynical, almost proud of his personal mediocrity, lacking in erudition despite his Stanford education. His powerful family had made a "success" of Lido by installing him as the president and chief executive officer of Grandinetti Chocolate and insisting that he live in that ostentatious Pacific Heights mansion. Dee found him friendless, obnoxious and misogynistic. His ex-wife had left years earlier, disgusted.

So, without other purposes in life, he threw himself into that one activity which felt best and provided gratification fastest. He asked nothing of Dee except that she make herself available to him, and the reward for him was her inevitable violent writhing and thrashing, her labored breathing and sweating body. She usually simply lay below him, arms at her side, eyes closed as she felt his long, stiff phallus inside her, taking to where she had never been, even through her episodes of onanism at home while her family slept.

He came in and reached down to fondle her breasts. "Lovely. Beautiful." He often marveled at her body. When he gave her oral sex, he stared with fascination at the exquisite tone of her stomach and thighs. If his own body was ugly, he certainly had a capacity to appreciate hers.

"Are you mine?" he asked.

She smiled. "I am right now."

"But I mean at all other times. Are you truly mine?"

She giggled. "Nobody *owns* anyone."

"I hate it when you get philosophical. Maybe I'll get used to you in a decade."

"I doubt it," she said.

"What are you thinking about?"

"Fucking our brains out."

He frowned. "Potty mouth."

She shrugged. "What do you expect from a white-trash Western Hills girl? If I can do it, I can say it."

He arched an eyebrow. "Oh, *can* you do it? I hadn't noticed. It seemed I was doing all the work."

"Well, that's because I'm inexperienced. I was just a sweet little virgin when we met. You corrupted me when you picked me up in the Tenderloin that day. You got me stoned and broke my cherry, you dirty old bastard. Otherwise, I would have remained pure for life."

He laughed. "Like hell. You were going to get it on with Red from Florida. Betcha my cock is bigger than his."

"Probably. Does the FBI know about that lethal weapon you have down there? Do you need a license to carry it?"

"Do you want to know what I'm thinking right now?" he asked. "I'll tell you: I think you need to broaden your horizons. We're going to start on that right now." He left the room.

Dee just wanted to shower, dress and go home. She'd had her fun for the evening.

Presently he came back, dressed. "Take a shower and put on your clothes. We're going out."

"Should I put on that new white dress?"

"No. I don't care how you look tonight."

She did as told, and they left the mansion. In the Mercedes, Boylan drove straight down Broadway Street, towards the Bay Bridge. North Beach. Dee hated all those raunchy strip joints.

They reached North Beach, and Dee shuddered at the glare of neon and electric signs. Big Al's. The Condor. Adam and Eve. He and She Love Act. Miraculously, Grandinetti found a parking space right in front of the Lowell Brothers' Theatre. Grandinetti took her arm and led her inside.

"Is this the place that used to get busted all the time?" Dee asked.

"Yes. Best show of its kind, though. The place looks like a New Orleans brothel."

"Smells like one too," Dee muttered. "Yuck."

She had imagined all of these places to be lurid flesh pots where bikini-clad predators hustled tips from men too shy or ugly to get girls any other way. I don't like these places, she muttered to herself. He doesn't expect me to dance nude...?

"Evening, Chuck," said Grandinetti to the manager sitting in the cashier's booth. Chuck wore a white shirt, black bow tie and black slacks.

"Lido!" Chuck said, shaking hands. "I thought they ran you out of town."

"They did. But I sneaked back in."

Chuck laughed. "Same old Lido. Hey, if I had your money, I could make jokes, too."

"So, is it twenty-five dollars apiece as usual?"

"No, man," Chuck said, shaking his head, "this one's on me. Go right on in." Then he looked at Dee. "How old is she, anyway?"

"Old enough to know better." Grandinetti took her down a well-lit, mirrored hallway.

The place reeked of marijuana, perfume and an unmistakable gynecological odor. They entered the main showroom. It was called the Ecstasy Room, and consisted of a series of private booths with windows that looked out into a long, rectangular chamber. Grandinetti and Dee squeezed into a booth together.

Her throat was dry. "May I have something to drink?" she asked.

"They don't serve drinks here," he said.

"I mean water."

"Not even that." He peered through the window, into the chamber. "Anyway, who needs refreshments? This is a cultural experience for you, sweetie. The Lowell brothers consistently provide the finest in live adult erotic entertainment. This place opened in 1966."

"Yeah, and I bet they haven't cleaned it once," Dee said. She did not want to spend the rest of her evening sharing a booth with Lido in a North Beach scumatorium.

"I've known the owners for years. They opened this business in the mid-Sixties, and today it's more popular than ever. Most of these strip joints will fold because they can't compete with the Lowells. They would be angry if they knew I called this a strip joint. They think of it as a kind of antiestablishment place where people can celebrate the miracle of the female body. Don't think all these sex palaces are the same, sweetie." He paused. "This place is from another era. The owners are authentic Haight hippies, and that's where their sensibilities lie. They also make money by selling sex, and that's what so irks the authorities. If you find you need to know about the other sex palaces, ask me; otherwise, you might end up in some downright ugly places. That would be a shame." He looked down at her. "Are we having fun yet?"

"I'm coming in my pants."

He chuckled.

She sniffed. "I smell Lysol."

"You certainly do. And you don't want to know what the Lysol is covering up."

Bump-and-grind music started up.

"Showtime," Grandinetti muttered.

They watched as a young woman with honey-blonde hair sauntered into the chamber, which was bare except for a hospital bed. She was dressed in an immaculate white smock and pretended to be oblivious to the faces in the windows surrounding her. She went to the bed and smoothed its already smooth sheets, then plumped up its pillows.

"Here comes the good part," Grandinetti said.

A young red-headed man limped in, wearing an authentic Army uniform.

Oh, shit, Dee thought. This is sick. Just way too fucking sick.

The music pounded and the Army man saluted the blonde, saying over the music, "Hiya, Miz Dee," and the nurse batted her eyes, Betty Boop-style, and waved him over to the bed. He nodded and eagerly went over, his cute dimpled face eager and none too intelligent. Dee closed her eyes and slumped against the side of the booth.

"Open your eyes," Grandinetti said. "I paid good money for this."

Dee said nothing but opened her eyes. She looked away for a few minutes. When she returned her attention to the show, the Army man was naked. His body was muscular and freckled.

The blonde tossed off her smock, threw her arms around him and they kissed. Then she kissed him all over, eventually kneeling and drawing his long, thick member into her mouth.

Dee, in spite of herself, found it erotic, the sexy way the performers' bodies moved, but she could not stand to watch it because of Grandinetti in the booth, and that she knew the performers were simply acting out Grandinetti's sordid fantasy.

"I gotta go," Dee said.

"The show is just getting started," Grandinetti said.

"Let me out. I'll wait in the car."

He let her by and she headed down the hallway, the way she had come in, and passed Chuck, who was busy with another customer. She reached the Mercedes, which he had left unlocked, and locked herself in. She stared for a while at the garish neon lights of Broadway Street's sex shows.

Grandinetti got in, nearly half an hour later.

"Pretty tasty show," he said. "You should have stayed till the end. It was bad manners to leave."

"You're an asshole." Dee was grateful that Grandinetti wasn't in a very talkative mood as he drove her back to Western Hills. They said nothing as the Mercedes came to a stop in front of Bud's Good Eats and Dee climbed out.

"So," Grandinetti said, "think about what you saw tonight."

She unlocked the gate and disappeared. When she reached the hallway, she found her mother leaning against Dee's bedroom door. Her eyes seemed rheumy, insane. Dee had never seen her mother look older or angrier.

"I know where you've been, what you've been doing. You won't get more than a few hours of sleep tonight. If you're too exhausted to work in the morning, I'll call in sick for you."

Dee shrugged. Inside her bedroom, she looked in her copy of *Looking for Mr. Goodbar* and couldn't find her bank book. Then she found it in *The Happy Hooker*. Its balance was just over three thousand dollars. Lido Grandinetti may have been a perverted asshole, but he was also a lifesaver.

Chapter 5

The Grandinetti mansion was completely dark. Everyone was elsewhere. The celebrations were everywhere tonight.

It was July 4, 1976. The Bicentennial. Jamey liked saving the evening's activities for tonight. He had his own reasons for celebrating; he believed by now he would be dead or in San Quentin. He was sweating profusely even though it was cool and the fog was surprisingly thick. Summer in San Francisco. His heart pounded as he and Bubba stopped the Kawasaki a block from the mansion and walked through the foggy gloom. He looked down at the black knapsack in his hand.

"We'll never get a better time than right now," he muttered as they reached the mansion and stood in front of the great white house. "America's birthday, everyone's got somewhere to go, hangin' out downtown, gettin' bombed." He smiled. "Well, candy man, *you're* gonna get bombed too. In a different way, of course." He chuckled.

He reached into the knapsack and pulled out a Molotov cocktail. His bare hands were slick and trembling as he took out a cigarette lighter. Bubba watched, his eyes wide, as Jamey ignited the oily cloth sticking out of the bottle's neck. The cloth caught fire immediately and, as agreed, Jamey handed the flaming object to Bubba, who had the more accurate throwing arm.

"No! I can't!" Bubba cried, throwing up his hands.

ENTREPRENEUR

Snarling, Jamey hurled the flaming projectile over the iron gate, through the dense fog, towards the Grandinetti mansion's big front window. The two boys then scrambled down the block and hopped onto the small motorbike. Jamey swore he could feel the exploded bomb's heat on his back as Bubba gunned the modest engine and struggled down the street. Now we're even, candy man. Bubba could barely steer, he was shaking so hard.

Bud Steeves climbed out of his truck at Fisherman's Wharf and looked out at the calm waters of San Francisco Bay, the majestic expanse of the Golden Gate Bridge almost directly overhead but greatly obscured by fog. He decided it was the right time for a swim, with all the stores closed because of the big holiday and all the people gone because you couldn't see fireworks in this fog that so often rolled in around this part of the city. America was 200 years old, Uncle Sam wasn't waging war on anyone at the moment and everybody was free to keep working, paying the IRS and doing a slow march to the grave.

Bud Steeves shed his clothes, slipped into the water and swam, his life seeming as murky as the fog surrounding him. His youngest son was a punk, wasting his life away picking fights and hanging around Market Street. Bud's Good Eats would survive till it died and customers would keep asking him to put more meat and less mayo on the sandwiches. The business of America is business, said Calvin Coolidge. Steeves peered out in the general direction of Alcatraz Island in the middle of the bay and swam vaguely towards it, his anger melting away as he muscled through the water. The Rock, he believed, was very much like himself: quiet, indestructible, unforgiving, unchanging. He felt a quiet kinship with the island, and sometimes wished he could move there, away from everyone.

ENTREPRENEUR

Paul stood on the sidewalk near the front door of Western Hills High School. Countless students milled around him, some lounged on the school's lawn. All were giddy and smiling, many were holding hands and kissing. To Paul, it was very much like the school spirit he saw whenever the Western Hills High Devils whipped another team's ass.

He waited for the red-white-and-blue fireworks to explode overhead. When they did, a deafening cheer swept through the crowd. Paul raised his lips to his trumpet and played "God Bless America." The crowd was utterly silent as the poignant trumpet music filled the warm summer air. Then they sang, at first some of them and then everyone: "God bless America, land that I love, stand beside her, and guide her, like a light from the sky up above..."

After another huge cheer, Paul launched into *The Star Spangled Banner*. This got his feet moving, and he did a march along the sidewalk as boys and girls eagerly followed him, first in a ceremonial trip around the school, then down the block, to Tower Street. As they paraded through Western Hills, the sky lit up with the crackle-pop of fireworks, and the boys and girls cheered.

Paul played with gusto and led his followers to

Miss Trinh's apartment building. He stood outside and peered up at the second floor, where he knew she lived. He didn't know what to play for someone Vietnamese on America's birthday, so he chose something ironic, *Hail to the Chief*. The window opened and Miss Trinh looked out at him and he played, so he played harder and as he did so the front door opened and a tall redheaded girl swept out, smiling, drawn to Paul's exuberant trumpet playing. Then Ms. Trinh just shut the window and disappeared.

Fuck you very much, Paul thought, shrugging. He finished the number, a girl threw her arms around him and kissed him, and the kids cheered once again. He smiled, wanting some more of that, and because she lived here, he knew where to get it. He played some more and moved on, the Pied Piper of Western Hills, as his followers stayed close behind.

Paul Steeves played on, giddy with American pride.

Donna Steeves wandered into Dee's bedroom and swore she could smell cigarette smoke. Outside, the noise and fireworks were getting to her. The Bicentennial meant nothing to her. Just another day off for everyone but her.

Dee had her makeup items on the dresser, though her coloring was so flawless that it really wasn't necessary to use cosmetics. Another painted lady. Donna sneered.

The bedroom was immaculate, but there was the odor of cigarette smoke. Well, so what if her daughter had secretly taken up cigarettes? Like mother, like daughter. She went to the bookcase and found the copy of *Fear of Flying*, where Dee had hidden her checkbook. Three thousand dollars. Donna had seen the cashier's check from Grandinetti before Dee had a chance to deposit it. For services rendered.

She took the checkbook out of *Fear of Flying* and put it inside her own tattered copy of *The Happy Hooker*. She smiled, wondering if her daughter would get the joke. Donna Steeves was still smiling as she left the room without bothering to turn off the light and close the door.

Dee was back at Pacific Point Army Hospital and the wounded soldiers were drunk. She liked them better that way. They were too weak to get boisterous and instead just fell asleep. Stronger men under alcohol would get less inhibited, but these ones, who were on painkillers, were simply put to sleep from the smuggled-in liquor. Some pea-soup fog had floated in and there was nothing to see outside. Many of the men had watched the nationwide celebrations on television, and Dee had feared a scenario in which the men's exuberance got out of hand and they began play fighting, then real fighting, and ended up making a war zone of the common room. But no. They soon grew bored with the TV coverage of the celebrations and the Bicentennial became just another day of recuperation. Dee was grateful for that.

A nurse said to her, "Tomorrow they'll pay for tonight, with those hangovers. Why don't you just go on home now?"

Dee nodded and went off to change into her street clothes. Just outside the hospital's large, imposing front entrance, she saw Red Tarlock loitering, smoking a cigarette. She walked past him, pretending not to notice him.

"Long time, no see, Dee," he said.

"Hello, Red." She stopped and offered him a small smile.

"Big day in the Yoo-ess-ay, huh? Yessir, that great lady called America finally did it. Went and turned two hundred years old. Lookin' better than ever, I'd say. Well, the good news just keeps on coming. Uncle Sam told me that I am being discharged tomorrow. Docs said I'm strong enough now that they can send me back to point of induction and my stitches won't come undone along the way. Very shortly I will be back in Florida, wondering what to do and where to go from there. Another confused, disillusioned Vietnam vet."

"Well, I would say you'll be glad to be home."

"Ain't that the truth. Anyway, I just came on by to remind you that if you ever happen to be in Florida, be sure to look me up. I'm sure to be in one White Pages or another." Then he said, "Damn shame you couldn't get over to see me that afternoon. I waited but you didn't show. I had to go it alone."

"I was afraid you'd bring that up."

Red stared for a moment at her breasts. "Damn, Dee, you're so gorgeous, it hurts to look at you." He shook his head and ambled away to a taxi that was waiting nearby.

Dee walked the few feet to the bus stop and waited as Red's taxi disappeared into the night. He had had the last word. Nice for him. Another perfectly awful day about to end. She couldn't wait for the bus to get here and deliver her home to Western Hills.

At the foot of the hospital's driveway, a dark car pulled up. It was Grandinetti's Mercedes—she knew by its license plate. She wanted to run into the hospital, down the street, across the Golden Gate Bridge. Just run. Somewhere.

The car's passenger door opened and Grandinetti leaned over, smiling. "Hop in, sweetie."

"Thanks, but the bus will be along in a minute or two." She hadn't seen or heard from him in weeks, ever since their night at the strip joint on Broadway Street.

"I thought we could get together and wish Lady Liberty a happy birthday," he said.

"I'm tired and want to go home."

"Dammit." He got out and went over to her. "Come on. Let's go to my house. It's only two minutes away. I know you want to."

She *did* want to. But she shook her head.

"Then I'll cut to the chase. I want to marry you. Now. We can fly off to Las Vegas and be married within a couple of hours. Just say yes."

She said nothing. The bus arrived at that moment, and she boarded it, walking right past Grandinetti. The bus lumbered away, and Dee knew that saying no to Grandinetti was the wisest thing she would ever regret.

They stopped in front of Bubba's house and Jamey got off. "Look," he said, "you can't say anything about tonight. Hear me?"

Bubba just stood there hangdog, whimpering.

"For Christ's sake, grow up!" Jamey snapped. "You tell anyone we torched the mansion, we're both fucked. And I swear to God, I'll pound you if you say anything."

Bubba nodded and went home. Jamey turned and jogged to his own front door.

He knew he wouldn't sleep that night. The next day the fire would be all over the news, and he prayed that Bubba would be man enough to keep quiet about it. Jamey had the overwhelming urge just to take off and hide. Jamey Steeves knew, he just *knew*, that he was really going to be swimming in a river of shit this time.

ENTREPRENEUR

Chapter 6

I hate this, Donna Steeves thought as she looked at the roast beef and Yorkshire pudding her husband had prepared. Only he likes it, and he makes it for everyone's birthday.

Bud Steeves was smiling. It was Paul's birthday. His oldest son was becoming a man, and so he had closed Bud's Good Eats for the day. Steeves usually ignored birthdays altogether, except for the dinner that was a tradition from his boyhood. The very recent Bicentennial may have had something to do with his heightened spirits; America's big birthday had made the whole country giddy. If Paul could turn 17 and America 200 at least once a week, Donna thought, things in their household would be that much quieter. He had bought Paul a fine new suit for his birthday and told Dee she could keep all of her salary from now on.

"From now on, we all eat together," said Steeves. "No eating and running off. We are a family."

They all sat at the dining room table, Paul sheepish and uncomfortable but smiling in his fine new suit—navy blue, with a white shirt and burgundy tie. Dee tried desperately not to roll her eyeballs at her father fawning over his fair-haired, star-spangled boy. She still wanted to move away and become her own woman. Jamey sat, a small smile spreading across his freshly washed face. Since the Fourth of July, he had been as close to being the model son as his parents could ever hope. He went to school, came home, locked himself in his bedroom to study and even offered to do some of the grunt work at Bud's Good

Eats. He couldn't work behind the counter, knowing that the customers didn't like him and certainly would never eat a sandwich he had made. Perhaps it was the country's landmark birthday that made them all, at least for now, a family.

To Donna Steeves, the ideal family was, and always had been, something of a cross between *The Brady Bunch* and Norman Rockwell paintings. Families did not fight, or did so with spirit and humor and kept their battles brief. They did not remain angry at each other for long. They dressed properly and showed each other courtesy and respect. Everyone lived long and stayed healthy. Nobody moved far from home, and if they did, they came back as often as they could.

These were simply the notions she had carried throughout life, not knowing if any such families existed and certain that she would never belong to one. She did not know her neighbors in Western Hills despite so many years in residence there; she was at once too bashful and too proud to acquaint herself with them. As the proprietors of Bud's Good Eats, she and her husband, by all outward appearances, had succeeded in business and marriage while other local couples went broke and split up. Yet she waited on them, making their sandwiches until her arms and legs ached.

Her life with her husband, Dee and Jamey did not strike her as a family that anyone might envy. She could see little of value that any of them had given her, and she was quite sure she had failed them on any number of levels.

It was up to Paul. He was the one who would make them all proud. In his new blue suit, white shirt and red tie.

Bud Steeves was meticulous in setting down the dinner before them all. He had made everything himself, and his wife was just as glad to sit in the living room throughout the afternoon. Finally he took opened a couple of bottles of Napa Valley red wine. "A toast," he said. "To my splendid son Paul. May he set the world on fire."

Jamey, remembering his July Fourth exploits with the Molotov cocktail, nearly laughed out loud at his father's choice of words.

They all clinked glasses and sipped the good red wine.

Steeves did not say more about his predictions for Paul's glorious future. But it was clear to all that Paul would rise at something, and soon, to a place where everything that had eluded his family in Western Hills would be theirs for the asking.

Paul did not much like roast beef and Yorkshire pudding. In fact, he could think of no food that he would call his favorite. Still, he cut the food, ate it and sipped at the wine. On this, his birthday, he made resolutions to himself: he would never get fat, drunk or married. He would live a clean life of hard work, right thinking and self-denial. He would never make any of the mistakes that had fouled up his parents' lives.

He had returned to the house near Ms. Trinh's to find the girl who had kissed him on the Fourth of July. He loitered there, wondering what any resident who recognized him might think. People sometimes got pretty spooked by neighborhood youths just hanging around and might call the cops. But within minutes, out came his reward. She was tall and redheaded, with pale green eyes and big breasts and the sincere smile of someone who hadn't yet learned about how difficult life could be.

Her name was Nancy Hollandsworth. She had just moved into Western Hills from Arizona because her father worked for the government. She linked hands with Paul and they bounded down the street together. She had kissed him on the Fourth because she admired his trumpet playing and patriotism. Paul, naturally, had been delighted by the kiss;

he could still remember the moment of her smooth lips pressed against his and her open, toothy smile.

She adored music and had sung for years in her school choir. She said he played the best trumpet she'd heard since Miles Davis, and he half-promised to have her as the guest female vocalist when he and his band next played. The entrepreneur in him thought it a grand idea, having a tall pretty redhead with big boobs fronting the band.

Nancy liked boys who had direction; she saw immediately that Paul knew who he was and what he was about. She thought it was unusual and exciting for someone his age to know himself so well. His father's prediction unnerved him a bit, about Paul's "setting the world on fire." How, precisely, would he do *that*? He was smart, certainly. But the world was full of people whose smarts had gotten them absolutely nowhere. Setting the world on fire required something special: imagination, vision, stupendous luck. His parents were humble people, so he could count on them only for moral support.

One of his talents was the ability to recognize the potential in other people. At school, Dennis Chung could barely spell kat and narrowly avoided having to take English at summer school, but he had an amazing aptitude for physics, biology and chemistry. He effortlessly aced tests that made Paul sweat. Dennis would doubtless win a scholarship to Caltech, Stanford or MIT. His success in the natural sciences was inevitable. Dennis Chung hadn't chosen his path; it had chosen him.

Paul could do many things well and a few very well. He could play the trumpet, had played in the school band but was no Miles Davis, and he was competent on the electric guitar but would never make anyone forget Jimi Hendrix or Eddie Van Halen. His bandmates, musically, were as good as he was or even better; together, on a good night, they could get on stage and have fun making danceable music, but they were now as good as they likely would ever be.

In sports, he had made the basketball team, but San Francisco—indeed, California—was a big place; there were better players around, much better, whose athletic achievements made the local newspapers and reminded him of his own mediocrity. Willie Buttilla, a senior who played forward for the Devils, was academically mediocre. But he stood six-seven, and, on the court, had lightning speed. He was one of the most talked-about players in the Bay Area. People watched Devils' games just to watch Willie fake opponents right out of the gym. He was nearly perfect from the free-throw line and could hit jumpshots that left crowds breathless. The campus paper's sports section often was a tribute to him. Willie would go from Western Hills High to the college of his choice, then to the NBA.

In English, Paul did better than Andrew Jay, mainly because Andrew was abrasive and ugly and the teacher didn't like him. Andrew disliked the teacher and flunked everything but English and journalism. But you merely had to read his passionate, eloquent articles in the school paper, which captured everyone's imagination, to know that someday Andrew Jay would win a Pulitzer Prize.

Paul had the gift of leadership, of bringing out the best in those around him. He excelled at making life look easy and never complaining. But making it look easy took hard work. He hid his studying better than the others did and made a special effort to be personable even when feeling adolescent moodiness. He worked out to stay in shape and didn't eat the greasy stuff the other kids devoured. He was always elected to student government because of his popularity and willingness to do the things everyone else agreed was desirable but too much trouble: when Western Hills High started having school plays after a dozen-year hiatus, Paul singlehandedly began doing all of the publicity and much of the logistical work; when others got involved, he supervised them. If Paul Steeves was in charge, it would be done right, the first time. He also organized dances and other functions.

Why he did such things mystified him in many ways. At times, he was ambivalent about the whole human race. He had many admirers but few true friends. His personable aloofness simply made people value him that much more. At times he wondered if he really cared all that much for his own family. He lived with them, but in many ways his parents and siblings weren't much different from the people he saw at school every day.

Although considered uniformly handsome and certainly popular enough to date whichever girl he wanted, Paul was insecure about his appearance. He disliked his long, lithe body, which looked girlish when compared to the bulk of some of the other jocks at Western Hills High. He thought his skin was too dark, his nose too big and face too narrow. He disliked his slurry California speech and envied the Eastern lockjaw he heard sometimes on the news and knew that if, by some miracle, he ever attended an Ivy League school, the moment he opened his mouth he would inadvertently reveal himself for what he was: a kid from working-class San Francisco who had no business being among the young lions of the East.

Nancy aside, he'd had little experience with girls. He had never been in love, and his infatuation with Miss Trinh had been humiliating. So he seemed aloof and uninterested; he could have all of them, so he wanted none of them. In truth, he feared having an intimate relationship in which he lowered his guard and the girl discovered that Paul Steeves, at his core, was nothing special.

He envied Jamey. He was bad, tough and mean. His brother had it made. Everyone already hated or feared him, so he could say what he liked and not give a shit. Jamey had seduced neighborhood virgins, been threatened with beatings by their brothers, but nothing had come of it. None of them wanted to mix it up with Jamey Steeves. And if they got a couple of guys to help work Jamey over, Jamey could easily get help from other local badasses. Next thing you knew, a neighborhood gang war had started in Western Hills, and nobody wanted *that*.

"Tastes great, Dad," Paul said of the roast beef and Yorkshire pudding, providing the expected compliment. He gobbled up his food and held out his plate for a second helping he didn't want.

Dee's stomach turned as she nibbled at her leathery roast beef. What do I say, and how do I say it? She had just gotten her two weeks' notice at Grandinetti Chocolate. Reason for layoff: Shortage of work. Dee and another woman had been laid off. Profits were down, expenses up, cocoa beans from South America were less abundant than expected, the energy crisis was sending fuel costs through the ceiling, blah, blah, blah.

The human resources manager, Mrs. Watts, had called her in and laid her off with what bordered on disbelief. Why was the highly efficient Deirdre Steeves, of all people, getting the heave-ho? She seemed more surprised when Dee, who knew that Lido Grandinetti was merely retaliating because of her rejection of him.

Dee said to Mrs. Watts, "I wasn't going to spend the rest of my life here, anyway."

She wondered what she would tell her father. She would have to tell him tonight, while he was in a good mood over Paul's birthday. Best to come out with it and hope he doesn't go ballistic, she decided. But I'll wait till I finish dessert.

The birthday cake was Paul's favorite, the fresh-fruit kind with real whipped cream. Steeves set it down and they all sang "Happy Birthday to You." Then the doorbell rang.

"What the hell...?" Steeves said. "Nobody ever rings that bell."

"I'll check it out." Dee hurried downstairs, certain it was Lido Grandinetti, all dressed up, with his Mercedes parked just behind him. She wanted him to see her with her hair up, dress up, at home with her family. She wanted to tell him to fuck off forever, or to elope with him that night. She would decide as soon as she opened the door.

But it was not Grandinetti. It was Bubba Ozinski's father and, next to him, a middle-aged man in a San Francisco police uniform.

"Hello, Dee," said Ozinski, looking very grim. He gestured to the cop. "This is Captain Geary from the Western Hills precinct. Is your father home? We need to speak to him right away."

"Just a moment." Her heart pounding, she ran upstairs and blurted, "Dad, there's a couple of men at the door. They won't say who they are..." She thought it best to lie; if she said a cop was there with Bubba's father, Jamey would simply bolt out the back door.

"Always something." Steeves rose and lumbered across the room and down the stairs.

Steeves faced the two men. "Yeah?"

Ozinski said, "I'm Bobby Ozinski's father—"

"I know. Bubba's the fat kid who runs around with Jamey." Steeves nodded at the cop. "Geary. What's up?"

"May we speak in private?" Ozinski asked.

"This is private enough for me," Steeves said.

"This is a *very* delicate matter..." said Geary.

"Look, you boys speak your piece so I can get back to dessert." Still, he relented and led them to the door that opened into Bud's Good Eats.

Donna Steeves wondered what was going on downstairs. The men had obviously gone into the deli. Paul was getting anxious to get to Nancy's place.

"Must be important," Donna said. "Dee, who's there?"

"Dad will tell you when he's done."

"Tell me!" she snapped.

Dee swallowed hard. "Mr. Ozinski."

Donna frowned. "Bubba's father?"

Jamey continued eating cake, silent.

"Who else?"

"Captain Geary."

"The police?" Donna looked at Jamey.

Then Steeves called up from downstairs, "Jamey, come down here now."

Jamey slid out of his chair and bounced downstairs, as if this summons were expected. The other three Steeveses just stared at each other. Paul had a feeling he wouldn't be seeing Nancy after all that evening.

Jamey encountered silence and darkness in Bud's Good Eats. Mr. Ozinski and Captain Geary stood side by side at the rear of the small deli.

"Do you recognize this?"

Geary held out the Molotov cocktail Jamey had thrown at Grandinetti's mansion on the Fourth of July. The bottle, still full of clear fluid, was sealed in a clear plastic bag.

Jamey groaned. Oh, God, that fuckin' Bubba and his big fuckin' mouth.

"I'm sure it has your fingerprints all over it," Geary said. "Apparently you threw it in heavy fog and didn't see that the front window at the Grandinetti mansion was open. The bottle just flew into the living room and landed on the sofa. Then the fuse burned out, fortunately."

Jamey closed his eyes.

"Let me explain," Geary continued. "Mr. Grandinetti is a reasonable man. He doesn't want trouble. He reported this to our Pacific Heights precinct, and before we could begin an investigation, Bobby Ozinski wisely confessed to his father, who reported it to us. Mr. Grandinetti left it to me to handle this matter in the way I saw fit. So my offer to you is this: leave San Francisco immediately and never return. Then you won't have to go to jail."

"I'll answer for him," Steeves said. "He'll be out of here within the hour if Grandinetti will forget about this."

Geary looked at Ozinski and said, "Okay." They left the deli. Bud Steeves walked up to his son and, scowling, said, "You stupid little bastard, you almost ruined my whole life just now." He reared back and threw a right cross at Jamey, who saw it coming and could easily have ducked but it crash into his right eye. He staggered backwards but did not fall. He then grinned and steadied himself, his eye already beginning to swell. He raised his hands like a boxer and approached his father, who raised his hands as well. Jamey faked with the left and Steeves flinched, then Jamey came in with the right and blackened his father's eye.

"We're even," he said.

Steeves, in much greater physical pain than his son, covered his eye and tried to focus on Jamey, who had taken worse beatings from tougher guys. The visit from the cop, the order to get out of town and the punch from his father—all had meant little to Jamey Steeves.

Steeves addressed his son as best he could despite the excruciating pain spreading through his sinuses and mouth. "Okay, get packed. Paul will go with you to the

Greyhound station. Go to your uncle's place in Sacramento. I'll call and let him know you're coming." Then he staggered into the backroom, put some ice chips into a plastic bag and pressed it to his eye. Jamey grinned, his own eye burning somewhat, as he watched his father struggle up the stairs to fetch Paul.

A few minutes later, Steeves and Paul came down together. Paul looked from one black eye to the other, then back again, his face white and his movements anxious, as if expecting one of them to throw a punch at him, too.

"Paul packed your bag. I gave him money for your ticket. It's a three-hour ride to Sacramento. Your Uncle Jack will be there to meet you. If I ever see you here again, I will call the cops." Steeves then headed back up the stairs.

Jamey grinned. Sacramento, here I come, as if there's no trouble for me to get into up there.

He and Paul walked up Tower Street and took the bus to Market Street, where they got off and headed towards the Greyhound station. The night was clear and quiet, with some downtown workers on the street heading home to families and dinner. Paul felt envious of his brother; it was his birthday and yet Jamey, the baby of the family, was getting out first. How unfair!

"How come you and Dad punched it out?" he asked.

"I got Dad pissed."

"How?"

"Ask him. He'll be happy to tell you." Then, "Mind if I ask you a question? A personal question?"

Paul shrugged. "Go ahead."

"Ever been in love, Paul?"

"No. There's time for that."

"Ever *made* love?"

Paul said nothing.

Jamey tsked. "You're the only Steeves virgin left."

"Really? I didn't know Dee had a guy."

"Her boss. I found out by accident. Bubba heard this rumor that Grandinetti was banging my sister. So we went to check things out. Word got back to Dad...and here we are."

They reached the bus station, just off Market Street. Jamey sat in the waiting room and plopped a quarter into the coin-operated television bolted to his seat. Paul went to the ticket counter to pay the fare to Sacramento. The state capital wasn't where *he* would have gone, but it was away, and that was where he wanted to be, too.

He came over and handed the long white envelope to his brother. "It's an express trip, three hours. Guess I ought to be getting along now. Not too safe for a lone white boy."

Jamey stuck out his hand. "Thanks. Happy birthday."

Paul shook his hand. "Have a nice trip."

Back out on Market Street, Paul hurried to get the bus back home. When it arrived, he boarded and gazed out the window, losing himself in thoughts of a new life, in another part of San Francisco or, like Jamey, in another city altogether. He got back to Western Hills and noticed that Bud's Good Eats was dark. He thought the restaurant should have had a sign posted in the door: "Closed tonight in honor of Mr. Paul Steeves's Birthday."

Happy fucking birthday to me, he thought, opening the iron gate and traipsing up the stairs.

Dee waited in their living room with her suitcase. She smiled. "I'm leaving too. Want another trip downtown, to that hideous Greyhound station? I'm going to Los Angeles."

"What about your job?"

"Laid off."

"Let's go."

They stopped at the Rusty Nail, a tavern where there was always a taxi waiting for a drunken fare. The aging car lumbered along till it reached downtown. Next to Paul, Dee looked radiant and eager. He envied her but wondered what she would do in L.A., where they had no Uncle Jack to take her in. Did Dee have any money or connections she hadn't told him about? He smelled her sweet perfume and saw her blonde hair pinned up, her young breasts jutting. So Grandinetti had been her first? Western Hills' fairest maiden had been ravished by the rich asshole who'd had a hundred other Dees. Then he laid her off, for whatever reason. Well, the creep didn't deserve her. If he ever tried to contact Paul about Dee's whereabouts, he'd say go to hell and hang up.

The cab arrived at the Greyhound station. Dee paid the driver and he unloaded the suitcase from the trunk. She looked up at the station's neon sign and its huge running-dog logo. She sniffed. "God, this area is so creepy." "Smells like a bathroom out here."

"Jamey loved it here."

"Figures. Say, let's go for a drink. There's a bus to L.A. every hour. I'll catch the next one."

"I'm underage. They won't let me in."

"So am I. We'll lie. We look old enough." They went into the Travelers' Tavern, right next door to the bus station.

The bartender swished over. He wore a handlebar mustache and a gold earring in each ear. "May I help you?"

"Two rum and Cokes, please," said Dee.

The bartender looked at them doubtfully for a moment but did not ask them for identification. He went away to mix their drinks.

Dee reached over and gently kissed Paul's cheek. "Happy birthday." Then she asked, "Did Jamey say why he had that fight with Dad?"

"No, but they sure beat the hell out of each other."

The bartender came back, Dee paid him and he left. She clinked her glass against Paul's. "Here's to ya."

They sipped in silence.

"You're the only one I'll miss," Dee said.

"Then why do you have to go?"

"Because I have to get away from someone."

"Grandinetti."

Dee made a face. "Sneaky bastard..."

"He used you."

She shook her head. "We used each other. He bought me meals I could never afford on my own, drove me around in a Mercedes and flattered me."

Paul sneered. "He's ugly."

Dee smirked. "Not so bad."

"Sounds as if you liked him."

"I liked *it.*"

"Then why leave?"

"Because if I stayed, I would become Mrs. Lido Grandinetti, and then soon I would become his ex. Better to put this all behind me right now."

"And what's in L.A. for you?"

"No Lido, Mom or Dad. With my Grandinetti work experience, I'll find a new job." She paused. "You should get out as soon as school's out. You'll grow up, too. Become your own man."

Paul frowned. "I *am* my own man."

"No. You're fraudulent. As bad as Lido, in your own way."

"I resent that."

"Well, at least now you're standing up for yourself."

He left the bar without saying goodbye. Walking down the street towards the Western Hills bus stop, he felt tears stinging his eyes. He boarded the bus and got off on Tower Street. He had been found out. Dee had had enough backbone to tell him the truth about himself, and her reward was to escape them all, escape Western Hills, forever.

Donna Steeves sat in the kitchen, smoking one Winston after another and staring at the mess on her table. Roast beef, Yorkshire pudding, vegetables, birthday cake, all of it cold and stale. The hoodlum and the whore are now gone, she thought. But my Paul is still with me for another year. If my husband, out for his nightly swim in Fisherman's Wharf, drowns, it will be the perfect day.

ENTREPRENEUR

Chapter 7

Jamey awoke with a start from his forbidden nap as a noisy taxi sped by. It had to be a taxi; who else would be out on the road at this hour? He got up out of the uncomfortable folding chair and stretched his legs, wondering if the security supervisor would drive by that night to check up on his newest guard, Buford James Steeves, Junior. Jamey looked up at the clear, starry sky. He didn't know the exact time and didn't care; what difference did it make? Out here, one hour was the same as the next.

He stretched some more, looking down and laughing at his black nylon windbreaker. On the left breast of his jacket was a plastic oval badge, and on the back the word SECURITY stretched across in big white fluorescent letters. Not exactly Jamey's idea of gainful employment.

Yep, Uncle Jack, that astute British businessman, had sure put his nephew to useful, gratifying work, wandering around this fenced-in construction site that someday soon would be an apartment building, or an office building, or whatever the hell it was supposed to be. And just to make sure his new guard didn't fuck off anywhere during his shift, Uncle Jack had made sure to padlock the fence. All Jamey could do from midnight till eight in the morning was eat his meal, drink his coffee and listen to his portable Panasonic. There was a smelly portable toilet that he dreaded using, and the weak light over the guard's desk made it impossible even to read the newspaper. Well, *that* was fucked.

ENTREPRENEUR

Jamey reached down and checked his radio. It was battery operated, and as usual he had fallen asleep in the hot arid Sacramento darkness with the radio on. The batteries weren't dead, thank God. He would have to look into investing in some rechargeable ones. He had a feeling he would be spending many more nights at construction sites before moving on to better things.

Sacramento, Jamey decided, was a strange place. America was the most important country in the world, and California was the most important part of America, and Sacramento was the capital of California, so it would figure that Sacramento would seem really big and important. But no. Sacramento seemed like a bunch of scrubland, with suburbs, a freeway, lots of government buildings, brown parched land but not much else. Well, that was all right by him, but it would all change. You just had to give it a little time, and Sacramento would grow up. Anyway, it was a shitload better than San Francisco, cramped and crowded, foggy and faggy.

He was hungry, so he reached into his lunch pail and took out a submarine sandwich. He smiled. Nice big sandwich filled with lettuce, cheese, tomatoes and meat. He turned up the radio and munched away to the Rolling Stones. Actually, his job wasn't so bad at this hour, with the music playing and no one but him awake and a few cars driving by. It was like spying.

The sandwich was fresh and delicious, prepared by Maria, the Browns' housekeeper. She was close to forty and prematurely graying, a handsome slim woman from South America with a warm smile and the nicest set of boobs Jamey had ever seen, and she showed them to him a lot. She made him great meals and smiled at him often. She seemed to consider herself pretty lucky, working for a living as the Browns' housekeeper, like this was some kind of dream-come-true job for a lowly woman from Latin America. Maria really seemed to think the Browns were her natural superiors.

Uncle Jack and Aunt Virginia learned quickly enough that they couldn't keep Jamey indoors at night, so Uncle Jack installed his nephew as the all-night, locked-in security guard at his newest construction site. Uncle Jack was not a subtle man.

Jamey spent little time at his new home. Rather than work all night and sleep most of the day, like most nightwatchmen, he slept through his shift and moseyed around town till it was time to work again. He thought at first that Uncle Jack must be amazed at his capacity for going without sleep, but then it occurred to him that he wasn't fooling anyone; Uncle Jack guessed he mostly slept on the job. The site really needed no guard; what else was there to do but sleep and listen to the radio?

Jamey didn't have many friends yet, but in his wanderings he had joined some pickup softball and football games and eventually caught the eyes of a few local girls. He usually went to Gold's Gym right after work and pumped iron for an hour. He was getting prodigiously muscular.

With the other boys, he was moderately popular because he kept his mouth shut and his hands to himself. He told them he was from San Francisco but left because he hated it, and the other kids didn't ask questions. At home, Uncle Jack and Aunt Virginia asked no questions about why he had come to live with them, and their two sons stayed out of his way. All in all, it wasn't a bad deal; he was finally away from Mom, Dad, pesky Paul and conceited Dee. It wasn't a bad deal for Uncle Jack, either, who paid only minimum wage and seldom saw his teenaged nephew.

Nevertheless, Jamey in time volunteered that he had dropped out of Western Hills High and had hung out with the wrong crowd. He didn't tell them he was the worst member of that wrong crowd.

Uncle Jack nodded. He said it was indeed a difficult situation and that Bud Steeves had done the right thing in sending the boy away from San Francisco. "That awful place. It's Sodom and Gomorrah. How can they stand living there?"

He believed Jamey was on the right track but needed more familial support. Why hadn't any of them called? It wasn't natural that a family should just banish one of its own over personal problems. Uncle Jack was a devout family man, adoring and indulgent with his wife and children. He confided to Jamey, "Your father is my brother-in-law, you know. I married his sister...well, I came to America from England years ago, made it and tried to help him out, but he was stubborn and he struggled, and that's what makes him feel so inadequate. Who knows?"

The key to success in life, Uncle Jack concluded, was optimism. "Don't hate anyone. I don't hate the Vietnamese, Soviets, Cubans, blacks, Mexicans. I didn't even hate the SLA. Look, mate, if anyone with money wants to buy anything from me, I'll sell it to him and shake his hand. That's the only way to go if you want success in this life. That's the best advice you'll ever get from me or anyone else."

Jamey finished his sandwich in the darkness and looked up to see the glare of headlights as a car slowed down. He smiled, knowing it was the Nordstrom twins, Charlotte and Gigi. They lived with their mother and father in one of Sacramento's bigger houses and as the parents slept the daughters sometimes stole the car keys and went joyriding. They were tall blonde girls with small high breasts and big dark eyes who loved screwing every boy they could. Jamey couldn't get over how the girls had so much independence; Mr. and Mrs.

Nordstrom obviously did not know about their daughters' nocturnal car voyages and scarlet reputations. He had balled both of the girls, and so had most of the other boys they knew. He still couldn't tell them apart sometimes.

"Hi, Jamey," one of them called out from the rolled-down window. He could barely see them through the flimsy bars of the portable fence, so he stood up and grabbed at the fence like a prisoner clutching heavy iron bars.

"Hi, Charlotte," he said.

"I'm Gigi."

"Yeah."

"Listen," Gigi said, "we know you have a big club. We wanna join." She giggled.

He laughed. "I'd love to share it with you. But you know I'm locked in here till eight."

"Oh, come on. I can't believe a big strong guy like you is trapped inside that silly little fence. You could rip it in half easily."

"Yeah, but my uncle would shit a brick."

The girl let her eyes wander around the site for a moment. "You have a really, really stupid job. I'm sure you could find something much better if you put your mind to it."

"I'll tell my agent to get me a better gig."

The girl giggled again. "You're funny, Jamey. But I'm serious about your getting a better job. This isn't work for a smart grown man."

Jamey had told them he was twenty and had finished high school but was having too much trouble finding himself to get on the career fast track. "Maybe this is my true calling. Nighttime security work. Walk softly and carry a big stick."

Gigi laughed loudly. "Yeah, you've brutalized us with your big stick a few times. By the way, we're having a barbecue at the park tomorrow afternoon. Promise to come?"

"I'll do my best."

"Do better than that. Four-thirty tomorrow. I will be deeply disappointed if you don't show up. Gotta run." She revved up the engine and screamed off.

Jamey sat down again and opened his lunch pail, to see what sort of dessert Maria had put inside. He groped around and took out what felt like a slick piece of paper. It was a photo of her, smiling, and on the back it said, "Think of me always. Love, M."

He smiled and slipped the photo into his wallet. "I'll do that," he murmured. A picture and a personal note on its back from a thirtyish woman who apparently had quite a little crush on sixteen-year-old Jamey. "Sorry, Nordstrom gals," he said in the darkness. "I won't be at your picnic. Something tells me I just got a better offer."

The Bay Area Boyz played *Pretty Woman*, and Paul showed off for Nancy with his best guitar riff as she sat at a rear table. Although he couldn't see her, he was very aware of her at the back of the room, listening to the band and doubtless keeping time with her foot as she always did. The Bay Area Boyz was Paul's band although he wasn't its best musician. He thought that any William Morris agent who heard them would say, "Your name is clever, but you guys really need to practice."

They had this gig, for tonight only, at the Balboa Community Center, a large hall tucked away in the south end of San Francisco. Paul wasn't thrilled about this one-nighter; it didn't pay well but they needed the experience, and California, being one of the world's music capitals, was filled with competing bands. You took what you could get.

This dance was an informal affair that Paul guessed served mainly to get the Balboa kids off the streets for the evening. The kids danced freely and exuberantly; the floor was always full.

Paul played the final chords of the song to robust applause and announced the band would be taking a break. He set down his guitar, left the stage with the others and made a beeline for Nancy, eager to get out of the stifling community center. They joined hands and exited into the parking lot. Nancy never seemed to notice other guys, and her hand was strong and firm in his, supportive and affectionate. "When you play that guitar," she murmured in his ear, "I forget about everything else. Music makes me so horny."

Paul chuckled. He led her out into the parking lot and chose the cleanest, shiniest car. He pressed her against the door of a long dark car and sealed her mouth in a kiss. His hands seized her breasts; all Paul and Nancy ever did was kiss and grope. He started to wonder when that wouldn't be enough, at least for him. After several minutes their lips parted and Paul reached behind her. The car's door opened with a soft, gentle click. "In here," he said in a weak, throaty moan.

"It's not your car—"

"Who cares?"

He pulled her in. The car's interior was dark and smooth and leathery, filled with the smell of a new car and some sort of cologne. They resumed making out. Paul closed his eyes in the darkness and took great comfort in the strong embrace of Nancy's lean athletic arms, her warm fresh breath, her clean, shampooed hair.

"Get your sweaty, horny little asses out of my car!"

Paul hadn't even heard the car's door being opened, but the deep, masculine voice sounded annoyed yet somehow amused. He and Nancy looked up.

"After all that guitar playing, Mr. Steeves, I would have thought your hands might like a rest."

He knows me, Paul thought. From where? Then the man climbed into the car, and in the bright interior light he saw the black hair, the deep-set dark eyes, the long narrow body and beautiful clothes. Lido Grandinetti. Why the hell was *he* here?

"Just ignore me. I'm on my way back inside. Just came in to get my cigarettes. Make yourselves more comfortable. But please clean up if you make a mess."

Paul blushed. Grandinetti disappeared in an instant, leaving him and Nancy once again in the darkness of the car.

Nancy frowned. "Where does he know you from, Paul?"

"Lido Grandinetti. The chocolate king. He knows my sister. *Knew* my sister. You want to pick up where we left off?"

She shook her head. "Not now. Let's just go back in."

The two traipsed back into the community center. Grandinetti greeted them with a small smile, leaning with his back against the bar. He was dressed in a tan linen sportscoat and off-white pleated slacks. He looked stylish, wealthy and jaded, so unlike these T-shirted kids. Paul nearly laughed. Didn't the scion of Grandinetti Chocolate have anything better to do on Saturday night than hang out in the Balboa Community Center? With his fine clothes, fancy car, money and experience, he could at least seduce one or two of these young virginal cuties to validate his evening. Dee was right, Paul thought. Grandinetti, in his own megabucks way, *was* pathetic.

When the band finished at one o'clock and packed up, Grandinetti came by. "Paul? Do you have a ride home?"

"Usually we all just cram into Ned's van."

He shook his head. "Well, tonight you'll do no cramming. You'll travel back to Western Hills in style."

Paul shrugged and nodded, his brow sweaty. He went over to Ned Farley, his bandmate, and said, "Ned, we won't be joining you guys for a bite as usual. Got a family friend to drive us home. See ya."

Grandinetti threw his arm around Nancy and said, "Yeah, Ned, see ya. Take care of the guitar and stuff, will you?"

In the car, Nancy sat between Paul and Grandinetti; Ned had agreed to take the guitar and amplifier back home in the van. Paul loved the beauty of the Mercedes and how smoothly it traveled out of the parking lot and through the streets. His father's pickup truck, his pride and joy, was such a rustbucket compared to the Mercedes, and while Bud Steeves slaved away to keep his truck on the road and his family afloat, Grandinetti took his material blessings for granted. So said Dee.

Grandinetti drove very slowly, as if in no hurry to reach Western Hills and conclude his evening. "You sounded good tonight, Paul. Quite professional for a bunch of high school kids just trying to make a buck."

"We've gotten better," Paul said. "I don't know if we'll play together that much longer. High school's over next year and there *are* other priorities, you know."

"I thought you might turn pro," Grandinetti said.

Paul laughed. "No. The musician's life? Not for this guy, thanks very much. Anyway, I'm not good enough."

"Ah. Perhaps I'm just no judge of musicianship. But Deirdre insists you have talent. What *are* your plans, Paul? Tell me honestly."

"Straight to bed. I'm really beat."

Grandinetti laughed. "No, I mean your plans for the *future*, once you're out of high school."

"College is where he should be," Nancy said. "He's consistently on the honor roll."

"'Consistently'?" Grandinetti said. "Is that so, Paul?"

"Yessir," he drawled. "All you have to do to make the Western Hills High honor roll is blow enough kisses at the teachers." He felt Nancy's elbow jab his side.

"I'm sure the honor roll is an admirable achievement, much deserved," Grandinetti said.

"Yes," Nancy said.

"Anyway," Grandinetti continued, "*where* are you planning to go to college?"

"Where did *you* go to college, Mr. Grandinetti? Or *did* you go?" Nancy asked.

"Call me Lido. I went to Stanford. If you like, I can contact Stanford and maybe pull a string or two. It's quite hard to get in otherwise."

"There are plenty of quality schools in the Bay Area," Paul said.

"But only *one* is called Stanford. And that one fact makes all the difference, as you'll learn soon enough."

They stopped at Nancy's house. "There you go, young lady," Grandinetti said. "It's been a treat meeting you."

"Thanks." She bounded out of the car and towards her front door, Paul following. At her doorstep, he leaned towards her for a goodnight kiss, eyes shut and lips puckered. But when he felt nothing and opened his eyes, he found her white-lipped with rage. "'I'm on the honor roll because I blew kisses at enough teachers.' How could you *say* that in front of that prick? Doesn't he feel superior enough as it is?"

"Do we have to get into this right now?"

"Is Dee's name really Deirdre? How come *he* knew her real name? Sounds like the local rich playboy is getting nice and chummy with the whole Steeves clan."

Paul sighed.

"I'm not your kind. Go back to Lido Greedo over there. I think he's getting lonely for his bud." Nancy's eyes danced in the yellowish porch light. "He wants to send you to Stanford, huh? How will you repay him? Oh, but that's none of *my* business." She opened her front door and disappeared.

Paul dragged himself back to the car. He got back in and shut the door.

"Is everything all right?" Grandinetti pulled out from the curb.

"Women," Paul muttered, shaking his head. "Fuck."

Grandinetti guffawed. "Are you referring to Nancy? She's a good one, I can assure you." They crept along to Tower Street, then to Diego Avenue.

"Turn here." Paul gestured to his right.

"I know the way."

Of course you do, Paul thought.

Grandinetti sneered a bit, peering through the windshield. "All these apartments and little stores with their ostentatious iron gates! As if anyone here has anything worth stealing." He paused. "Say, is Deirdre still in town? Shame we had to lay her off."

"She's gone. She didn't say where she's living. I hear from her now and again."

Dee was staying at a place called the Los Angeles Women's Residence and loved her new city. She was looking for film parts and meeting new people all the time and her letters bounced with enthusiasm. Away from Western Hills and her family. Paul knew that was the source of her newfound happiness.

"Well, give her my best. She has my number, you know. Remind her that I'm only a call away. She said you like to play tennis. I have a lifetime membership in one of the better clubs. Would love to play a few sets with you sometime. Interested?"

"I'll get back to you."

He nodded. "Fair enough."

At the Steeves' iron gate, two steps from the window saying Bud's Good Eats, Paul opened the door and was gone in an instant, with just a short wave to Grandinetti for the ride.

"Dee, you're the only *native* Californian I've met since I moved here," Luanne Buckelew said. A tall, bone-thin Kansan, she spoke in a rich Midwestern twang Dee found charming. Luanne was another stage-struck out-of-stater who thought her gaunt good looks would get her a Hollywood acting career. She had made decent money modeling but was getting too old and her gigs were getting fewer and farther between. Dee couldn't model because she was too short and voluptuous. Luanne consoled her by saying that modeling was boring, anyway.

The two women were sitting in the waiting room at Segal Associates, a talent agency Robert Segal had founded years earlier and sold just before his death. The new owner kept the name because of Segal's reputation as a shrewd and ethical agent. Dee had gotten the call at the Los Angeles Women's Residence and been overjoyed that a real agency liked her eight-by-ten enough to want to meet with her personally. But she also knew that she had no acting experience, her AFTRA initiation fee had been awfully high and she had absolutely no personal contacts within the entertainment industry.

Luanne was saying, "I've heard all about the casting couch. Might not be the worst way to go if it comes down to getting a good part or remaining an extra for life." She had worked plenty in films, but always in tiny, non-speaking parts, as a background girl, a piece of human furniture. She had grander ambitions but was in her thirties, too old to model but still holding out Marilyn Monroe-like hopes for the silver screen. "You could grow old as an extra," she had told Dee.

Dee sighed, sitting in the waiting room. Segal Associates was large and impersonal, filled with wannbes, dreamers, show-offs. Still, she loved being here, meeting new people and living in such a different new world. The women seemed genuinely friendly and eager to help, the men short and surprisingly often quite overtly homosexual. Dee had not been prepared for that.

But she knew, every day, that moving to Los Angeles had been the right thing to do. Gone forever were the lonely days and nights in Western Hills—the fog, hills, Bud's Good Eats, Grandinetti Chocolate, weird Lido. She ate little and guzzled Perrier, went for long walks and did aerobics at a local studio. Her honey-blonde hair shimmered in the sun; her skin soon tanned to dark bronze. People frequently mistook her for a native. Dee Steeves, L.A. girl.

She watched with interest as the door behind the secretary opened and a man, clearly the agent, emerged with a tall blond man in a powder-blue sports coat. "I mean it, Tommy: keep the faith. I'll get you back to work just as soon as I can." The agent's voice was filled with false cheer and professional, empty optimism.

"That's what I need to hear, Mr. Burwitz," said Tommy. His voice was deep and mellifluous, perhaps better suited to radio than movies. A born performer, a big strapping blond man with a voice to match.

"Have we let you down, Tommy? Ever? Answer me that." The agent laughed, a man who could afford to laugh at those who filled this office every day. Dee was surprised by the agent's loose and relaxed manner, considering how stressful his job was supposed to be.

Tommy cleared his throat and addressed the room at large: "Let it be known, to all, right here and now, that this man"—he tapped the agent on the shoulder—"has never let me down in my long and distinguished career as an extra. I would be better off today if he *had* let me down."

Everybody laughed, including the agent. "This man speaks the truth," said Burwitz.

"Furthermore," Tommy said, "I suggest that you all settle down and marry Marines." He pointed to a group of young male hopefuls. "Especially you."

"Always the kidder," Luanne said. "And always the drinker. Right, Tommy?"

"Work is the ruination of the drinking class." He looked over at Dee, who was standing nearby. "And who's this?"

"Oh," said Luanne. "Tommy Wilhite, Dee Steeves."

"Don't tell me you're an actress. Go home, Dee Steeves. Stay barefoot and pregnant till you're forty. This business isn't good enough for you."

Luanne rolled her eyeballs. "Oh, no, here we go again. Tommy Wilhite, the angry actor."

"I'll spare you. I promise. No rants today, Luanne."

"Thank God."

Wilhite smirked. "You're welcome." He dropped down onto one knee and grabbed Dee's hand. "Miss Steeves, will you marry me? I don't make much money but I'm good in the sack and life will never be boring around me."

Dee played along. "Not much money? I can't have that. I need a husband who will support me in grand style."

"Then will you at least have an affair with me?"

"No ring, no fling."

The agent had disappeared back into his office. His secretary picked up the phone. She looked up and said, "Ms. Steeves, Mr. Burwitz will see you now."

Dee took a deep breath as she stood up. She felt anxious, unsure of herself possibly for the first time in her life.

"Be assertive. Tell the man what you want," Wilhite said. "Insist on script and director approval. If he balks, tell him to eat shit."

Dee grinned as she went past the secretary's desk and entered the agent's office. "We'll wait for you," Luanne called out.

"It'll have to be outside," the secretary said. "That's all the business we're doing for today."

Inside, Burwitz said, "I'm going to give you the first, and most disappointing, acting offer of your life."

"Well, I may give you the most disappointing performance of your life. I don't have much acting experience."

He waved her off. "So what? Tell you what. I need to know two things: first, do you have a dark dress? Something suitable for a party?"

Dee shrugged, frowning. "Yes, I brought one down."

Burwitz nodded. "Second thing is: do you smoke?"

Was this a trick question? "I haven't smoked since..."

"But if you light up, you won't choke to death?"

Dee laughed, but the agent took out a package of Camels and tossed it to her. "Show me."

So she took out a Camel and lit it with the lighter on his desk. She took a long, deep drag and held the smoke in her lungs for a few moments before exhaling a huge cloud of smoke. The hot tobacco smoke felt good in her lungs, relaxing, its smell making her mind flash back to all the cigarettes she'd smoked at Grandinetti's.

Burwitz smiled. "That's all I need: a pretty girl smoking in a dark dress, around other pretty girls and their handsome men. A ludicrous part, really. A party scene."

Dee left the office and walked down the stairs. Segal Associates, she thought, was a crappy place, considering the glamorous nature of the industry. Her heart pounded as she walked, her brow sweaty. Low pay, no exposure, a party girl having a cigarette. The scene would probably not even make it into the final cut. Oh, well. It was better than zero, which was what Luanne and Tommy had gotten.

Outside, on the sidewalk, Luanne and Tommy were waiting for her. "So, who's going to give you your first screen kiss? Richard Gere or Robert De Niro? Or maybe Jane Fonda?"

"I'm going to be a party guest who stands there smoking and pretending to make small talk." She made a face. "Hooray for Hollywood."

"Let's celebrate anyway," Tommy said.

The three walked down Western Avenue, brown palm trees shooting up towards the merciless, blinding Los Angeles smog.

The "celebration" consisted of Tommy and Dee sipping a split of Napa Valley wine in an anonymous bar reeking of stale cigarette smoke. Luanne had left, saying, "I have other things to do."

"What next?" Tommy asked Dee. "If we keep our clothes on, we can go to a party on La Cienega. Without our clothes..."

"The La Cienega thing sounds good." Dee saw that Tommy could be most provocative. Did such bluntness really get him anywhere? Actors. Eccentrics. Well, she guessed, most people who knew him were used to it. She guessed she would get used to it, in due time.

"Now that you're on your way professionally," Tommy said, sipping at his glass of champagne, "we need to concentrate on your personal life so that you will become a well-rounded, fulfilled young woman. Where are you located, at present?"

"The Los Angeles Women's Residence."

"Oh, *that* place. Do you like it?"

Dee shrugged. "It's cheap and convenient. What more could a girl ask?"

"Got a boyfriend?"

"You cut right to the chase, don't you? No, I just got into town."

Tommy grinned. "So there's hope for you. Or for *me*."

"Aren't you married?"

Tommy shook his head. "Giving divorce a chance."

She paused. "Not seeing anyone at all? How old are you?"

Tommy took a deep breath. "I'm thirty-five."

"Where are you from, originally?"

"Noo Yawk City," Tommy said. "Dad's a retired ophthalmologist, Mom died long ago. After a couple years at NYU, I decided to let Hollywood exploit my prodigious talent and incomparable good looks. A dozen or so years later, I'm still pluggin' away."

"But you don't make that much money, Tommy. How do you support yourself?"

"Dad. His eye practice thrived, and the guilt money to me, his luckless scion, arrives monthly. It's enough to cover the rent, food and car." He laughed, his eyes downcast.

"Dad also kept me out of the service, which was just as well. Had they sent me overseas to kill the Viet Cong, they would have had to bring me back in a body bag or a straitjacket."

Dee nodded. Vietnam was something she had learned far too much about during her days at the hospital.

They finished the wine and Tommy said, "Let's find a few dozen more unsung Los Angeles watering holes to sample."

"Better still," Dee suggested, "let's go have a party at *your* place."

"Better still, indeed." On the street, down the block, they saw Luanne emerge from a taxi.

"Hey!" Dee exclaimed. They watched as she disappeared into a building.

"And there goes Luanne. So let's get on with the business of having a good time."

They got into his car and headed out for the party he'd mentioned. She was still wearing the party dress from the audition. "Am I overdressed?"

"There's no such thing as overdressed here in L.A."

"Hope I won't offend your friends when they see me in this."

"Oh, they'll try to seduce you within minutes. And that will offend *me*." He looked around. "Delightful as the West Beverly is, there are a number of other watering holes nearby. Let's do some bar-hopping, shall we?"

Dee shook her head. "No more for me tonight."

"OK. Women are wiser, I've always said. I'll drive you home, if you like."

"Are you OK to drive?"

"No. I should be drunker to drive."

Outside, they climbed into his Plymouth. "On second thought, let's go to my place. The beloved Cedric Hotel."

Dee shrugged as Tommy sped down the street, a vision of palm trees and sunshine and pastel building facades. Cars, cars everywhere, the fine art of walking lost or at least ignored here in the hot, heartless City of Angels.

They easily found a spot in the surprisingly spacious parking lot of the Cedric and walked under its imposing marquee.

"It was probably meant to be a movie theater, originally," Tommy said. Inside it was imitation-wood paneling, palm trees, a ludicrous chandelier. Cheap, made to look opulent, its architect scrambling to please his client who demanded Hollywood in the tradition of the West Beverly Place, the Pacific Palace, the other stylish hotels Dee had just visited. Tommy went up to the front desk for the key as Dee waited by the entrance. A tall building, imposing, with nonstop traffic; soldiers went by, tourists, transients on budgets, cops on the lookout for prostitutes, none of them looking happy to be at the Cedric Hotel.

At the elevator the awful truth was confirmed: the Cedric was merely a cheap, dingy transient hotel despite its moderately stylish lobby. The budget had lasted only to the eighth floor; at the ninth, Dee and Tommy stepped out into a narrow and depressing corridor; the threadbare carpeting revealed splintered floorboards. As Tommy unlocked room 910, they could smell a faint odor of stale cooking even though hot plates were forbidden by management.

"This is awful," Dee said.

He nodded. "But the price is unbeatable."

Dee had no great desire to see the room. It probably had a single dim bulb overhead and shiny, greasy, yellowed walls. She felt claustrophobic, as if she could simply reach out and touch each of the four walls. Which, of course, she probably could.

Tommy began unbuttoning her blouse, his touch light and quick, his movements quick in the blackness. She could feel her clothes pulled from her body, shivered at the room's stuffy closeness. Out of habit, she reached behind her and unhooked her bra, then pulled off her panties. Gently she placed Tommy's hands on her breasts. "I take it you're not altogether a virgin," he murmured.

"Less experienced than you think."

Just then the telephone rang. "Just ignore it," Tommy said. But the shrill ringing continued. Dee said, "Tommy, pick it up. *Please.*"

Tommy lifted the receiver. "What?"

"Mr. Wilhite, this is hotel security. We saw you escort a young lady into your room."

"Not me," Tommy said. "I'm gay."

"Please, Mr. Wilhite. We've been through this before. You know the house rules. If we come up there and find a woman in your room..."

"She's not a real woman, just a tranny. Her dick is bigger than yours." Then, "OK, you win." He hung up the phone and turned to Dee, who during the conversation had put her clothes back on. "In the future, we'll have to make better arrangements."

Downstairs they sauntered through the lobby and got into Tommy's car. They drove downtown and spent the entire night at one of the few remaining twenty-four-hour movie theaters, both drowsing periodically. At dawn they returned to the car and headed back to Hollywood, to the Los Angeles Women's Residence. After a brief kiss, Tommy sped off, back to the Cedric to catch up on the sleep he had missed. Hideously fatigued, he could barely see straight as he navigated his way home.

Chapter 8

Maria's strong hands eased the tense muscles in Jamey's neck as he lay in bed. "Feels good?"

"Mmmm." His eyes were closed and he lay naked on the bed, enjoying Maria's strong hands on his body. There was no all-night security patrol to dread tonight; they had the place all to themselves. It was sunny and warm outside, hot even. Jamey couldn't have cared less. He had no intention of leaving the bedroom anytime soon. They were all alone in the house. Uncle Jack and Aunt Virginia away on a camping trip.

Maria's hands kneaded the muscles in his shoulders and back, then farther below. She put on some sort of lotion, like baby oil, that smelled fine and felt even better. The exhaustion from those all-night patrols went away.

"You're stiff, Jamey," Maria observed as she massaged his legs. Turn me over and find out just how stiff I really am, he thought with a smile. "Those long hours, Jamey, all night, walking around. That's unhealthy," she said.

She told him to turn over onto his back. He opened his eyes and smiled up at her. Maria was a tall, thin Latin woman with surprising strength. She was a housekeeper, a damn good one. Jamey wondered how she had learned to become a masseuse. She doused her hands with baby oil and massaged his face, his neck, his chest. "Close your eyes," she ordered, and massaged him in other places. As she progressed, he arched his back, wanting to cry

ENTREPRENEUR

out, wanting to writhe, thrash from side to side, but Maria had him pinned down. Finally, at the moment of climax, he wanted to scream, but all that came out was a deep moan. In a moment or two she pulled off her own clothes and lay on top of him, her arms around him. They lay together there, silently.

At these times, Jamey thought with a small smile, a cop could show up at the door with the news that Uncle Jack, Aunt Virginia and the kids had been killed in an auto accident and Jamey would just shrug and spend the rest of his young life spending his uncle's money, living in his house and making love with his housekeeper.

In due time they silently got up and Maria pulled the sheet off the Steeveses' bed and smoothed it out. Jamey went into his own bedroom, the attic, and lay down, staring up at the angled ceiling. If he had one problem these days, it was that he didn't get enough sleep. His work kept him up all night and Sacramento was like an oven during these spring months. There was no window and the heat was stifling; he drifted in and out of sleep all day, sweating constantly. Still, he smiled, thinking of the San Francisco family he would likely never see again and the charming Mexican girl who was giving him succor. A guy tosses a firebomb through the window of the richest man in town and they punish the culprit by sending him into the arms of someone like Maria...well, that was the kind of justice that made Jamey Steeves proud to be an American.

Even with their big fan Uncle and Aunt had trouble sometimes coping with these hot Sacramento nights. Uncle Jack brought home beer by the case and drank it all up, although Jamey secretly helped himself and Uncle never said a word although he must have wondered why his beer always disappeared so quickly.

After their loving she disappeared downstairs. These were the minutes he hated. She was the first woman he had learned to care about, someone who didn't know him as

Western Hills' worst hood; why must they act so covertly here? It angered him that he was not free to take her out or even be seen in public with her. If Uncle Jack or Aunt Virginia caught them together, it would surely end their relationship; he could hear Aunt Virginia on the phone, ordering his father to drive up from San Francisco and pick up his good-for-nothing hoodlum for a son. He was a minor, he had no rights, he had to take orders from others till he was eighteen.

The Muscle Man.

Maria stood before him, smiling. "You've worked hard. Your body needs sustenance. Come get some."

He nodded and followed her downstairs, naked. At the kitchen table was a tablecloth and one of Aunt Virginia's fine dishes, her best china. On it was a hamburger, plump and blood-red, covered with lettuce, a tomato slice and rings of uncooked onion. Next to it was a small mountain of freshly cooked French fries and a pitcher of iced tea. Jamey poured himself a glass and drank it down. "There's no sugar in the tea," he said.

Maria giggled. "You're already sweet enough. The burger is rare and the onions uncooked...as you like it, right?"

"Right." He smiled. Aunt Virginia would have a heart attack if she saw his bare ass on her chair, eating off her expensive plate. Well, what Auntie didn't know wouldn't hurt her. The smooth covering of the seat felt nice against his bare bottom. "Maria, you really should work at a restaurant where you would be appreciated instead of slaving away for these creeps."

She grinned. "Someday soon, when you become a very rich man, you can take me to San Francisco and buy me the finest restaurant in town. OK?"

He nodded gravely. "Yes, I will." His voice was sober. If all he had to offer was a promise, he made damn sure it was a sincere one.

"Anyway, there are worse places to work, Jamey. Why do you think I should be dissatisfied? A big clean house, work I can do well, a sexy lover to make me feel good. Life is fine for me."

Jamey shook his head. "But we have to sneak around! We can't go anywhere because you'd be fired."

Maria shrugged. "Tell me where we could go that would be as much fun as we have in the bedroom?"

"There are movie theaters around..."

She sneered. "They are all the same, no? Boy meets girl, boy loses girl, boy gets girl again. In this house, at least, boy gets girl whenever he wants."

The next day, Jamey, as always sleeping at work, used the company phone to call the local radio station and asked them to play a song dedicated to Maria.

Paul's thighs and calves burned. Sweat poured from his face and neck, down his back and legs. He smashed the ball at Lido Grandinetti, who panted as he returned the shot. They went on for several minutes until Paul sent him an impossible volley and Grandinetti dropped his racket in defeat. They met at the net and shook hands. Grandinetti looked so ashen that Paul feared he was about to collapse.

"They taught you well," the older man said when he had his breath back. He mopped his shining face. His hair was plastered to his skull. "Let's sit."

ENTREPRENEUR

Paul nodded. He wore proper tennis shorts, bought at the tennis club by Grandinetti, along with white socks and matching sneakers. He looked identical to all the other young men at the club. Which was precisely the point.

"If you show up on the court with cheap shorts and colored socks," Grandinetti had told him, "everyone here will know you don't belong at my club, and I can't have that. So I'll treat you to the Pacific Heights Tennis Club's official uniform."

The tennis apparel had been frightfully expensive, but Paul knew he looked great, and he believed that you played better when you looked like you belonged in the game.

The two sat side by side on a courtside bench. "You made me work, Paul," Grandinetti said. "My doctor keeps after me about getting exercise and staying in shape, but frankly, I'm too lazy to extend myself and most forms of exercise bore me silly."

Paul looked around. "Well, this is certainly the finest place I've ever played tennis." He tugged at his sweat-drenched white shirt. "And thanks for the whites."

Grandinetti offered him a small smile. "Glad you like it. Now, how about a shower? Then maybe a drink at my place? Better still, we can stop by Fisherman's Wharf, pick up some things and have a seafood feast."

"A shower would be nice." Paul said nothing about the drink. He showered and changed back into his khaki slacks and gray pullover and stuffed the soaked, smelly tennis outfit into his totebag. He rejoined Grandinetti in the lobby and didn't object when they drove to Fisherman's Wharf. Sitting in the car as Grandinetti went into one market or another, Paul looked out at the bay and Alcatraz, then over to the Golden Gate Bridge, knowing this was where his father liked to get away from it all by swimming under the bridge. He half expected that some night his father would swim in the bay and either be overtaken by the currents or merely keep swimming till he drowned. Man with a death wish.

Grandinetti returned with a smelly package in white paper. "We'll eat well tonight," he said, placing the package in Paul's lap and starting the car's powerful engine. He drove up to his mansion, making casual conversation but getting no replies as Paul gazed out the window at the fabulous residential display of San Francisco wealth. Such homes! And tonight he would dine in one!

He had never actually been to the mansion and was unsure of where it was. His eyes bulged with wonder as Grandinetti pulled up to an estate that resembled the White House. A heavy iron gate, a generous lawn and a flagpole. A huge window, pillars. Dee had spent so many evenings here, naked and in the arms of one of the city's richest men. Paul wanted to giggle.

Grandinetti said, "Get out here, Paul. I have to park the car in the garage, but I want your first impression of the house to be through the front door, like all other guests. Just step out, ring the buzzer and wait to be let in. Jennings, my butler, will look after you."

The Mercedes disappeared around the corner and crept up the hill Paul shrugged and went up the stone steps. He looked around, still not quite believing that he was here, at the Grandinetti mansion. It was Lido Grandinetti's great good fortune to have been born into all this, and his and Dee's luck to have shared a tiny bit of it. Paul pressed the buzzer and opened the instantly released gate.

He entered a large, well-lighted marble hallway.

Next to Grandinetti was Jennings, an aging man all in gray. "This," Grandinetti said to the butler, "is another Steeves, Paul, sister of the one whom you had the pleasure of meeting."

Jennings merely offered Paul a courteous smile. Grandinetti said, "Jennings, would you mind going upstairs and seeing if you can find my tennis outfits? Two of them, I think, would fit Paul perfectly. And get the tennis rackets, if you can find them. Paul here is quite a tennis enthusiast. We've just been playing."

Jennings nodded and was about to leave when Grandinetti, still holding the seafood package, handed it to the servant. "Also, give this to Mabel and ask her to do something wonderful with it. I bought far too much. I hope Paul will be joining us. Well, Paul?"

"I have a date with Nancy tonight," he said.

Grandinetti waved him off. "Nancy is a very understanding, thoroughly gullible and totally infatuated young American female. Make up some bullshit excuse and she'll believe it."

Paul nodded, rubbing his arms. "May I use the phone?"

"Naturally," said Grandinetti. To Jennings, he said, "Also, bring him a sweater. With only that windbreaker, he's freezing in here. Start a fire, too. We're going into the study."

Moments later they were in the study. Paul smiled with gratitude. Oh, was it cold! The study was a massive room with mahogany paneling, huge velvet curtains, a grand piano, leather furniture. It all looked old but carefully maintained—perhaps new but made to look old, Paul mused. On the walls were oil painting of Wild West scenes, and on one wall, taking up virtually the entire wall, was a meticulous oil of the Golden Gate Bridge on a brilliantly sunny day. A gigantic bookshelf was packed with leather-bound volumes of what Paul presumed to be first editions of classics, signed books written by long-dead men and women. It was a magnificent room, except that one end of the room, right below the big window looking out past the flagpole and onto Broadway Street, was bare. There should be something, Paul thought. The room looks asymmetrical. He spun around.

"Wonderful."

"Glad you like it. But it's too much like a museum for me: very beautiful, very cold, dead people on the walls."

Dead people on the floor, too, Paul thought.

"Let's have a drink," Grandinetti said. "Bourbon?"

"Fine." Dee had ordered liquor just before taking the bus out of Paul's life. She was now in Los Angeles because of the tall, spoiled man pouring booze at this moment from the bar by the bookshelf. Maybe Paul should thank Grandinetti on Dee's behalf for giving her the motivation to leave Western Hills and strike out on her own. Dee had written that she had gotten a tiny part in a movie and had moved out of the Los Angeles Women's Center. The letters arrived care of Paul's friend Ned Farley's house. Dee asked Paul not to say anything to their parents about her life in the City of Angels.

Grandinetti handed Paul a crystal glass half-filled with bourbon. "Call Nancy." He gestured to the telephone by the bar and sat down in one of the deep leather armchairs on the other side of the room.

Paul picked up the phone and called, hoping that Nancy's mother would answer and say that her daughter wasn't in. Presently, however, Nancy answered, her voice exuberant. "Paul! I'm really looking forward to tonight!"

He felt a stab of guilt. "Nancy, I'm afraid we'll have to postpone tonight."

"Why?" Her voice was nearly a moan.

"Complications. I hope you understand." His voice sounded much cooler than he'd hoped.

"Kiss my ass." Click.

"Yes, tomorrow is another day, kiddo. I'll make it up to you." Paul felt Grandinetti looking at him. He sipped at his bourbon and said, "I'll show her a good time tomorrow night."

Grandinetti smiled. "Thanks for joining me. I hate evenings here alone. Maybe that's why I got married years ago. Too bad it didn't last."

He sipped at his drink and motioned to the vacant area below the huge front window. "The furniture people had a hell of a time getting the silk-brocade sofa out of here. Did you hear about that? While we had the window wide open to air out the room, some idiot threw a Molotov cocktail in here. Anyway, the firebomb burned part of my sofa and went out. Jennings found it, the bottle of gasoline completely intact but the sofa somewhat burned. They said it would be easier to remove the sofa altogether. The police wanted to know if I had enemies or had been targeted by any terrorist group. I told them that I was the richest guy in town, so naturally I had enemies. Would've been a shame if all those those first-edition books had been burned, but the rest of it could have gone up in smoke and I wouldn't have minded." He chuckled. "Even if I had been one of the casualties."

"You wanted to be burned to death?" Paul asked.

"Well, no. Not really. Anyway, a simple little Molotov cocktail wouldn't have destroyed this place. It's indestructible. Like the Grandinetti fortune."

"Then why keep living here? Why don't you sell it?"

Grandinetti laughed. "Who could afford to buy this white elephant?" He closed his eyes. "My family asks only that I make a daily appearance at the candy factory and try to stay out of trouble. So all I do, when not wasting my time at Grandinetti Chocolate, is wander these rooms and read those books. 'Once upon a midnight dreary, while I pondered, weak and weary, through many a quaint and curious volume of forgotten lore...'"

"Poe," Paul interjected.

Just then Jennings came down with a bundle in his arms: the freshly laundered tennis outfit Paul had worn that day, along with a couple of other similar things and two tennis rackets with plastic covers. On top of all this was a light-gray V-neck sweater.

Grandinetti laughed as he spotted the sweater. "Oh, did I buy that once? I didn't know. It's perfect for you, Paul. Good thinking, Jennings."

Jennings smiled and left the room. Grandinetti turned to Paul. "When I go shopping, I buy everything that fits." After a pause he said, "Would you like me to show you around this museum I call a home?"

Paul nodded. The place was enormous, opulent and spectacular, something out of the movies. The difference was that this was all real, not a bunch of facades and shiny pieces of junk the actors pretended were priceless art objects.

In the hallway was a coat of arms. "That's something you will find in all mansions," Grandinetti said. "During the war I'm sure they would have appreciated my donating it to the Army so they melt it down for bullets or whatever. In fact, they would have probably appreciated me along with it, to stop bullets. Well, they got neither. Too bad." They walked a bit farther and he opened two large doors. "The ballroom. Another must for a residence like this."

The ballroom seemed as big as the Balboa Community Center, where Paul and the Bay Area Boyz had played. The chandelier certainly looked real and took Paul's breath away. Grandinetti turned on its lights and the chandelier burned feebly.

"This room does not get much use," he said. "Maybe because having five or six hundred guests over to the Grandinetti mansion presents certain logistical problems. There's almost no parking up here in the Pacific Heights, or anywhere else in this city. The rich and powerful of San Francisco won't take a taxi to anyone's home just for a night of dinner and dancing, and since there's nowhere to park the limos, what can you do? So they just stay at home or find someone else's party where there's somewhere to park." He leaned against the finely paneled wall. "Besides, there's only me here, and I'm not worth the trouble of visiting. Speaking of seeing people, do you see much of Nancy? Are you an item?"

"One doesn't like to be thought of as an item."

Grandinetti smiled. "Touché!" Then, "I certainly hope she didn't feel threatened by me, by the fact that I showed up that night to meet you and caught you in my car. Tell her I'm merely a family friend with no designs on her."

"I'm sure she hardly gives you a thought."

Grandinetti laughed. "Touché again!" He surveyed the ballroom. "I should have that chandelier cleaned up and throw a big fine ball. Call it Bloomsday. Do you know what and when that is, Paul?"

"June 11, from Joyce's novel *Ulysses*."

"And have you read *Finnegans Wake*?"

"I didn't like it, so I put it down."

"San Francisco is my Dublin. I share Joyce's ambivalence when it comes to hometowns.

"Let me show you the gun room." They went upstairs to another paneled room, this one smelling quite pleasantly of oil and metal. Racks of shotguns and hunting rifles locked behind glass, trophies all over, antlers on the walls, in beautiful condition, obviously carefully maintained every day just as the unused ballroom was. "I don't use any of these things anymore, but my family says I have to maintain it. Oh, well."

Grandinetti sighed and eyed Paul for a moment. "Do you like all this, Paul? My house, my car, everything?"

Paul nodded.

"Do you want it all? And have you thought of how to get it? What will you do for a living?"

Paul paused. "I've thought plenty."

"Well, let me tell you something. Law is where the money is. In America, one cannot do business without attorneys. Entrepreneurs and other businesspeople have to stick their necks out, risk their own money. Lawyers don't, and their fees are staggering." He changed the subject. "Have you heard from our girl Deirdre?"

"I'm expecting a letter at some point."

"We'll have to visit her. Anyway, let's leave the gun room. It's too damn depressing in here."

Paul watched as Jennings set the dinner table in front of the fireplace; at least they'd eat where it was warm. The silverware looked incredibly fine, and so did the china. He guessed Grandinetti didn't get many visitors. Crystal wineglasses, candleabra, the works. Paul wanted to use the men's room but didn't know quite how to ask Jennings.

He got up and sauntered over to the window to look out at the clear Pacific Heights evening—the lighted Golden Gate Bridge in the distance, the twinkling Fisherman's Wharf down below. Paul was here, in the fabled Grandinetti mansion, next door to the Gettys or Aliotos, the big white house owned by the legendary family still the cream of San Francisco high society, even if Lido was now decadent and lecherous.

Grandinetti was still infatuated with Dee and apparently had no offspring. What if he, deranged by lust, had his will changed and then died and the Grandinetti mansion became the Steeves mansion? Weirder things had happened. Paul grinned as he sipped at his drink.

Grandinetti returned in a tweed jacket of a different color. "I freshened up," he said. "A moment ago," Grandinetti continued, "you admitted wanting to own my house. Trouble is, I can never keep it warm. Care you guess why?"

Paul nodded. "Because hot air rises, and your ceilings are too high. The top half of the floor is too warm and the bottom half too chilly."

Grandinetti bowed. "Absolutely right. Tell me, how did you become so smart?"

"Public education."

Grandinetti said, "Paul, you look about ready to burst. Do you want to use the men's room?"

"Yes, please."

Grandinetti chuckled. "Well, if you follow Jenkins, he'll show you to the men's room."

Coming out of the bathroom, he heard, "Dinner is ready."

The cook had made the seafood into a wonderful-smelling stew. Jennings had poured white wine for them both, and Paul hoped that was the last of the evening's alcohol. His head was starting to ache and he hoped Grandinetti wouldn't talk throughout the meal, especially about Dee. He also hoped the seafood stew wasn't just the first of a five-course meal. He hoped that someday he would have Grandinetti's lifestyle without all that pessimism. He shot a look up at Jennings, who must surely know that he, the tall, lanky kid dining with the boss, was the younger brother of the beautiful blonde the boss had been screwing. What did Jennings think of that?

"So, now that you've seen a bit of *my* world, let me hear a bit about *yours*. Have you heard from Dee? I'm very concerned about her."

"She promised me she would stay in touch. I imagine she's just getting settled into her new situation."

"She told me she wants to be an actress, so I'm guessing she's somewhere in Los Angeles."

Paul shrugged.

"Well, if she wants to act, the Grandinetti name has some influence in Tinseltown. Tell her I would be happy to call in some favors with those producers and directors. It might mean the difference between an Oscar and chronic unemployment."

After dinner both Grandinetti and Paul declined on dessert. Grandinetti slumped into an overstuffed chair and had Jennings put on classical music Paul did not recognize. Then he drifted off, eyes open, as the music played on. Paul looked over at the pile of clothes he had been given and wished like hell he could just get Grandinetti to hurry him down to Western Hills so he could call Nancy and apologize for standing her up. Never again would he take her company for granted. Not after an evening with Lido Grandinetti.

Paul sat as the music played and the fireplace crackled and Grandinetti lost himself in Schumann, or Haydn, or whoever it was. When the music ended he looked up and said, "Well, Paul, are you ready to go home to Western Hills? Maybe make up with Nancy and start anew?"

"That would be fine."

Together they walked out to the garage, climbed into the Mercedes and headed out silently to Western Hills. When they reached Tower Street, Grandinetti pulled up in front of Bud's Good Eats. "Well, here you be."

"Thanks for everything. I had a nice time."

Grandinetti responded with a small smile. "We'll do it again. Often, I hope. Look, would you do me a favor?" He gestured to the dark-brown totebag on the backseat. "I've put all your new things in there, plus something I picked up once for Deirdre. Would you give it to her? It would mean a great deal to me."

Paul nodded. "Sure, when I find out her address."

"Good. Say, want to go someplace for a coffee right now? It's really not all that late, and the mansion can be so dreary..."

"Thanks, but I have to get up early. Six o'clock, to be precise." He wanted to get away from Grandinetti and let the evening's events sink in. He was mildly surprised at his own ambivalence about one of San Francisco's richest citizens, who apparently offered him friendship and brotherhood and had even seemed willing to use his influence to help him along in life.

"Six o'clock?" Grandinetti asked, genuinely surprised. "Why so early?"

"To help get Bud's Good Eats ready for the breakfast crowd." Paul couldn't help but roll his eyeballs at the prospect of the morning routine.

Grandinetti looked past Paul, at the vacant, locked, thoroughly humble-looking little delicatessen on the darkened street. He could see that the man was casting an appraising eye over his home turf. It was still fairly early but Tower Avenue was dark except for streetlights. Bud's Good Eats was just a dusky crevice between a parking lot and a tailor's shop, whose proprietors ate lunch regularly at Bud's. He could imagine what Grandinetti made of people who got up at the crack of dawn to eke out a living at a small neighborhood business.

"Western Hills certainly does go to bed early, doesn't it?" Grandinetti said.

"Most of San Francisco does, in my experience."

"Yes, I suppose. Say, what do you do at Bud's Good Eats to help it stay afloat?"

"Oh, I make sandwiches, toast bagels." He smiled. "You oughta see me clean up. I do it better than anyone."

Grandinetti chuckled. "Sandwiches, bagels, cleanups? Somehow that all seems a bit beneath you."

"Well, I like to think I was made for bigger things."

"Indeed. And what might those bigger things be?"

"Don't know yet. What are *you* cut out for?"

Grandinetti frowned. "Damned if *I* know. I've gotten good at dressing like a millionaire and pretending to run California's premier chocolate company, though. If you should ever discover your true calling, or mine, I would like to know. Time is running out for me."

Paul eyed him. "By the way, how old *are* you?"

"Guess."

"Forty-five? Forty-eight?"

Grandinetti threw back his head and laughed. "You're worse than Deirdre!" He paused, "I'm thirty-nine. Prematurely graying, alas. It makes me look older."

Paul thought it was his bored, jaded attitude that made him seem older. Perhaps it was also the superior attitude Grandinetti's parents had instilled in him that made him isolate himself from the rest of the world and become a prisoner of his own loneliness.

"Thirty-nine," Grandinetti said. "Forty is just around the corner. And not so far off for you, either. Do you think you'll be significantly different from the way you are today? Or maybe a bit more like me? I suspect the latter."

Paul shook his head. "We're miles apart. I'll be nothing like you when I'm forty."

"Oh? Will you be so much better?"

"I'll certainly try."

"What specifically do you find lacking in my character?"

Paul took a deep breath. "You've had all the resources, advantages, opportunities. You've done nothing with them."

"Really? Won't you give me some credit? Haven't I done moderately well in not squandering the family fortune? This car? The mansion? My clothes, my Stanford degree...?"

"No, and that's my point. You've had everything and done very little with it."

"And if the tables were turned, Paul, would you have done much better?"

"I think so."

Grandinetti chuckled. "You're quite the confident one, aren't you? My family's wealth and status were all that mattered. They decided early on that I would marry, and that my wife's family would have money, too. That narrowed it down somewhat, as you might imagine. When the inevitable divorce occurred, it was acceptable because at least I was divorcing someone from my own socioeconomic class." He looked off into the night. "Imagine if I had fallen in love with and married a beautiful young penniless maiden who had only herself to offer..."

"Whom you laid off," Paul said.

"She thinks that's why I laid her off. Well, she's right. But she didn't say *why* she wouldn't marry me. Do *you* know why?"

"None of my business." But then he added, "You were wrong for each other. From different stations in life. Rich boy and poor girl. Like a bad novel. Doomed from the start."

Grandinetti leaned over and looked Paul squarely in the eye. "When you see her again, I want you to tell her that I still love her deeply and want to marry her."

Paul looked away. "I gotta go. Six in the morning comes early." He unlocked the car's door and got out.

"Whatever you do," Grandinetti said, "please take that bag with you and don't forget to give Deirdre that...item."

Paul reached over and pulled out the bag, marveling once again at its fine smell and feel. It was also heavy, bursting with fine, expensive clothes that were now his to keep. Why did the good, high-priced stuff seem to weigh so much more than the cheap stuff?

"It's been the most exciting evening I've had in some time, Paul," Grandinetti said. "I can't remember when I had such a workout on the tennis court."

"Goodnight." Paul walked away and unlocked the family's iron gate. Once inside, he unzipped the bag and immediately found a white silk dress—the "item" that Grandinetti wanted so desperately for Dee to have. Beautiful, low cut, lacy.

"Paul, is that you?" The voice came from upstairs.

"Yes, Mom." Time for fast thinking. How to explain to her this beautiful bag and all the goodies inside? Better not to explain at all. "I forgot something," he blurted, and went back outside.

He hurried over to Ned Farley's home a block and a half away. It was a good thing that the lights were still on. The Farley family was always among the last on the block to retire. Mrs. Farley was a thin, amiable woman who delighted in having the Bay Area Boyz practice in her basement.

"Paul? Is that you?" Ned asked, stepping outside.

"Ned, I need a favor."

"Name it."

Paul thrust the zipped bag at him. "Hold this for me till I come back for it."

Ned's face lit up. "One expensive overnight bag you've got here, Paul. Looks and feels like a million bucks. Got a new babe? Is Nancy yesterday's news?"

Paul made a face. "It's all Dee's stuff that she bought behind Mom's back."

Ned opened it and took out the white dress. His eyes bugged out at the plunging neckline. "I believe you, Paul. Only Dee has the equipment for this kind of apparel."

"Put it back in and hide it somewhere safe. Promise?"

Ned smiled. "Yeah. Just make sure you can get us some more gigs. I think we're getting sloppy."

Paul shook his head. Ned never got rusty. He was easily the best musician Paul had ever known, and had the talent to become a professional. Paul thought it would be a terrible shame if Ned didn't fully realize his potential.

"Just thought I would let you know that I saw Nancy this evening with some other guy. I asked her about you. She just sneered and walked away."

"No sweat."

From there he walked down the street to the Tower Street Diner, which stayed open till late. He slurped down a chocolate milkshake and read the newspaper. Scanning the day's top stories, he thought for a moment that a journalism career might be fun, but then reminded himself that the job paid very little and was probably full of frustration. Oh, well, he would just have to go off to college and maybe there he would learn what he was meant to do.

Jamey felt good, *real* good, as he got out of bed, careful not to wake Maria. He put on his clothes and carefully navigated his way out of the bedroom. He was so thirsty and his throat was so parched that he could barely swallow. There was only one thing to do.

Uncle Jack loved beer and kept his refrigerator full of cold bottles of Beck's, so Jamey reached in and grabbed one, then popped it open and took a long, greedy drink. The soothing alcohol went to his head instantly as he stood in the utter darkness.

"Jamey..."

The quiet voice came from only an inch behind him. Suddenly the kitchen light went on and there stood Uncle Jack, in his pajamas. "Hello, Jamey."

Jamey gulped. "Uncle Jack. What's goin' on?"

Uncle Jack smiled. "Let's sit down and chat a bit."

"I'm kind of tired." Jamey knew that he reeked of sweat from lovemaking, and that Uncle Jack almost certainly knew he'd just been with Maria.

"Jamey, let us sit and chat and drink beer. Like two grown men. We've much to discuss." He reached into the refrigerator and took out a bottle for himself. Then he motioned for Jamey to take a seat, who reluctantly did so.

Uncle Jack sat down next to him, closer than Jamey would have liked. "It is very late, Jamey. Past midnight, you know." His voice was deep and solemn.

Jamey cocked an eyebrow. "Is it?"

Uncle Jack nodded. "Indeed it is. A young man needs his sleep if he is going to put in a good night's work in a few hours."

"I'm just a security guard. I don't exactly work, I just roam around that construction site and think pleasant thoughts all night. You know that."

Uncle Jack smiled. "Whatever you say. But I'm curious: Since you work nights and never seem to be here with us, what do you do with all that free time?"

Jamey shrugged. "I amuse myself, exploring the city."

Uncle Jack chuckled. "Exploring the wonders of Sacramento? I'm afraid it does not compare to the wonders of San Francisco, especially in the wee hours, which you surely know intimately."

"Uncle Jack," Jamey said. It was now his turn to be condescending. "If I'm just out wandering around the streets of Sacramento till dawn when I'm not at work...well, how is it *your* business?"

"Jamey, I have taken you in and given a good new start to a very bad little boy, haven't I?"

The boy blushed. "Huh?"

Uncle Jack's small gray eyes bore down into him. "I have taken a little smartass from Frisco and put good food in his stomach and a clean house to live in. Yes or no?"

Jamey just drank his beer and said nothing.

"Yes or no? A little troublemaker who is destined to die young or rot in prison. He gets a second chance, right? He has a steady job, which is more than he deserves, even though he probably thinks he's better than us. He goes out at night, and by fighting dirty, beats up guys bigger than himself. Here he gets a home, plenty to eat, is treated with courtesy. Am I right? Yes or no?"

Uncle Jack's anger mounted. He was a big, strong man, his chest stretching the cloth of his pajama top. Jamey figured Uncle Jack could take him in two minutes if it came down to a fight.

"Yeah, Uncle Jack, you're right."

"You're damn right I'm right. And all I ask in return is that you respect my rules. That means getting your ass off the street and into *your own bed upstairs* at a decent hour so that the neighbors won't start dragging my good name through the mud."

Your own bed. Jamey grimaced.

"I know that this isn't the sort of house you're used to," Uncle Jack continued. "We don't roam the streets till all hours and fight and steal and whore around. My wife and I don't live like your mother and father, who have to work late and rise early to fix sandwiches for every bit of lowlife that walks in the door. I am a successful businessman, respected and admired. We're the cream of society, such as it is in a place like Sacramento. I'm rich and will get richer. My wife and sons are envied by all their friends, and rightly so. You can't believe how bright my children's future is. Do you *really* think I'm about to jeopardize all my hard-earned status over a two-bit piece of trouble like you?"

"I hear you, Uncle Jack." Jamey felt his nerve returning. His voice sounded light and cocky.

"You weren't wandering about town tonight, Jamey. You were in *her* room. Not for the first time, I might guess. God only knows how often you two go at it."

Jamey smiled. "Well, is it a crime to like sex?"

Uncle Jack gave a short, menacing laugh. "I won't have you crawling into my housekeeper's panties whenever your little thing gets hard. You stay away from her from now on."

"You can't make me."

"Oh, can't I? I can reach over right now and break you in half. But I won't. Either you promise to stay away from her or I'll make her promise to stay away from you. Well...?"

Jamey thrust out his chin. "We love each other."

Uncle Jack laughed again, a hearty guffaw as if at something genuinely amusing. "Love? Is that what you call it? How much will she love you when I tell her that I'll call immigration and have her deported to Latin America? Hate to tell you this, my boy, but she's an illegal. One phone call and adios, Maria." He chugged on his beer.

"Bastard."

Uncle Jack grinned. "I've been called much worse. But it's for your own good. You don't understand how immoral your behavior is, and neither does Maria. I don't blame you. Even now you're a better man than your father, which is no compliment at all. Can't imagine what kind of people your siblings are. But they're not *my* problem." He got up and stretched. "Finish your beer, Jamey. Have another one, if you like, but then it's off to bed for you." He patted his nephew on the shoulder and strode out of the room.

Jamey finished his beer and soon went up to the attic. It was another stifling Sacramento night, a night for tossing and turning. He wished it wasn't his night off. He started to think he'd never sleep well again.

Hours later, the blinding sun burned through his window and Jamey, groggy, dressed and came downstairs. He wanted desperately to see Maria and say something, anything, but Uncle Jack was already at the breakfast table, reading the paper. He looked up and smiled.

"Jamey, sleep well? Have some breakfast."

"The usual," he said to Maria, who disappeared into the kitchen. Jamey felt uncomfortable in the company of Uncle Jack and Maria but his appetite won out. He always felt hungry and Maria's breakfasts were always wonderful.

"The world is just so full of conflict." Uncle Jack stared at the front page, his voice emotionless. "But the alternative is no human race, and that is no alternative at all."

Maria soon came back with Jamey's bacon, eggs and toast. Jamey looked at her and she looked at him, but her face betrayed little expression, just a prim, indifferent smile, like a bored waitress. He ate ravenously and drank two tall glasses of orange juice. He would come back later that day, when Uncle Jack was out at one construction site or another and Aunt Virginia was out and the boys were at school.

"Going back to bed so you'll be fresh for tonight?" Uncle Jack asked.

"Nope," said Jamey between gulps of food. "Going into town for the day. I'll catch a nap later."

"Well, be a good boy." Uncle Jack shot him a smile and a wink so genuinely good-natured that for a moment Jamey wondered if their awful conversation over beer had simply been a bad dream. But no, it wasn't a dream. Uncle Jack was just a good actor with his smile and wink.

Jamey finished breakfast and left just as his two lanky, pallid young cousins came down for breakfast. "My boys!" Uncle Jack enthused, kissing them each on the forehead.

Jamey rushed back in the early afternoon when he knew Uncle Jack and Aunt Virginia were away and the kids were at school. It would be only him and Maria. Perhaps they could talk things through, or perhaps they would run away together right there and then. Or perhaps they'd merely go back to her room and communicate in another manner.

He reached the house and could see through the window that Maria was in the living room, doing housework. She always wore a white uniform, like a nurse. With her dark coloring and slim figure, she looked incredibly sexy.

"We can run away, Maria. We have options."

She shook her head. "Options? The teenaged security guard and the illegal housekeeper have options?"

"He's such a fucking pig." Jamey clenched his fists.

Maria nodded. "And a jealous one, at that."

"Meaning?"

"You have done what he has wanted to do for over a year." She gestured to her lithe, white-clad form. "Do you think you are the only male in this house who desires me? He resents you."

"Well, too bad for him."

She shook her head. "No, too bad for us. The next time he tries, he will succeed."

Jamey burned with rage at the image of big, virile Uncle Jack ravishing Maria. Uncle Jack was a chauvinistic, two-faced pig, but Maria, being a woman, must surely find him attractive on some level. Blind with fury, Jamey turned and ran out the door as Maria continued her housework.

Chapter 9

Dee drove down the street and headed up La Cienega in the late-fall coolness. She stopped at the corner grocery store for a six-pack of beer and then headed for her apartment. She hoped Tommy was home. It was always nice when her lover was there to greet her. She imagined what they would think back in prudish Western Hills if they knew she was living in Los Angeles with her boyfriend.

Dee had become so busy as a very minor player in movies that she scarcely had time to eat or sleep. Well, she was getting experience and, paying her bills. She looked forward to bigger parts and more money. She'd had offers to work on the stage, but she wanted film and TV parts. Live audiences were too scary, and she enjoyed being supervised by a skilled, patient director.

She bounded up the four flight of stairs and unlocked her door. "Tommy? Tommy, honey?"

"Hello, Dee."

"Paul!" Wide-eyed with surprise, she put down the beer and came over to throw her arms around her brother. "What are you doing here?"

"I was in the neighborhood..." Next to his hand was a beautiful large brown tote bag that Dee seemed to remember from somewhere. She appraised Paul, her handsome brother, with his lovely dark hair and large brown eyes. "How long has it been? Seems like forever. So, what's happening?"

"Dad's working like hell. Mom's got too many aches and pains. Jamey is still in Sacramento, so far as I know."

"Do they know where I am?"

He shook his head. "They, uh, don't talk about you."

Dee rolled her eyeballs. "Very nice. Well. Don't you just love my spacious home?"

Paul looked around. "You rented a furnished place."

"How could you tell?"

"Because it's ugly as hell." They both laughed.

At that moment Tommy came in and kissed Dee curtly. If they had been alone, she would have wrapped her arms around him and initiated one of their endless makeout sessions. He stood over Paul and said, "How's your beer?"

Paul smiled. "Thanks, I'm fine."

Tommy shrugged and drained his can. Dee felt proud to have a tall, heavy-shouldered, blond, beer-drinking American male for a boyfriend.

"Dee," Tommy said, "Paul and I had a nice long chat while you were out. He understands that while I live with you, I have every intention of making an honest woman of you, when you say yes to one of my proposals."

"It's true, Paul," Dee said. "He *does* propose, and I say no or maybe later. He'll win out, eventually."

"But for the time being," Tommy pointed out, "we're having lots of fun shacking up."

"Plus, Tommy is legally married to someone else, which makes it that much more deliciously scandalous." Dee giggled.

Paul nodded.

Dee suddenly felt odd, sitting here with her live-in lover, explaining her situation to her younger brother who had just arrived and not altogether approving of everything. It seemed that Dee was carrying on as she had in San Francisco, although this time she wasn't a wide-eyed virgin and her paramour wasn't a jaded rich guy who was her boss. It was hard, showing off and impressing Paul with big blond Tommy when, in truth, they were just another couple struggling to get by. She worried sometimes that she might have made a mistake about rejecting Lido Grandinetti.

"Paul," she asked, "what brings you down here?"

"Just wanted to get away from home for a while." Then, "Dee, there's something in this tote bag I was asked to deliver to you."

"Who sent it?" she asked.

"Guess."

Dee opened the bag and took out the white silk dress. "Lido. Nicer than I remember."

"And cost more than I've ever made," Tommy said.

"Thanks, Paul. Tommy knows all about my relationship with Lido."

"That's the main reason I came down, if you want the truth," Paul said. "He asked me to deliver it. He was quite preoccupied with your having it."

"Tell him I'm delighted he went to the trouble. I really needed something beautiful to wear."

"He would be delighted if you would walk down the street with me to Haller's Bar and thank him in person. He drove me down here."

Tommy said, "Let's go see Lido who went to all the trouble to give something nice to my fiancée."

"Well, Tommy," said Dee, "you two can go give him my regrets. I've nothing to say."

"He's waiting for me. I have to go back to him with the news that you've accepted the gift but still reject the giver." Paul stood up and straightened his slacks.

"Take the leather bag, too. I don't want it, nice as it is." She handed it over and Paul took it. "Do you see Lido often?"

"Sometimes a couple of times per week."

"Are you friends?"

Paul grinned. "Not sure yet. I think he sees himself as my mentor or something."

"Well, be careful around him. You know how manipulative he is."

Paul threw back his head and laughed. "I'm afraid I'm not his type, Dee." He pecked Dee on the cheek and said, "Gotta run. Thanks for the beer."

In a flash Paul was down the stairs and out of sight. Tommy said, "Nice guy. Awfully mature for his age."

"He's always been that way, maybe to compensate for the other two of us."

"Very businesslike, if you ask me. Alas, he will thrive in this cruel world and enjoy his stay, while temperamental artsy-fartsy types like us will always complain of the world's injustice."

"Were you dressed when he knocked?"

"Nope. In my bathrobe."

"He must've wondered about you. Undressed and home in the middle of the day while the rest of us were out working in the cruel world."

"I told him the truth. He bought it." Tommy had a job as the film critic for an obscure but important-sounding newspaper, the *Los Angeles Daily News*. He could go to Westwood Village, watch a new release, write a review and call it in. It worked well for him. It didn't pay well, but he also got some acting work now and again. Each month, with the arrival of

Tommy's check from home, they managed to have enough money to live on and keep Tommy's aging car.

"Did you tell my brother about your screenwriting?"

"No. He'll find out." Tommy's screenplay was only half-finished and he seemed to think he would have to revise every word. He handed her the dress. "Put this on."

She did, stepping into the other bedroom. Dee found it embarrassingly revealing in the bosom, nearly exposing her nipples. It was tight and sleek, and with her blonde hair and tan and voluptuous figure, she looked magnificent. Letting her hair down so that it tumbled about her shoulders, she asked herself: *Who is this woman?* This woman was worldly and mature, someone who knew herself well, not the child who labored away at Grandinetti Chocolate and gave her paychecks to Bud Steeves. Not the naïve girl who gave her virginity to Lido Grandinetti and spent endless hours writhing underneath him. This was the *new* Dee Steeves, the woman who refused to see Lido Grandinetti again regardless of the material bribes he offered her.

She liked this new woman a great deal. She pirouetted for Tommy. "You like?"

"Me likes," Tommy said. "Me wishes I could buy you such nice stuff."

"Honey," she drawled, "it don't matter who *bought* it so long as I *got* it." She moved closer to him. "Give us a kiss. It's been *hours* since our last makeout session."

"No wonder I'm so horny." He took her into his arms and enveloped her in a deep kiss. He pulled himself away long enough to say, "Let's get you out of this garment and into your birthday suit."

In a moment she was naked. They went into the bedroom and made gentle, careful love. Tommy, conscious of his size, always wanted to be sure he didn't harm her. She recalled her nights with Grandinetti, who didn't care if he did hurt her, and if he thrust too hard and she gasped, he thrust even harder. Tommy was meticulous, like Grandinetti; he picked up after himself and couldn't tolerate messes. He wasn't lazy so much as complacent about himself and his plans. If you didn't know where you wanted to go, you often went nowhere at all. They were a good match, if not a permanent one. Dee was eager for the future and all that awaited her in life. Did it include Tommy Wilhite? She didn't know.

She cuddled him after their lovemaking. "Wonderful."

"I need a smoke." Tommy reached over and lit up a Pall Mall. Dee thought how much like an overgrown kid he looked, smoking like a naughty boy, his blond hair mussed, a light growth of stubble on his face. "Now that we've done what we were obviously brought together to do," he said, "you should maybe tell me how your day went, since you're the only one of us with a life at the moment."

"He hit on me again," she said matter-of-factly of the star of the new film in which she was slightly more than window dressing. The star was married and thought to be a credit to the film industry. When they were alone, he practically mauled her.

"Can't fault his taste in women," Tommy said.

"He slapped my sweet ass, that's yours to defend."

"What! Your sweet ass! I'll murder the rogue. I'll call the police."

"Well, I wish you'd do *something*."

"Violence resolves nothing," Tommy said.

She gently punched his stomach. "Wimp."

"Well, you're a tough broad from Western Hills, so why don't *you* handle the matter?"

Changing the subject, Dee said, "The agent says he can keep me working till I collapse. Maybe even better parts..."

"Hollywood has discovered Dee Steeves. Don't forget to thank me for my alcoholism and wimpiness when you step up to accept your first Oscar."

"Well, I may have to take a rain check on all that additional work. I went to the doctor, and I'm pregnant."

"Let's celebrate with a beer." He hopped out of bed as if she'd just confessed to having cancer.

Maybe I should have held it off for later, she thought. He's so insecure right now. If he really panics about this, I'll suggest an abortion or adoption. I couldn't go through with it, but I'll say it anyway.

He came back with another can of beer and settled into bed. The light was bright. Good. It was important to see the look on Tommy's face as they talked this out. Dee had always believed in non-verbal communication as the source of a person's actual feelings. Words lied but faces didn't.

Tommy said, "It's time I grew up and became a daddy. If my wife won't give me the divorce immediately, so what? The world won't come to an end. You will soon have two children to look after. Is that acceptable?"

She looked at him with mock gravity. "Eminently acceptable." She kissed him and tugged at his old, frayed robe. "Before the child arrives we'll have to get you a new one of these. I won't have any child of mine seeing his father in that old rag."

Paul stepped into the bar and thought Grandinetti was going to have a heart attack when he saw the expensive tote bag. "Paul, did she refuse the dress?"

"No, Lido, she took it. She was grateful. She just didn't want the tote bag."

ENTREPRENEUR

They were probably the only two heterosexuals in the bar. The other customers, all males, looked with some interest at the two new arrivals. Grandinetti, expecting to see Dee, wore a smart orange shirt, tan jacket and khaki slacks. He looked lean and tanned, obviously in preparation for a reunion with his lost love. The gays in the bar looked at Paul and Grandinetti for several minutes.

"Two Budweisers," Grandinetti said to the bartender. Ordinarily he drank nothing but bourbon and thought beer was a workingman's swill, but today he wanted to be on Paul's good side. Paul loved ice-cold beer, the only kind of alcoholic beverage he did like. He was surprised at how he infrequently bartenders carded him.

The bartender brought over the beers and Grandinetti paid for them. "So?" he asked Paul.

"She didn't want to see you but her new boyfriend did. She works as an extra in movies. The visit wasn't long. I didn't get that much information."

Grandinetti nodded and sipped at his beer. "They live together? Is that what you're saying?"

"Yes. They have a large two-bedroom apartment and some ugly furniture. They make do."

"Her lover...what's he like?"

"Pleasant enough, I guess. Blond guy who likes beer."

"What's his name? What does he do?"

"Tommy Wilhite. Part-time actor who writes movie reviews for some newspaper."

Grandinetti swigged at his beer and wiped his mouth with the back of his hand. "Tell her if she unloads this loser—"

"Lido, she's *happy*. You should be, too. You're a tall, handsome, rich man. Why not just find yourself a new lady?"

"Maybe I want my old lady back." Grandinetti's eyes narrowed. "Let's go to her place right now to see Deirdre and Tommy. I can ask her point-blank to let me buy her the best goddamn penthouse in Beverly Hills."

Paul shook his head in disgust. "You're hopeless."

"Spoken like a true member of the distinguished sandwich-making Steeves clan from elite Western Hills."

"Aw, fuck you." Paul turned away but Grandinetti grabbed his arm.

"I'm sorry, Paul. I'm just spoiled and disappointed and I thought Deirdre would have me back and we would live happily ever after. I really thought so. Look, let me buy you dinner. The trip down here doesn't have to be a total waste. We can go to the most overpriced steakhouse in town and ogle whichever celebrities have the misfortune of sitting in the next booth."

As they were leaving a young man in a lumberjack shirt came up to them and said, "If you're going, can I come?"

"Piss off, Mary," Grandinetti said.

"Excuse me?" The young man snarled.

Grandinetti wheeled around and punched him so hard that the man dropped instantly to the floor, not even moaning. Grandinetti muttered, "I don't like your kind. It's unnatural." He turned to Paul. "Let's go before another one of them wants to sodomize us."

After dinner at a restaurant where dinner for two cost more than Dee and Tommy earned in a month, Grandinetti and Paul went to a noisy, garishly lit nightclub called the Casbah.

"It's the hardest goddamned place to get into in all of Los Angeles. God knows why," Grandinetti said.

The Casbah's bouncer smiled and let them both in. The pushed through a crowd of fashionably dressed young people and settled into a table close to the dance floor. Grandinetti ordered weird imported beer for them both. Paul sipped his, thinking that if Lido got drunk, Paul would

have to drive them back to the Bay Area. Grandinetti had taught Paul to drive Mercedes, and Paul drove it much better than Lido did. Lido certainly seemed to have an unlimited amount of time to spend with the younger brother of the woman who obsessed him, and Paul guessed that was the source of much of Grandinetti's unhappiness.

"Lido!" said a young woman in a black leather evening dress as she approached their table. "Lido Grandinetti! They told me you were dead and buried!"

"You mean I'm not?" Grandinetti stood up and offered a small embrace to the woman who clearly appeared to want more than a hug. "Nice to see you, Whitney."

"Nice to see me?" Whitney mocked, giving Grandinetti's arm a tiny punch. "After so long, it's just 'nice'? Why do you hurt me so, Mr. Grandinetti?" She shot Paul a little wink that said *I love teasing this big bastard.* "Who's your slender young friend with the big brown eyes? Ain't I your best friend anymore?"

"My friend is Paul Steeves. Paul, this is Whitney something."

Paul stood up and quickly shook Whitney's outstretched hand. Whitney was heavily made up and wore lots of jewelry. She licked her lips as her eyes bore straight into Paul's, as if she'd like to eat him with a spoon. Poor little rich boy Lido Grandinetti. So lonely that he had to make friends with people like Whitney.

"Come join us at our table," she said.

"No, thanks," Grandinetti said, suddenly no longer in the mood to party. "It's late and we must be going." Within seconds, they were out the door. Paul, standing there on the sidewalk as the valet ran off to retrieve the Mercedes, wondered what they were going to do now.

"Sorry about Whitney," Grandinetti muttered. "I could tell she liked you."

"Maybe too much," Paul said.

Grandinetti chuckled. "Much too much, I would say. A young guy like you shouldn't be in those decadent places. Next time you'll have to bring Nancy."

Paul knew Nancy would never consent to a trip anywhere with Grandinetti. She called him Lido Greedo or the Old Man with All Dollars and No Sense. The events of this trip would not have surprised her in the least: Grandinetti bugging Paul to help him get Dee back; failing in this mission, punching out a homosexual, eating an outrageously expensive dinner and being accosted by an overly friendly nightclub patron. A typical night on the town with Lido Greedo, Nancy would have said.

"Maybe I should make it a long-term goal to make friends with Deirdre and Tommy and come down here often," Grandinetti was saying as he pulled the car onto the street and began the long drive north. "Maybe I'll bring you down here with me and we could double date with them."

"Whatever." Paul buckled his seat belt. "Aren't you too drunk to drive?"

"I'm way too drunk to let *you* drive."

Jamey sat back against the half-completed building and, for the tenth time, rubbed his aching ribs. The sun was rising and his all-night security shift was ending. He wasn't cold anymore and had lots of energy from the coffee he'd drunk all night. It would have been the start of a perfect day but for his aches and pains.

No more fighting, he had admonished himself. Well, so much for that. He had gone to a local dance and kept a football player's date on the floor half the night. When he started groping her ass, her boyfriend pulled them apart and hauled Jamey out the door. The guy was big and strong but a bit slow and didn't know how to fight dirty. After several of Jamey's kicks and elbows, he was out cold. But he'd gotten in a few good punches and Jamey was still smarting.

Uncle Jack was in the construction office not far away. He ignored Jamey now, because his nephew knew about his nightly visits to Maria's bedroom. Uncle Jack left him alone so long as he said nothing to Aunt Virginia. Jamey had no intention of saying anything, but it was fun just the same to have Uncle Jack by the balls.

To make a point, Jamey had started refusing the delicious lunches Maria had packed for him. He'd go into town and have something to eat before work, and that would keep him till the next mealtime. Soon Maria stopped preparing the lunches altogether.

Uncle Jack stepped out of the construction office and told Jamey, "I'll be at my other site if anyone asks." Then he disappeared into his car and drove off.

Jamey wandered around the site for a few more minutes until a familiar car came by.

"Hello, Jamey," said the driver, a fortyish woman with long reddish hair.

"Elaine," Jamey muttered.

"Ready for a ride later on?" she asked.

"Why not now?"

"Well, isn't that wrong? To leave your post, I mean? Won't they fire you over that?"

"Naw." But Elaine was right: in security, abandoning a site was one of the worst things a guard could do. But what *would* Uncle Jack do?

ENTREPRENEUR

Elaine's husband was a man known to participate in all-night poker games and chase his girlfriends. He was successful, like Uncle Jack, and cared deeply about doing business and reinforcing his reputation as a fun-loving man's man. Elaine had found her own interests in life, and Jamey Steeves was one of them.

"Tell you what," Elaine said. "Just to be on the safe side, I'll come get you at midnight, when you're officially off and then we can have ourselves a real nice party."

The boy grinned. "Yeah."

Elaine smiled and drove off. Jamey wandered about for the rest of the shift, looking forward to his "party" with the married woman Elaine.

Jamey sat at the bar of the Tally-ho Tavern and guzzled down his second beer, still not quite believing that the bartender hadn't carded him. California could be fun that way. He thought it was great to drink while still a teenager. Did all the Sacramento bars serve people without asking for ID? If so, Jamey thought it was a great policy. He daydreamed about his adventure last night with Elaine and looked forward to the next one. He also wanted another beer and was going to order it when he heard a deep voice behind him.

"Buford James Steeves?"

"Huh?" Jamey asked, turning around.

"Are you Buford James Steeves?" The deep voice belonged to a burly cop.

"Who wants to know?" he said, regretting it instantly. Bars didn't seem like the right place to talk back to cops.

"You gonna be difficult with me, kid? Is that how it's gonna be?"

"What's your problem?"

"I will ask you one more time: are you or are you not Buford James Steeves?"

The boy sighed. "Yes."

"I have a warrant for your arrest."

Jamey laughed aloud. "On what charge?"

"Underage drinking, for starters," the cop said. "I'll bet you don't have a scrap of ID."

"Sorry I didn't card him," said the bartender.

"No problem." To Jamey he said, "Let's just go down to the police station and sort things out."

"I want a lawyer," Jamey protested as the cop pulled him to his feet. "I have rights, you know."

"Yes, you have rights. You have the right to a lawyer," the cop said, handcuffing him. "You're gonna need one, a damn good one."

When they reached the police station, the cop said, "Actually, the charge is statutory rape. We'll forget the fact that I found you in bar. I'll contact your Uncle Jack and he'll get you a lawyer."

In the lockup, Jamey met the only other prisoner, a tall, emaciated man in for vagrancy. Over a dozen vagrancy busts for him in California alone, he boasted.

Donna Steeves carefully steered the family's pickup truck towards Sacramento in the rapidly descending dusk. She had been for driving years, taught with much reluctance by her husband; Bud and she had fought after literally every lesson. But she had learned and gotten a driver's license, though it was Bud who did all the driving to make pickups from suppliers and deliveries to the delicatessen.

Bud had refused to have anything more to do with Jamey and had called his wife a fool after she hung up the phone with a promise to Jack that she would promptly come up to

Sacramento to deal with Jamey's newest outrage. Bud had expressed concern about Donna's ability to drive all the way up to Sacramento by herself but had ultimately allowed her to get into the pickup truck and drive off.

Donna thanked heaven when she saw the sign saying ENTERING SACRAMENTO COUNTY. Not far now. She hadn't brought much with her, mainly because Jack had insisted that Jamey already had enough clothing and had probably outgrown what was back in Western   Hills.

Uncle Jack paced the comfortable living room of his house, waiting for Bud's truck to arrive from San Francisco. That fucking Jamey was beyond belief. Virginia had just stopped her I-told-you-so's, and he had to admit she was right. Take in some kid nobody wants and you're just going to have lots of trouble, she'd said. You can't take a loser and bring him up to your level because he'll simply drag you down with him.

He felt ill as he waited in his comfortable home for his brother-in-law to show up and help straighten out this mess. Uncle Jack didn't pretend to be without contempt for Jamey's family; Bud and Donna were low-class folks from San Francisco whose reputation down there was nothing, so they didn't appreciate how much Jack and Virginia had to lose.

But Jack couldn't believe his eyes when, finally, the pickup truck pulled up his driveway and as the car door opened a tall, slim woman emerged. Jack groaned. Donna. She had come instead of Bud. Shit.

"Alrighty," she said, breathless, as Jack opened the door. "I have the money."

"Why didn't Bud come?"

"Why should he? He doesn't care about Jamey."

"And *you* do?"

Her eyes narrowed. "I'm his mother."

"Well, he's in lockup till tomorrow morning. We'll have to hope we can make this thing go away just with the money."

"Let me get this straight," Donna Steeves said. "My son had sex with a girl and now she's pregnant. Statutory rape. So I have to hand over ten thousand dollars to her father so he'll forget the whole thing even though the girl is naughty and there's no guarantee that Jamey is the father?"

Jack nodded. "That's right. And there's no guarantee that he'll accept the bribe."

"Unless he needs money."

Jack laughed. "He's Arnold Briller, who's making a mint off of Sacramento's rapid growth. Your money will mean very little to him. He just wants to slap Jamey and you across the face. His daughter is unmarried and promiscuous and now pregnant. Someone has to take the blame for this, and Jamey Steeves in a relatively short time has made himself a reputation as a first-class womanizer and troublemaker. Arnold Briller needs to save face."

"Is Briller a reasonable man?"

"He's a successful, greedy man with an image problem because of his daughter. I'm a successful, greedy man with an image problem because of my nephew."

Donna laughed. "I certainly hope he doesn't try to send Jamey to prison even after he takes my money."

Uncle Jack shook his head.

"We'll see." Donna sighed.

Uncle Jack had never seen her look so old. She put in hard days at Bud's Good Eats just to make a living and put up with Bud's moods. And what comes of it? Jamey becomes a hoodlum and she has to drive up to Sacramento to bribe her son's way out of trouble.

ENTREPRENEUR

Nobody deserves all that heartache and hardship, Uncle Jack said to himself as the two of them got into his car and drove over to Arnold Briller's stately home some blocks away with three thousand dollars in cash from Bud's Good Eats stored for the moment in the pocket of Donna Steeves's old, worn wool coat.

The other prisoner introduced himself as Grant. "It's easy to remember. Just think va*grant*." Grant said he was from San Francisco, just like Jamey, and he seemed to know so much about that city and its fun places that Jamey was amazed they hadn't met before.

Then Grant said he had worked for Grandinetti Chocolate's marketing department and Jamey was skeptical until Grant spoke at length about daily life there much the way Dee had, although he probably hadn't known Dee. The man spoke with the lively intelligence of someone who could have had a lucrative career but instead dropped out of society altogether. Jamey didn't want to get too chummy with him.

"I left Grandinetti Chocolate with no regrets," Grant was saying. "I was in marketing, which was the easiest job in the world because everybody loves candy in the first place. I just thought of different ways of preaching to the converted. But I got disillusioned. I had to deal occasionally with Grandinetti, the laughingstock of the place. He didn't know the first thing about the business. Grandinetti had solid people behind him, so his work was done. All he had to do, and all he *could* do, was nod yes and rubber-stamp things and sign his name. His family had tons of wealth and was big in stocks and bonds and what-have-you. He had to do *something* for a living because he was a Grandinetti. He was as unhappy and incompetent as you can imagine. Every bit a prisoner as you and me, Jamey."

"Me, I turned it in and decided to work when I had to and take it easy the rest of the time. The consequence is jail time when things get rough. But I'm still better off than a corporate corpse like Grandinetti. I'm convinced of that."

They heard a voice and looked through the bars to see the on-duty cop. "Buford James Steeves," the cop said. Jamey rose and walked through the open door, which clanged shut behind him.

Donna Steeves was waiting in the sergeant's office with Jack and his lawyer, a middle-aged man with a shrewd face who seemed to be smiling with genuine mirth, as if this were all highly amusing to him. Jamey was startled by how old and haggard his mother looked. It was the first in ages he had felt anything like empathy for anyone in his family.

Jamey and his mother exchanged smiles but neither knew what to say to the other, so they did not speak.

"This case is now history," the lawyer said. "The parties concerned have reached a fair agreement."

The sergeant grunted, as if he had some comments to make on the lawyer's appraisal but would keep his mouth shut.

"You're good to go, Buford James Steeves," the lawyer said.

"Really?" Jamey asked. "Just like that?"

The lawyer nodded. Donna Steeves said nothing as she, Jamey and Jack left the jail and headed out to Uncle Jack's car.

"Did you have to bribe someone over this whole mess?" Jamey asked in the car.

His mother spoke up. "Ten thousand dollars. The girl's father looked at it like was pocket change."

"Dad must be furious."

"He stayed home. He wants nothing more to do with you. It's that simple."

Jamey nodded. "All that money to get me out of jail? Why did you do it, Mom?"

After a pause, she said, "You weren't meant to rot behind bars."

"Your mother is driving home tonight, Jamey," Uncle Jack said. "And you are moving out tonight. Understand?"

"I hear ya," Jamey said.

In the attic bedroom Jamey had his few things packed within minutes. His mother had started back for San Francisco right away and now Jamey was faced with the choice of where to go next. He would make his selection when he got to the bus station. Back to San Francisco, he thought with a chuckle. No, thanks, not in this lifetime.

He bundled up everything and stuffed it into his tote bag. Downstairs, Uncle Jack was waiting for him; Aunt Virginia, the kids and Maria were nowhere in sight, which hardly surprised Jamey. Uncle Jack tossed him a small wad of bills that didn't look to be more than fifty dollars. "Here," he said. "Go."

Jamey walked out into the Sacramento evening and headed out over to the Greyhound station. He remembered the evening he arrived here and was met by Uncle Jack. Now he was leaving, after having made so much trouble for everyone, and was off to his next adventure. He looked up at the departures board and made what, in his opinion, was a very fine selection indeed.

Chapter 10

The wind howled as Paul's teeth chattered in the early-morning cold of Western Hills. Being the temporary proprietor of Bud's Good Eats was hideous work. He hauled the last crate of vegetables out of the old pickup and carried it into the delicatessen. His muscles ached and he nearly fell asleep even as he walked. How had his father managed to do this every day for so many years? It was bad enough to drive all the way to the Embarcadero before dawn to get the better fruits and vegetables just in from the San Joaquin Valley. The Bay wind ripped right through you. Then, after making the purchases, he had to drive all the way back to Western Hills in the early-morning darkness. Then he had to unload the stuff and slice it up nice and fine for the customers' delicate mouths. Finally, open the delicatessen—and then the real work began. The customers didn't know half the hassles of operating Bud's Good Eats and Paul was beginning to wish *he* didn't, either. But he, dutiful son, had volunteered to give his father a break for the time being and let him sleep in. Fond father Bud trusted Paul implicitly and tossed him the keys.

The Bud's Good Eats tradition goes into its second generation of masochism, Paul thought as he sorted out the lettuce, onions, carrots, apples and oranges, then the varieties of bread and so on. Jamey had said to hell with it all, including the Steeves family in general, and had gone out to Sacramento. Maybe he had the right idea, although Paul knew that there had been trouble, big trouble, and his father had refused to help but their mother had not, going alone in the pickup with nothing, so far as Paul could tell. She'd come home right away, but it was obvious from their mother's heartbreak that this time Jamey had really made quite a mess. She had returned with the happy news that Jamey was okay and was going to move out Uncle Jack's place. Perhaps he had narrowly avoided a lengthy prison sentence or some other kind of awful thing. Paul chose not to speculate on such matters.

He thought briefly back to his recent trip to see Dee, who was making do as a film extra. Tommy, her boyfriend, was a fool, but they seemed happy and that's what mattered. Dee, in fact, made as much money sometimes as Bud's Good Eats. Paul knew this because now he did the books and saw, in black and white, the shop's finances. Prices could be a bit higher, the part-time help was overpaid, the fresh produce from the Embarcadero was no bargain either...didn't his father see any of this? Did he really think that raising prices now and again would drive away all the customers? Paul was glad that someday soon the shop would be sold, or something, and that he wouldn't inherit it.

Inherit it with a smile. Is that what Grandinetti had done with the candy factory? If so, he certainly had it better than Paul. Grandinetti, bored and restless, had headed out to Hawaii, saying, "Expect me back when you see me. I shall think of you as I turn the color of Grandinetti chocolate under the sun."

Paul snarled, chopping up some lettuce and onions.

He awoke to his father's unmistakable voice down the hallway. Bud was yelling. Paul was fully clothed and quite disoriented, but soon realized that he had fallen asleep immediately upon his return from school, and now it was in the early evening.

ENTREPRENEUR

His father was not yelling at him, but at his mother. Donna Steeves was yelling back. Paul sat up and listened, curious. His mother was not the type to fight.

Bud Steeves was throwing out his wife, at least throwing her out of their bedroom and as far as their absent daughter's. Paul frowned. Was this supposed to be punishment? Wasn't this what Donna Steeves wanted, an end to their years together in a conjugal bed? Paul supposed that Bud was enraged and acted on it the only way he knew how. He apparently was dumping her things into Dee's room and shouting, "Ten thousand dollars! I can't believe you took all that money to buy that punk's way out of trouble! Wasn't that Molotov cocktail at Grandinetti's place enough? So I send him up to Sacramento and it's more of the same, chasing everything in a skirt and getting her in trouble and while I am asleep my idiot sister calls and says, 'Please come pay off the tramp's rich father so we won't be scandalized and our boys can play Little League baseball without having anyone snicker.' So what does *my* wife do? She goes to the bank and takes out all that money which was meant for the college education of one Paul Steeves, who of our three children had a chance to become more than just trash. Are you a fool? Huh? Are you a fuckin' fool?"

"You want me out of your bedroom? Good!" Donna shot back. "Wish I could get out of this house, too! Dee and Jamey are lucky, getting way from here! That awful deli, this sad neighborhood, their wretched father! You think Jamey is so bad? Well, Dee was no better. She was screwing Grandinetti, her boss! He paid her well, in cash. She hid it, I found it. Jamey tried to set fire to his mansion. Maybe she was in it. That would have meant one fewer child for you to be ashamed of. As for me, I am now retired. I will not work at Bud's Good Eats. If it fails, good. There are other places people can eat. My working days are over! Maybe I will have my own phone connected here in Dee's room.

You want anything? You can call the operator and get my number." With that she shut and locked the door.

Paul got up and opened his bedroom door. He saw his father standing in the hallway, outside Dee's bedroom.

Steeves said, "Your mother doesn't love me anymore."

Chapter 11

The basement of Ned Farley's home was as romantic as a basement could be. They had fixed it up as a recreation room of sorts and threw parties sometimes. Whenever there was a Farley party, Paul was at the top of the guest list.

Nearly a couple of dozen young people had been invited. Some dancing, some necking, a few just visiting or listening to the music on the radio.

The Bay Area Boyz would disband soon. Some guys back from overseas duty had started up bands with which Paul's was unable to compete, so the bookings had declined significantly. Paul accepted the demise of his band. He believed that the best deserved to get the work.

A few feet away, Charlie Benton and Laurie Jones were dancing very suggestively. They bragged about being engaged but had no rings yet. Charlie fancied himself a tough guy from the neighborhood—"He's a tiger I want to tame," said Laurie. But ever since that night his mother had moved into Dee's room, Paul had been cynical about love, romance and marriage. He had decided there should be a law on the books: You must visit the Steeves household before getting your marriage license.

Nancy insisted on sitting on his lap. She was too tall for him to be comfortable this way and she wanted his hand on her butt, which embarrassed him. Nancy liked that sort of intimacy in public. She especially liked it when Paul cupped his hand behind her head and brought her face forward for a kiss in front of others, and she always tried to slip him the tongue. Nancy got angry and hurt if she tried to get friendly with her man and he said no. She would look around the room, as if checking to see if there was a guy around who would say yes. Sometimes a woman had to show her man that there *were* other guys in the world who found her attractive.

Nancy had applied to the University of California at Berkeley. A diligent student, she deserved to attend such a fine institution and they probably would accept her. She wanted Paul there, too, so they could share their collegiate experience while continuing their romantic relationship. He said he wanted to attend Stanford or the University of Southern California. Actually, he wasn't going anywhere because he had no money. Instead of Stanford or USC, he was going to stay in Western Hills and get a master's degree in the School of Hard Knocks. But Nancy and the others didn't need to know that just yet.

Paul and Nancy hadn't had sex yet. Were they the only virgins in Western Hills? He looked over the top of her head and surveyed the room, which was full of couples who had been together for a while. All of them envied Paul and Nancy as a charming, handsome couple and surely surmised that they were sleeping together. Paul nearly laughed out loud when he thought about his mother and father in separate bedrooms; his sister, the former mistress of candy king Lido Grandinetti; his brother, the would-be firebomber of the Grandinetti mansion. There was probably lots of other scandalous stuff that he didn't know. But mostly, his family meant three simple words to most of Western Hills: Bud's Good Eats, the upstanding family which made the thickest sandwiches and served the creamiest smoothies in town.

Yes, Paul had to admit, the Steeves family was different from the rest. But was that something to brag about?

Ned Farley came by and said, "We've got refreshments upstairs now. Come on up."

Paul smiled. "Okay." He was grateful for an excuse to get tall, sturdy Nancy off his lap. She was cutting off the circulation in his thighs.

Soon they all headed upstairs. Ned, like Nancy, was headed to Berkeley. He was a good guy who would certainly succeed: a political science degree, then probably law school. His father was a partner at a downtown firm and would surely put him to work as soon as he passed the bar exam.

The Farleys could have moved into a better neighborhood ages ago but stayed in Western Hills because his father had grown up there and had a sentimental attachment to the community. But Paul guessed that the Farley family would move about as soon as Ned started college. Ned would find a better band or simply forget about music. Paul was intrigued that the conventional belief prevailing throughout the nation for decades, that men should go to college and women should stay at home, didn't apply in the 1970s. Most of the girls had definite academic and career plans. At this party in Ned's basement, most of these kids had applied to the University of California and California State University campuses and even to out-of-state schools. At Western Hills High, Paul knew many kids, and even those whose aptitudes and grades were mediocre seemed to have prepared for the future by securing apprenticeships or some other kind of vocational training.

He figured they would laugh their asses off if Paul admitted that he was taking over Bud's Good Eats. Imagine! Paul Steeves, the honor student and all-around leader, staying in Western Hills and minding the sandwich shop.

Maybe I shouldn't have come here tonight, he thought as he stood with Nancy's arm around his waist. Maybe I should just cut them all loose. I have nowhere to go, I am a man without a future.

"Nancy," Paul murmured, "I want to go home."

She frowned. "But we're having fun!"

"I have a cold and I've been working at the deli too much and I'm about ready to fall asleep."

"Betcha if this was the Grandinetti mansion, you would want to stay. Bye." She waved him off and headed up the stairs with the others. She was easily the prettiest girl at the party and she was his. A winner. A keeper. Paul wondered, putting on his jacket and making his way to the front door, if sex, even one encounter, would resolve these awful spats. Their necking was often prolonged and so heated that his clothes remained damp for the remainder of the evening and they parted in frustration. Maybe if, the next time, he merely said yes...?

But no. He wouldn't participate in a clumsy grope. He had a stubborn romantic streak. There would have to be an appropriate setting, flowers, wine, music. They would both have to say wonderfully clever things and make love as adeptly as people with years of erotic experience. The sky would have to fall, the earth move, the mountains crumble...

I've got to stop reading trashy novels, he thought, walking home through the fog and wind.

He could see the lights on at the closed-and-locked Bud's Good Eats. Grinding, slicing, unpacking, sweeping, mopping; the drudgery never ended. Paul, hearing his parents argue the night he moved his mother into Dee's old room, had actually started to feel stabs of empathy for his father. Around the house he seemed like nothing more than a tenant at a cheap weekly hotel, watching his step around the others, saying nothing, keeping to himself. He spent more and more time at the delicatessen.

Against his better judgment, Paul went into their apartment, then went through the door that connected their home to the deli. He found his father sitting on a crate at the back. "Hey, Dad."

"You look awful," he said. "Catching a cold?"

"Yeah. Need some help here?"

"Not from a boy with a cold. Where you been tonight, all dressed up and with a cold?"

"Ned's party."

"Left early? Where's your gal?"

"Nancy wanted to stay."

"Where's she going after graduation?"

"Berkeley, probably."

After a pause, Steeves asked, "So, you want some good news or some bad news?"

Paul grinned. "Do I have a choice?"

"Well, the good news *is* the bad news. Depends on how you look at it. Mr. Blume came by today."

"The guy who owns this building?" Paul asked, surprised.

Steeves nodded. "He came by to tell me that Western Hills ain't so broke after all. It's the up-and-coming neighborhood in San Francisco, so they're razing the whole block and replacing it with fancy apartment buildings. Bud's Good Eats will be history as of September 30."

"So we'll have to move."

"Yes, sir. Like I say, it's good news or bad, depending on your point of view."

"And what will become of *you*, Dad?"

Steeves shrugged. "Maybe I can steal some more Mafia money and retire in comfort."

ENTREPRENEUR

"Huh?"

"That's how I got my start here in San Francisco. Remember I told you I came of age in the Midwest? Well, I had this go-nowhere job in Chicago as a baggage clerk at the train station where you can check your things even if you're not traveling. So this sleek guy comes in with a satchel he wants to check for a few hours. Really nice satchel, too, and of course it's locked. Well, you don't have to be a police dog to smell the cash inside that satchel. He's a Maf guy and there's money in the satchel. The train station is a good place to hide money for a short time in case the cops come by. So I give the guy his baggage check and soon as he goes, so do I. Out the back door, never to return. My heart is beating so hard I think I'm gonna drop dead, right? But I get back to my room and with my screwdriver and pocket knife I manage to pry open this beautiful satchel, but when I'm done it's not beautiful any longer." He chuckled. "Inside is several thousand in cash, like I figured. This is Mob money, so I gotta leave the Windy City. I go to Greyhound and take the bus out here. Met your mother on that trip. She must've thought I was the weirdest guy in the world. Never did I put down that broken satchel and I didn't sleep a wink, worrying about whether or not the Mob would track me down." He paused. "That's why I got so mad at Jamey. He's too damn much like me."

"That's an awful story, Dad," Paul said. "If I had known that, I would have broken out into a cold sweat whenever someone in a trenchcoat came in or a fancy dark car drove by. I'd have expected guns to start blazing."

"Naw, they would have spared you. They wanted me. Just walk into Bud's Good Eats and shoot me point-blank." Steeves rubbed his chin. "Not a day passes that I don't think of that satchel."

"Well, stop. Put it behind you, Dad."

"Oh, I have some bright new memories that will keep me going for years. Like going up to the merchant teller and finding that a cashier's check has been drawn for ten grand by your mother. So I know where your brother is but not where your mother is, but I have to figure that she's gone to rescue Jamey. I call Jack and get the story. She's going to give some rich guy all that money so he won't put little Jamey in prison over his pregnant, underage daughter. I can picture your mother going into his big house and humbly offering all our money so's he won't make trouble for Jamey. She probably offered him sexual favors, too."

"Dad—"

"You wanna know where your future went? Ask your mother. She gave it to a rich Jew in Sacramento." He fixed a level gaze on his son. "Paul, I'm proud of you. You're a smart fella, a real winner. Ambitious. You won't be happy with a simple life. I'm just so damn sorry that you won't have that money for college."

"I'll get by."

"I'm glad this operation of mine is coming to an end. I couldn't bear to have you wasting your life fixing sandwiches here, waiting on rude people, biting your tongue like your mother and I did. It isn't nearly good enough for someone like you." He shook his head and muttered, "So long, Bud's Good Eats."

His son laughed. "Paul's Good Eats."

Steeves groaned. "God forbid."

"Well, these decisions about where to go and what to do don't have to be made by tomorrow morning, right?"

Bud Steeves reached out and touched his son's arm.

ENTREPRENEUR

"Here's your inheritance. No money, but some good advice. From now on, Paul, look out for number one. Understand?" His grip tightened. "To hell with unselfishness. Hear me? Let the damn preacher man squawk about that on Sunday morning. Get what you want, you hear me? Don't lose sleep over it if you have to step on some toes along the way. They'd step on yours with pleasure." He was breathing hard by now, clutching his son's arm. "Don't take shit off nobody, Paul. And for Christ's sake, don't let the bastards grind you down—"

"Dad! Enough!" Paul pried off his father's hand. "You're a little drunk and very tired. Maybe you should call it a night. I'll work down here."

"I just told you: Paul Steeves does *not* waste his valuable time in Bud's Good Eats. You go upstairs and I'll keep at it down here." He thought for a moment and scratched his head. "So Jamey's out of Sacramento and headed God knows where. Don't I have another kid to account for?"

Paul chuckled. "Dee."

"Yeah. The blonde girl, right?"

"Yessir."

Steeves looked at him.

Paul shrugged. "In another city. Doing okay." A wannabe starlet, pregnant with her married lover's child. Paul had recently gotten a letter from her, care of Ned Farley. Bud Steeves didn't need to know these things. Paul wished his father goodnight and went upstairs as Steeves drank some more vodka.

Donna Steeves rose and made sure both Paul and Bud Steeves were sound asleep. She didn't want them, or anyone else in San Francisco, to hear her. She went into the closet and took out her best white dress and a pair of sandals. She put these on and emerged from what had been Dee's bedroom. She went slowly down the stairs holding her keys to the sturdy old pickup truck. When she reached the curb she unlocked the pickup's door and crawled in. Her heart beat furiously as she turned on its ignition, dreading the chance that Steeves would wake up and look out the window. Instead there was no sound or movement from the apartment above the delicatessen. She took one last hard look at the words BUD'S GOOD EATS creeping in gold-block lettering across the narrow darkened window.

Goodbye, goodbye.

She pressed on the accelerator and the pickup rolled down Tower Street. It was well after midnight; there was no traffic as she negotiated an endless series of streets and hills. Finally she reached Fisherman's Wharf and parked along the street. It was dark and quiet. The sky was clear and starry but a chill in the air surprised Donna as she got out. She left the keys in the ignition but turned the engine off and walked with some caution.

Fisherman's Wharf, a thriving commercial district popular with tourists throughout the world, was deserted for the moment. What would she say if a cop came by?

But nobody did, and she made her way past the jagged rocks and sand of the beach to the waterline of San Francisco Bay. She plunged in. The water was so cold that it took her a moment to catch her breath. She looked up and saw the Golden Gate Bridge. Was anyone up at this hour and driving across? No matter.

Donna let the current carry her out under the bridge and beyond. She had always been a strong swimmer and rolled over onto her back, looking up at the stars and the moon. Impulsively she ripped off her dress. Now she was naked. It seemed the right thing to do, somehow. She smiled, filled with relief, her first genuine smile in many years, as the current

took her farther, farther, out into the vast emptiness of the Pacific Ocean and eternity.

PART TWO

Chapter 1

Los Angeles, 1980

Jake Palladino sat back and read the newspaper in his small office at the Wilshire Men's Club, glad to have this late-morning downtime and especially glad that the owners of the health club were generous enough to spring for a good air conditioner. Los Angeles could be such a hot, brutal bitch.

Palladino folded back the paper and read slowly as the cold, refreshing air blew into his face. A former heavyweight, he had been called the Great White Hope by some and the Great White Dope by others. He hadn't lived up to his early promise and once or twice nearly had his brains scrambled by this or that black or Latin boxer. Still, despite his broken nose and cauliflower ears, he was a moderately handsome aging man, proud of his cleft chin and full head of salt-and-pepper hair. He liked it when people remarked that his droopy eyes and deep voice reminded them of the actor Robert Mitchum. Some of the members, middle-aged guys trying to stay in shape, loved to pound away at Palladino in the ring, not altogether realizing that he was letting them hammer at him and could easily have taken out any of them at any time.

What concerned him at this moment was that nobody wanted the job he had listed in the *Times*. He stared at it now. *Assistant required for exclusive men's health club. Interesting work for the right person, good neighborhood, full-time employment.* Well, he conveniently neglected to mention that the job paid only five dollars per hour, but that was better than the minimum wage of only three bucks or so. This wasn't the worst deal in town.

Just then his phone rang. Someone was downstairs, asking about the job. A young guy, a kid really. "Send him up," Jake said.

The kid swaggered into his office. He was blond, with broad shoulders. Handsome, with a lot of attitude, the kind Palladino had seen on the faces of the boy models in the GQ ads.

"You the boss?" the kid asked.

"Maybe." Palladino looked the kid up and down. "Do you know how to box?"

"I fight a lot, if that's what you mean. That's kind of why I'm here. I don't have any gear."

"Well, we do. Put some on and get into the ring."

The kid shrugged and disappeared into the locker room. He reemerged in boxing trunks, headgear and boots. One of the employees tied the kid's gloves. Palladino was impressed at his broad, heavy shoulders, tight stomach, thick, sinewy arms, long legs. Pushing two hundred pounds, but he would need a year of weight training before he could call himself a professional heavyweight boxer. Also, the kid was barely six feet tall, if that, and his reach was limited. Over the years the boxers had gotten much taller. Six-four, six-five had become a common height in the sport.

In the ring, Palladino nodded. "Okay, let's go."

The kid charged at him like a street guerrilla and threw a left jab. Palladino blocked the jab and sent him backwards with a soft right. Well, the kid needed to learn some technique. But he came right back and traded punches for a few minutes, even tagging Palladino a couple of times with shots that made his headgear vibrate. Afterwards, he said, "You got any verifiable employment references?"

"No, not really."

"Well, you got a job." Then, "Tell you what. If you want to work here, just keep your mouth shut and your eyes wide open. Think you can do that?"

He kept his mouth shut and his eyes wide open for the longest single period of his entire life. He learned quickly enough that after his main duties were done, it was a good idea to make himself useful by running errands for Jake or anyone else who wanted something done. He smiled till his lips ached and was endlessly diplomatic with everyone, especially the older members. The club reeked of wealth, both old and brand new, and Jamey liked to walk through the private reading and gaming areas where members could read and relax. In those air-conditioned, perpetually darkened, mahogany-paneled rooms were expensive leather armchairs and huge oil paintings of the early days of Los Angeles, before its insane growth and unchecked sprawl, hilly and golden land, open to all. Jamey was quick and efficient and could do what little was expected of him in almost no time. His work done, he sat in Jake's office and listened to the old guy tell stories of his boxing career.

Palladino did not ask about Jamey's background. He did not want press for phone numbers of personal references, and Jamey was not eager to tell about his endless months on the road, up to Seattle and Portland and down to Tijuana. He was particularly reluctant to tell about Reno, where he took a job as a bellman and made good money steering whores towards guests until the girls' pimp objected and threatened to kill him. There were temporary jobs as a manual laborer where he often punched out coworkers over trivialities. Jamey decided he did not ever want to grow up. To him, growing up meant growing old and getting boring.

Jake saw the boy's potential and let him use the punching bags during slow periods. Jamey learned quickly the difference between street fighting and boxing, and soon punched the bag with speed and efficiency. He also lifted weights religiously and grew even more muscular.

Jake at some point began to truly see Jamey as a viable heavyweight boxer, and when the urge hit him and there were no members around, the two men would get into the ring, where Jake would teach Jamey shrewd defensive tactics and how to use moderate height to his advantage. He showed the youngster how to duck and bore into a much taller opponent, and how to roll with punches and duck away from them. Jake wouldn't let Jamey step into the ring with any of the club's members, because he wasn't sure that the kid had enough self-restraint yet to avoid harming them. But there were pickup basketball games, and Jamey participated when an extra man was needed, and he always played more poorly than necessary but made it look as if he were going all out. Through his interaction with members and his consistent losing performances, Jamey practically doubled his salary in tips.

He also discovered that Palladino had sent word to the cook that the new hire was a serious boxing prospect who needed to bulk up, so Jamey sat in the kitchen eating the same scrumptious chops, steaks and stews that were served to the members.

The Wilshire Men's Athletic Club's membership consisted mainly of doctors, lawyers and accountants who wanted to prevent their paunches from getting any larger. They engaged him in conversation and told him anecdotes about their old days at Johns Hopkins, Yale or Stanford. Jamey took discreet messages from wives and lovers and acquired a reputation as someone who could keep secrets and respect confidentiality.

ENTREPRENEUR

For his part, Jamey simply went along to get along. He did not see his days at the club as valuable experience towards a career of any kind, nor did he regard the people he met there as potential contacts. If he was a gentleman, it was only out of common sense. There seemed every reason to be the resident good-natured tough guy. He had been a rebel and a misfit for long enough to know how difficult and exhausting such an existence was; compared to then, these days were easy. He was content simply to maintain the status quo. When Palladino started encouraging him to sign up for amateur boxing matches just to measure him against other, similar fighters, he shrugged and said he would think about it. He would have to start training then, and that was hard work.

His only real expense was for rent of the room in skid row that he hoped to be able to vacate soon. He was grateful to be so muscular and aggressive-looking when he went home at the end of the day. His hotel was at the corner of Fifth and Stanford, a scary, creepy place, far worse than San Francisco's Tenderloin. L.A. was also horribly expensive, with few affordable places even in the worst neighborhoods. Once he got into town, he checked the *Times* every day for job openings, and soon came across Jake's ad.

He liked some club members more than others, but treated them all with the utmost respect. He pretended to remain ignorant of them and their personal business, but inevitably he would come to his own conclusions about these men, especially when he saw the ones, not significantly older than himself, with flaccid breasts, protruding stomachs and sagging buttocks, men whose necks were reddened by women's bites and who threw temper tantrums over lost racquetball games.

Jake, contemptuous of them all, nevertheless was a shameless toady. A third-generation Angeleno who despised rich people but especially the newly rich ones and those from outside of California, movers and shakers who had come here to exploit the land and the economy. But his job was to be nice and professional, to stay on everyone's good side, and could patronize them with dignity.

"This guy here," he said as a member entered the locker room, "is the biggest inside trader on the West Coast. He takes advantage of all his investors, only they don't know it yet." Then he called out to the man, "Long time, no see. Been pulling long hours these days, huh?"

"Keeping busy, that's for sure."

"Well, don't let the bastards grind you down," said Palladino.

The man laughed.

Jamey paid attention to his boss, watching and listening as Jake taught him to deal with this exclusive clientele and their fragile egos. He genuinely liked the ex-fighter and considered him an adept actor, playing a part day after day, always convincing. The old guy could have made it in Hollywood.

Jamey personally liked a member named Waller, an amiable middle-aged guy who owned a chain of travel agencies. They would play racquetball even when other members were around even though club employees were supposed to be invited to play only if there was no one else around. Waller and Jamey played hard, and Waller usually won except when his age caught up with him and he faded quickly. Then Jamey could beat him easily. "B.J. the lion-hearted," Waller called him. Afterwards they would go for a beer in the men's lounge. Waller's advice to was, "Be frugal, always. That lion's heart you got beating in there is going to get old and slow down before you know it."

The trouble came when he had been there for several months. He had a thief and troublemaker's sense that things weren't as they should be when he went to his locker and could tell that someone had been through his things. Nothing was gone, but someone had definitely poked around in his clothes and personal belongings. Well, there are dishonest people everywhere, he thought as he changed into his sweats and went for a workout.

When he came back, he found a pink slip taped to his locker with the words SEE ME, J. Palladino. Jamey knocked on Palladino's office door.

Inside, Jake said, "We got trouble. I just got a report that someone lifted a Patek Philippe from a member's locker. You know what a Patek Philippe is, kid?"

Jamey shrugged. "A watch."

Palladino laughed, bitter. "Oh, shit, it's more than just a watch. There are lots of cars on the road that don't cost as much as a Patek Philippe." He paused. "Also, there's been a rash of thefts over the past while. It's that asshole Niebuhr, he's the one says his precious little fuckin' watch was stolen, now he's making a federal case out of it."

"So, where do I come in?"

"Well, Niebuhr claims the thefts happened since you started here."

"Oh, fuck."

Niebuhr was a tall, stocky younger man who was high up with International Megaplex, the huge movie theater chain. He had wrestled and boxed during his college days and still worked out practically every day. He frequently sparred with Jake, and when they were in the ring Niebuhr went at his opponent hard and dirty, viciously punching below the belt if he couldn't get inside on Jake. The older man emerged from these sessions wincing and holding his groin. Jamey watched, disgusted.

"Oh, Niebuhr's a real son of a bitch," Palladino said. "He made me search your locker. Good thing you didn't have anything remotely resembling a fancy watch in there." He paused. "Did you take the watch?"

Jamey held up his left forearm and showed his wrist. "Timex is all I got."

Palladino shrugged. "I don't know what the hell to tell that guy."

"Everyone goes through that locker room any number of times per day."

"And everyone's got a combination lock on his locker."

"Shit, Jake, those stupid locks are the easiest thing in the world to get past. Still, they're better than nothing. Anyway, if you like, I'll quit. Maybe it'll take the heat off you."

"You don't gotta do that. Just be aware that there are people around here who don't completely trust you."

Later on, when they had a friendly racquetball competition upstairs and virtually everyone was there, Jamey made his rounds. One of the members not upstairs was Winthrope, a new member who had gone to medical school back East and was now a rising cardiologist in Los Angeles.

Jamey padded into the spacious locker room in his sneakers and saw Winthrope at the wrong end of the room, jiggling a paper clip into a lock that clearly wasn't his. The lock popped open and B.J. rushed up to him, still unseen.

"Put that down, sir," he muttered.

Winthrope looked at him, his face white with panic. "Yes, all right."

"So *you're* the one," Jamey whispered.

"Yes."

"They thought it was me."

"That's too bad. I apologize," Winthorpe said.

Jamey knew he couldn't simply reveal Winthrope as the thief. No matter what he said or did, he would lose his job. Nobody liked a rat.

"Put the lock back on," he told Winthrope, who obeyed him. "Now, listen carefully," Jamey said, his eyes boring into Winthrope's, who was much smaller than him and practically shaking with fear. "If anything else goes missing, I'll finger you, and your reputation won't be worth shit. Understand?"

"Yes," Winthrope whispered.

"Finally, I want ten thousand dollars from you, payable by this time tomorrow."

Winthrope laughed. "I don't have it."

"Bullshit. You're made of money."

"And if I refuse?"

"Then I'll go straight to Jake Palladino and tell him about what I saw ten minutes ago. I'll meet you in the Beverly Grand Hotel tomorrow night. Bring cash. A packet of C-notes. Hundred-dollar bills."

Winthrope, sneering, nodded and stalked out of the locker room.

Jamey reached the Beverly Grand in plenty of time and sat in the lobby bar, nursing a beer and marveling once again how easy it was to drink in California when you weren't yet of legal age. He was dressed in his best clothes; he believed in committing extortion with style. He watched the main entrance carefully, eager to see Winthrope.

You had to step into a load of shit to find yourself paying out ten thousand dollars to clean it up, he reflected as he sipped at his beer. Usually, that deep smelly shit you stepped in had something, or everything, to do with sex or money. Fortunately, Winthrope had lots of money and could part with it without suffering too much. Jamey felt no moral compunction about taking the man's money. As far as he was concerned, the money was honestly earned by the Steeves family at Bud's Good Eats, then made its way to old man

Briller in Sacramento because of his slutty daughter, and now it was coming back to the Steeves family. He pictured his mother's face as he put the money in her hands. Maybe this would improve his father's opinion of him, too. Or not.

Kleptomania puzzled him. Homosexuality did, too, and he'd seen enough of that in San Francisco. He had repulsed by those males who wanted to touch him, especially when all that sweet female ass was twitching around everywhere. Back in Western Hills, his buddies had often urged him to join them in fag bashing—charging into city parks, or the notorious Castro district, to beat up queers blowing each other in the bushes or alleys. No, thanks, said Jamey. He couldn't figure out why the fairies did their thing in public, where they were vulnerable to the cops and punks. Why didn't the faggots get their perverted rocks off in private? Or maybe they liked the danger of doing it in public places.

Still and all, maybe it was sheer boredom that compelled a guy like Winthrope to steal stuff out of lockers. He seemed like such a winner—handsome, rich, smart, a prominent man who was a credit to the community.

Just then Winthrope walked into the bar. He was wearing a navy blue suit and a striped rep tie. He had obviously just come from the office or the hospital. Jamey caught his attention and waved him over.

"Mr. Winthrope," he said.

"Let's get this over with," said Winthrope.

"Fair enough."

"I want you to know," he said uncomfortably, "that I usually don't do such things. I have a problem. I'm getting professional help—"

Jamey put up his hand. "None of my business, sir. Please don't explain. I'm not your judge."

"Then why are you blackmailing me?" Winthrope frowned as he withdrew a thick envelope and handed it over.

"Because you have so much and I have so little." Jamey slipped the envelope into his breast pocket.

Winthrope looked angry, repulsed. He said, "Doesn't this bother you? Demanding money from a man who can't control his own behavior?"

Jamey shook his head just the tiniest bit. "Sir, I could shake you down right here in this bar and not lose a moment's sleep over it."

"Sociopathic little punk," Winthrope muttered.

Jamey patted his breast pocket. "Thank you for this."

"How do I know you won't be coming back for more?" Winthrope asked, suspicious.

"Because I'm not leaving the area, now that I have some money. Anyway, thanks for the contribution. Buy you a drink?"

"Up yours," Winthrope muttered, getting up and walking out of the lounge. Jamey smiled again, patting the new bulge in his jacket pocket.

The bus pulled into the San Francisco Greyhound station and Jamey, entering the lobby for the first time in a long while, remembered his conversation with Paul and how his eye burned from his father's punch.

He walked down Market Street, amazed at how unchanged it seemed. Did you miss me? Or did you even notice that I left?

He passed by Amazement, the big arcade in which he had spent so many evenings. Would they recognize him in there?

He walked past the Tenderloin. His legs uncramped and the walk felt good. But from downtown San Francisco to Western Hills was too far to walk, so he boarded the Western Hills bus and gazed out the window for the half-hour ride.

The bus eventually lumbered onto Tower Street and he got off. The fog was a bit lighter here. Tower Street now looked curiously new in places, like a struggling old neighborhood on the upswing.

He blinked in disbelief as he looked at where Bud's Good Eats and the Steeves home should have been. Instead there was a new-looking apartment building that occupied the entire block. He walked further, about a block or more, till he found the Genoa Grocery Store where he had bought or stolen many things. Old lady Genoa was still there, minding the store.

"Ma'am...?" he asked.

"Yes?" She showed no sign of recognizing him.

"I haven't been here in some time. My family used to have a business here. Looks like they've torn it down."

"Family business here? Which one? Most of the old stores are gone."

"It was a delicatessen."

She frowned. "Bud's Good Eats?"

"Yes!"

"Oh, *that* place. You one of Bud Steeves's kids?"

"Yes. You knew me as Jamey."

"Little punk."

He said nothing.

The old woman scratched her head. "Well, lemme see. The Steeves girl left, the pretty blonde, and the tall boy, the nice one, moved out. The mother threw herself in the bay. Her dress was found somewhere in the water…"

"Oh," Jamey muttered as he wandered out of the store. Dazed and heartbroken, he felt like a stranger in his own hometown. He was sure he could easily find Paul or his father in the phone book but decided against it. He had wanted to see his mother again, to have her see him in his nice clothes and neat hair, returning the money. That was the point of the trip. That was all that mattered. He was too late.

ENTREPRENEUR

Chapter 2

South Bay, 1982

"This is *our* century. The United States is the world's foremost military and economic power. Our hegemony is unquestioned. But we have certain responsibilities. We must defend our friends and stand up to our enemies. Just because we are on top does not mean that conflict is no longer possible. In order for our future to be glorious as our present, we must not succumb to arrogance and complacency."

Senator Kay Roth, as tall and poised as a faded movie beauty, stood at the podium as she addressed the graduating class of People's University. Capped and gowned in the audience under a cool blue June sky, Paul Steeves sat and listened. Don't worry, Senator. No arrogance and complacency here. Just a tired young guy with a crabby old father for a roommate.

Kay Roth, the junior senator from California, had graduated from Stanford and probably couldn't have found People's University on a map. California had chosen for its senators two tall Jewish women, liberal Democrats who had married well. The newspapers said that their husbands had bought them their senate seats and predicted that Roth would become America's first woman president, if she wanted that.

Senator Roth went on talking, but Paul stopped listening. Next to him sat Paul Hankowsky, known to all as Hank, his best friend over the past four years. Hank, a wirehead from Reno, was a stocky, bearded, friendly man who had chosen People's University because it was just far enough from, and close enough to, home. A gifted design engineer but an apathetic high school student, he had been rejected by Berkeley and Caltech. Hank wanted to do big things in California, where he claimed they offered limitless opportunities to those with brains, brawn and balls.

"Stick with me, Paul," he had said over beers. "We'll own California in a decade."

Paul regretted having no guests at the ceremony. Nancy had graduated from Berkeley a couple of days earlier and moved to southern California. Paul's father, in one of his snits, simply refused to attend because he thought Paul would be embarrassed to have him there among all those smart, successful people.

Lido Grandinetti, too, was a no-show. Four years earlier, he had written letters and made phone calls to Stanford but failed to ensure Paul's acceptance there. Paul felt relieved that Lido's connections had let him down. People's University had been good enough, thank you very much.

Grandinetti refused to attend the ceremony ostensibly on ideological grounds. "I despise that bitch," he'd said of Senator Kay Roth. According to Lido, Roth had done entirely too little on Capitol Hill to look after the financial interests of California's moneyed elite. "But come by for a drink after the ceremony, Paul, and we'll figure out what to do with you now."

Paul *knew* what to do with himself now. He and Hank had just finished building the world's first usable, marketable personal computer. They had done so in the back office of Amazement, the video arcade where he worked and sometimes slept. Scavenging parts from surplus stores and working endless hours on schematics and programming, they had met their self-imposed deadline of graduation day. They fashioned the machine into something fun and affordable—they *needed* to make it into something everybody could enjoy and, eventually, would consider absolutely essential to a happy life.

The senator finished her speech to polite applause. On the stage was Professor Toni Freeman, head of the philosophy department. Paul grinned at what Professor Freeman must have thought of Senator Roth. Freeman, the closest thing People's University had to a celebrity, was a lanky, handsome, graying black woman who had been born in Alabama or Georgia, raised in upstate New York and spent time in prison for antagonizing the Establishment over civil rights.

She had written acclaimed books on being black, being a woman, being an American and being an academic. She often spoke in class about the hypocrisy of her native land. "This country absolutely depends on debt and irresponsible spending. It couldn't exist without blind, insatiable consumption." Freeman was the only woman Paul had ever heard of to be on the FBI's Most Wanted list because of her political affiliation with the Communist Party and her friendships with George Jackson, Huey Newton and Medgar Evers.

Easily the most interesting and provocative of all Paul's professors, Freeman probably belonged at Berkeley in 1962 alongside Mario Savio, standing on the roof of a car, demonstrating against the upright, uptight Cal authorities. But these weren't the crazy, radical 1960s, and this was just People's University, where the students were mostly concerned with four gets: get in, get through, get out, get a job. In Freeman's lectures, Paul took careful notes and listened with keen objectivity. He received an A in her course. Paul was fascinated by people whose views differed so much from his own, and he believed that when he became a hotshot high-technology entrepreneur, he would understand his critics and skeptics that much better because of his willingness to keep an open mind. His major, however, was business. The professors were boring but they taught you what you needed to know.

ENTREPRENEUR

Freeman apparently sensed right away that Paul Steeves, the tall brown-haired student who always looked as if he'd been up most of the previous night (which, of course, he had), was a serious and earnest student. She had often seemed to speak directly to him and had even, once or twice, asked him to consider majoring in philosophy.

At the conclusion of the ceremony, Paul and Hank said hello to a few people and headed for Hank's Ford in the parking lot.

"Lots to do," Paul said.

"People to see, asses to kiss." They both guffawed.

Paul pulled off his gown and tossed it into the backseat. "Glad I'm dressed up, going to see the man."

Soon they were on the northbound freeway, towards downtown San Francisco. Hank, as always, drove fast, with little regard for safety. Soon they reached their exit and crept towards Market Street, countless cars in front of them.

"I hate this fucking traffic," Hank said. "You nervous about seeing Bayliss?"

"Nope."

"Wonder what's gonna happen."

Paul screwed up his face like Marlon Brando in *The Godfather*. "He'll make me an offer I can't refuse."

They reached the crowded, seedy stretch of lower Market Street and saw the entrance to Amazement, busy and noisy on this mild, clear afternoon. At night, the lurid pink-neon blaze of the arcade's big sign was visible from a dozen blocks away. Hank stopped for a moment and Paul got out. A sheet of newspaper flew by his head and drifted out into the four lanes of Market Street. He stepped over Orange Julius and Taco Bell debris and hurried past panhandlers huddling by storefronts.

ENTREPRENEUR

He entered the perpetually dusky cave of Amazement and, as always, was immediately assaulted by the games' electronic sound effects which, blended together, formed a kind of insane rock music. The air was laden with the salt-and-sugar smells of candy, chips and soda. NO FOOD OR DRINKS ALLOWED said the sign above the attendant's cage.

The attendant smiled and gave him a congratulatory high five. "Mr. Bayliss is in the office, waiting for you."

"Yeah." Paul used his own office key to let himself in.

He found Fred Bayliss behind the desk, sneering at the latest Pacific Gas & Electric bill. "This goddamn place burns up almost as much power as a Vegas casino."

Paul smiled. Bayliss had complained many times about everything.

"Sit down, Paul. You probably know why I asked you to drop by." Fred Bayliss was a big, beefy man, as tall as Paul and twice as broad. A third-generation amusement-parlor proprietor, he was largely unsentimental about his business and employees, indifferent to the degeneration of lower Market Street, unafraid of the Bloods and Crips who stayed till dawn and spent their crack money playing Donkey Kong and Pac-Man. For security purposes, Bayliss had adapted his games to accept tokens, not quarters. Twin token machines, as big and impenetrable as safes, squatted at the entrance; customers who smuggled in screwdrivers and jimmied open his games would not get his money. The tokens were five for a dollar, the best deal in town. Whenever players got high scores, the games spat out small red prize tickets, redeemable for prizes in Amazement's Plexiglas display case: family-size Hershey bars, Sony radios, Seiko watches and other items. Every other morning, a Loomis guard carrying a .38 caliber handgun emptied stacks of twenties from the token machines in this funky, smelly section of Market Street.

"How did graduation go?" Bayliss was asking.

"It was a little too warm out, but we survived. Senator Roth gave us a nice pep talk."

"No M.B.A. school?"

"I'm in debt up to my ass."

Bayliss chuckled. "Well, you've had enough schooling, so far as I'm concerned. This is for you." He reached into his drawer and took out a long, slender box containing a Cross silver ballpoint pen. A nice pen. Paul had seen nicer ones.

"Thanks, boss." He'd hoped, insanely, for the mint-condition 1962 Mickey Mantle baseball card in the display case. Available to the customer who won an unwinnable 5000 prize tickets.

"Paul, you have been ideal here. You've never bitched about working graveyards and you've always been conscientious. Remember back in 'Seventy-nine, the White Night riots? The queers and blacks came by here, looking to trash the place, and we had to close. You stood here by me, and I never forgot that."

Paul nodded. While the city was still reeling over the mass suicide, nine days earlier, of cult leader Jim Jones and his followers in Guyana, San Francisco Supervisor Dan White, clinically depressed and plagued by anxiety after a Twinkies binge, brought a handgun to City Hall, crawled in through a window and killed Mayor George Moscone. Then he shot Supervisor Harvey Milk, the city's first openly gay official. White was convicted only of manslaughter; outraged, the gays rioted. Paul helped Bayliss secure Amazement's seldom-locked glass doors and pull-down steel gate, standing in front of the display case, watching as the young men prowled around 1 Market Street, rattling the arcade's gate and doubled over with maniacal laughter.

"I was never so scared in my life as that night," Paul said to Bayliss.

"I'm getting damned tired of coming out here so often from my home." Bayliss lived across the Golden Gate Bridge, in Marin County. "Then driving down to Oakland and San Jose to check on the other arcades. By now, you know pretty well how my business operates. So, how'd you like to assume that hassle for me?"

"What would my title be?"

"Is general manager OK?"

"I accept." Paul anticipated the offer and did not altogether want the job. "And I have something for *you* in return for all you've done for me over the past four years."

He went into the rear of the office, reached behind one of the video games and carefully lifted the newly completed Cherry computer prototype. His heart thundered in his chest as he carried the light new machine over to Bayliss and placed it on the desk. Hank perhaps had a right to be there as well, since he, much more than Paul, had built the machine and could better demonstrate its capabilities. But Bayliss disliked the bearded, smelly electronics freak who seemed to be there very often.

The computer had turned out perfectly. The two young men had stayed up many nights, programming it, soldering its guts together and agonizing over its visual appearance. Its handsome beige plastic case, a molded box four inches deep, gleamed in the room's harsh light. Paul had ensured that its top was removable to facilitate access to expansion slots, a circuit board and memory connector. The machine was correctly proportioned and Paul was convinced it would be easy enough to mass produce.

"What the hell *is* that?" Bayliss asked.

"A personal computer." Paul plugged it in and turned it on. It hummed quietly to life and its screen lit up. "Let me show you what it can do—"

"I'm not in the mood."

"Okay. But the possibilities..."

Bayliss sat back. He ran a hand through his graying hair. High technology overwhelmed him. He bought no-brainer Atari games all the time and his customers loved them—but personal computers...?

"Well, it's a nice computer, Paul. I hope you two will be very happy together."

Paul smiled and shook his head. "No, I said it's *yours*. We'll build others. Take it home for your daughter. When's her birthday?"

Bayliss frowned at the machine and pointed at the well-designed logo of a burgundy cherry with a stem and a tiny square of light reflecting off it. "A *cherry?*"

"Yessir. Meet the Cherry computer."

One night, Hank and Paul had puzzled over names. They wanted to emphasize the computer's user-friendly quality.

"We should give it a name that says, 'Anyone can use it. Even a cybervirgin,'" said Paul, a mischievous glint in his eyes.

"The computer for cherries!" Hank replied.

"The Cherry computer!" they cried in unison.

Bayliss looked at the computer as if he wished it would grow legs and run away. Or maybe he wanted his legs to be younger so he could run away. "So, Paul, you'll accept the promotion? I'm glad of it. I'm glad to have you as my new G.M."

"I'll start on Monday morning."

"Oh, you can take a week off."

"Monday morning, nine sharp. But promise me you'll take the Cherry. It means a lot to me." He loaded the computer into Bayliss' car and, minutes later, was back on Market

Street, waiting for Hank to complete his zillionth trip around the block. The afternoon was cool and beautiful and breezy; even lower Market Street looked good today.

Hank pulled up. "So...?"

Settling into the car, Paul showed his friend the pen. "Bayliss gave me this pen, and I gave him our computer. Fair trade."

"Where does that leave us?"

"As of this moment, Hank, I would say we pretty much have Fred Bayliss by the balls. But he doesn't know it yet." The two young men laughed as they pulled away.

Bud Steeves was at his usual spot by the bay window. Paul had said he would come straight home, but such a popular guy would always be detained by friends and admirers. Soon Paul would probably move and deposit his old man into some old folks' home. It would be just like him.

Months after Donna Steeves' suicide, Bud's Good Eats had closed forever to a deafening silence. Only Bud and Paul were left; they moved to an apartment building in the Avenues, two rooms and not nearly enough seven square feet. Paul needed a job. The unemployment office referred him to Amazement. Fred Bayliss had only graveyard work available, but paid well above minimum wage. He did not mind if Paul napped in the office; the buzzer outside the office door would wake him if a customer needed assistance. He also wanted Paul to make a walkthrough or two each shift, if only to remind the customers that once the cops had made *their* walkthroughs, someone was still looking after the place.

Paul needed the income, so he continued working at Amazement after enrolling at People's University. He replaced father's truck with a new Honda motorcycle, which he parked next to the back door of Amazement. During his graveyard shifts, he worked a little, slept a little, read his textbooks and helped Hank with building the Cherry. He slept away the weekends on the sofa he and his father had moved from their old place. Bud Steeves had seen very little of his son over the past four years.

Bud pulled his paisley robe around his neck and smiled suddenly, reminding himself that Paul had finished college depsite these obstacles. A winner, a true winner, as they all knew he was, destined to go far in life.

His son had plenty of plans, but Steeves didn't know the specifics. Paul had been with that girl Nancy for quite a little while now but they seemed to have grown apart, what with him at People's University and her at Berkeley. They should never break up. What could it hurt, even if the marriage was unhappy? Bud Steeves knew about unhappy marriages.

He heard a car outside and looked down as Paul climbed out in his navy graduation suit. He had a nice figure for apparel—tall, slender, long legs.

Minutes later the door opened and Paul strolled in.

"Here I am, Dad. Four years older and thousands of dollars poorer."

"Let's track your mom down and show her that her mistake with that money didn't do any harm."

Paul looked sad. "Dad, you know about Mom. The cops found the truck down by Fisherman's Wharf. That guy in his boat found her dress..."

"Doesn't mean a thing. We hire a good private eye, he'll find out that it was all just a hoax. She'll come back, when she finds out you got that degree."

Paul sighed. "Look, are you OK for dinner and whatever else you might need? I'm going away for the weekend."

"How you getting down there?"

"With Hank, downstairs. He's waiting right now. Later."

"If there's an emergency, how will I reach you?"

"You'll be fine, Dad."

"But what if I need something from the store?"

"Then get off your butt and go to the store. Put it on my tab. Later."

Steeves scowled. "Just stay away from that tramp Dee. A disgrace to our family."

"Whatever."

Bud Steeves watched from the bay window as Paul and Hank sped off towards who knew where, leaving him behind. He knew his days with his son were ending soon.

The car cruised up through Pacific Heights, to Grandinetti's mansion, which looked more majestic than ever on this clear afternoon, though Paul had seen it so often that it now failed to impress him as much. The house was whiter than white, the beautifully manicured lawn greener than many golf course. A springtime wind whipped through Old Glory. Paul loved it that Grandinetti had a huge American flag on a pole in his front yard.

"Pull in here," he said.

Hank's mouth dropped open. "Jesus, Paul! So this is where he lives?"

"Yes. Lido Grandinetti. The chocolate king of San Francisco."

"I love his nuts. So you know the owner of one of the world's biggest candy companies. I'm fuckin' impressed."

"He's been good to my family." He devirginzed my sister. He tried to get me into Stanford. "He wants us to have a drink with him."

ENTREPRENEUR

Grandinetti had given Paul his own key to the massive iron gate. He let himself and Hank in. They rang and Jennings immediately opened the grand door with the words, "Good afternoon, Mister Steeves. Please come in."

Paul and Hank entered to the strains of violin music. The music suddenly stopped. Grandinetti appeared and Jennings disappeared.

"Hello, Lido," Paul said.

"Welcome, Paul." Grandinetti smiled. "Got through the pageantry all right?"

"Sure. Wish you could have been there," Paul said.

"Ah, well. I promise to make it up to you. Let's have the champagne."

"Lido, this is Hank, from school."

The two men shook hands. "Hank, I hope you'll join us."

Hank smiled. "Happily."

As Jennings reappeared to pop the cork and pour the wine, Grandinetti asked, "Did she send you all off into the real world with a compelling speech?"

"The senator? Sure," Paul said. "She warned us against complacency and arrogance."

Grandinetti smirked. "Maybe I should have attended after all. I would have demanded ten minutes for rebuttal."

The two young men laughed in spite of themselves. Hank's eyes rolled as he tried to take it all in.

"I want one day to have what you have, Mr. Grandinetti."

"Do you? Then one day, Hank, perhaps you shall have it. And please call me Lido."

After they drank to happiness, success and the future, Grandinetti said, "So, what are our plans for this evening? If you're hungry, I can get us a table anywhere in the city.

Ernie's, L'Etoile, the Blue Fox? If you're especially nice to me, I will even pick up the tab."

"Actually, Lido," Paul said, "We're just on our way out of town. We're doing a little celebrating elsewhere."

"Will you see Deirdre?"

"Maybe."

"Give her my best and congratulations. What's her child's name again?"

"Caitlin."

"That's right. I should send the child a gift. When I was born, my present was stock in my name. Don't know if Deirdre would appreciate that, though."

"When I was born," Hank said, "someone gave me a stock certificate that, by the time I was four, was worthless."

Grandinetti laughed. "At least they thought of you. Isn't that what mattered?"

"No," Hank said.

Grandinetti laughed again. "I like your candor." Turning to Paul, he said, "Since you're leaving in a minute, I'll give you a surprise: I have you and Nancy booked for the summer at my condo in Monaco. Frankly, you look like shit. You need to sleep late, have fun, make love. Monaco is the perfect place to relax and rejuvenate. This is my graduation gift to you. Then you can come back and make your plans. I'm pretty sure I can help you get into law school somewhere next year. I'm serious. I would love to see a smart young man like you go places in this world. At the same time, I would hate to see you languish in mediocrity by making bad choices. What do you say?"

"No thanks, Lido," Paul said. "I've already made a commitment starting Monday morning."

Grandinetti's eyes narrowed. "Really? Where?"

Paul said, "I'm going to work full-time for Bayliss as general manager."

"Amazement." The word oozed out of Lido Grandinetti's mouth like sludge. "So I guess it won't be the lawyer's life after all for Paul Steeves."

"Guess not." Paul had heard, many times, Grandinetti's thoughts about the advantages of a legal career. 'In this country, there is a need for lawyers...' Etc. & etc.

"No lawyer here, Lido," Paul was saying. "I'm going to stay the course for the time being."

"What a shame," said Grandinetti.

Paul shrugged. Not long afterwards, he and Hank were back in the Ford, heading down the coast.

"He was kind of pissed at you," Hank said. Then he slapped the steering wheel. "Jesus, Paul! Why didn't you go to *him* for the Cherry startup money?"

"Because he might have said yes." Paul, naturally, had already considered that option. But Grandinetti, drunk and garrulous one evening, had confided that while his family was very rich, *he* wasn't. He had wanted to put the mansion on the market but it wasn't precisely his to sell. He had a nice car, fancy clothes and plenty of pocket money to fritter away. But freeing up large amounts of family money for investment purposes? No can do. He would have to get the written consent of Grandinetti family members who thought him a fool. So Paul didn't broach the subject again. Other people could, and would, come through with the money.

I wish these people would get the fuck out of my house, Dee thought as she surveyed the living room and then watched as yet another couple entered. "The bar is in the kitchen," she said, as if reading their minds. Luanne Buck, seeing the chaos in the kitchen as guests reached over each other for glasses and bottles, had converted the room into a makeshift bar and mixed the drinks herself, quickly and efficiently. Tommy had gone out to get more beer and ice, the two things they ran out of the fastest. Soon enough, the guests would get bored and head for another party.

Dee wondered why Tommy invited people they scarcely knew. She cringed as some well-dressed young man discreetly poured his watery drink into one of her favorite large potted plants. Then he spat into the pot.

When the place was clean, it was a wonderful, stylish L.A. apartment, with hardwood floors and salmon-colored walls. Tommy paid the rent from his inheritance he received from his recently deceased father, a New York City ophthalmologist. Dee looked over at Paul, wondering what he thought. She suspected that he now considered Dee and Tommy her social and professional inferiors, and their guests tonight were entertainment-industry types. Some of them were still into "getting it" at est. They talked about the changing face of American cinema and what it might mean to the younger actors, directors, writers and producers fortunate enough to penetrate the holy clique. They all openly coveted money and status and thought Hollywood was the center of the universe.

Paul was interested in getting his money and power through Cherry Computer. He stood in a corner, listening to Josh Hawkins, who often came to Los Angeles on business. She knew they were talking about that computer Paul and his friend Hank had secretly built in the back office of that shitty Amazement place where her brother worked, and that the sleepy-eyed, sharp-minded Josh was somehow in on it. Josh ate, slept and lived money.

For Dee, this "party" was a disappointment. Chinese food a case or two of Michelob would have been more fun. She and Paul could have gotten shitfaced and contemplated the meaning of life.

Completely ignored for the moment, Dee slipped out of the living room, strode down the hallway and disappeared into Caitlin's room. When her daughter was born, she and Tommy moved to a two-bedroom apartment at Beverly and La Cienega. They shared one bedroom and the other one became a nursery, then a small child's room. In the room sat Caitlin's bed, a dresser, her toys and a small table where Dee worked, her tools being a pad of paper and a pen. She kept her typewriter in her own bedroom, despite Caitlin's insistence that its clack-clack-clack did not bother her. Better to bother Tommy than their child.

When she turned on the bedroom light she saw that Caitlin was awake, gazing out at her mother with a characteristic smile.

"Noisy out there," the four-year-old child said. "Who is it?"

"Daddy's friends," Dee said, coming over and sitting at the edge of the bed.

"Not your friends, too?" Caitlin asked.

Dee pouted. "I don't have any friends."

Caitlin pouted back. "I'm your friend."

Dee laughed and bent down to kiss the child's forehead. Facially, Caitlin from every angle was Tommy's daughter: blonde, with large round gray eyes, upcurved pink lips forever formed into a smile. Dee wondered when, if ever, her little girl would begin to look like a Steeves.

The laughter and clink of glasses continued as Dee went to the small desk and picked up the freshman biology textbook she had been reading for the past week. Tommy's essentially estranged father had been kind enough—or felt guilty enough—to remember his son in his will. While they were hardly rich, they now had the money to relax and reprioritize for the next while. Dee had stopped seeking acting jobs because she had a child who needed her around all the time, or she felt the need to be around her child all the time. She had acted in one sitcom pilot that the producer had taken to the Las Vegas convention but the networks had called it too insipid, even for prime time television.

She was the first-string critic for the important-sounding but obscure *Los Angeles Daily News,* having inherited the job from Tommy. Bored one morning, she revised his copy, and did so for the next several reviews. The paper's entertainment editor wondered why the reviews had suddenly gained such eloquence and insight. Tommy said, "Dee, you do them from now on." She did, and the paper even began using her byline.

Lately she had become fascinated by the human body and health. When not looking after Caitlin or popping out to Westwood to review a film and wander around UCLA, she took biology courses with a vague plan to get a degree within five years and apply to medical school. The party-animal life her husband so enjoyed tired her. She enjoyed the intellectually enriching milieu of academia, especially after an evening of Tommy and his friends.

She heard the gentlest rapping on the door and turned around to see her husband enter the room. "The hostess with the mostess." He was dressed in a sports coast and khaki slacks and loafers. His hair was still thick and blond, though his features were starting to bloat from drinking. Tommy Wilhite, the eternal adolescent. Or, perhaps more accurately, the eternal college boy on academic probation.

"Our friends were worried about you. We were going to send out a search party."

"Friends? I thought they were just moochers looking for a free party. And they found one. *Party at Dee and Tommy's.* It would make a great B-movie. Or a great C-plus movie."

Tommy offered her a thin smile. "Paul is looking for you, too. Please rejoin us."

"Go out there and tell them that you're taking them all out to dinner in Beverly Hills with our retirement fund. They'll instantly forget about me. These folks really have their priorities straight."

Tommy asked, "Why?"

"Why what?"

"Why are you being such a cunt?"

"Just because I'm reluctant to entertain a bunch of freeloaders?"

"Maybe you're just tired."

"Or maybe it's PMS, or that I'm just not getting any."

"Enough." Tommy glowered.

She sashayed out of the room. He let out a huge sigh and followed. In the living room, Hank, the technical wizard, was heehawing with some bimbo from downstairs. Paul now stood in a corner with Nancy, a new arrival. She was dressed in a red T-shirt and matching shorts that showed off her big breasts, small bottom and pretty legs, and she wore a pretty purple scarf in her red hair. She looked spent and sunburned, as if from a day at Disneyland. Nancy now looked nothing like the vivacious, engagingly awkward teenager Dee had first met several years earlier. Nancy was a woman now. Dee felt saddened; Nancy had been in much too big a hurry to become an adult. Better to remain a child for as long as possible.

Dee guessed that Nancy and Paul were back together and doing their best to make it work out. Obviously Nancy hadn't met the love of her life while at Berkeley. She went over to say hello to them but was intercepted by Tommy's old friend Andrew Wellman, vice-president of entertainment at one of the Big Three TV networks. Wellman, handsome and deep-voiced, had started out as an actor, then moved into programming. When the network was in the Nielsen ratings toilet, Wellman was offered the chance to run things, and he quickly improved the network's numbers, mainly by buying situation comedies with wide and lasting appeal.

"Fun party," he deadpanned. "You should have had the good manners to invite me over sooner."

Dee gazed at him. "Do you believe in love?"

"Huh?"

"Nothing. Just a rhetorical question."

"You know, Dee, I like your reviews in the *Daily News*."

"I aim to please."

Wellman said, "I want to make one observation. In your reviews you sometimes come across as malicious. You really shit on a lot of people who have given a great deal to the American film industry."

"Pauline Kael pisses people off, too," she said.

"You're not Pauline Kael."

"I'm much cuter."

"You certainly are," said Tommy, stealing up behind her and wrapping his arm around her waist.

"I've got to go. Do the right thing, Dee," Wellman whispered into her ear as they embraced. He was gone in a second.

"Boy, was he pissed," Tommy said. "What did you say to him? No, don't tell me. Forget that I even asked."

Dee walked past him and approached Paul and Nancy. "Are we having fun yet?"

Nancy said, "I still can't believe what I've just heard. Tell Dee."

Paul shrugged and turned to his sister. "I'm going to work full-time as general manager at all three Amazements. I start Monday morning."

Nancy bristled. "All this time, I thought once the school thing was out of the way, you'd get ahead."

"I *am* getting ahead," Paul said.

"Tell Dee the rest, why don't you?"

Paul sighed.

"Yes...?" Dee asked.

"Well," Nancy said, "Grandinetti wanted to send us to Monaco for the summer. Monaco! For the whole summer! But Paul said Mr. Bayliss needed him bright and early Monday morning. Turned down Monaco just like that!"

Just then, someone said, "Dee, we need help with the stereo." She said to Paul and Nancy, "Hold that thought" and went over to see what was wrong with her expensive AM/FM record player. The equipment was full of knobs and dials she herself didn't understand. After playing with one or two for a few minutes, the music came on. By the time she thought to look for Paul and Nancy, they were gone. She didn't care if she never had another party, considering what a mess her guests left behind.

In the kitchen, she asked Luanne for something to drink. "All that's left is Bud," Luanne said.

"Okay."

Luanne, tall and blue-eyed, was still a knockout from fifteen feet away, but up close you could see that she was battling middle age. She had enjoyed the evening, mixing the drinks and flirting with the men and women who entered the kitchen. "I loved that guy Andrew Wellman. So self-assured and handsome. Does he need his drink freshened? Does he need anything at all that *I* might be able to provide?"

"He split, Luanne."

"Shit. Alone?"

"Yes."

"Then maybe he'll be back."

"I doubt it."

Just then two of the male guests entered for drinks and Luanne beamed at them, Andrew Wellman already forgotten. Dee wished she, too, could shrug off things and people instantly.

Paul and Nancy walked down La Cienega Boulevard on a perfect L.A. evening. Minutes earlier, Nancy had left Dee's place with the words, "Well, Paul, if you're staying at the arcade and not taking me to Monaco and it's all a done deal, I'll see you around." She brushed past Paul and slipped of the apartment altogether. Paul followed her and soon caught up with her.

The chic boulevard didn't do much to help their mood. Paul usually liked evening walks in Los Angeles, enjoying the stylish Mediterranean architecture and palm trees. But right now, he thought that anyplace else in the world would be preferable to this. A part of him just wanted to turn around and walk away. They had both changed so much in the past four years, and become so preoccupied by so many other things, that they would surely never be able to rekindle the flame that had burned so brightly for them once. But Paul still cared for Nancy and wanted to be with her.

"You're cheating on me," she said. "That's *got* to be the reason you're staying on at that big stupid video arcade. You're doing some cute girl there, some black girl from Hunter's Point."

Paul laughed. Nancy could sound as coarse as any guy. "I think I already explained it. You know how hard Hank and I have worked on the Cherry..."

Nancy laughed. "You think you two will get rich with that computer? Who will buy it? Every guy has invented *something* that nobody wanted. And since we're clearing the air about things, I want to know; why haven't we made love yet?"

"Huh?"

"We've been together for five years and you haven't yet made love with me. I'd say that's pretty peculiar behavior. And frankly, Paul, *you* need that Monaco vacation." She took a key out of her pocket and dangled it in front of him. "I'm at the West Beverly, room nine-ten. How about it?"

Paul shook his head. "No, not this way. Not in anger."

"Or you just don't like women." Her eyes were merciless, her smile small and mean. "Are you a fairy, Paul? You've lost so much weight, and you have those dark circles under your eyes. Maybe you have the Gay Plague. I half expect to see you break out in lesions. I saw that cot and blanket you keep in Amazement's office. Maybe you and Hank have been doing more than building a computer all those nights."

He snarled. "Fuck off."

"Nancy and Paul, the neighborhood's last remaining virgins. I'm offering you my hot, horny young California body tonight. Let's join the human race."

Paul groaned.

"While we're making plans, Paul, let's call old man Bayliss and tell him to shove Amazement. Then we'll call Grandinetti and say we'd be delighted to spend the summer in Monaco. We'll get married there. You can go to law school and I can have a baby. We'll pretend we're normal people." She thrust out her hand. "Deal?"

Paul drew a deep breath. "Nancy, I can't do that. I have a feeling big things are about to happen. The Cherry means a lot to me. You and I can keep going together and make plans. But we have to accommodate each other, too. Just be patient, all right?"

Nancy shook her head. "No more patience here. Love me tonight or lose me forever. Well?"

She hailed a taxi and was gone in an instant. He walked back to Dee's, where she had a bed made up for him on her sofa. All the guests would be gone, except for that Okie broad tending bar in the kitchen and giving him the eye.

He had often wondered about himself and Nancy. Would stay together, and if they didn't, how, and when, they would break up. Now he knew, and found he did not care.

Luanne had no financial worries and her bedroom was filled with old, handsome furniture. Her huge bed was soft and immaculate, although Paul didn't like her satin sheets. *Not bad*, he decided as he lay naked in her bed. Her high standard of living surprised him because she was losing her looks in a hurry, and that goofy Midwestern drawl was quite a turnoff.

He inhaled the air's heady perfume. Luanne had asked him to walk her downstairs to her apartment and, once there, wrapped her arms around him and given him a long, deep kiss. She disappeared into the bathroom as Paul, unsure of what to do, stripped and crawled into bed. He heard the shower on. Luanne was washing off that strong perfume and garish makeup. Good.

Paul looked around the room and caught his reflection in a mirror. He looked away, not wanting to see himself in this brothel. He was sure, for the longest time, that his first lover would be Nancy, and minutes earlier he was truly at a loss to explain himself when she demanded to know why he hadn't made some attempt at a seduction.

Sitting now in Luanne's bed, he resolved to forget about Nancy. Now was as good a time as any to begin his sex life, and this woman had experience. Luanne would probably expect nothing from him afterwards; she would *want* to be rid of him as soon as their loving was over.

The shower had been off for only a few seconds when the door opened and she came out, her body long and firm, breasts small and pert, hips narrow, legs and underarms hairless, mature face white and glowing in the muted lighting. She was scrubbed free of makeup. Paul couldn't decide if she was pretty; she was every bit as tall as Nancy but lacked the other woman's big breasts and youthful radiance. The size and shape of a woman's breasts mattered to him greatly.

Paul felt his groin burn instantly, his heart pound, his pulse race. Luanne sauntered over to the bed, casually threw back the covers and scrutinized his priapus for several moments. Finally her lips curved into a small smile and she murmured, "The college boy with the three long legs." She slipped into bed, reached over and, with the lightest touch, stroked his member. He ejaculated at once, involuntarily, violently. He then sat still, naked and filthy, grimacing as sweat ran down his chest. He wanted to dress and leave but felt paralyzed.

"Sorry."

"No worries. You need foreplay." She leaned over and wrapped her arms around him, her soft kiss irresistible. Paul sighed and closed his eyes, wishing she wouldn't call him college boy. Paul and Luanne. Who knew? Dee had frowned when Luanne left the party with him.

He got it up, got it in, kept it going. He pinned her to the bed, stayed inside her and pumped, harder and faster, till finally she cried out, "No more!" He gave till he had no more to give, and the two lay for the longest time in a sweaty heap.

"Was that your first time, Paul? It just seems weird that you've gone this long without nooky. That tall redhead? Nancy? Dee said she was your girlfriend. Big titties. Nice ass. You sure you never fucked her but you've been together forever."

He shrugged. "We've come undone."

"Too bad for Nancy. Tommy says Dee is just unreal in the sack." Luanne paused. "I'd wet her down in a heartbeat."

"Ewww."

Luanne laughed. "School's out, college boy. Welcome to the real world. Tommy and I used to fuck, then he met Dee, but he still comes by for a quickie. Frankly, I'm surprised you and Dee didn't do each other back in Western Hills."

Paul made a face. "With my *sister?*"

"Worse things have been done by better men."

"This conversation is getting way too bizarre." He got out of bed.

Luanne chuckled. "Oh, you're just a frustrated product of provincial San Francisco. This here's L.A. You're just a bumpkin, like I was when I first came here from Kansas." She paused. "Say, my buzz wore off. Go fix me a drink, OK? The booze is in the kitchen."

Paul did as told, pleased to end this humiliating conversation. He wanted to get fully dressed, or at least put something on, but Luanne would just ridicule him more. So he fixed her a drink and brought it back into the bedroom. Paul Steeves, the naked cocktail server.

"Drink up."

"Thanks." She looked at him. "Whatcha doin'?"

"Getting dressed."

"Stay the night?"

"No, thanks."

"Please? I need someone tonight. Dee told me you were gonna stay the weekend. You can go home when the sun comes up. I hate nights alone. I have depression and insomnia, and I'm all out of Valium and Seconal. If you leave, I'll have panic attacks and run naked through the streets, screaming your name."

"You'll survive." He knotted his tie and tucked in his shirt.

"Bastard!" She threw her glass at him but missed.

He left the apartment complex and checked his watch: nearly three. He was relieved to be in the safest part of town with all-night city buses. He got the next one to downtown, walked the two or three creepy blocks to the Greyhound station and bought a one-way ticket for the three-fifty a.m. express to San Francisco. He had slept maybe ten hours in the past three days. Boarding along with the other handful of passengers, he settled into his seat and dropped off to sleep. He woke up only when the bus pulled into the San Francisco station. He slept away much of Sunday, too, and on Monday morning, at eight sharp, he showed up at Amazement for his first day as general manager, natty in his dark suit. He even hung his framed college diploma on the office wall. He promised himself two things that day: that he would never work another graveyard shift, or fuck anyone even remotely resembling Luanne Buckelew, as long as he lived.

Chapter 3

Jamey set the combination of his lock at zero, as always. The men's club had a new rule that everyone must have a lock on his locker, even though a few of the more trusting members had stored their belongings in lockers and left them unsecured. Management also reminded everybody that once each person's property was in a secured locker, if anything was stolen, no one could blame management.

Jamey changed into his sweats and got ready for the day. Palladino was hung over and couldn't do the calisthenics class, so he told Jamey to fill in for him. Jamey said fine; he would lead the class and do the exercises along with them. He loved to watch the hard-headed, cold-hearted, soft-bellied members sweat and strain through the regimen of sit-ups, push ups and jumping jacks. Palladino would also probably want him to do the day's sparring. When Jamey finished with the workout and went into the room where they did the boxing, he saw Palladino and Niebuhr putting on their gloves. Palladino looked pale and sweaty, but Niebuhr didn't seem to notice or care. Jamey had learned much about sparring with the members. You had to lose and make it look good. Most of the members were weaklings who loved to put on the gloves and think they were actually beating the other guy.

Jamey hadn't spent any of the money he had blackmailed from Winthrope. He was unfailingly polite to all the members and went through his daily life saying yes, sir and no, ma'am.

"Come over here and help with me with these gloves," Palladino said to Jamey. Ten feet away, Niebuhr already had his gloves on and stood there, impatient. He was tall and fairly muscular and walked with a military bearing. He had been in the Army for several years and boxed while studying at Yale. He was dark and handsome, with a deep voice and a commanding presence. His family had been rich for generations and if he had been raised to think that acting was a noble profession, he could have been a Hollywood action hero like Clint Eastwood or John Wayne. Niebuhr, the guy who had accused Jamey of stealing his money, seldom looked at or spoke to him.

"All right, sir," Palladino said as he ambled over to Niebuhr.

The member nodded and rushed over to him, jabbing at Palladino's head as if trying to knock him to the floor. Unwell to begin with him, Palladino tried to bring up his hands to ward off the blows. But Niebuhr just knocked away the old man's hands and hammered away.

Son of a bitch, Jamey thought. But he said nothing and wondered why Palladino didn't just end the session and walk away. But then Niebuhr hit him with a combination of punches and Palladino ended up sprawled on the mat with blood oozing from his mouth. Niebhuhr just stood there, as if expecting their session to continue.

Palladino gestured to Jamey. "Help me up and get these gloves off me. I don't feel so good."

Jamey did as told. When the older man's gloves were off, he said, "I apologize, Mr. Niebuhr, but that's the best I can do today."

"Your best isn't very good," Niebuhr replied. "It wasn't worth the trouble of putting on the gloves. What about you, Steeves? Think you can last a few minutes with me?"

Steeves. Jamey had done his best to make sure that nobody knew his last name. How had Niebuhr learned it? Jamey looked at Palladino to see if his boss wanted him to spar with Niebuhr, who would be a vastly different opponent from the soft-bodied guys who comprised the majority of the club's members.

Palladino, his face darkening with the deepest Italian contempt, looked over at Niebhur. "If he wants to, Jamey, I think you should accommodate him."

He laced up the gloves for Jamey, who felt the usual fear, exhilaration and anticipation he experienced whenever he got into a *real* fight. He smiled politely at Niebuhr, who was tapping his feet on the mat.

Palladino slapped at Jamey's gloves. "Begin."

Niebuhr charged at Jamey, looking like Robert De Niro in *Raging Bull.* Badass, Jamey thought as he ducked from the jabs and kept away from the right cross. Niebuhr was a couple of inches taller and about ten pounds heavier than Jamey. He was also quicker than Jamey would have guessed, and he landed a solid right to Jamey's jaw. Jamey hadn't been in such a serious altercation in so long that he really was not prepared for someone like Niebuhr. The man dodged and weaved, and landed a couple more solid punches to Jamey's head. This big bastard isn't just screwing around, Jamey told himself as he exploited the taller man's height and went in low, landing punches to the middle and the occasional blow to his head. But Niebuhr fought him off, and the two men kept on pounding each other. Niebuhr was damn strong, and he could defend himself well.

Jamey tried to glance at Palladino, to see if his boss would end the sparring match. But no.

Then I'm gonna take you out, Mr. Rich Guy, Jamey thought. You want to fight? I'll give you my best, and my worst.

The match continued. Niebuhr fought like someone who had been on a college boxing squad. He hit hard and often, even if his technique was was a bit unorthodox. Jamey clinched him and pounded him in the groin. Take this, Tough Guy, he thought as he went for Niebuhr's kidneys. Here it is, College Boy. You sure you can take much more of this?

Their faces were both bloodied when Jamey landed the roundhouse that Niebuhr could not overcome. Niebuhr backed off and swayed, smiling stupidly, throwing slaps at the air. Jamey danced towards him, ready to drop the big man with one final right cross. But then Palladino got between them.

"Good workout, gentlemen. I think we've all had our exercise for the day."

Niebuhr blinked a few times and seemed to get over the beating he had just taken. He snarled at Jamey and Palladino. "Get these damn gloves off me," he said. Palladino did as told and Niebhur walked out of the room.

"He was," Jamey said. "Real pissed."

"Too fuckin' bad for him. He'll get over it."

For several days, nobody said anything about the fight. Jamey and Palladino thought that Niebuhr felt too humiliated to having been manhandled by that kid who cleaned up after everyone.

"So far, so good," Palladino would say when another work day had ended and there had been no trouble from Niebuhr.

But on a Tuesday, another employee went up to Jamey and said, "Palladino wants to see you in his office. Says it's urgent."

Jamey knocked on Palladino's door and went in. Palladino was at his desk, counting cash. His face full of regret, he handed some of the money to Jamey. "Here's what we owe you. Niebuhr made some trouble today. He demanded your termination. We gotta let you go."

Jamey nodded as he pocketed the cash. He thought this gig was going to last indefinitely. "You should have let me knock him cold."

"I suppose."

"What's going to happen to you, Jake?"

"Nothing. You're the fall guy for this one." Then, "Remember what Fitzgerald said: 'The rich are different from the rest of us.'"

Chapter 4

The alarm went off and he snapped awake. His sleep had been light, not altogether restful. And, as always, he had an erection that simply refused to go down.

This was the biggest day of his life. He had Federal Expressed the manila envelope to Bayliss' Marin County home several days earlier, and his boss had faxed him a terse note: *We'll meet at Amazement.* The note was chilling. In the manila envelope, Paul had said everything. What if his plans just suddenly went haywire?

He stayed under the covers for a few more minutes, wondering just how the meeting would go. Oh, hell, he thought, just get dressed, go in and hear what the old man has to say. He smiled in spite of himself. When you sat at the poker table and held four aces, it was impossible to suppress a smile.

First thing was to go for a jog. Paul, years earlier, had run casually at Western Hills High. He had stopped mainly because the volume of work at college had taken all his time. Ironically, he now ran at Western Hills High again. It had become nearly an addiction, literally; he ran till the endorphins flooded his brain and his high stayed sometimes for hours.

Once in his track suit he got onto his motorcycle and drove the fifteen minutes to the athletic field at the university. There, Langston Raymond was waiting for him. A stocky black boy, he had seen him running one morning and shyly asked if he might join him.

"Looks kind of suspicious, a black guy running by himself here. I might be hassled. Be different if we ran together."

He agreed and had come to think it might be a wise idea.

"Hi, Langston," he said.

"Hello, Paul."

And they ran. Paul truly had come to view these before-work runs the way a drug addict might see his morning trips to score from his dealer. Paul came to score a high that cost no money and was created by his own body. He and Langston jogged at first, then gradually ran harder and faster, one lap after another. Soon they were running fairly hard, and in their final laps they broke into a hell-for-leather sprint, Paul bursting through the wall of pain as his feet, legs and back burned excruciatingly and his heart threatened to explode in his chest. Once the endorphin high kicked in, he was all smiles.

"See you tomorrow, Paul," he said.

"Goodbye, Langston."

He went home and took a long, hot shower. In the bathroom mirror he coolly appraised himself, looking closely at his good-looking body and big brown eyes that won him many compliments. He knew it was important to look good and stay in shape. People had no excuse for being fat.

After toweling dry, he put on his best blue suit. Fully dressed, he went into the living room and said good morning to his father. If he failed to do so, the old man grew crabby and morose, complaining about his health, his lack of happiness and the indifferent doctors who prescribed medications that were overpriced and ineffective. "How's the weather outside?" Steeves asked.

"Foggy and miserable. Go back to bed today, Dad." They had begun pretending that Steeves had a life of some sort, that he normally spent the day at the park feeding the pigeons, or socializing, or at least doing something moderately useful.

His father seldom combed his hair and had lost so much weight that his pants came up practically to his shoulders. His face was wrinkled and lined and there was usually much stubble on his face. But still he didn't seem to have any major health issues except age and hatred of the rest of the world. He would surely live past eighty, and Paul accepted that, though he wished the old man would find it within himself to find a better outlook on life. The next decades would be that much better if he could.

Looking up from his coffee, Steeves said, "I dreamed that Jamey was back. Whatever became of him?"

"As I recall, you sent him up to Sacramento and then he got into trouble and Mom drove up there to help him out. Uncle Jack gave him the heave-ho. I assume he left Sacramento altogether."

"Maybe we should try to track him down. I would like to see him once more before my time is up."

"You'll outlive us all, Dad." Paul rose from the breakfast table. "While I'm at work, think of what you might like for dinner. We'll get whatever you like. I promise." He was out the door moments later.

The sky was gray and some kids were playing one noisy game or another in Amazement as Paul entered, carrying the morning paper. He said hello to the teenaged attendant on duty and disappeared into the office. With Bayliss' permission, he had had some video games repaired and put back on the floor and had gotten rid of others, so that the office was now bare, the way he liked it. There was just the desk and two chairs, some shelf space and the toolbench. A number of old newspapers sat on the shelves, brought in and read by Paul but still there because he had neglected to throw them out. Paul had gotten rid of all the pinball machine Bayliss ha bought; the video games generated much more revenue and couldn't be abused or tilted as easily as the pinball machines.

He hadn't seen Grandinetti in the longest time, although he had invited Lido to dinner. Grandinetti said no, as petulant as ever. Paul wished the guy would just grow up.

He opened the newspaper, sat back and read. One good thing about his job was that he stayed on top of current events on company time. Leonid Brezhnev dies. Paul wondered how much longer the Soviet Union could survive; were Iron Curtain reforms inevitable? The PLO and Israelis clash, again. Joe Montana is the new savior of the 49ers.

The newspaper's stock market pages made him smile. Josh Hawkins was doing great things with Paul's modest investments, insisting that the stock market, even at its most erratic, was the best way to go. Young, rich and powerful—that, too, was the best way to go. Paul thought for a moment as the phone rang.

"Hello?"

"Paul Steeves?"

"Speaking."

"This is Toni Freeman." She sounded anxious.

Paul sat up. "Yes, Professor. What can I do for you?"

"Well, I need to see you privately, as soon as possible. Would that be all right?"

"Yes. Why don't you drop by?"

"No, let's meet somewhere else. The Cable Car Club?"

"OK. Twelve-fifteen?"

"Fine." Freeman hung up.

The Cable Car Club? Paul puzzled over that one. It was the establishment blocks away done entirely in leather and mahogany and mirrors, a place where they could mix any cocktail under the sun and where men in dark suits and maroon ties congregated over plots to oust their bosses. Paul had gone there once with Nancy, who dismissed it as a boring boys' club where they sprayed aftershave as a room freshener. Well, at least it was just down Market Street, convenient enough, and Freeman sounded upset. He agreed to see her.

He made a walkthrough of Amazement. The arcade was recessed from the street, artificially dark and noisy, free of windows and clocks. Its daytime patrons were whoever happened to be there with some time to kill. Sometimes office guys in polywool suits came down in play. At night it was almost exclusively black boys in windbreakers who knew it was the only fun place open at night.

Paul was the big white man now running the place, grateful to be a head taller than most of his customers as he passed by them and tacitly reminded them of who was boss. Working the night shift for four years, Paul often wondered if the younger ones' parents knew where they were, or cared. Also, where the hell did these little street urchins get the money to play video games all night? The police came by often and walked through the premises with Paul. They were glad to see the street kids in Amazement till dawn, rather than wandering around downtown or elsewhere. At least this way, the cops said, the kids aren't spray-painting their gang affiliations all over every surface in town.

Every other month, Bayliss had Paul over for dinner at his Marin County home. The dinners themselves were quiet occasions; the family didn't speak at the dinner table. Suzi Bayliss, an intense young woman who seemed to stare at Paul throughout dinner, made it plain she wanted to date him. He seemed afraid to ask her out and she was not about to encourage him. It almost made him laugh, the notion of marrying the boss's daughter. Well, he often thought these days, this guy ain't marrying anyone. At least not yet. Recently he had received an invitation to Nancy's wedding. She was marrying a man he had never met, and he wondered what possessed Nancy to invite him to an event he quite obviously would not wish to attend, but to be a good sport he sent a telegram of congratulations.

To help forget about her, he threw himself into his work and found that as he did so the days, then weeks, just flew by. If he wanted a new girlfriend, the world was full of young women. Well, those young ladies would just have to wait. Paul Steeves was on a mission to change the world.

Just then he heard a key slide into the lock and saw the door open. Fred Bayliss ambled in, quiet and unsmiling. Paul went to get up.

"Sit down." Bayliss eased into a chair on the other side of the desk. He opened his briefcase, took out the manila envelope and dropped it onto the desk.

"This." He frowned. "Who has seen it?"

"Just you and me." And Josh Hawkins, of course.

"How did you find out I have undeveloped property in South Bay?"

Josh found out. "I'm not at liberty to say."

"Pleading the Fifth. That figures." Bayliss touched the envelope, as if afraid of it. "Paul, is this some sort of takeover attempt?"

Yes. "No, sir. It's just a business plan for Cherry Computer. Hank and I want you as our third founder. Your principal role would be to provide the start-up capital and business guidance."

They had no use for Fred Bayliss' business guidance. It was his money they needed; they wanted his wallet open and his mouth shut.

Bayliss eyed him. "Paul, you are asking me to make a huge financial commitment. You've initialed the deposit slips and do the sales reports. You *know* we do great business here at the bad end of Market Street. Today, Amazement packs 'em in with video games. Before that, we had pinball machines, and before *that* we had postwar fun machines everyone loved. So now you want me to jeopardize all that and go into the computer business? Why would I do that?"

"This is the future of the universe."

"Says who? You and Hank? Look, most people in the world have never been near a computer, and we've all survived."

"People way back when survived without cars, TVs and telephones, too." Paul leaned in closer. "Mr. Bayliss, my suggestion is this: make an appointment with Byrnes and Wilkinson and speak to their people about this. If any of them has any vision, they'll agree with me."

Bayliss sat back and ran an anxious hand through his hair. "Let's say I sign the papers making Cherry Computer a reality, with you, me and Hank as founders. Your business plan says we rent a South-of-Market warehouse, get cheap labor and start making computers. When our sales are good enough, we go public, float a stock issue, and use the capital to build a computer factory on my South Bay land, which I was thinking of selling. This would be a major investment. It would require most of the money I have, period."

"Yes," Paul said. "Dammit, do you want to keep running a hangout for street punks or do you want to change the world?"

Bayliss, startled, looked up, his face red, as if his very manhood had been challenged. When his composure returned, he took out the meticulously typed sheets detailing the plan. "All that square footage! All that tooling equipment! You sure we'd need all that?"

"Positive."

After shuffling through the papers on his desk for what seemed half an hour, Bayliss put the business plan back into his briefcase and stood up. "Get back to work. I feel a migraine coming on. I'm going home."

Paul left the office and beamed as he did his walkthrough of Amazement, knowing he had just gotten Fred Bayliss to help him change the world.

The plan was not quite as complicated as Bayliss thought, but it was involved just the same. Paul had read about Josh Hawkins in the newspapers and called him for a complimentary consultation. Josh declined on the consultation—his bosses refused to give away company time—but agreed to meet with Paul for a beer. He loved the idea of making and marketing the computer but admonished Paul to make Cherry Computer a small, viable company before attempting to expand.

"Two college boys who built a personal computer from scratch? Nobody with investment capital will touch it, because it's totally new and unproven," Josh had said. "But make a bunch of computers and sell them to the department stores and let word get around about how much fun the machines can be. *Then* you'll be able to go public and become properly capitalized."

The problem, of course, was the catch-22 of startup money. The warehouse, labor and supplies required to produce those first machines would need cash no bank would provide.

"Bayliss has the bucks," Josh stated. "Go to him. Threaten to quit if he won't go along with you."

Hawkins was so convinced of the computer's success that he even wrote up the business plan on his own time, a service for which he normally charged a small fortune. He hadn't charged Paul and Hank a cent for anything yet. Josh's brokerage house and Bayliss' firm would handle Cherry Computer's initial public offering, and both firms would be paid handsomely.

Bayliss had enough South Bay land for Cherry's factory. Josh felt that floating a public stock issue would be the thing that made the old man go along with the plan. When he died, his family would not be hit with huge inheritance taxes; they could sell of stock as the need arose. As Josh guided him, Paul laughed at how American business worked. Money protected itself, and Uncle Sam protected it, too. If you were struggling financially, too bad. If you wanted to make money, you had to *have* money in the first place. Cherry Computer would get loans upon providing proof that it didn't need them.

At the appointed time, Paul walked down Market Street and into the Cable Car Club. He spotted Professor Freeman easily, who sat alone in a corner nursing a glass of white wine.

"Thanks for coming." She seemed anxious. "Sit down, please."

"Hello, Professor." Paul thought the aging woman, taken out of her milieu, seemed frail and uncomfortable.

"Hungry?" Toni Freeman asked. "They serve full meals."

"But not very good ones." Paul remembered that it was an expensive joint. "Lunch isn't necessary. I can get something later." Freeman clearly had plenty on her mind. Better to get this over with.

"You're doing great," Freeman said tersely, her remark more an observation than a compliment. "Amazement isn't my kind of place, but it's one of the most successful businesses in town. The upscale department stores on Union Square must envy your traffic. Ever go into those fancy places? There's such personalized service because the staff outnumber the customers." Freeman chuckled. "But Amazement? The kids love it. It's 'cool.' Never closes, brings in the newest brainless games, and the street urchins come in."

"We're doing okay."

"And I congratulate you on wisely declining my invitation to join the academic world. It's cliquish and fiercely competitive, and so misogynistic! Sometimes they make room for a token woman."

Paul was surprised. He had the impression that Freeman had delighted in introducing her students to the world of economics, or at least that world as she perceived it.

"Do you really consider yourself only a token woman at the university?"

Freeman nodded. "Lord, yes. They needed at least one woman there and I was as good as any. They've practically said so, right to my face. But that will change. In the future, there will be many more of us. They gave us the vote, didn't they?" She offered a small, barely audible laugh.

"Is it as bad as all that?" Paul asked.

"Not at all, not at all," Freeman said. "Most of them are quite honorable, ethical, conscientious people, especially in business. But so many of the best didn't come home from the war just a few years ago. So many of those who are left are calculating, designing, cheating on test papers. Avaricious youngsters with no shame."

Paul smiled, thinking of how he had just bullied Fred Bayliss into providing Cherry's startup money.

"You're a winner, Paul." Freeman sipped at her wine. "I knew it when you were my student. You knew why you were there. You meant business, so to speak. So many of the others were there by default—they had nowhere else to go and they were too spoiled to take on unskilled jobs. I felt like a babysitter, quite frankly. So you left me with an excellent impression, and that's why I've come to you." She leaned in closer and spoke very softly. "I have a problem, Paul. A *big* problem."

Paul nodded. "Anything I can do to help, Professor."

"Did you hear what I just said?"

"A problem. A big problem."

Freeman stared at him. "They are out to destroy me."

"Who?"

"My political foes have put together a file on me to force me into an early retirement."

"Nonsense," Paul said.

"Oh, do you think so? They have shown me the file."

"And what's in it?"

"Things I have said in class. Trivial financial contributions to organizations that were not what they seemed. Remarks I have made, taken out of context. I have acquired my share of enemies along the trail and they are trying to get me out of the school."

"I'm still not clear on the exact nature of what your so-called enemies have against you."

"Have you heard of the Red Scare?"

"For Communists? Of course."

"Well, I'm becoming a victim of the witch hunt."

Paul nearly laughed aloud. "You, a Red? How could anyone think such a thing?"

"In this paranoid climate of America? It's all too easy. Plus, I'm a woman, and just as People's University needed a token woman, the Commie-hunters need a token target. Apparently McCarthy's successors are equal-opportunity persecutors."

"This is the first I've heard of it."

"Well, it's there. Everyone in government and academia is so obsessed with finding potential Reds that they've even set up an investigative body within People's University to weed out the suspected 'traitors.' Nice, huh?"

"And what do you want of me?" Paul asked, not liking the reluctant tone or phrasing of his question.

"I have a hearing coming up next week. Be there and speak up for me, Paul. Say what you will. Let them know that a conservative, up-and-coming businessman who recently graduated from People's University was a student of mine who disputes what is being said about me. That is all."

Paul thought of how Fred Bayliss might react to seeing his prudent, discreet, look-out-for-number-one general manager speaking out publicly in defense of some aging philosophy professor, risking his own incredibly bright future at Freeman's request.

Unable to think of anything else to say, Paul said, "I will do that, Professor. You can count on my full support." He glanced at his watch. "Unfortunately, it's nearly one o'clock and I have to get back to work."

Freeman instantly stood and grasped Paul's hand. Her grip felt clammy and tight, desperate. "Thanks so much, Paul. I knew you would say those exact words. Now, get back to work and make us all proud."

Paul left the Cable Car Club. He looked back through the window and saw that the waiter was standing before Freeman, who apparently was ordering another glass of wine.

ENTREPRENEUR

As he walked back down Market Street, Paul pitied Freeman, aging spinster who had lived for her work and her chance to train young minds, who because of her outspokenness, was in danger of having it all taken away. What a way to go into old age. Paul felt glad he hadn't eaten an overpriced Cable Car Club meal at the old lady's expense, but now he was ravenous and ducked into one of his favorite burger joints. After a cheeseburger and a chocolate shake, he went back to work. After Freeman's distressing news, he was glad to watch hordes of kids plunk tokens into machines, having fun, no worries. The chatter of voices, the flailing greedy arms, the green banknotes peeled off and fed into the token machines' metal mouths. Paul felt gratified, too, as if the cash were going into his own pocket. I love money. I love it, I love it, I love it.

He now wished that he hadn't agreed to help Freeman. He wanted to be obligated to no one. He just wanted to watch Cherry Computer come to life, then watch it expand into the American business phenomenon of the millennium. I want to change the world.

Minutes later, he read the day's mail back in his office. In it was a note from Dee, who always wrote to him care of Amazement so that their father wouldn't read the letters.

"Paul, please come down to L.A. I'm in trouble. Big trouble. Love, Dee."

Paul closed his eyes and sat back in his swivel chair, massaging his temples. What next?

Halfway back to Western Hills that evening, he forgot that he had promised his father "something nice" for dinner. So he pulled the pickup truck into the nearest grocery store and bought a couple of small steaks, two tiny baked potatoes, a small can of peas and a brick of vanilla ice cream. He won't be shy about telling me he doesn't like this meal. Well, he can eat this or go hungry. At home he prepared the meal and the old man ate it uncomplainingly, perhaps sensing his foul mood. He washed down his food with two cans of beer and retired early. Before dozing off he looked back with much disappointment on the day's events. The only thing that went well was the early-morning run with Langston.

Monday, and the subsequent days, brought nothing new. Bayliss came by once or twice and they went through the arcade's business, saying nothing of the Cherry business plan. Naturally, Paul did not bring it up either. Atari had sent over new games and Paul was busy supervising their installation.

He called Dee to let her know that he had received the note and would get down to Los Angeles as soon as he could but could not be more specific. He waited for his sister to spell out the nature of her problem so that maybe they could resolve the matter at least partly by phone, but Dee said nothing about what was troubling her.

Professor Freeman didn't contact him, but he suspected that a call was imminent. He felt angry at Freeman for enlisting his support. Paul wanted nothing to do with her and a board of feisty academics or patriotic zealots wanting to crucify an aging woman teacher just for having political views they found disagreeable. Things could get ugly if there was more to Freeman's activities than she'd let on at the Cable Car Club that day. And Paul couldn't afford to be thought of publicly as a radical sympathizer; it would undermine everything he had worked toward.

His workdays became long and frustrating. He mentally relived his encounter with Luanne Buck and felt obsessively horny. His breakup with Nancy nagged at him. He slept poorly, tossing about, having perverse dreams of sitting before a microphone beside Freeman, both of them dressed all in red, he explaining to a stern, blue-suited panel including Bayliss, Lido Grandinetti, his mother and Nancy that yes, he was a terrorist-sympathizing Commie just like Freeman and damned proud of it. His dream metamorphosed into an erotic interlude with Luanne Buckelew, who drawled, "Are you *really* a Commie?"

On Wednesday morning, Bayliss called him in. There was little in the way of ceremony as he spoke. He had the manila envelope's contents spread neatly in front of him and looked resigned.

"Paul, you win. I've been talking to my lawyer and he wants to ask you a bunch of questions because your ideas, as submitted to me, are too brief. But, dammit, you seem to have something here, a very feasible project. We're taking a stroll down to Montgomery Street tomorrow at three."

"Tomorrow at three?" That's when Freeman wants me. "That was fast."

Bayliss nodded. "I want to get started on this thing immediately. We can rent a South-of-Market warehouse while we commission an architectural firm to design a South Bay factory. Get that goddamn computer mass-produced and into the department stores."

"OK."

Bayliss frowned at him. "Aren't you happy?"

"I'm thrilled." He tried to smile at being told what he already knew. Even the lawyers, whom he considered fools, admitted that the Cherry computer was a winner. When you had a winner, you expected to win.

They shook hands and Paul left the office, more concerned about Professor Freeman and how to tell her that she might have to face things alone.

The phone rang. Toni Freeman sounded serene. "Paul," she said, "you're off the hook."

"Excuse me?"

"I mean I have quit. I'm no longer going to teach. I have retired. It's for the best. Goodbye." Click.

Chapter 2

Caitlin felt annoyed that her mother walked her all the way up to the school's door and then back to the car. "Why can't I do it on my own?" she asked.

"Because," Dee said.

"What kind of answer is that?"

"It's the right kind of answer for an eight-year-old."

"Mom, it's the Nineteen-eighties. Kids can walk to and from the car by themselves." The child sighed, as she often did when having to go somewhere or do something with her mother.

Dee blamed her parental anxiety on Los Angeles, a big, brutal place compared to Western Hills. She was not yet ready to cut the umbilical cord; leaving Caitlin alone, even for a moment, made her nervous. Let the damn kid resent the mothering, which would end soon enough. They got into the car and Dee checked Caitlin's seatbelt to make sure it was snug. "I already adjusted it, Mom," she said. "Well, it doesn't hurt to check," said Dee.

They drove home in silence. Dee felt nostalgic for the days when her little girl was soft and warm and lovable, not some growing kid with a mind and mouth of her own who questioned her mother at every turn. It was hard to be assertive with your daughter when she was nearly as tall as you and could sense it immediately when your confidence started to fade.

When they reached the apartment building she saw Paul's new car, no doubt with Josh Hawkins. These visits were becoming more frequent. Paul was saying little these days, but was doing some sort of big deal he had talked Bayliss into, and Josh was the architect behind it all. Whatever was going on, they both seemed to think it would make everyone involved filthy rich. It probably would, too. Josh wasn't often wrong about these things.

Paul had a key to the apartment and had let himself in. He, Josh and Hank were in the living room, sharing a bottle of champagne.

"Hi, girls!" Paul called out. "Surprise! Are you glad to see us?"

"Hi," Caitlin muttered. Dee had noted Caitlin's ambivalence about her uncle. If the kid didn't like Uncle Paul, how would she feel about Uncle Jamey, if she ever met him?

"How did it go?" Dee asked.

"Great. Fred Bayliss made me a rich man today." Paul let out a chuckle. His eyes glittered with excitement. He was breathing hard. "Co-founder of Cherry Computer. Chairman of the board." He chuckled again and gulped down champagne.

"It's official, Dee." Josh Hawkins nodded, sipping his wine. "We got the warehouse in South-of-Market. Amazement is mortgaged to the hilt. We're going to build the factory down in South Bay."

Paul, for his part, looked so wired that Dee guessed he wouldn't sleep for weeks. Both Hank and Josh, Dee had concluded, did not sleep, ever.

"Get your big blond hubby to come in with us on this, Dee," Paul was saying. "Go to the bank and borrow the money. Invest in Cherry, get rich and tell the world to kiss your ass."

Dee shook her head. "Tommy wouldn't risk his inheritance even if Josh here told him to do so. He's completely chicken about taking financial risks."

Paul made a face. "Wimp."

Dee smiled. "That's my Tommy." Then she disappeared into the kitchen.

Paul sat back and turned on the TV and flipped through the channels. Eventually he settled on ESPN and watched, bored, as the announcer went through a quick rundown of boxing events for that evening. "This man"—they showed a graphic of a blond, crewcut fighter—"B.J. Steeves, will be at the L.A. Civic Auditorium tonight, pitted against—"

Paul's mouth dropped open. *"What?"* The graphic disappeared from the screen, replaced with that of a mean-looking black fighter.

"Did you say something?" Dee asked, entering the room.

"Something wrong?" Josh asked, not paying attention to the TV screen.

"Dee, did you ever hear from Jamey?"

"No, thank God."

"Well, he's in town. He's a boxer. Gonna fight tonight at the Civic."

"I hope he gets his butt kicked," Dee said.

"May I ask what all this is about?" Josh said.

"We have a strange, and estranged, brother named Jamey," Paul said. "Haven't seen him in years. Apparently he's now B.J. Steeves."

Dee smiled. "How clever. I have other names for him."

"You guys wanna go to the fight tonight?" Paul asked.

"Not me," said Josh. "I see enough carnage and gore in the boardroom every day."

"I think I'll pass, too," Dee said. "Wait a minute."

She left the room, got the Los Angeles phone book and returned, horrified. "B.J. Steeves. He's in the book. He lives here! That does it. I'm moving to Nebraska."

Paul groaned. "All these years I thought he was dead or something. What bliss I knew."

"We made a special point of never knowing where he was," Dee said to Josh.

"He's a boxer," Josh said.

ENTREPRENEUR

"Always was in fights, as I recall. Anyway, I'm going to find out." Paul dialed Ticketron. As he was taking out his American Express card to order tickets, he glanced at Dee, who reluctantly nodded that she would accompany him.

"Okay. We're all set." Paul hung up.

Dee expelled a huge breath. "Well, as I live and breathe! Our darling little B.J. 'Jamey' Steeves, the terror of Western Hills, has made it to the boxing big time and we didn't even know it."

Just then the phone rang again and Paul answered. It was Tommy.

"Hey guy! How's my favorite millionaire?" He sounded boozy. A woman giggled in the background. "Tell my missus that I'll be missing dinner tonight. OK?" Click.

"Was that my hubby?" Dee asked. "He'll not be home for dinner?"

Paul just smiled.

"Let's try some of that Moet Chandon, Josh," Dee said. Half an hour later she changed into a sporty denim skirt and white blouse.

"Everything but T-shirts is too fancy down here," said Josh. "But you look great. Show yourself off." After a moment he said, "Hope Jamey breaks a leg."

"You mean his neck," Dee said. She wondered what to wear to a prizefight. She and Paul drove out to the Los Angeles Civic Arena in Paul's new white Plymouth. He had finally traded in the old pickup truck.

There was a preliminary bout as Paul and Dee took their seats. Dee was dying for a cigarette but knew that the Civic was a non-smoking facility. She was wearing what she thought was a sporty outfit but nobody paid her any attention; most of the people were vulgarians dressed like Vegas pit bosses sitting with their dolled-up whores. Dee thought boxing was as civilized and sensible as the Vietnam War, where young men who didn't know better went off to war essentially to defend American corporate ideals overseas. Here, tonight, young men with nothing to lose mixed it up in the ring for pay.

Paul saw things differently. He said that boxing, like many other things, was worthwhile if you knew what to watch for and recognized that the fighters, if good, were actually well-trained athletes. He saw a genuine beauty and art in the way Muhammad Ali had fought, and the same of Rocky Marciano. But the two men they were watching in the ring now weren't doing much more than dancing around and trading occasional punches. The guy who did less dancing and more pretend punching would probably be the winner. Well, Dee thought, at least this was better than seeing two guys basically beat each other's head in. To her, no matter who the pugilists were, boxing was little more than a street fight.

The preliminary bout went the distance because the two fighters were unable or unwilling to hurt each other. One won by decision, and quickly the main bout was announced. Dee and Paul sat and watched as two men, one black and the other white, climbed into the ring. The white man slipped through the ropes and bounced a bit on his feet. He turned around. Dee, for the first time in several years, saw her brother Jamey.

When Jamey's robe slipped off, Paul Steeves, who prided himself on envying no man alive, suddenly envied his younger brother's buffed-up physique. Paul, steeped in sedentary work, had neglected exercise; even his laps around the track had virtually stopped. If there was anything he disliked about himself, it was his skinny, bony, unmuscular torso. His kid brother had obviously spent the past year or more lifting weights with the same dedication that Paul had shown in starting up Cherry Computer. Jamey still had a boyish, smooth face and that familiar cocky fuck-you smile. He now wore a crewcut. His shoulders were massive, his stomach tightly muscled, his legs strong and chiseled.

His opponent, Jonny Cordova, was a lanky young black man, intense and fidgety. The two stayed in their corners and received instructions from their handlers. Dee stared in wide-eyed, fascinated revulsion at her brother's Arnold Schwarzenegger physique and eagerness to fight in front of a crowd of crude strangers. She had always feared B.J.'s defiance and anger, his readiness to pummel others over the merest slight. Here he stood now, half naked, ready to pound this young black man into oblivion for the titillation of the rubes in attendance.

"Kill him! Kick his ass!" someone or other shouted every time one of the fighters, it did not matter which, landed a particularly damaging punch or seemed to capture the fight's momentum. Dee felt nauseated and appalled by the simple fact of being there.

The bout lasted nine rounds, out of twelve. Jamey, battered and bloody, was cut in a couple of places but bled all the way down to his chin. It hardly slowed him down. Cordova had clinched him throughout the fight as his energy flagged, but in the final rounds he simply tried to avoid his opponent. Jamey moved in repeatedly, aiming devastating blows to Cordova's stomach and arms, then jabbing mercilessly at his face. Dee was sure her brother could have ended the fight at any time but chose to prolong it for his own sadistic thrill. He knocked Cordova down, who got up slowly and nodded to the referee that he could continue. Jamey bounded over and assaulted Cordova with a handful of punches that sprayed the audience with Cordova's sweat. Then he reared back with cartoonish exaggeration and hammered the young black man with a right cross that sent him across the ring. Cordova somehow became entangled in the ropes and, technically, remained on his feet, free to take more punishment. Jamey, determined to give his fans their money's worth, charged at the supine fighter and pulverized him with a series of hooks. The crowd cheered. Dee leaned forward and retched, violently and dryly, into her lap. Flashing through her mind was the jaundiced sign saying HOTEL and the awful smells of the Tenderloin that evening so long ago. But tonight was far, far worse.

The referee stopped the fight and raised Jamey's right glove in victory. The booes were deafening. The winner beamed and danced back to his trainer, who wiped his face clean. Cordova, amazingly, was still conscious but required assistance in getting into his robe and out of the ring. Out of the corner of her eye, Dee could see judgmental Paul with his arms folded across his chest, disappointed. Paul liked a good show; he appreciated pornography when it was erotic, avant-garde films when they were compelling and ate exotic cuisine when it looked and smelled good. He had come to the Civic to see an exhibition of pugilistic prowess. But he got only a barroom brawl with the more vicious man victorious. "C'mon, let's go," he was saying.

Dee stood and went a step towards the exit. Paul grabbed her arm. "I meant, let's go *see him*." Paul Steeves, honor student from Western Hills, alumnus of People's University, co-founder of Cherry Computer, always knew what to do and did so without procrastination or hesitation.

She let out a shocked laugh. "Why?"

"Because he's our brother."

"He stopped being our brother years ago."

"No." Paul took her by the hand and led her to what was clearly the dressing-room entrance. The security guard stopped them. "Got a pass?"

"Better than that," Paul said. "B.J.'s our brother."

The guard spoke into his radio. "Go ahead," he said presently.

The two went inside and met their brother, who was seated with his eyes closed as a doctor took a close look at his face. "No stitches this time," he said. Then Jamey opened his eyes and said, "Hey! Is that you?"

"It's us," Paul said. After brief, awkward hugs they said, because they could think of nothing else, "Good fight."

"Come into the dressing room," he said. They went in. "Let me introduce you folks." Jamey scratched his head as if trying to remember who was there. "My brother Paul and sister Dee. My wife, Honey; my manager, Mr. Wasserman...."

"Hello," Honey said.

"B.J., you didn't tell me you had family right here in California." Wasserman said.

He shrugged. "I kinda forgot." After a pause, he added, "Mr. Wasserman, you think anyone noticed tonight that I'm not black?"

Wasserman laughed. "Tonight went so well that they wouldn't have cared if you were polka dot. You looked great tonight. Get a reputation and we'll be able to go to Vegas and Atlantic City. Better opponents and bigger purses." Wasserman was a tall, thin man in a beautiful dark suit. He had graying thick hair and a sharp nose. The manager clapped his fighter on the back. "You get reacquainted with your family and I'll see you tomorrow. Fair enough?"

"Sure."

Paul could see that his eyes were bloodshot. Do you take_steroids, brother? "I'm impressed by your career rise. How did it all happen?"

"After Uncle Jack booted me out of Sacramento, I bummed around a lot and got even better with my fists. Started working at a health club. Got lots of experience and found me a missus—"

"He means me." Honey pointed grandly to herself. She pointed at her breasts which billowed out of her low-cut dress. "Finest pair of titties in L.A., right, B.J.?" she said, shooting an envious glance at Dee's own high, firm bustline.

Jamey winked at his wife. "You know it. Them's bodacious ta-tas, baby girl."

Dee rolled her eyeballs.

"Did you know we have a kid?" Jamey was saying. "A boy. Buford James Steeves the Third. Big handsome kid. But I'll be sure to teach him not to hang around boxers and pick up their bad habits and vulgar manners."

"Tell you what," Dee said. "I'll wait in the hallway."

"Don't mind if I join you," said Honey, following closely behind.

A moment later, Jamey said, "Well, Paul, just you and me again. You married yet?"

"Nope. Too busy trying to take over the world."

"Dee hitched yet?"

"Yes. Has a tall, cute girl, too. Caitlin."

"Is she still a stuck-up bitch?"

Paul glowered. "Is not and never was. She did her best back in Western Hills and she's become a great wife and mother. You should be proud."

"Oh, I guess I didn't see her virtues, seeing as how she always judged me and treated me as an outcast. I did my best, too, believe it or not."

"No one judged you."

Jamey spat onto the floor. "Shit. You judged me every goddamn day of the week, all of you. That's why I always ate dinner so fast, to get away from your condescension." He took a deep breath. "And now you've condescended to see me here tonight. I'm *so* honored. You look pretty prosperous, too. Rob a bank or something?"

No, but I'm going to buy one soon enough. "I make do."

"I bet." Jamey thought for a moment. "Say, I went back to Western Hills awhile ago. Bud's Good Eats is gone."

"Yes. They tore it down. Along with everything else from our adolescence."

"I went into the old grocery store and the woman said Mom died."

Paul nodded. "Drove out to Fisherman's Wharf at midnight, parked the jalopy and jumped into the Bay with her best dress on. Nobody knows exactly why."

"Dad still alive and kickin'?"

Paul smiled wryly. "He's my roommate. We've got a crappy apartment out in the Avenues."

Jamey threw back his head and laughed. "The Avenues! No better than Western Hills! The hotshot is living with Dad! That's funny."

"Oh, Dad's mellowed. We get by."

"Does he ever mention Mom?"

"No, never."

Jamey continued to sit and think, as if whatever was inside his head was too much fun to abandon just yet. He looked up and smiled at his brother. "Still in Western Hills. With Dad."

"How do you feel after a fight?"

"Like it's my birthday. I like to win, just like you." He paused. "Pretty good show tonight, though, huh?"

"Not my thing." Paul didn't want to say that his brother was too lacking in technique ever to defeat a genuinely talented opponent.

Jamey laughed. "Yeah. You're a lover, not a fighter."

"So, how long have you and Honey been married?"

"Few years, I guess. She was big as a beachball with our kid when he got hitched. Kid's a cutie, a boy. But I already told you that. I didn't want no girl, but don't tell Honey that." He stared at Paul. "I don't like women that much."

Paul just smiled. "I'd like to see your boy sometime."

Jamey clutched his chest, having a mock heart attack. "Good God! You would condescend both to see my fight *and* meet my poor humble offspring? I can't believe it!"

"I'm trying to be nice to you. Please do the same for me."

Jamey stood up. He had on a light-blue shirt, black leather coat and dark slacks, plus boots that added a couple of unnecessary inches to his height. "Whatever you say, dude. Say, you hitched yet?"

"No," he said.

"Girlfriend?"

"No." He frowned.

"We've both got good memories, huh?"

"Yes. And we treat each other with such dignity."

"Well," Jamey said, "maybe your problem is that you're too busy trying to take over the world."

Jamey pointed past the closed door, to the hallway. "How about Dee? Is she still a knockout, or what? Couldn't believe it when I saw you two by the guard out front. She still is a fox. Hasn't changed at all. Unfortunately."

Just then they heard a knock at the door. "I'm *famished*, B.J.," Honey called through the wafer of white-painted door.

"I hear ya." He motioned for Paul to get up and the two walked into the hallway to rejoin the others. They kept walking, at Paul's suggestion, all the way out to the parking lot, to his car. Paul drove all the way to Jamey and Honey's house, Jamey giving directions.

"Wanna get some dinner at a place nearby? Great Mexican food," he said.

"Maybe later," Paul said.

"Paul's right," Dee interjected. "He lives up north and I have a busy day tomorrow. A rain check, OK?"

Paul was surprised at how rattled, really upset, his sister sounded. He would have liked to join Jamey and Honey for dinner and a drink. After all those years apart, such an evening would have been agreeable. Maybe he and Jamey could have discussed their familial issues and gotten things resolved. That would have to wait.

"Tomorrow, then, Paul," Jamey said. "Five o'clock. Right here. All right?"

"Sure. I'll be here."

Jamey nodded and helped Honey step from the car. They murmured their goodnights and in a twinkling had disappeared into their apartment building. Dee moved to the front seat and they drove in silence back to her place. Paul wanted to listen to the radio as they drove down Hollywood Boulevard; he disliked television but loved the intimacy of radio, especially in the car. When they reached the curb of her street, Dee grabbed Paul and burst into tears.

Paul held her for what seemed an eternity, not sure just exactly what had caused her to cry so. No doubt something to do with their brother—but had their reunion been so awful? After a while, Dee, scarcely looking at her sister, emerged from the car and hurried up the stairs to her suite. Paul followed up the rickety stairs, escaping the emptiness of the night.

Inside, the sitter beamed, overjoyed that they were home and she could now leave. Tommy wasn't home yet, she explained, and Caitlin was fine. She had tidied up the place a bit but wasn't sure if she wanted the newspaper on the coffee table moved. Dee excused her and watched as the girl went out to meet her ride, which was already downstairs.

Without asking if he was thirsty, Dee handed Paul a can of beer. She turned on only a couple of lights, keeping the living room shadowy, and settled into an overstuffed chair as Paul remained standing. They both drank quickly, the beer icy and refreshing in the humid Los Angeles evening. The front door was open, the screen door shut. The air outside felt oppressive. Paul stifled a belch and looked out the window as the outline of a palm tree. Los Angeles, California. You can have it, man.

"He did his best tonight," Dee murmured.

"What was with those tears, anyway?"

"I was just weeping for us all. Our lives seem so screwed up. Tragic. Especially his."

"His? He's got a career, a wife, a child—"

"He's already getting punch-drunk and his wife is a slut. He's the same old prick," Dee said. "Like I said, a tragedy. Ours. It's all our fault."

Crap of the family, Jamey had called himself. Well, maybe. He was a dysfunctional Steeves, acting out in protest over the way his father and siblings had treated him.

"Weird family," Dee said. "Even you, Paul."

"Me?"

"You're a megalomaniac. You want it all. You absolutely want it all."

"Is there something wrong with that?"

Dee shook her head. "I'm not just talking about money, power and fancy cars. That's substitute gratification. Your life in its own way is as empty as mine, Jamey's, our parents'." She pointed her finger at him. "You are a sore winner."

Paul tugged at his fine dark linen jacket. "Well, megalomania has its benefits."

"Sure, be glib. Go back up to San Francisco and tell Josh Hawkins to make you some more money. Kiss Fred Bayliss' ass some more and maybe he'll retire tomorrow so you can be King Shit all by yourself."

Paul drained the last of his drink. "I'm getting another. Want one?"

"Yes. And if you get drunk enough, maybe you can lose your inhibitions enough to tell me to shut my mouth and stop picking on you."

Paul disappeared into the kitchen and came back with two full cans. "Well, you *are* being a bitch tonight."

"It's just because I have a loser for a husband and my youth is slipping away and I'm growing disillusioned with life in general." She leaned in said, "I've been balling other men. Isn't that awful?"

Paul smirked. "Shame on you."

Dee tsked. "You disappoint me, Paul. I was so eager to see you go into shock over the news of my wanton behavior."

"Seriously, Dee, what does Tommy think of your playing around? He must know something."

"Tommy is past the point of giving a damn. He lives for his own pleasures, like booze and broads. At least he's no hypocrite. He doesn't fault *me* for doing the same things *he* does." She took a deep breath. "He's still looking for the big score and to gain some sort of fame. If he came across the original New Testament, instead of preaching it, he would try to hustle it around town to the film studios. The guy is totally without ethics. He prides himself on being a loser. He says he is an innocent in this brutal world, and that explains and excuses all of his failures."

Paul groaned.

"How come our marriage is hanging by a thread? That's what I really want to know."

"Because you're a modern woman and that's a fatal flaw. Anyway, that day you called and wanted me to come down immediately—remember?"

Dee nodded. "Yes. I said we had resolved the matter."

"Well, what *was* going on there? You never said."

"I was going to file for divorce from Tommy."

"So why didn't you?"

Dee paused, as if trying to remember. "Because I was too busy with other things to go through with it. So the feeling passed. But I almost wish it hadn't."

Paul sat down and looked at his sister. "Do you still want to leave him?"

"At times, yes. More frequently now than before."

"So just do it. What's the problem?"

"I'd need custody of my daughter," Dee said. "And Tommy says absolutely, positively not. So we're biding our time."

Paul nodded. "I see. And you want me to look around for some resolution to this that will get you a divorce and custody?"

Dee smiled. "Yes, please."

Paul nearly regretted making the offer as soon as he uttered it. He wouldn't have made the gesture had it not been for Dee's rattled, emotional behavior in the car earlier that evening. They listened for a moment as, outside, a police siren blared again, far in the distance, chasing down one bad guy or another on the mean, hot streets of Los Angeles. Ah, life in the City of Angels! Paul looked at his watch. Past midnight. It would be another sultry one till dawn, then heat up for another torturous day. He longed for the comparatively cool Bay Area.

"I wonder if her real name is Honey. His wife," Dee was saying. "He seemed genuinely happy, if only for now. Maybe we should have gone out and eaten Mexican with them. Learn about how a happy marriage works." She smirked.

Then they heard the heavy pounding of the stairs that was enough to make the whole apartment gently shake.

"Speaking of tall, fair and drunk..." Dee murmured.

Presently Tommy opened the screen door and stepped in. "Hi, Paul," he said. He didn't slur his words. He ambled across the room and bent over to kiss Dee. Paul watched him carefully. He's got so little confidence for such a big man, he thought for the millionth time. He had always trusted and respected tall men; it was the pipsqueaks with little-man complexes you had to worry about.

"So, what's news?" Tommy asked. He knew Paul, not L.A.'s biggest fan, didn't come down unless for a specific reason.

"He came down to celebrate some good news," Dee said.

"Oh, you mean that Cherry Computer now exists?" Tommy said, looking at Paul.

"Exactly."

"Well, that's just grand," Tommy said. Pointing to the can of beer in Paul's hand, he asked, "Any left?"

"In the refrigerator."

Tommy went and got himself one. "Nearly out. Need more." He peered around the room. "You got it dark in here. Just like a cocktail lounge. Kind of romantic. Maybe low lighting is what we need, Dee." He chuckled.

"Excuse me a sec," Dee said. "Must go to the little girls' room." She left the living room and disappeared down the hall.

Tommy went over to Paul. "Is she angry that I missed dinner with you folks?"

Paul shrugged. "She's a big gal, Tommy. She gets over things."

Dee came back in and said, "Tommy, you missed all the fun tonight. We went to see my brother fight at the Civic Auditorium."

Tommy's eyes widened. "Dammit, I didn't know he was in town! They should publicize these things better."

"Not only that," Dee added, "but we got to go backstage and congratulate him."

Tommy laughed. "And did he give you his autograph? Did he dedicate his next fight to you?"

"She's not kidding, Tommy," Paul interjected. "I'll tell you about it sometime." He felt tired and awkward, standing there in this dimly lit apartment with this unhappy couple while his clean bed at the Beverly Inn awaited. Dee had often invited him to stay with them, but Paul much preferred to stay at the Beverly, where he and Josh could each get a deluxe suite and get the concierge to arrange fun outings for them.

"A prizefight tonight?" Tommy seemed puzzled. "Dee never wants to go to those kinds of things with *me*, and she goes out only when she has to do a review for the paper."

"Well, don't sweat it, Tommy," Paul said as he went out the door.

Many more surprises in store for you, my friend, Paul thought as he walked down the stairs to his car. He promised to help Dee with getting a divorce and custody. He would get Josh Hawkins on it right away. Josh was a born fixer; he innately knew what to do in every situation. Josh would put Dee in touch with the right private investigator, who would covertly accumulate information against Tommy Wilhite that would compel any judge to take his girl away from him and put Caitlin in her mother's custody. That good-natured, confused blond bear of a man would be heartbroken, divorced and all alone in this world in a matter of months, thanks mostly to Paul Steeves. Once inside his car, he put on the radio and put Tommy Wilhite and his imminently crumbling world out of his mind.

Chapter 3

Jamey was feeling okay. Or at least he wasn't feeling too bad. The two quick shots of vodka in the morning may have helped, as did the substantial breakfast. In fact, this was the first day of what looked to be a fine future for him. He looked at his reflection in the airplane's window and saw a big, good-looking guy. He looked past his reflection and saw the Pacific Ocean, with the California coastline alongside it. He felt peaceful, being several thousand miles above the world and its stupid, petty problems. Maybe he should look into becoming a pilot? Terrorists beware. Badass boxer in the cockpit. The thought made him smile.

Another thought that made him smile was the packet of hundred-dollar bills in his pocket. Taking care of business.

He took out a bill and looked at it, felt it. Crisp, new, meticulously printed, made from some mysterious kind of silk-paper, he'd heard. And it spent just fine, thank you very much. He shook his head in admiration as Benjamin Franklin's austere portrait looked out at him. People kill and die for you every day, Benny. You're the man.

He shifted in his seat, feeling a little bit angry at the world. Honey had bitched and moaned over dinner about the sudden appearance of two siblings about whom he had never said a word. Was he so ashamed of her, she wanted to know, that he could not bear to tell her about his family because she might actually want to *meet* them someday?

"Those two looked at me like I was some big-titted, small-brained bimbo who couldn't make a buck without taking off my clothes," Honey had said, her mouth half full of a beef enchilada. "I tried to be nice but those two acted like they couldn't stand to be seen in public with me."

She had been silent over dinner and sullen when they got home. In bed, she rolled over and went to sleep without a word. Well, that was Honey. Up and down like a goddamn roller coaster. With her heart-shaped face and big heavy breasts and mane of light-brown hair, she was more than pretty if not beautiful, but she was starting to get heavy and she wasn't the world's greatest lover. She winced whenever he put his tongue in her mouth and nearly fainted once at the mere suggestion of taking him into her mouth or up her ass. "What do you take me for, a skid-row whore?"

As always, when he got to thinking about women in general and his wife in particular, he started thinking of his sister Dee and that night in Grandinetti's mansion as he spied on her beautiful blonde body years ago. She still looked great. No tummy, titties still firm filling out that white blouse, face like a fuckin' cover girl, betcha she could suck the chrome off a trailer hitch…His cock grew stiff as he sat in the airplane. Was it incestuous to think such thoughts? Well, so what? Deirdre Steeves Wilhite. *There* was a hot number, so long as you didn't have to live with that hoity-toity cunt every day. What was her husband like? Must be a devoted guy, to be with her for so long.

Shit, life threw you curveballs sometimes. He couldn't get it out of his mind. Teach yourself to play the game, punch your way up through the ranks and finally get represented by someone reputable like Wasserman, appear at the Civic and win…then two assholes from home show up and it's like you're Mr. Nowhere again. Well, that go-getter Paul,

Daddy's special boy, was going to have a visit from his kid brother and they were going to resolve some longstanding issues.

As the plane touched down at San Francisco International Airport, Jamey was tempted to board a connecting flight to Sacramento to go look up the only soul who ever gave a damn whether he lived or died. His beautiful Maria would be delighted, but not surprised, to see that he had become a successful man. Now, *there* was a reunion he wanted.

But when he left the plane, he got into a cab and headed into downtown San Francisco, to his special appointment. Maria would have to wait.

Dee stared as her daughter Caitlin toyed with her food. She hated discipline the kid but was damned if she would let this nonsense go on for much longer. Caitlin didn't like like many foods at all, not even crap like chocolate and potato chips. But you had to eat, and you had to obey your parents, and Dee was not about to let Caitlin get away with things. That girl was a smart one; soon enough, if given an inch, she would take a mile or two.

"Hurry up and eat," Dee said.

Caitlin looked up at her. "Why do I have to go to the symphony?"

"I believe it's called a field trip. Schools do that sometimes, you know."

"Well, it's a dumb idea. School is a dumb idea. Most of those kids are jerks."

"That's the wrong attitude."

"I don't care."

Dee let out a huge, exasperated sigh and resisted the urge to reach across the table and slap her child. A clever child, she told herself, is something of which to be very proud. Didn't the pediatricians all say that?

She checked her watch. "Well, I better get you off to school."

"You seem really panicky, Mom. Why are you in such a hurry?"

"I've got things to do today."

"Seeing Daddy today? He's not around much."

No, Mommy's going to be seeing some other man today, sweetie. Dee wondered if her daughter sensed this and was trying to prolong the morning so that the planned rendezvous wouldn't materialize. But Dee couldn't allow that to happen. "Meal's over. Got to get busy now, honey."

Caitlin put down her fork. "Wish I could go wherever you're going. That symphony will bore me to sleep."

Dee was bathed in sweat after dropping off Caitlin at school and speeding home. Her clothes were damp; she smelled stale and dirty. She pulled off her sweater, shirt, jeans and shoes within seconds and scampered into the shower. She briskly lathered up her hair, face and body, then stood under the hard, hot spray for minutes. Stepping out, she dried her long blonde hair and looked at herself in the mirror. Thanks for the metabolism, Mom, she thought, admiring how slim her hips and tight her belly had remained despite pregnancy and a general lack of exercise. Missing dozens of meals over the years, accidentally or not, had something to with it. Her breasts, in her opinion, were still youthfully jutting and capped with smooth bright-pink nipples. Not too bad for an old married broad with a kid. Not bad at all.

She went into her bedroom and took out a handful of condoms. They were the best form of contraception for her, ribbed and deeply arousing when she and he were going at it as hard as they could.

ENTREPRENEUR

As she put on her bra and panties, she thought back to the night before at the fights. Jamey and his masterful boxing, blond figure in her mind's eye, stirring her loins. She wanted him, Tommy, to make love to her; she would have initiated it had he not been in a deep slumber. By and by she had dozed off, and that was that.

Dee selected a pink linen suit and matching skirt with a baby blue blouse. Far from a whore's attire, but sexy and sunny and sultry. She had carefully deodorized and perfumed, then brushed her blonde hair and dabbed on lipstick.

Outside, she got into her car and drove northwest, to the Hollywood Hills. She turned on both the air conditioner and the radio, enjoying the music and the engine's powerful hum. She was glad for the new car as she climbed the hill, up into the hazy air above Hollywood.

Jackson Worthy lived on Beechwood Avenue. When she reached his home, she put the car in park and stared at the house for a few moments, feeling her heart pound. How long had it been since Tommy made her feel this giddy and girlish?

Outside, parked a few feet from Dee's, was Jackson's handsome dark Oldsmobile. Inside the house, her man awaited. Must not let him wait. She turned off the ignition and got out. Jackson's mortgage was crippling, but he *had* to have it, so it was his. That was how Jackson Worthy did things. How many times had she made this brief walk to his front door? Dozens? No two times were quite the same.

She knocked and he answered, slowly opening the door with a smile, dressed only in his bathrobe and sandals. After a brief peck on the lips and a soft "Hi," she sauntered in.

There was stationery everywhere: Jackson's writings; ideas for books; race-related essays that would appear in *The New Yorker* and *Paris Review*, to provoke and startle much of America; disarmingly funny short stories the literary journals and certain other magazines begged him for. A fiendish worker, Jackson Worthy, one of America's premier writers and not quite forty years old. He was also black, and much of his work concerned being black in America.

People said he was the best writer around. Dee believed he would get even better.

"Have you had lunch?" His voice was low and quiet.

"Yep. Not hungry."

"Afraid I haven't bothered to eat for a few days. The muse visits and..." He threw up his arms.

She shook her head and smiled. "Jackson, you're as bad as Caitlin."

Jackson and Dee had met when she, promoted to entertainment reporter for a major Los Angeles newspaper, attended a press conference where he discussed his latest novel. She found him quite full of himself, overly impressed by his own intelligence and good fortune. But the man could write like a demon and Dee stayed up all night reading *Soul Food for the Man,* of which she wrote a glowing review. Not long after, Jackson's publicist called and said his client wanted to meet with her for an exclusive interview. Just the two of them. Interested?

She agreed and went to his hotel suite at the West Beverly Inn. They ordered room service and Jackson sipped beer. He sat sprawled on the sofa, telling anecdotes and jokes as Dee, in the loveseat facing him, laughed till her ribs ached. He told her of his childhood in Harlem, his early ambitions to become a preacher. She didn't bother to take notes, and soon they both stopped pretending this was an interview. They were on a date. Many others followed.

Eventually she made love with him, mainly because she was lonely and confused and depressed, and because he wanted to know her—who she was, and what she did, and why.

She took his interest to heart, feeling that he cared about her. Maybe he was the only man in the world who truly did.

Jackson sat at the breakfast table and munched on warmed-up pizza (she found his diet abominable and resolved to improve it). He appraised her with large, round brown eyes. He was a tall man, broad and muscular, with glistening ebony skin and fine features, big soft lips and a smooth, hairless jaw and upper lip. I sure seem to like the big guys, she told herself. There was a gentleness about his eyes and smile that sometimes detracted from his imposing appearance and lent him a deceptive air of weakness. He was the exact opposite of weak. His work thus far had been limited to the written word; he'd spent countless hours agonizing over his prose. He was branching out now, into screenwriting, an original work. He was temperamental and perfectionistic, like most other highly successful people. His way or no way.

When the pressures of being Jackson Worthy got to him, he hid out in his home. Dee felt she had found the man she wanted, and if the world had a problem with a white woman loving a black man, too bad. This wasn't Mississippi, and 1962 was a long time ago. It was foolish to care about such trivial things in this brief life.

He swallowed a chunk of pizza and smiled. "So, how's my best girl today?"

She smiled back. "I'm glad to see you're happy."

"Actually, I'm cranky as hell. Come over here. I need succor."

As always, she walked over and sat on his lap. "Tell me what's wrong," she whispered.

"The bastards are grinding me down."

"Poor baby." She reached over to her purse and took out a cigarette. As she put it into her mouth, he took it out. "I won't have you smoking in my house. You know that."

"Sorry. I forgot."

"Why do you smoke, anyway?"

"Right now, because I'm frustrated, in love and a wanton woman. Good enough reasons?"

Jackson chuckled. "Try to be more direct, dear. We should try making love at night sometime. Interested?"

"Can't do it if my husband comes home, and lately he's been coming home often. It's just a game I'm playing. I'm pretending to be I'm married." After a moment she said, "That picture where the director wants some new dialogue? Does he think it's good otherwise?"

Jackson nodded. "Oh, yeah. And let's hope it all goes well. I need to make more money."

"Maybe I should call Paul or Josh about you. They're really doing great with this Cherry thing." One evening, she had entertained Jackson with the tale of Paul and Fred Bayliss and their grand designs for the computer factory in South Bay.

He shook his head, rueful. "Those two guys were born to make money. I was born to spend it." A moment later he said, "Apparently it's chic to be black in America right now, at least for me. Everyone wants my thoughts on everything. I basically keep repeating myself, changing the words each time. But they always want to hear more." He looked at Dee, still on his lap. "I wonder when they'll get sick of me."

She kissed his nose. "Never."

He had emerged from the Montgomery Street meetings drenched in anxious sweat. Even his underwear was damp. He wanted to leave San Francisco for a couple of days. If he had known it would be this overwhelming, and that the lawyers would set his head spinning the way they did, he would have said to hell with it and contented himself with a life as Amazement's general manager.

Lawyers, Paul thought. What assholes. They spoke an incomprehensible language, made obscure allusions and wouldn't give you a straight answer to the question, Nice day, huh?

Paul's eyeballs ached and perspiration trickled down the small of his back as the legal eagles in dark suits and sober ties spoke of tax loopholes, acceptable compromises, collateralization. Paul wanted to yell at them, or punch them out. Maybe he should have brought Jamey along, to do the honors.

Paul knew that he had made the right career choice. Lido Grandinetti and his rhetoric about law school, lawyers and Paul's future. What did Grandinetti know?

Next came the architects to design the Cherry factory down in South Bay. Josh Hawkins had recommended a firm of young hotshots housed in a converted Nob Hill mansion. They were already in high demand, with many contracts and glowing write-ups in newspapers and architectural magazines. They had won several prestigious awards for buildings in San Francisco. Paul liked most of their work and liked them, too, and carefully considered their drawings for the huge Cherry factory. But these guys were San Francisco architects who designed Victorian things with lots of concrete and ornamentation. Cherry represented the new, not the old. Cherry would need glass and chrome, lots of it, to capture as much South Bay sunlight as possible. Paul was building a huge, spacious facility. The young Nob Hill architects frowned at him. Paul didn't care. He was the boss. He made the calls.

He smiled as he sat at his desk in Amazement's office. The arcade was still thriving but all the video games in the backroom had been removed and the whole room was Paul's interim office. The temporary Cherry factory was operating at full capacity in their South-of-Market rented warehouse. Paul hated going to the warehouse because he couldn't concentrate there, with the noisy assembly line and the clattering of plastic on plastic, so he decided to stake out Amazement's backroom for the time being.

He studied the drawings of the factory's front entrance, where an enormous red neon sign proclaimed CHERRY COMPUTER. That's what they needed. Not that he especially *liked* the sign, but he knew it was a necessity, big and bold. The factory would be located near the freeway, and he wanted as many eyeballs as possible to see his company's name in big, brash, unmistakable letters.

Fred Bayliss, concerned with his advancing age and confused about his place in this exotic new business, made it clear that he was not to be disturbed unless Paul needed his signature for something.

Paul secretly wanted to close or sell the Market Street Amazement in the next few years. Good riddance to the punks and losers with nothing better to do than play video games. Sell the arcades and put their managers to work at Cherry.

He looked at his watch and reminded himself that his brother had called and wanted to see him here at Amazement and not over dinner. Would he bring his wife? That tacky woman, Honey. He sure hoped not.

Suddenly the phone rang. Paul picked it up. Josh.

"Paul, I have the number of a private investigator, very experienced in what you want. Probably unreasonable rates, but you get what you pay for."

Paul took down the information, thanked Josh and hung up, not wanting to prolong their conversation. Josh always looked forward to a few minutes of gossip, but Paul felt too tired. Jamey was coming here. Whatever for? It was time for his arrival. He looked at the drawings again and got angry at Dee for accusing him of being on a power trip. Was he a "sore winner"? Maybe, but what of it? Yes, he enjoyed things, he did have big plans for the future and being young and healthy and smart in the present. He tolerated rooming with Dad in Western Hills for the time being. Still, Dad had been in his corner all along. Dee, with her boozing, ne'er-do-well, soon-to-be ex-hubby—what did *she* know about happiness and fulfillment?

Dee was fashionably unhappy, like so many other people Paul knew. Bitch and moan and look for the quick cure, go to the psychiatrist and expect him to make everything all right. Expect sex and the orgasm to compensate for your lack of self-discipline and direction. Above all, blame everyone but yourself. Well, Paul Steeves knew better than that.

Just then he heard a knock on the door and promptly opened it, still dressed in his dark-blue suit and a maroon tie that he'd worn for the day's business.

"Jamey, come on in." No Honey. Good.

"Thanks." They both noticed the slight echo. "Empty in here."

"Gonna stay that way for a while."

"So you're now the president of Cherry Computer *and* the night manager of Amazement?"

"Well, the night manager job isn't really a job. I just come in here to get away from the craziness at the warehouse."

"Don't close out Amazement. I spent much of my youth here, you know."

"It makes too much money to be closed."

Jamey nodded and cleared his throat. "Let's get down to business." He reached into his pocket and withdrew the packet of bills. "Think fast." He flung it into his brother's chest.

Paul looked inside the envelope. "Hundred-dollar bills? Must be thousands of dollars here. What's going on?"

"Ten thousand dollars, Paul," Jamey said. "There it is. The money for your great future."

"What are you talking about?"

Jamey took a deep breath. "Years ago, in Sacramento, I had a little trouble. Remember? So Mom drove up and paid off some rich people to make the trouble go away. She paid them off with the money for *your* college education, then she drowned herself."

Paul shook his head. "No. You don't have to do this."

Jamey laughed, bitter. "What you got there is dirty money. One night, I happened to catch some fine, upstanding citizen giving in to a moment of weakness. So I extorted that money from him, not unlike the way Dad acquired the capital for Bud's Good Eats. He ever tell you that story?"

Paul sighed deeply. "Look, I got the damn degree and everything else worked out okay. Shit, this is foolish."

"I *am* foolish, and so are my motives. Still and all, we've come full circle, and now I have paid you off. I have fulfilled my obligation to you. I want nothing to do with you ever again."

"Let's talk about this." Paul wondered if his brother, riled enough, would hit him. "I don't need this money. I'm set for life. Use it yourself. Save it for your kid."

Jamey's eyes narrowed. "Don't worry about my damn kid."

"Well, I'm not taking that money, period."

"Yeah, you are," Jamey said, "even if you carry it around in your rectum."

Paul blushed. They both kept their distance from the money, as if it were something incredibly disgusting or dangerous. Paul placed his hands on the desktop, his eyes surveying the dark wooden desk and chair. "Now, look, we're acting like a couple of little kids. Enough, okay? Maybe we didn't like each other much back then, and I'm sure I was a son of a bitch to you—"

"Damn straight."

"But that's all in the past, so let's move on. It's a cold world out there. As brothers, we should try to get along. That's just the way I see it."

"After Dad hit me and kicked me out, where were my two siblings? Huh?"

Paul looked down. "I'm sorry for that. We let you down, and we shouldn't have. Dee regrets it too, you know."

"Does she?"

"Yes, even if you don't think so. Last night at the fight, we had a reunion by accident. We're the only siblings you'll ever have. We're yours, and you're ours. It sounds clichéd, but it's true. We are obligated to each other."

Jamey again pointed to the envelope full of bills. "That's my obligation. All done. I can survive on my own."

"Whatever you say. Still, I can help you now. I stand to make a mountain of money, and I can help. I'm no neurologist or psychiatrist, but I do know that head injuries are bad, and boxing is full of them."

"I'll get by."

"Just reminding you of how it is."

"Thank you so much, Dr. Steeves."

"You know, since I have such power now, I could get you aboard with Cherry. A cushy job, lots of benefits."

"Wow."

"Be serious, Jamey."

ENTREPRENEUR

"I don't need your help or your pity, Paul. Now I gotta go. My wife and kid are expecting me."

"Like I said at the fight, I *would* like to see your kid. How about dinner? All of us—on me."

"You should take that money and get some chick drunk enough to marry you." He walked to the door and opened it, then turned around. "Don't hesitate to come see me fight again. If Dee is writing a review, tell her to say nice things about me. But don't try to sweet-talk the security guard again, because I won't let you in."

"At least try to make it over to see Dad. He asks about you."

"Oh, I'm sure he cries himself to sleep every night because of our estrangement."

"We're in the phone book. Can you remember that?"

"Maybe I'll come by sometime. Maybe not." He disappeared, shutting the door softly. The room seemed much more spacious without him.

Paul put the envelope with the money in his pocket. He'd think about what to do with it later. Jamey was the angriest person he had ever met, and how long would be stay that way? For the rest of his life? Anger is seductive; it feeds on itself. The Steeves family, a modern American tragedy. Shakespeare couldn't have done better.

He felt tired and believed he could get to sleep now, despite Jamey's unsettling visit. He took out the drawings one last time and sighed. Words spoken in an office, pencil markings on paper, ink on forms—all these elements would conspire to create Cherry Computer, the future of American business. Miraculous. And at the center of it, as well as the cause of it: President Paul Steeves, a man who had married his job.

His phone rang again. "Paul, it's Tommy. Dee wants to know if you'd like to come down here for dinner this weekend."

"No, Tommy, I'm dead tired."

"Fair enough." Click.

In the months ahead, he knew, Tommy Wilhite would not be calling with dinner invitations. Keep your friends close and your enemies closer, Tommy. Paul went home and crawled into bed.

Chapter 4

"Jamey, life is too short to stay mad," the letter read. Jamey rolled his eyeballs at the masculine, barely legible handwriting. "Paul gave me your address in Los Angeles. Please contact me. Love, Dad."

He laughed aloud. *Love, Dad.* Oh, yeah, whole lotta love in that old man's heart. In the kitchen, Honey was trying out a new recipe and seemed to be having little success, judging from the clanging of pots. The kid, with his mother, was laughing heartily.

"Daddy's here," he called out, slumping into an easy chair and wondering if he should read the letter and toss it, or just toss it. Honey came in with flour on her chin.

"What's that you got?" she asked.

"A letter."

She made a face. "Well, duh. I mean, who's it from?"

"My father."

"Yeah, sure."

"Look for yourself." He shoved it into her face.

"God, that's awful handwriting. What's it say?"

"It says my daddy loves me and wants me to come home."

"Really?"

Jamey rolled his eyeballs. "Go back into the kitchen and do whatever you were doing."

ENTREPRENEUR

Once she was gone, he read on. "As you know, Paul and I live together now, and he has told me all about your evening together at the Hollywood Bowl. I must say I am impressed that you have found a way to make a living, if I don't approve of your methods. Anyway, I never thought you were a serious enough person to have a trade of any sort, but your brother assures me you are making do. I only hope you are not mixed up with the wrong people, and I think that famous Don King may be the wrong kind of people, from what I have read in the newspapers and elsewhere. So please stay away from people like him.

"Furthermore, Paul tells me you are now married and have a little boy. I hope you *are* in fact married and not just living with this woman and lying to everyone, for that would make your child a bastard, and that would be a bad thing. I suppose you know by now that your mother simply took off one night with our truck, parked it at Fisherman's Wharf and threw herself into the icy bay. She did not leave a note and I try not to think about it too much.

"My health is deteriorating almost daily. If I felt better, I would insist that Paul drive me down to Los Angeles to see you and your family. He has finally gotten rid of that rickety old pickup your mother used on her suicide mission and replaced it with a fine new car. I want him to start driving me to church so that I can explain myself and my adverse circumstances to Our Father because I believe our meeting is imminent. You will be glad to know that your brother takes wonderful, indulgent care of me and grants my nearly every wish. But he is very busy with work now and has little time for me. He goes to Los Angeles often and, if you want to know the truth, leaves me to fend for myself. He said you were mean when he saw you, and I don't guess I blame you. Paul, like all successful businesspeople, is aloof and to the point, not someone with a big heart. But that's just how it is.

"I do not want to see my daughter again or hear her name, as she has brought shame to our entire family. But my two other children? They're another matter. Back in the old days, I was too tired and drunk and cranky to treat you better than I did. So let's start all over again."

Jamey's hands were sweating all over the inexpensive white stationery. He took a deep breath and thought, Could my old man really be turning over a new leaf? He did not hear the racket Honey was making in the kitchen as she struggled with cooking. Maybe, he thought, I'll just drive up there, collect the old guy, bring him down here, put him up and show him the sights. Take him to the biggest, best church in town and show him what today's Jamey Steeves is all about.

Terrence McArdle sat behind the desk of his office, which, to Paul, looked like something out of a cheap movie. "You asked, I got."

I paid, you provided, Paul corrected silently. "Looks complete to me," he said, perusing the report.

McArdle laughed. He had a mirthful, musical laugh, not suited to private investigative work, or to police work, which he had done for many years. But the looked the part: tall, rangy, silver-haired, deadly serious. "Very easy work this time. Mr. Wilhite didn't do anything secretly. Didn't seem to care if the whole world watched."

Paul didn't look up. He read and sighed.

"If Mrs. Wilhite gets a decent lawyer, the divorce will be easy and clean. But she must get out of that apartment as soon as possible, with Caitlin. Immediately."

The conversation dragged on for a few more minutes. McArdle had tapped phones, watched covertly, stuck his nose into Tommy Wilhite's private doings and spoke to strangers about things that were nobody's damn business. Then he had it typed up and proudly presented it to one of the family, Mister Paul Steeves, who had paid him to pry into Tommy's life. No room for ethics these days.

By the time he got back to his hotel room, Paul decided to call Tommy's office. After being put on hold for an eternity, his brother-in-law came on the line, nicely lubricated. "Hey, bossman! What's the good word?"

"Tommy, you must come to my suite right away."

"Paul, I'm *married*." He chuckled.

"Forget the jokes, Tommy. Come over now."

Click.

Tommy looked angrier than Paul had ever seen him. "Been spying on me, huh?" he muttered, going through McArdle's report as he sat in Paul's hotel room.

Paul nodded.

"Well? What now, bossman?" Tommy licked his lips. He cleared his throat loudly.

Paul reached into his pocket and took out a large blue bow he had bought downstairs, in the shopping arcade. He peeled off its slick backing and stuck the bow on the cover of the report. "Happy birthday. Merry Christmas. Whatever."

"What...?"

"It's yours now, Tommy."

"You're not giving it to Dee or a lawyer...?"

"It's yours. Burn it, shred it, give it to your wife if you want."

"Does Dee know about all this?"

Paul smiled. "She sort of commissioned it."

"So why are you letting me off the hook?"

"She'll have to get her divorce without my help."

"Dee ordered the report," Tommy mused. "Gee, and all this time I thought she *liked* me."

Paul laughed. "Keep your sense of humor. It becomes you."

"What would become me now is a drink."

"I can see that."

I don't fuckin' believe it. He sat in his car and peered again at the apartment building where Paul and Bud Steeves lived. The place was no improvement over their home in Western Hills. Jamey walked up to the iron gate of the shabby and depressing building. Another wood-and-plaster special, painted some shade of blue but so faded now that it was nearly gray. What about all that big money Paul said he was going to make?

Naturally, Jamey didn't have a key, so he looked up Steeves on the directory, found the button and buzzed. Nothing. He tried again. Still no answer. Either Paul had taken him out for a while or the old guy just wasn't hearing the buzzer. Probably the latter.

Jamey took out his penknife. Looking left, then right, he slipped its steel blade into the lock and swiftly jimmied it open. Old skills become useful at the oddest times.

Upstairs, he knocked loudly several times before he heard the door chain rattle and the deadbolt lock slide away. You're getting too trusting in your old age, old fella.

"Dad?" Jamey swung open the door and saw his father. Not really his father, but a withered old man, looking vaguely like him, whose pants went up to his armpits and were held up with suspenders.

"Jamey!" came the small cry, and the old man's narrow, atrophied arms feebly went around him. This was the first time in his life he could remember Bud Steeves hugging anyone, much less him. He felt a catch in his throat as he gently, awkwardly returned the embrace. He could smell soap, ointment and old age.

"Come in, son, come in." Steeves led Jamey into the apartment. It was large and dark, with high ceilings and artisans' flourishes on the walls. It was also old and musty, like their long-gone place on Tower Street, and filled with new, handsome furniture, doubtless provided by Paul. While he was *out* buying all this new stuff, Paul might've spent a few bucks on a nicer apartment in a better neighborhood, Jamey thought.

"It's been so long, son," Steeves was saying as he motioned for the younger man to sit in a large, overstuffed chair. His voice was hoarse and unclear from ill-fitting dentures. Sitting there, Jamey could fully appreciate how small his father now was. He felt amazed that before him stood his once domineering, volatile father, who had inspired such hatred and fear in him and hit him so viciously that evening so long ago.

"How did you get up here?" Steeves asked.

"Oh, there was someone downstairs, so I said I was your son and you weren't answering, so he let me in," he lied.

"No, I mean, how did you get *up here?* To San Francisco. You live in Los Angeles."

"I drove. Got a new car."

Steeves smiled. "All that way!"

Jamey smiled back. "All that way. It was fun." This was no lie. He had a new car and loved to drive. The drive up the coast was over before he knew it.

"You have grown into a big, handsome fella. I was big and handsome myself. You must take after me."

Jamey nodded. "Guess so."

"Hear you have a child," Steeves said.

"A boy."

"I want to meet him."

"Soon enough. Maybe when I get back."

"Where you going?"

"I fight. We're leaving in a month or so."

"Well, save your money. That business, I don't trust it. Shysters and such, you know. And tomorrow you may not be so tough, and then where would you be?"

"I'll remember your advice." Looking around, he added, "Jesus, Dad, I can't believe this apartment at all..."

"Paul is moving us, but who knows when? He's so busy with business, you know. He always goes off for meetings. But you can't fault him for wanting to make a buck. Guess he's his father's son that way." He smiled.

"Well, I hope he can part with some dough to get you into some better place to live. Maybe Palm Springs."

"You've turned into a handsome man," Steeves said again, as if he hadn't been listening. "And a good man. Always thought you would, even though there were folks around here who swore you'd be in the morgue or prison before you were old enough to drive a car. Remember that stuff about the Molotov cocktail and the Grandinetti mansion? I figured all along that fat kid Bubba put you up to it, but someone had to be the fall guy, and as usual it was you. A person must choose his friends carefully in this life."

Jamey smirked. *I knew you would turn out to be a good man, Jamey-boy.* "Those days are long gone, Dad. Best not to think about them anymore. I've put all that behind me."

"What kind of woman is your wife?" Steeves asked.

"Oh, she just loves me and dotes on the kid nonstop." He was surprised by his own answer. Funny how you answered questions you didn't expect to be asked.

"Well, that's good. Need lots of love to keep a marriage going. Need lots of love to keep children on the right track."

Yeah, sure, a lot you knew about being a loving father. Jamey looked at his watch and said, "Look, why don't I take you to lunch? I have a car, you know."

Steeves beamed. "Lunch? Someplace Italian, maybe?"

His son grinned. "If you like."

On the drive home to Los Angeles, cruising along the highway, the window down and the wind whipping through his hair, Jamey scarcely heard the radio blaring as he dwelled on the afternoon with his father. He felt as if he had just been to a high school reunion and approached by a bully. The bully, once formidable and remorseless but now weakened by age and humbled by life's adversities, had come up to him, hand outstretched, smiling and eager for friendship. What could you say?

Over lunch, Steeves accepted his son's offer of a cocktail. He had cut out beer almost entirely and became mildly intoxicated, chuckling at one point and saying, "Let's go to the Tenderloin, buddy. We'll shoot some pool, bust some heads and drink a few beers." Immediately afterwards, they drove around the city. Steeves, who had driven his pickup truck to the Embarcadero every morning for years to pick up supplies for Bud's Good Eats, recognized almost nothing in San Francisco now. He stared with wide-eyed wonder as they drove slowly through the city. Jamey kept driving, through one neighborhood after another. When they reached Sea Cliff, Steeves looked out at the mansions perched overlooking the Bay and said, "Thieves and liars. That's how they made their money."

But later they were back on Market Street and went by Amazement. Steeves whispered into his son's ear, "Kind of a cheap-looking place, don't you think? Hope Paul makes that computer company into something better than this."

They wandered into Union Square and stopped in Bocassio's, one of the city's toniest shops. Steeves fell in love with a Swiss-made wallet, and Jamey bought it for him even though all the old man had to put into it was his Social Security card, expired driver's license and fifteen dollars. Still, he was delighted with the gift and tossed his old wallet into a nearby garbage can.

Steeves talked nonstop during their visit, telling his son about stealing the Mafia money back east, of coming out west with a headful of dreams, of his happy early years with his wife and his regrets that her life became so bad she ended it in San Francisco Bay.

"Don't make the mistakes I made," he said.

"I won't, Dad. I promise." When he drove his father home, he said, "I'll get on Paul about a new place to live. You deserve better than this."

Then Steeves went into his bedroom and came out with a framed picture of a young couple. "Our wedding picture. It's the only one I have. Keep it."

Jamey reluctantly accepted it.

"In certain ways I think you're the only child I have left. Paul has become a different person. All that power! It's gone to his head, you see. He wants to own the world. He's greedy, and I don't trust greedy people. But you and I are survivors. No one gave either of us anything and yet we've pulled through."

Jamey said nothing but and gave his father a gentle hug and went to the door.

"Do you know," Steeves said, "I haven't had such a nice time in ages?"

Jamey took his time driving home, disturbed by his visit with his father. He didn't know what to make of the old man, but was ashamed that his father thought he had turned into an honest and respectable man. Better you didn't know, he thought as he steered the car down the California coastline.

PART THREE

Chapter 1

Los Angeles, 1990

As sunlight streamed into her Hollywood Hills bedroom, Dee woke up and stretched. She put on her robe and sandals, then walked down the hallway, through the kitchen and out the door, where she was greeted with a commanding view of Los Angeles, spread out endlessly before her. She saw some brownish smog in the air but it was generally a pleasant morning. She smiled at the scent of wet grass and fresh flowers.

Below her, miles below, was the apartment building where she had lived with Tommy. I've moved up in the world, she thought, enjoying the play on words. She reached down and picked up the copy of the *Times* that had been delivered minutes earlier.

This is where I have always been meant to be, she thought. And inside was the man she had always been meant to love.

For the moment she was the only one up. She couldn't stand the thought of breakfast, not even coffee, and even the maid was still asleep. Caitlin needed her sleep, especially considering how big a day this was for her. Jackson, once in a deep slumber, could not be awakened by anything less than a major earthquake. He often hogged the blankets or even the bed itself, his long muscular body stretching well over the edge sometimes. Dee sometimes wondered if he would actually fall out of bed. If he did, the impact of hitting the floor would fail to wake him, too.

ENTREPRENEUR

Jackson dreaded mornings even more than Dee did. He was often crabby but mellowed quickly, as if the rising sun warmed his mood.

She picked up the rolled-up newspaper and brought it inside. Dee was a Democrat by default who distrusted Republicans and wanted Jackson to get out and vote. Dee knew about Paul's experience People's University professor and felt alarmed about what sort of place her country had become. Her cynicism about American politics appealed to Jackson, whose politics were highly unorthodox.

Jackson, publicly, was a writer whose heartfelt, insightful essays on race relations appeared in top magazines. The world had labeled him a civil rights advocate. Privately, he was a libertarian who favored abortion, optional taxation, elimination of the Executive branch of government and the legalization of marijuana. He opposed capital punishment and conscription, gun control and privatized medicine.

"There is only one party, the Property Party," he said. "It's divided into the Democrats and Republicans. I'll toss a coin. You vote one way and I'll vote the other. We'll cancel each other out."

Jackson and Dee's neighbors never invited them over. She sometimes wondered if it was because they were an interracial couple, but Jackson was indifferent to parties, anyway. Often, they didn't go anywhere. Which was just fine with her, since life with Caitlin and Jackson occupied all her time and mental energy.

Their intensely private life also made her wonder if Jackson feared that his white wife undermined him in some way, made him seem someone who had embraced the enemy.

"I am a man and a writer, in that order. I am not a political or civic leader of any kind," he stated. As an undergraduate at Columbia, he had written a James Joyce-inspired collection of short stories based on his childhood, *Harlem*. After graduating, he wrote a highly successful novel, then a second, and a third. Dee suspected there were plenty of people eagerly waiting for Jackson to fall on his ass.

Would it happen, and how would he cope with it?

Dee was Jackson's biggest supporter and most conscientious editor. She read every word he wrote and gave him candid, extensive feedback. He paid careful attention to her. He had just made his foray into films with a screenplay, not a tense examination of blacks and whites but a fast-paced comedy about a white cop and a black convict pursuing a murderer. The script worried her, though she couldn't say why, but something was missing. She dreaded being solicited for her opinion, telling the truth so far as she knew it but unable to expand as he pressed her for ways of improving his work.

She went back into the bedroom and watched him sleep. Soon she would have to wake him. He and Caitlin both had plans today, and this would be their last morning as a family for some time. Perhaps forever.

She went into the living room and sat on the sofa to read the paper. She instinctively turned to the sports section, to see which horses were running where. Jackson loved the track and the Las Vegas casinos. He loved gambling in general, craved the excitement and risk. He took a scientific approach and won consistently. He had paid for their entire wedding trip with his winnings at baccarat.

The paper said that Jamey was fighting at a major Las Vegas hotel. There was no picture of him, and Dee hadn't heard a word from or about him since their meeting in Los Angeles that awful evening.

She hoped Jackson wouldn't read the paper too closely and want to see Jamey fight. She heard the maid in the kitchen, and went into Caitlin's room to wake her. She found her daughter sitting up, in her pink T-shirt and panties, running her hand through her hair.

Long wavy blonde hair, precocious body, wide innocent sweet face, fair flawless skin, deep-pink lips, narrow shoulders and hips. A ripening beauty.

She had already packed. Ready to go. Dee suspected her daughter was happy to leave home. Too much turmoil: divorce, remarriage. She did not expect Caitlin ever to come back to live with her on anything like a full-time basis. School, probably college, then a place of her own.

"Big day for you, huh?" Dee said, kissing her

daughter on the head. Want some breakfast?"

Caitlin shook her head. "I'm not hungry, Mom. Maybe I'll have cereal and juice."

Dee smiled. Caitlin was always so ladylike and refined. The girl's friends were attractive, poised, endlessly polite, like Caitlin herself. Dee smoked, chewed gum, spoke in slang and profanities. She had been an easy lay for a rich guy in San Francisco and a few others since. She wanted better for her daughter. Fourteen-year-old, Caitlin, so far, had been the good girl her mother wanted her to be.

"Excuse me, I have to brush my teeth."

The girl stepped past her mother. After developing breasts, she refused to let her mother see her naked. She was uncomfortable with her ripening body, yes, but Dee also suspected it had something to do with Jackson. They had lived together before marrying, and Caitlin did not like that...but Jackson's color, Dee believed, manifested itself in her shyness. Better not get naked. There's a black man in the house.

She went back into her bedroom. Naturally, Jackson was flat on his back, sound asleep. He never snored or talked in his sleep. Dead and fit to be buried.

Dee leaned over and kissed his neck, again and again. He snapped awake. "Huh?"

"I'm giving you artificial resuscitation, sweetie."

"In the middle of the night?" he muttered.

"It's breakfast time."

He groaned.

"You slept long and well," she assured him. "You were in bed with me all night, and we were naked, and all you did was sleep."

"Then why do I still feel like complete crap?"

"Because you didn't fuck my brains out like you were supposed to. But there's time now."

He shook his head. "Time, yes. Desire, no." Mornings were out for him. Mornings were not for love. Still, he pulled her down on top of him and pecked her lips good morning. "Listen, you said something about my script—the new one..."

"Oh, *please*, Jackson." Dee said. "Work, work, work. It's seven in the morning—"

"Seven is a good time to work. Talk." He spoke with levity and a small smile, but she knew he meant business, literally.

She thought for a moment. "OK. Early on, you know that scene where the cop gets the con out of jail and they put their cards on the table?"

"Yeah, I know it. It's just the most important scene in the whole project."

"Well, it's not funny enough. They're both being too heavy, too tough. You need a cute, clever smartass sort of exchange in order to establish the rapport between the two characters."

The film had already been cast and there was much excitement about it in the trade papers. Justin Aldridge, a veteran director with two Oscar nominations, was using this as his comedy debut. A brilliant young black actor from Broadway comedies, Lamar Stone, was making his film debut as the convict, and longtime tough-guy character player Robert

Chisholm, deep-voiced and prematurely white-haired, was playing the cop. And of course Jackson Worthy was writing the whole thing. Everyone speculated it would be a marvelous triumph, considering the quantity and quality of talent involved.

"Uh huh. Anything else, boss?"

"Well, yes, since you asked. In the barroom scene, where Lamar's character is cutting up and winning over those tough guys so they don't beat the shit out of him and Robert?"

"Yes…"

"Well, Lamar's lines are too Stepin Fetchit. He's making quite an ass of himself to make those drunken white guys laugh. Frankly, I'm sure he'll will demand rewrites immediately."

Jackson sighed deeply. "You cunt."

"The truth hurts, huh?"

"Wonder if it's too late to get an annulment. Gotta find me a woman who will say I'm right even when she knows I'm wrong." He tossed her aside and got up, naked, and headed to the bathroom. "Don't you know anything about the fragile male ego?"

"No, but I know a little about angry directors and inadequate screenplays."

"Two months' obsessive work down the goddamn drain," he said as he closed the door.

They reached the airport and parked the car. "We're a bit early. Let's have a cup of coffee." Caitlin seemed eager to get back on the road, up north, to begin the next chapter of her life. She was dressed in a pink blouse, blue sports coat and gray skirt. She filled out her clothes well, looking womanly and confident. Jackson was already mentally in New York, dealing with the editor who had summoned him for revisions on his latest novel. He was also scheduled to make an appearance on a local TV show, debating issues with Norman Mailer. He did not know precisely how long he would be in Manhattan, and he was already getting antsy, which was why Dee had insisted upon driving to the airport. A distracted Jackson was a dangerous thing to have around.

"Jackson, if you're all set, we can be on our way," Dee said, thinking her husband might wish to be alone right now.

"A cup of coffee."

They marched off to the coffee shop, Dee walked between Caitlin and Jackson. Jackson walked with what Dee secretly called his "boss nigger" swagger, his face set in a businesslike, bemused expression that made white people avoid him. So far as Dee could tell, their world was very tolerant of her relationship with him; but of course, this was Los Angeles and Jackson Worthy was a celebrity, the kind of person a tourist hoped to meet.

"You may be ambivalent about moving out, especially at your age," Jackson told Caitlin as they sat in the coffee shop. "But once you've had that independence, you'll love it."

She offered him only a small smile. Jackson was generally cool and cerebral with her, making casual observations he doubtless thought were pearls of wisdom. Dee felt he regarded his stepdaughter as just another adult (another *white* adult?). Dee couldn't tell whether Caitlin, loved, tolerated or detested Jackson, or whether she was merely indifferent to him. Jackson was always polite to the girl but nothing more, giving her plenty of space, letting Dee do the parenting. He lived for his work and his wife; the kid may have been excess baggage he supported financially. Dee reminded herself, often, that she had left Caitlin's alcoholic father to take up with a black man and dragged her daughter along. If the child was withdrawn and perhaps angry, should that be surprising?

Jackson was not the world's easiest man to live with and the couple had squabbles, but Caitlin was never the issue. Plus, Jackson insisted that American public education was a joke and that the girl must attend a private school, even if at his own expense. They never spoke of this matter, but Dee felt certain her daughter knew Jackson was paying the bills.

"I'm looking forward to school," Caitlin said.

"It'll be better than any public school," Jackson said. "Speaking of which, I want you to take this." He reached into his jacket pocket and produced an envelope. "Guard it with your life."

She thanked him and put the envelope in her own jacket pocket. Then she looked at Dee. "We should be going."

They headed to the gate and Dee said to her daughter, "Wait here a moment. I want to say goodbye to Jackson."

Caitlin stepped up and gave her stepfather an awkward but firm little hug.

"I'll be at the Plaza," Jackson told her. "Don't know for how long. If anything comes up and your mom isn't available, call me. Reverse the charges. Promise?"

Caitlin smiled. "Promise."

Dee looked closely at her daughter's face and saw warmth, affection, belief in her stepfather's concern for her. We'll become a family yet, she thought as Caitlin walked slowly down the hall and stopped, pretending to look out at the jets waiting to take off.

"You gave her money," Dee murmured.

Jackson nodded. "Emergency money. If she has it, she won't need it. Follow my logic?"

Dee shook her head.

He smiled. "Good. It'll give you something to think about on the drive up the coast. Tommy's meeting you in the Bay Area, right?"

"Yes. He thinks it's better if we take her to school as a couple. More respectable, you know. They don't have to know we're divorced."

"Well, don't fuck him tonight."

Dee glowered at Jackson. "God, what a disgusting thing to say."

He cocked an eyebrow. "Well, you know how divorced folks are sometimes."

Dee turned away from him but he grabbed her. "Sorry. I *was* being disgusting. It's a streak in my nature that manifests itself at the worst times." Then, "Just one thing: if your ex wants to talk about me or us, just kindly refuse comment, OK? I'm still getting used to this unconventional arrangement, being the only black guy in someone's family..."

Her face softened. "You're forgiven." She kissed him.

"And promise you won't enjoy life at all till you see me again. Hear me?"

She smiled and pecked his lips again. "Promise."

Tommy stood at the curb and waved with a wide smile, looking OK for a middle-aged alcoholic. He wasn't wearing sunglasses and his eyes were a clear blue. At least he's managed to stay sober, Dee thought. The drive had taken several hours but Caitlin and Dee enjoyed their trip up to San Francisco. Now it was just a matter of crossing the Golden Gate Bridge and heading into Marin County.

Tommy bent over to kiss them each hello. Up close, Dee was disappointed to see just how much her daughter resembled him. Where am I in her face? she wondered. Tommy had been most understanding (or perhaps merely indifferent) about their divorce. She wanted out? Well, if she wasn't happy with him, she should go her own way. She wanted custody of the kid? Take her; she should be with her mother. She wanted to marry this black guy? Far be it from humble old Tommy Wilhite to stand in the way of true love.

Dee would stay in a hotel that night, while Caitlin slept on her father's sofa. Both Tommy and Caitlin wanted it that way. Dee felt left out and unwanted but agreed.

Sitting in her suite at the ultra-swank Pan-American Hotel, Dee read the message from Paul: "Sorry, but I am unavailable for dinner tonight. Maybe tomorrow?" That bastard. Whenever Paul and Josh Hawkins came down to Los Angeles to unwind and have fun, Dee had been hospitable and asked for nothing in return. So now high-and-mighty Paul couldn't pull himself away. Business first. Bastard.

She wanted to call Tommy and invite herself to have dinner with him and Caitlin. But that wouldn't do; if they wanted her around, they knew how to reach her.

Dee was not especially glad to be back in the Bay Area. All those years in Los Angeles had taught her that she was not a true San Franciscan, that she had no desire whatsoever to return here.

Now she was a grown woman, aging but still beautiful, intelligent and sophisticated, wise if jaded. The Pan-American's smooth beige walls seemed to offer little comfort as she thought of her daughter a mile and a half away, and her husband in New York, three thousand miles away. She looked for a moment out the window, unimpressed by its panoramic view of the city. Presently she would go downstairs, to the hotel's four-star restaurant downstairs, and have the most delicious overpriced dinner in town. Alone.

She put on her modest charcoal-gray dress and brushed her hair, self-conscious that she would be eating without her child or former spouse, who would be eating together and did not wish for her to join them.

Just then the phone rang, and she answered, eager. At last, someone had come through to eat with her.

"Hi, Dee." Josh Hawkins. "I'm downstairs. Paul said you were up here and, hey, I was in the neighborhood. Maybe I could take his place? For dinner?"

She stayed on the line, silent.

"Dee?"

"Yes, I'm still here. Look, it was a long trip and I'm kind of tired..."

"You were waiting for Paul to come have dinner with you. I'm here instead. We can eat right down here."

"Akiro's?" She immediately brightened up.

"Akiro's."

"You have reservations? That place is always packed."

"You're staying here, Dee. Just call their direct line. They always keep a table to two clear for hotel guests."

"I'll give it a try."

"I'll be waiting." Click.

Shit, she thought. Josh Hawkins thinks the whole world revolves around him. She sat and watched TV for close to half an hour before she called the restaurant, secured a table and went downstairs to join Josh.

"Paul felt really awful that he had to cancel out on you," Josh said as they sat in the muted elegance of Akiro's. "He feels he doesn't see you often enough."

"Ain't that a shame."

"I'm telling you the truth. Want some more wine?" He caught the waiter's attention and signaled for a fresh bottle. Despite its Japanese name, Akiro's was French-Californian in menu and décor, a vision of subtle burgundies and golds. *Playboy* magazine named it one of America's finest restaurants. Akiro Yamamoto, its owner, had been murdered in an unsolved case only months after the restaurant's opening, and his widow bravely carried on.

Dee and Josh, entering Akiro's, were led to the last vacant table, theirs only because, as Josh had said, she was a hotel guest. Dee could see the place's appeal; the restaurant was big yet cozy, the ceiling high and tables spaced widely apart. Eavesdropping was impossible. The perfect setting for a seduction.

"Paul is devoted to you completely. You must believe that," said Josh, completely devoted to those who could help him advance professionally and financially.

"I must be a hell of a woman," Dee drawled.

"Frankly, I blame you for Paul's being a bachelor. You've set the bar so high—"

"Oh, please. Then why won't he take time out from business to have dinner with me?"

"Because he's being pulled in every direction over the new computer." Cherry's newest machine, the Suzi, named for Fred Bayliss' daughter, was still in production and presented challeneges Paul had not anticipated.

"That's my brother. Work like hell for a few decades, then have a nervous breakdown or a massive coronary."

Josh looked cross. "What about your husband? Worthy, right? He's as bad as Paul. You're up here, but I don't see him at our table, having dinner with his missus. Where *is* he?"

"He went back to New York. His agent got him booked on a couple of talk shows. He'll be back soon as he can."

"Oh, well, that's entirely different. You can make a living by writing novels and essays about being black and if you neglect your loved ones it's all right because you're doing it for the cause. But if you run a computer company and bust your ass and sometimes have to take a rain check on dinner, you're a shameless workaholic with misplaced priorities."

"You're defending Paul and yourself. You're two of a kind," Dee said.

"Damn right we are. Proud of it, too. Not that I feel I need to defend anyone. If Jackson Worthy wants to think he's nobler than I am, well, maybe he is. I'm just a guy who makes money for people and gets new businesses off the ground to prevent another Great Depression, while Jackson is going around telling everyone how to make America into Martin Luther King's Promised Land. But Jackson Worthy's message is seductive as hell and he's manipulated his position very well. He's worked his magic well on you, too. He's romantic, I'm practical. If I had been some sort of social crusader instead of a money man, you would have married me long before you met him."

"I seriously doubt that," Dee said. "This wine tastes good. Got some more?"

"Yeah." Josh poured her another glass. She smiled and sipped. He sat and sulked. Josh usually wasn't one to sulk. Even in bed, he had a stud's technical proficiency and detachment, not letting his feelings get in the way of a fine performance. Josh had access to so many women, so why should she matter to him?

"I completely fucking blew it," he muttered. "I should have married you when we were involved. You know?"

"When we were involved," she said, "I was already married. Remember?"

He snarled. "That didn't stop you from divorcing Tommy and marrying Jackson. *Remember?*"

She nodded. "Don't ask me to explain, because I don't understand it myself."

They took time out for a moment. Then Josh said, "When I heard about you two, I read his novels. The man *can* write."

"No kidding."

"I'm glad you're not biased." He offered her a small, mirthless smile.

"Josh," she asked softly, "where *is* this conversation going?"

"I apologize if I'm being a jerk. I regret it. Let me try to be a gentleman. All in all, are you happy in your life?"

Dee smiled. "Ecstatic."

"Good. My former paramour, a frustrated product of financially pinched Western Hills, has found ecstasy with a tall, dark—"

"I'm leaving." She stood up.

He grabbed her arm and pulled her back down into her seat. "You'll miss your chocolate truffle. Tell me about your life down there. What do you do to occupy your time?"

"I spend my days longing to be back in financially pinched Western Hills, slaving away at Grandinetti Chocolate, doing thankless clerical work. Seriously, I have an ambitious husband and a teenaged daughter. I have many things to do. More important things to do than chat up my former squeeze and listen to his bellyaching because things didn't turn out his way." She stood up and marched out of the restaurant.

Once back in the hotel's lobby, she cooled off and pressed the elevator button. Poor little rich boy. It made her feel gratified, knowing that she was married and in love and got to spend her mornings waking up next to Jackson Worthy, while Josh was still another hound, smug and rich and horny, wanting what he couldn't have.

Upstairs, back in her suite, she called the Plaza in New York but was told that Jackson wasn't answering, although he had checked in. She took out a pad of hotel stationery and a pen and began to write. "Dear Jackson, I tried to call but you weren't in and I started feeling lonely. Maybe it was a bad idea for me to come up here, to my hometown which at best fills me with ambivalence and at worst makes me cringe. Caitlin snubbed me and stayed with her father and tomorrow we will go up to her new school and pretend we are a happily married couple. Caitlin will probably hate her new school and although she doesn't know you are footing the bill she no doubt suspects it and may blame you for forcing this upon her. I wanted to go to New York City with you but that wasn't possible. How I wanted to see New York City through your eyes! Instead, tonight Caitlin and Tommy had dinner without me so I went downstairs to the expensive snob restaurant and happened to bump into the rich man who was my first lover and he said some entirely unfair things about you and us, and I know you're really trying very hard to teach me not to give a shit about other South Bay hang-ups and insecurities but I am a slow learner. When I call again, you had better be in or else I might just hop a flight out there and there'll be a knock at the door and it'll be me, expecting a good explanation for not answering my calls. Love & kisses, Dee."

She put the letter aside, intending to mail it the next morning. Then she undressed, crawled into bed and dreamed about a man who was tall, dark and handsome.

"Dee, are you ready to go? It's us. We've already eaten." Tommy sounded rested and happy, eager to start his day. He sped by in his car and picked her up, and the three drove across the Golden Gate Bridge, to Marin County and Heavenly Valley School for Girls.

They reached the school within minutes. "Red-brick colonial, nice pillars," Tommy said, showing off his modest knowledge of architecture. "I assume those old mansions are dormitories. Can you believe how green it all is? I mean, is this a school or a country club?"

After parking the car they went up to the main building where everybody had clustered. A smiling woman welcomed them all and shook their hands. She gave Caitlin a colored lapel tag and called out, "Pamela Baker" to some older girls. A petite, pretty girl with dark hair came over and introduced herself all around. The woman who had summoned her said, "Caitlin, this is Pamela. She'll show what you need to see and tell you what you need to know. Remember: *your* problems are *her* problems. Don't hesitate to bug her."

Pamela smiled. "Exactly right, Caitlin. Don't be afraid to shake me awake at four in the morning to ask me about something that easily could have waited till later." Then she said, "Where's your stuff? I'll help you to your room."

The two girls disappeared and the woman turned to the next family and greeted them with the same charm she had just shown the Wilhites.

"Pamela seems like a sweet girl," Dee said. "But what a high-pitched voice. And she came up to about Caitlin's chest."

They all walked to Brown Hall, where Caitlin had a room. It wasn't much, but it was a new environment and had two bunk beds, dressers and wardrobes. Another trunk was already stored there. "I see your roommate is already here," Pamela said.

Dee was soothed by the soft music from a girl's room down the hall. She hoped Caitlin would be happier here and that her new roommate wouldn't be a bitch, lesbian or slut. Well, considering Caitlin's height and sturdy build, that probably wasn't going to be an issue. She was filled with despair; her child leaving her. They would never relate to each other in exactly the same way again.

"You'll meet your roommate in due time, of course. In fact, now it's lunchtime, and parents are welcome." Pamela smiled. "Hungry, Mrs. Wilhite?"

Dee knew better than to say, "Why, child, I'm not Mrs. Wilhite. We're divorced. I'm now Mrs. Worthy, and we'd love to join you for lunch downstairs." So she said, "Well, Pamela, I think it's lovely that the school wants to extend that gesture. Whoever said there's no such thing as a free lunch?"

Pamela giggled. "By the way, Caitlin, I would suggest investing in a heavier blanket than the one they provide. The housing people here seem to be from San Diego and think because it's California it's got to be balmy all year round."

All three offered polite laughs and then heard a bell.

"Well, that's the bell for lunch. Just behind where we first met when you signed in. I'll be there soon, but I have a few other things to do." She offered Caitlin a ladylike but firm handshake. "Remember, if you've any questions, I'm Pam Baker. Gotta run." With a big winning smile the petite brunette went off.

"Now *she's* a nice girl, Caitlin," Dee said.

Caitlin paused. "I hope it wasn't just an act."

"Well, *that's* a cynical thing to say."

The girl shrugged. "Just being honest."

"Well," Tommy said, sweating and swallowing, "I guess we should be going, seeing as how you're in your new home and are eager to go to the dining hall for lunch and get to know the others..."

"Yes, let's go now." Dee's voice sounded strained. She had been dreading moment: the unofficial end of Caitlin Wilhite's childhood. Dee had always reassured herself that she and Caitlin had been close and that once the physical separation had happened that closeness would be forever compromised.

Dee virtually threw herself into her tall, sturdy daughter's long arms, promising herself she would have dignity and refrain from crying. Then Caitlin offered her father a polite, firm hug and murmured, "Thanks."

Dee and Tommy took one last, long look at their daughter, who she seemed eager to see them go. They turned around and headed down the stairs and out of the building, silent but holding hands. Dee wondered, as she often had, how Tommy really felt about her marriage to a black man—hadn't it made her suddenly repulsive to him? Could he really stand to touch the hand of a woman who so often touched a black man so intimately?

In the car, they drove without speaking. Dee got lost in her own thoughts, pleasant and otherwise. Then Tommy pulled over to the side of the road and burst into desperate, convulsive tears. She leaned over and held him, and they gripped each other tightly, as if in some sort of competition. Dee wondered exactly why Tommy wept; was it for Caitlin and her newfound independence, or his own failures, his inability to live without alcohol? Or was it merely his depression over middle age and a wasted life?

"Smile, Paul! Smile more! This is your big day! Cherry Computer now has its own factory!" The photographer maneuvered in front of Paul, Dee and Josh as they walked across the vast parking lot and headed towards the vast sign saying Cherry Computer, an electrical sign with a ferocious blaze in the night sky. Even now, at two in the afternoon, the sign was a spectacle. Just across the way, visible from the parking lot, was another equally impressive facility, Grandinetti Chocolate.

Josh had made Cherry Computer happen as much as Paul or Hank. But only Josh had the business acumen to progress beyond having a nifty toy sitting in Amazement's office, so Paul had gone to him, and Josh led him through the minefield that was American business. Paul told him of the two rich guys in his life: Lido Grandinetti and Fred Bayliss. Josh wasn't surprised to learn that Grandinetti lacked personal access to the large amounts of liquid capital necessary to start up the business, but *was* surprised, after a difficult and covert investigation, to learn that Bayliss, owner of vulgar video arcades, owned other things, including a large parcel of South Bay land. Bayliss also had plenty of credit at his bank. Josh whistled as Paul told him the amount of Amazement's monthly revenues and its relatively modest rent at the wrong end of Market Street. Josh guessed, accurately, that the old man had more than enough resources to start Cherry Computer. Paul just needed to bully Bayliss a little bit into freeing up those resources so they could be used to change the world with Cherry Computer.

Dee saw it all only as a sort of scene from a pirate movie: tall, swarthy Paul and cold-blooded, sleepy-eyed Josh, with swashbuckling derring-do, hopping onto Bayliss' treasure ship when he isn't looking, grabbing him by the balls and applying the squeeze. Bayliss could have told them to fuck off, of course. But he hadn't, and here they were.

Paul worked like a fiend to make sure the computers were sold as fast as they could be built. The business and high-tech media often did not know quite what to make of this handsome new toy and practically allowed President Paul to dictate their coverage. Ah, American business.

Dee, alienated from Tommy, had begun a brief affair with Josh, until their essential differences and geographical distance caused their relationship to erode. At about that time, she had gotten the call from the newspaper to interview Jackson Worthy.

Paul stood and looked ahead as the photographer snapped away. He looked peaceful and prosperous under the huge sign, and the photographer was careful to shoot upwards so that the big red sign appeared directly over Paul's head, once again reminding the world: Paul was *The Man* and Cherry was *The Company*. Inside the lobby was a prototype of the Suzi.

He had broken with tradition by not debuting his new machine at San Francisco's Moscone Center. Paul Steeves, Cherry Computer co-founder and boss, wanted to show off the Suzi at their immaculate, gleaming new factory, sending a message to the world that

Cherry Computer was doing just fine, would do even better and would be around for a very, very long time.

When he saw Dee and Josh arrive, he broke into a huge smile and waved them over. Dee thought he looked the way he should, a tall, handsome, lonely man who was living out the remarkable success story everyone had predicted for him.

She wondered about her brother. He wasn't human, somehow; he had some sort of commodity missing in him, never getting too angry or happy, always on an even keel, always making friends and seldom enemies. Dee would have liked her brother a great deal more if he'd been a pain in the ass once in a while.

"Looking good," the photographer said, almost gushing.

"Let me introduce a few people," Paul said. "This is my sister, Dee Worthy, and my financial adviser, Josh Hawkins. This..." Grinning, Paul snapped his fingers at the young woman photographer.

"My name's Marni Duggan." She smiled, as if at a private joke.

"Quite an accent you've got there, Marni," Dee said. "Are you British, Irish or Scots?"

"Canadian." Marni smiled and stood up, a medium-sized girl with straight black hair, large, sparkling blue eyes and a wide, toothy mouth. She moved smoothly despite all the photographer's equipment draped over her body.

"Let's go inside, Dee," Paul said.

Cherry Computer was arguably the coolest new company to work for in the Bay Area. Every Stanford or Berkeley graduate wanted to work for Paul Steeves and Paul Hankowsky, those two humble guys from People's University. Paul believed that the free publicity alone would be crucial to the Suzi's success. People would want to know why it was so much more expensive than all the other desktop computers. Paul prayed that many customers would not be averse to spending ten thousand dollars for the newest, hottest gadget.

"Grandinetti wants to move his factory to Nevada or Arizona. It's cheaper there," Paul was saying. "I imagine he'll be here today."

Dee groaned.

"I need to speak to the bandleader," Paul said. "They're not playing loudly enough. I can actually hear myself think."

Soon the band started up with *America the Beautiful.*

"My brother certainly is certainly the detail man, isn't he?" Dee remarked to Josh.

"That's why he's *The Man,*" Josh said.

Paul came back to them with a tall, red-haired, tense young woman. "Everyone, you know Suzi Bayliss, the chairman's daughter."

"Paul has told me all about you," Suzi said, stiffly shaking Dee's hand.

Dee also remembered Hank, Paul's pal from People's University. Hank had overcome the huge technical challenges in designing the first Cherry. His family had a mining company in Reno but he had bigger things in mind for himself. Paul told her Hank had invented the Cherry computer and wanted to be more involved in the company's daily operations but Hank was a designer, not a manager.

Paul was hoping that Hank would just keep designing cool things and not get any ideas about running Cherry Computer.

Paul said, "Suzi, where's your dad?"

"He went home," she murmured, uninterested in the question but interested in the questioner. "I think he's mad at you."

Too bad for him, Paul felt like saying.

"He didn't like that dark-haired girl hovering all over you, taking your picture and not his. He said it's as much his day as yours."

"Well, your dad is now one of the richest men in California. That should assuage him just a tiny bit."

"Not Dad. We already had enough money. Tell him that you're not his enemy."

Paul nodded. "In the meantime, we're all going for a drink soon. Wanna come?"

"Oh, you know I don't drink."

Paul turned to Hank. "You and Josh take Suzi around, mingle and look really important."

Hank smiled. "Come, Suzi, let's go have a free Coke before they're all gone."

He took her arm and led her away as her feet moved with his but her eyes remained glued to Paul.

"Why did you send her away?" Dee asked.

"I want her to marry Hank," Paul said.

Dee stared at her brother. "Are you serious? Does she really have designs on him?"

"Well, *he* has designs on *her*."

"Silly me for asking."

"You and Jackson are a couple of romantics." Paul thought for a moment. "Maybe we need a romantic or two who use Cherry computers. Would Jackson be willing to featured in one of our ads?"

"I'll ask him."

Paul supervised virtually all of Cherry's advertising. He had just executed a campaign featuring print ads in which famous people were pictured using their brand-new Cherry computers. *Look Who Picked a Cherry*, the captions said.

ENTREPRENEUR

Dee knew that Jackson would never go for the idea. He'd consider it the worst kind of selling out. Still, Paul and Jackson had met several times and Paul quite liked him. Paul told Dee privately that Jackson struck him as the love child of Professor Toni Freeman and Malcolm X.

Josh Hawkins, earlier that day, had looked worried and said, "Paul, I really hope this new computer, the Suzi, goes over well. It's the most expensive model yet, and I'm not sure it's any better than the others." Paul worried, too.

Paul, Josh and Dee went inside Cherry's wide-open glass doors and were greeted by a new-building smell that pleased Dee and made her giggle. Incredible, immaculate newness. The white floor was utterly without scuffs. The assembly line was impeccable. She felt giddy, and imagined the frenetic activity of this computer factory as it cranked out machines for the world.

Too much, too many, she thought, taking a deep breath to steady herself. She had often thought during her days across the road at Grandinetti Chocolate and its endless activity, all day and night. Just too goddamn much.

"Congratulations on your new factory," she said to Paul. "It's remarkable." They walked up one aisle and down the next. The glint of machinery and the antiseptic, artificial smell started to irritate Dee.

"We'll make better machines, smarter ones, faster ones. Then, who knows?" Paul smiled. "Time for you to go, huh?"

Dee nodded. "Jackson promised to call me at eight o'clock. We both get irate if we don't have our evening chat. Josh, mind driving me back to town?"

Josh smiled. "Happy to do it."

The phone rang as promised back at the hotel that evening, but it wasn't Jackson. It was the NYPD, telling Dee that Jackson had been shot dead outside a Manhattan TV studio by someone in a car who had sped away. The cop wondered why Jackson Worthy, controversial figure that he was, hadn't arranged for some sort of personal security. He added that Jackson's murder had been reported on all the TV stations everywhere by now.

She thanked the cop for calling and gave her Los Angeles number since he would need to contact her further. Then she hung up and sat in the darkness for the longest time.

Chapter 2

Las Vegas, 1985

Wasserman hollered, in the final minutes of the sparring session, "Kick his ass." Jamey nodded and, bearishly ponderous, came at Leonard "Forever" Young, who was undefeated and planned to stay that way. Young was training for a bout two days away, and Wasserman needed to see if he could withstand some of this Jamey's best.

Young was six-three and prodigiously muscular; his forearms and legs were impossibly striated, his chiseled body shone like burnished ebony. He was handsome enough to have chosen Hollywood instead of boxing. He floated just inches away from Jamey. He spat out his mouthpiece and tapped his strong black chin, his eyes glittering with mischief. "Come on, guy, hit me! One free shot!"

Jamey, enraged, reared back, but Young dropped to his knees and cackled as a big glove flew over his head.

Hearing laughter—the sparring session was well attended—and angry that his opponent had ducked, Jamey tried to kick Young in the face, but Young easily caught the boot in his glove and pushed it backwards, sending Jamey sprawling across the ring and into the ropes.

Wasserman said, "OK, gentlemen, that's enough."

Jamey spat out his own mouthpiece. "I haven't finished."

"You haven't started," Young retorted.

The only satisfaction Jamey got from Leonard "Forever" Young was in screwing Young's wife while the contender was out jogging. Jamey left the ring, showered, dressed and headed down the hall into the vast casino and bar of their host facility, the Silver State Hotel and Casino, which was no Caesar's Palace. Well, at least they had decent rooms at the Silver State, and the management had agreed to supply all the complimentary beer the boxers and their entourages could drink. Jamey made a beeline for the bar and ordered a Michelob, because the TV commercials said it was the most expensive beer in America.

He settled into a comfortable casino chair and gazed at the people playing slot machines. Honey called regularly, always bugging him for money even though she was making good money as a stripper in Los Angeles. She said he must be some sort of celebrity by now, and couldn't he pull some strings and get her jobs as an actress or something? He kept neglecting to return her calls, and at times even forgot he was married. Maybe she did too.

Getting drunk didn't seem like such a bad idea to Jamey. Wasserman, the only person he had to answer to, wasn't around, and all Wasserman cared about was that Jamey somehow manage to get up in the ring and spar with his new hotshot, Forever Young.

Thirsty, Jamey downed several beers, then closed his eyes as the casino's powerful air conditioner soothed him. His mind traveled back to another gambling town recently visited—Atlantic City, New Jersey.

Jamey, back east, had been winning fights against progressively better men, when Wasserman learned that another heavyweight up-and-comer, a former Bronx streetfighter named Mike Tyson, needed an opponent. Or, rather, promoter Don King was looking for an appropriate opponent for Tyson, and approached Wasserman. Did Jamey want to mix it up with Iron Mike in New Jersey?

Wasserman said yes. So they went to Atlantic City and Jamey began training, ecstatic but horribly nervous. He'd already heard much about the brutal, relentless Tyson. At the weigh-in, he was pleased to see that, at exactly six feet, he was much taller than Tyson, who was listed at just over five-eleven but was maybe five-nine. Still, Jamey was big and competent but Tyson was massive and frightening.

Wasserman said, "Stay in your room when you're not training. I don't want you to be distracted by the glare of publicity." Jamey did as told, but later learned the fight was largely ignored. Nobody in Atlantic City, or anywhere else, took the bout seriously. Tyson was going to be the Next Big Thing, and B.J. "Dynamite Hands" Steeves, like Pinklon Thomas, James "Bonecrusher" Smith and Mitch "Blood" Green, was just one more bum for Tyson to pummel before fighting Michael Spinks for the title.

Tyson entered the ring without a robe; he wore only his signature black trunks, matching shoes and red gloves. He looked intense and murderous, and fixed his opponent with a blank stare from the opening bell. Jamey, who had feared no man inside the ring or out, now was overcome with terror of Tyson's piledriver fists and violated ring decorum by chickening out. He danced around anxiously and jabbed the air surrounding Tyson. The crowd booed, and in one round, after the bell, Tyson, in a display of adolescent exasperation, slapped him with an open glove and yelled, "Fight or go home!"

In his corner between rounds, Jamey sat breathless and perplexed, his mouthpiece out for the moment. All he could say was, "He'll kill me." His trainer, whose lips were half an inch away from Jamey's ear to prevent anyone from reading his lips, replied, "Then just keep moving. Don't slow down. If he can't catch you, he can't kill you."

Jamey kept away from Tyson, round after round. Both men stopped trying to make a fight of it; Tyson saw that his opponent wanted only to complete the bout.

The decision, of course, was unanimous. The crowd booed and threw debris as the two fighters left the ring. Jamey boasted to himself repeatedly that he had just gone the distance against one of the world's best young boxers. The next day, he heard the jokes made at his expense on the TV sports reports that "'Dynamite Hands' did more running than a career politician."

Well, he thought, *at least Iron Mike didn't punch me silly*. Unfortunately, Wasserman and King had negotiated a very Tyson-friendly contract; Jamey's payday, after taxes and other deductions, was a fraction of what he expected. With part of his purse he bought something he enjoyed a great deal: a cell phone. He signed a three-year contract and made good use of his new toy. He memorized his number and had business cards printed, which he gave out freely. He was never too busy to take a call.

He watched the action in the casino and wondered for a moment if Paul or Dee had watched Tyson vs. Steeves on HBO and what they thought. His brother was in the papers nearly every day now, Chairman Paul in South Bay with Cherry Computer, the company everybody was creaming over. Paul would just shake his head and say of his brother, "No comment."

Jamey felt good under the bright lights of the Silver State's casino. Then he heard his phone ring in his jacket pocket. He answered it.

"B.J., get out of town!" Young's wife Bea shrieked into his ear. "He knows about us!"

"Huh? How?"

"Oh, fuck, don't be an idiot! He knows lots of people here. Someone told him!"

Click.

Jamey, quickly sobered, put down the phone and weighed his options. Fight or flight, literally. Young, like Tyson, was tough and vicious and insanely jealous. Fleeing would be cowardly, and would mark the end of his career, but at least he would still be in one piece.

Well, fuck, he thought. Either way, I'm through as Young's sparring partner. Might as well piss off before he gets here.

Jamey started to get up, then heard an angry voice.

"Motherfucker!" Young barked. "Outside, Steeves. You die now." His eyes were glittering with rage. "I know what's been going on with my woman."

"Huh?"

"You been with my wife!"

Jamey nodded. "Yeah, you got it."

Young and Jamey marched out into the parking lot, where there were a few cars but no passersby. Young took off his denim jacket and dropped it on the pavement. Glowering, he charged at Jamey too hard and wild, his punches missing as his man easily ducked and weaved. Then Young tired, rushed at Jamey and threw a roundhouse swing that slammed into a van's side door.

"Owwww!"

Young collapsed, silent.

"Oh, shit!" Jamey turned around at the familiar voice and saw Wasserman in the doorway. The manager came over and knelt over the unconscious Young. He turned to Jamey. "You can't stay out of trouble, can you? You stupid asshole. Bea just called and told me what was going on. Thought I could get here before he totally pulverized you. But look at this—the wrong guy, the *important* guy, is on the ground! The useless sack of shit is still standing." Wasserman carefully looked at the fallen man's hand. "Broken. Broken goddamned hand. Broken hand of a boxer. You, Steeves, have just altered boxing forever. He'll never have the same manual dexterity, and who knows when he'll even be able to fight again?

"Steeves," Wasserman said quietly, "you have to understand that Young's career is very important to some very important and dangerous people. When his injury is revealed, these dangerous people will want to know what happened. And I'll have to tell them the truth: that you're totally responsible. They will want to *kill* you, Steeves. Leave immediately."

"I'm broke." Jamey sounded helpless.

Wasserman took out his wallet and withdrew a business card, which he handed to Jamey. "I know this guy out in Long Beach, a man everyone calls Butch. He runs the Commodore Hotel and provides personnel sometimes for the merchant marine. He can get you on a ship for Hawaii, Guam, the Philippines. Go to the Commodore, introduce yourself to Butch and give him my name. Never come back here, and don't call your old lady. They'll maybe be after *her*, too."

"I said I'm *broke*..." Sweat streamed down his face.

Wasserman handed him a hundred dollars. "Take this and go to the Greyhound station down the street. Buy a one-way ticket to Long Beach. Now. From now on you're a deckhand." The older man looked down again at the prostrate Young. "Now fuck off, Steeves. I have more important things to do than give guidance to some punchy asshole who's just disabled my top client. I know your room number. I'll have your bags packed and forwarded to the Commodore."

Jamey nodded and hurried out of the parking lot, then down the stairs and out onto the street. He jogged all the way to the Greyhound station. He bought a ticket, took a seat and waited for the announcement that his bus was boarding. He climbed aboard and took a seat. Whatever happened now, he knew he was no longer B.J. "Dynamite Hands" Steeves. He had come full circle. He was, once again, Jamey Steeves just another bum from Western Hills.

Chapter 3

They had a date for that day, but Marni called to tell Paul that she would be late. Paul said that was all right, he had a few things to take care of anyway. One of those things was calling Dee to make sure she was all right. They had had Jackson's body for the funeral and the police said they were investigating but nobody could provide information, which was another way of saying that everyone was afraid of stepping up and telling the cops anything.

Paul wanted to have Dee come up and stay in the Bay Area for a while so they could see each other on a daily basis, but Dee wanted to stay where she was. Jackson had no will and his ex-wife wanted half of whatever he had, which apparently wasn't much.

Paul had moved himself and their father into a mansion in South Bay, near the factory, and kept an apartment in San Francisco's Nob Hill that he used essentially as a weekend retreat for himself and Marni. They decorated it with Marni's pictures and some movie posters and secondhand furniture—she liked to decide the décor. The apartment was a hideaway from Bud Steeves, where Paul and Marni spent wonderful hours in the bedroom. Best of all, it was a secret from virtually everyone. Everyone knew he kept an apartment in Nob Hill and that he still looked in on Amazement occasionally. Bayliss had his mansion just across the Golden Gate Bridge and had become a hermit.

The phone rang, and Paul nearly said, "Hi, Dee."

But it was Fred Bayliss. "Paul, I need to see you up here at my home soon as possible."

"Fred, if this is about Cherry..."

"No. This is strictly a personal matter."

Paul frowned. Personal? Ever since Cherry Computer's founding, Paul and Bayliss had said little to each other. Rather than provide moral support, Bayliss had become remote and crabby, resentful of this young guy who apparently believed himself some sort of entrepreneurial Superman. Paul, far from being grateful to Bayliss, had manipulated and exploited him. Bayliss, like Dee, seemed genuinely phobic about entering the Cherry's South Bay factory and, in the very few cases where his involvement was required, insisted on deferring to Paul.

"Tell you what, Fred," Paul said. "I'll be up tomorrow evening. Fair enough?"

Sigh. "All right."

Click.

"Old fart," Paul muttered into the dead phone, rolling his eyes. He placed it back in its cradle and it rang again immediately.

"Paul, it's Dee." His sister sounded old since Jackson's murder. Old and tired. Paul wondered if she would ever regain her former exuberance. It didn't help that people were constantly reminding Dee about what a great man Jackson had been and how deeply his loss was felt. People wrote articles about him in the paper. They urged her to start the Jackson Worthy Foundation, or give her blessing to those who wished to do so. Dee thanked Paul for the money he sent regularly and told him that Jackson's lawyers and ex-wife were shocked at how modest his estate was.

"But that isn't why I called," she said.

Just then Paul heard a knock on his apartment door. "Hold on, Dee." He dropped the phone, opened the door for Marni and gave her a quick peck.

"Sorry, sis. You were saying...?"

"I'm worried about Caitlin. She sounded unhappy the other night when we spoke. She doesn't say much; you know how she is. She keeps it all inside. Maybe if you drove up there to see her...? It's not far."

Paul sighed. "I'm not her favorite, Dee. What would I say? In fact, what would *she* say? She'd just tell me everything was fine, and why didn't I go home and tell you not to worry?"

"Well, I can't ask Tommy. He'd show up drunk and make an ass of himself. But I'm worried. Would you try, for me?"

His sister's voice sounded so thin and reedy, so full of despair, that Paul said, "Okay. I have business up in Marin County tomorrow. After I get back, I'll call you."

Dee thanked him and hung up.

Paul looked across the room and smiled at Marni, who was sprawled on a chair, her legs extended, back straight, generous breasts hidden under a heavy wool sweater, straight black hair slightly mussed. No makeup, skin pink and white, blue eyes incandescent. She had dumped her camera and equipment at her feet and looked expectantly at Paul, eyebrows arched.

"And what," Paul asked, "do *you* want?"

"A Beck's would be very, very nice."

Paul came over and kissed her nose. "Be right back."

After getting her beer and sitting back, Marni perused the movie listings. She was an avid filmgoer and saw everything in town, with or without Paul. She always insisted on the biggest bucket of popcorn available and didn't seem to mind the vegetable-oil topping they called "butter flavor." She often added a huge candy bar and washed it all down with a giant Coke. Paul was lucky to get a few handfuls of popcorn and a bite of chocolate. He marveled at the sight of Marni, naked, a snack-devouring woman with an impossibly tight belly and the clearest skin in town. She never gained weight or got zits.

"Let's see how many movies we can see this weekend," Marni was saying. "I'm in the mood for a binge."

Just then the phone rang. Paul picked it up. "Hello?"

"I hate to ruin your weekend," Bud Steeves said, "but I'm having trouble adjusting the seat on this stationary bicycle and Doris says she's too arthritic to do it for me. I can't exercise otherwise."

"Gee, Dad, I guess you'll have to vegetate and atrophy till I swing by there...whenever that is. Bye."

Marni didn't have family members who imposed on her. She came from British Columbia, and she flew up there as often or seldom as she pleased. She had never invited Paul to see the apartment she shared with another woman and she mildly resented it whenever he asked her detailed questions about her life and how she spent her days. He had seen many samples of her photography; she was very talented. She could have a more lucrative career if she desired one, but Paul suspected she had a talent for all things but only a limited interest; photography now, something else later. To her, life was about variety, not drudgery.

She didn't ask many questions about Paul, either. Restless and garrulous one evening, he told her, in mind-numbing detail, all about his business career. She grasped the ins and outs of Amazement and Cherry as quickly as Paul explained them. She asked him why Bayliss had been reluctant to stand in the way of progress, and she recommended that he marry Bayliss' weird daughter Suzi if he wanted more, more, more—which quite obviously he did.

Paul felt intimidated. This beautiful young woman understood so much. Marni was agnostic; God was a what, rather than a who, and all conventional religions were ludicrous. She had many friends but did not wish for Paul to meet them; she met his friends and considered them acquaintances. Josh Hawkins? More show than substance, little more than a fast, able promoter, a bullshit artist.

"Josh is a misogynist," she said. "So are you." She frowned when Paul said, "I love you."

"But I *do* love you." Paul gently squeezed Marni's plump breast as they lay in bed one evening. They had just ended a movie marathon. After a couple of buckets of popcorn, a quart of Coke apiece and a couple of family-size Kit Kats, Marni still wanted Italian food.

Back at Paul's apartment, the San Francisco winds and fog had started up and they were both cold. He made them Irish coffees. Tipsy, they made love, slowly and deliberately.

"This is what I live for," Marni said. "Weekend afternoons of movies, popcorn, rich food, booze and sex."

"You could do worse." Paul smiled, thinking back to his years of celibacy and wondered if those years without sex were good or bad. His technique wasn't great—Marni nearly usually took charge—but his desire was enormous. She sometimes blushed at her lover's ardor. "You're the horniest man I've ever met," she said once.

"Marry me," Paul said.

Marni giggled.

Whenever the subject of love or commitment came up, she treated it with levity. Is she mocking me? Paul wondered. I am being jealous, he thought. I hate being jealous. Jealousy is for fools.

He got up and dressed as well. Marni had some music on. The singers sang "I love you" as smoothly and unconvincingly as a secretly homosexual leading man speaking those words as he gazed into his leading lady's eyes.

"Let's drink," Marni said. "Your hair's a mess. Keep it that way—it makes you look human. When you're all and dressed, you look too much like Josh Hawkins."

"Why are you picking on him?"

She ignored him. "I'm not movied-out yet. The one I want to see isn't far away—"

"If I go near one more popcorn bucket, I'll puke. Now, about what I said in the bedroom..."

"You want to marry me. I don't believe in marriage. Ask me something else."

"Then move in with me, dammit!"

Marni said nothing. Her hair was a bit messy, too, and she was only half dressed. Her bra was clearly visible from inside her half-buttoned blouse. Usually she looked, to Paul at least, feline and adult and even indestructible, with her lithe body and brisk gait. She looked young now, however, naïve and afraid of commitment. Paul knew that back in the bedroom, when he had said, "I love you," he had simply been telling the unavoidable truth.

"If you don't move in with me and stay with me forever," he now told his lover with a sigh, "it will destroy me."

Marni threw back her head and laughed. "God! Paul Steeves, creator of an empire, entrepreneur of the decade, will be 'destroyed' by this Canadian chick if she doesn't move in with him!" After a moment she looked at him. "Do you really expect me to believe that?"

"Sounded good when I said it."

They both laughed, and Marni said, "Spoken like a true executive."

"But I want an answer," he said.

"I'll give you one next week."

"Why not now?"

"Because I have been doing things you don't know about," she said.

"Such as?"

"I have a boyfriend. I don't know if I want to give him up just yet."

"You've all kinds of secrets, huh? Wonder what else you've hidden away I'll be shocked to discover."

Marni grinned. "Well, that's the major one: I've been screwing someone when I haven't been with you."

"That's a hell of a revelation, at any rate. Has he been to your place, met your friends, your parents...?"

She sighed. "You know, Paul, one of the things I've liked about you from the start is that you're so involved in your own life that you don't waste your time prying into *mine*. If you're going to turn into a jealous partner with questions all the time, let's just shake hands and say goodbye."

Paul said nothing.

"Well, it was nice seeing you again," Marni said, reaching for her coat. "Guess we've had our movies for the weekend, eh? Think about what I just said. If you can live with it, call me."

"Put your coat down. You win. It's movie night."

Driving across the Golden Gate Bridge under a gray sky, Paul thought not about Caitlin, whom he would see in a matter of minutes, but about Marni. The movie had been boring, they had done without popcorn, they had gone to a nearby restaurant and scarfed down unwanted meals and desserts, and they downed cocktails that made them feel sullen. They said little to each other, and if he hadn't known better, Paul would have sworn they'd just had a spat.

At the end of the evening he'd wanted to put Marni into a taxi but she would have none of it; and Paul just chuckled, watching her bound through the cool, gray streets of downtown San Francisco, an athletic-looking young woman who feared nothing and no one.

He went back to his apartment alone. Marni seemed to have taken all its charm with her. Paul went to bed and fell asleep at once and awoke to a gray, drizzly day that suited his mood perfectly.

He had called Heavenly Valley Girls' School and asked them to tell Caitlin he would be there to take her to lunch, and he showed up right on time. Dee said that the school, in good weather, was a place of stunning beauty, which was probably what attracted so many students and parents; but in dreary weather like today's, Paul thought, it looked gloomy and forbidding.

He pulled into the parking lot and puzzled over where in this expanse of buildings and green lawns he would find his niece. Then he heard young female voices loudly singing a hymn of some sort.

Paul frowned. Making the kids read and sing about the deity that they couldn't see, couldn't hear, couldn't touch, read all about Him in the book full of inconsistencies. At least back in Western Hills High, all he had to do was put his hand over his heart and face Old Glory and mouth the words, "I pledge allegiance..." or however it went.

Up drove a Cadillac, shiny black, much like the one Grandinetti had driven so many years earlier. From it emerged a man, trim and gray, jaunty, beautifully attired. Paid big bucks to send his little girl here. Wealthy school, wealthy state, wealthy country. Future wives of America's future elite. Bless their pampered little hearts. Paul's new Ford suddenly didn't look so good, next to this man's Caddy.

The man got out, leaving a woman in the passenger's side. Doing a parent's duty, here to see the daughter who, in an hour or so, will be itching to see Mommy and Daddy wave goodbye. From his car and clothes and walk, he was surely the CEO or something close to the top, a gentleman to his clients and a son of a bitch to everyone else.

"Excuse me," Paul asked, "where is Anthony Hall?"

The man smiled politely. A business smile, prim and gleaming white. He gave directions, after a brief hesitation. He hadn't visited his daughter enough times to know its location by heart.

The man paused. They could hear singing, a different hymn. "Good. Worship. Keeps the soul strong against the influence of those atheists, agnostics and communists."

Paul thanked the man and drove over to Anthony Hall, reading the plaque about Susan B. Anthony and her contribution to American society. When he opened the door he found a little boy scampering around in the common room. A little boy in a girls' school was not what Paul was given to expect. But just then a door opened and a lithe, suntanned woman came in and smiled at him. The woman had dark blonde hair hanging loosely about her shoulders and had a sort of fashionably slovenly appearance—jeans, sandals and a white shirt.

"Hi," she said. "Are you a dad?"

"No, an uncle. I've come to see Caitlin Wilhite."

The woman's face darkened. "Caitlin." She gave a small nod. Paul got the impression they had spoken about his niece a few times already. "We've been expecting you...or someone. Please come in. I'm the housemistress."

Paul now understood the presence of the little boy and the scattered toys. Whatever was going on with Caitlin wasn't due to neglect at the hands of this fresh-faced Earth Mother housemistress.

"The girls are at chapel. They will be back at any moment. My husband will be there too."

Paul sat and sighed. Why he was here? Dee had sent him. If there's a problem, just get good ol' Paul on it. But what could he do? This woman probably knew Caitlin far better than he did, and Paul didn't know what to say to the girl. Was she clinically depressed or just lonely and homesick?

"Caitlin is quite an attractive girl," the housemistress was saying. "Minds herself quite well, you know. Some of these girls...well, they're spoiled rotten and think they can get away with murder."

"Her mom is concerned about her."

"Yes," the woman said.

"Caitlin and her mother had their weekly phone talk and her mother thought she sounded really down, so she asked me to come up and have a talk with her. Maybe I can see what's going on and what can be done to help. Caitlin's mother lives down in Los Angeles. And her mother divorced and remarried."

"Well, times are changing," said the woman, "even around these conservative places where change is resisted." She laughed a bit. "Divorce and remarriage are facts of life."

"Caitlin's stepfather died not long ago." Murdered. Police can't find the killer, assuming they're trying.

The woman put her hand to her cheek. "Oh, that's awful. Maybe she's having some bereavement issues...?"

"Has she spoken about it at all?"

"Not to me. My husband will be back soon. Maybe he'll be more helpful."

Paul sat back and thought for a moment. "Is she having trouble academically? Is she being persecuted by the other students at all, that you know of?"

The woman shook her head emphatically. "Oh, no. She has no problems academically. And she certainly would not be any sort of target for bullying, if that's what you mean." She laughed. "She's nearly as tall as you. She's half a head above most of the other girls, physically. It's strange. Caitlin doesn't try to relate to anyone and scowls if anyone tries to get into an exchange with her. She has no interest in anyone here. Absolutely puzzling. Her roommate finds her frightening, frankly."

Paul raised an eyebrow. "Has Caitlin *been* a bully?"

"Oh, hardly. No. Just detached and withdrawn. No friends, no socializing. Just studies and stays quiet. She's quite formidable physically and we really emphasize health and physical fitness here. She could be quite a standout athlete, but she chooses not to participate. She doesn't participate in anything extracurricular, ever." Paul couldn't tell if the woman was troubled or fascinated.

"I'm hardly a psychiatrist, but I would guess her problem is depression of some sort. Maybe repressed guilt over something like her stepfather's death. Anxiety, too. My husband might know more."

They heard the chapel bells ring outside and Paul saw the first girls emerge and walk across the lawn. "If you don't mind," Paul said, "I'll wait for her in her room."

The woman told him the room number and Paul thanked her, thinking that maybe he would get some idea of who Caitlin was today visiting with her in her room. The housemistress seemed like a very caring woman. Paul certainly could not remember such an empathic person back at Western Hills High School. Jackson Worthy had insisted that Caitlin attend a private school, and Paul respected him for that.

When he reached Caitlin's floor he saw that all the doors were wide open, as he supposed they always were. At Caitlin's room he had little trouble figuring out which side was hers and which belonged to her roommate. On one side the bed was carelessly made, movie posters and whatnot papered the walls and a few articles of clothing sat balled up on the floor.

On the other side the bed was so perfectly made that any drill sergeant could bounce a quarter off of it. There were no posters of magazine clippings on the walls, and in fact no indication that whoever occupied the bed had any plans to stay there more than fifteen more minutes.

The paperback book sitting on the bed surprised him. A *Critique of Pure Reason* by Immanuel Kant. Why would a fourteen-year-old girl want to read something like that? No wonder she's depressed, he thought. Well, Caitlin obviously isn't making herself at home here, so maybe here isn't where she belongs. But I'll let her make that decision.

Paul didn't want to wait around and meet the girl who found his niece frightening, so he decided to wait for Caitlin downstairs, outside. The sun had broken through and the campus now looked colorful and homey. The girls, all dressed in red, white and blue, strode merrily across the grass. They smiled and bounced along the way rich happy eager kids often do. The haves, blissfully oblivious of the have-nots throughout the world.

He spotted Caitlin, blonde hair tumbling down, breasts already prominent, a mobile red slash of a mouth, everywhere on her face the looks of her father. Ladies and gentlemen, presenting Miss Tommy Wilhite Junior. Well, kiddo, Paul thought, at least you're taller than they are. If they piss you off, just beat the shit out of them.

"Hi, Paul," Caitlin murmured, casually shaking the man's hand. "Thanks for coming by. But you didn't have to."

Hi, Paul. Whatever happened to Uncle Paul?

"I have to be up here in Marin anyway to meet with the old guy Bayliss, so I thought I would drop by. We can have lunch now, right? I'm famished."

Caitlin nodded. "Actually, there is a pretty good place not far away I would love to go to now. Claudio's?"

Paul nodded that he knew the place.

"My father took me to Claudio's when he was up here last," Caitlin was saying.

"Oh? And when was that?"

"Well over a month ago. He was supposed to come up again, but he has this new job and he says they're running him ragged."

"So, let's go. Do you have to tell anyone here that you're leaving town for a couple of hours? Get anyone's permission?"

"No. It's none of their business, anyway."

Paul couldn't help but notice that as all those other girls walked past them, none of them acknowledged Caitlin in any way and she utterly ignored them. So this is how it is, Paul thought. She really is an outcast. My sister wasn't exaggerating.

They got into Paul's car and drove off, through the carefully paved road, past the beautifully maintained grounds and majestic buildings under the partly sunny sky. Driving away from the Heavenly Valley School of Marin County, offering all the scenic beauty and Tender Loving Care that money could buy for America's queens of tomorrow. Beside him sat Caitlin Wilhite, fourteen, sullen and withdrawn, Heavenly's only dissatisfied customer. Paul sighed and gave thanks that he was no longer a teenager.

"My father," Caitlin was saying between huge bites of steaming, fragrant spaghetti. "He couldn't make it up to see me because he had a hangover. He always does. He's such a hopeless lush."

"That's not a very nice to say." Paul was surprised by her appraisal of Tommy and her refusal to call him Dad.

If Caitlin was too alienated to make friends and play sports, she was quite willing to eat. She had ordered a platter of spaghetti slathered in meatsauce and an entire pitcher of iced tea to split between the two of them, although Paul was sipping his first glass and Caitlin was slurping down her third. Claudio's was a place for eating, with its red-checkered tablecloths and efficient waiters and open-air kitchen where diners could see their meals being prepared.

Paul wondered how he would like being a parent, if it ever happened, and whether he would want a son or a daughter. Probably at least one of each. Would his child at fourteen be withdrawn and aloof and alienated like Caitlin, or a happy, exuberant girl like the ones at Heavenly? And could Marni and he have a child? He really didn't know Marni's true financial situation, just as he did not know all that much about her in general, but Paul had more money than he could spend, and they could offer their children every possible advantage. But those questions didn't need to be answered over lunch at Claudio's.

"How's your food?" he said finally as Caitlin silently devoured the pasta.

"Yummy." Then, "I don't like them at all. They brag about how their deb parties cost tens of thousands of dollars, how they travel all over the world and have fathers who run everything under the sun."

"And how do you deal with them?"

"I ignore them. What can I tell them? That my parents are divorced and my father's a drunk who will probably be fired again before the month is out?"

"What about your stepfather? Is he an issue?"

"Jackson? He's dead. At Heavenly, if they knew of him at all, probably thought he was just some big troublemaking nigger. I don't have anyone I can relate to. The Heavenly girls are just too elitist for me."

"Then what's the problem? Why are you so unhappy?"

The girl put down her fork and looked at him. "I hate Heavenly. I'll go crazy there if I have to stay."

Paul leaned forward and fixed the girl with an intense stare. "Caitlin, I need to know what's going on."

"That place is everything I hate. Jackson said American public education was a joke. Let his white stepdaughter grow up with her own kind and become a nice white lady."

"Do you think so?" her uncle asked.

She rolled her eyeballs. "I know so. They make us sit through church service to thank God for making them superior. 'Don't say what you think or act on any of your instincts or you'll burn in Hell.' Nice, huh?"

Paul grinned. "Charming."

"Jackson died flat broke, you know. So when Heavenly wants its tuition, will the Almighty write a check?"

Paul waved this off. "Oh, I can take care of that."

"Do you hate me that much?"

Paul sighed. "Just trying to help."

"You should have gone to Heavenly, Paul. Send your daughter there, if you have one. She'll like it."

He said nothing.

"Why am I in that stuck-up private school? My stepfather, a great man who championed social reform, has been murdered and my mom is still down in Los Angeles trying to cope with his murder and I'm at Heavenly, trying to pretend nothing is wrong."

For the first time, in their conversation and in their relationship, such as it was, Paul saw her niece's composure break. The girl's eyes were moist with grief and her face taut. "I don't know why you came here, but I'm going to tell you what: I am not going back to Heavenly. I am going back home, where my mother needs me and I need her." Tears streamed down her face as she spoke. "I'm sick of those snobbish girls and those teachers who baby them. I hate them all. I won't go back."

"Don't go back," Paul said, his voice soft. "Finish your spaghetti."

Caitlin shook her head and wiped her mouth with her thick white Claudio's napkin. "I'm not hungry and my food is cold. Let's just go back up to Heavenly so I can get my stuff and tell them I'm not coming back."

"OK."

They got back into Paul's car and headed across the wilderness till they reached the campus. "Do what you need to and we'll meet up again in the car," Paul said. Caitlin got out and disappeared, still in her red-white-and-blue Heavenly uniform.

Paul spent a few moments watching the girls walking around the grounds, smiling and carefree, enjoying the sunny, warm day.

He went into the Common Room and found more girls lounging around, reading magazines, playing checkers, listening to the radio. They made way for Paul, the older man. They were all pretty young women, or at least attractive, all well groomed and slim. America's young lovelies, set to marry America's young lions in the years ahead. Paul thought again of the daughter he had never had, someone who would love it here and be at home in this company. He knew that Caitlin was right: this was his sort of place, not hers. Well, was there anything wrong with fitting in and getting along?

He rang the bell and the old guy answered. He was tall and broad, wizened, with a faint sense of frustration about him. Paul could see such frustration in a middle-aged man, trying to cope with the endless problems of young women.

"Are you Mr. Hunnicutt?" Paul asked.

"Yes."

"I'm Paul Steeves, Caitlin's niece."

"Come in." The man's smile had relief all over it.

Paul held up his hand. "Thanks, but I've just dropped by to tell you that my niece won't be coming back to Heavenly."

"Not coming back? For how long?"

"Permanently."

"That's a shame."

Paul nodded. "Yes. But she'll be better off back home."

"It's as bad as all that, is it?"

"Worse."

"Shouldn't you speak to the headmaster about this before you take her away forever?"

Paul shook his head. "Wouldn't do any good. Would you mind notifying him of our decision?"

"I suppose I could."

Paul, eager to be away from here now that his business was done, smiled and stuck out his hand. "Thanks very much. I appreciate your help."

On the drive down to South Bay, Paul tried to think of the best way to handle the situation. Caitlin, sated by her good lunch and relieved by her permanent exit from Heavenly, nodded off immediately in the car. Paul drove slowly and deliberately down the highway, wanting to delay the inevitable meeting between his father and Caitlin. His evening was hardly over, and he grinned at the busy nature of the day: the drive from his apartment to Heavenly...the drive back to South Bay so Caitlin could stay for a few days before going back to Los Angeles...then back up to Marin County to learn about the bug that had crawled up Fred Bayliss' ass. Then he would go back, finally, to his San Francisco apartment for the night, to get away from all of them.

Driving through downtown San Francisco with Caitlin asleep in the passenger's seat, he made note of all of the city's luxury hotels—the Fairmont, Mark Hopkins, Clift, Huntington, St. Jeremy, Pan-American—and felt very tempted to deposit his niece in one at least for a few days. As pleasing as Caitlin might find the opulence of a deluxe suite with a magnificent view, a cold, lonely hotel room was not the last place for her after her experience at Heavenly. The girl needed a home for the time being, period. And putting her up in his San Francisco apartment, his love nest with Marni, with all their pictures together of cuddling and gazing at each other and the fragrant fog of their lovemaking apparent even to the tiredest nose...well, Caitlin didn't need to know about *that*.

He kept on driving and soon was minutes away from his big, fine South Bay home. What would his father say in the girl's presence upon their first meeting? "Whore's brat" was not beneath Bud Steeves. Paul knew he would just have to steal some courage and face the old guy, remind him of who was boss.

Fortunately, when they arrived at the mansion and he led Caitlin into the place, Bud wasn't in the living room, and certainly wouldn't be in the kitchen, and so he was definitely in his bedroom. That was a good place for him, Paul often thought. The confrontation wouldn't happen yet.

In the kitchen, Doris sat reading a magazine, and the room was filled with something delicious cooking. Doris was middle-aged, restless and convinced that she knew everything and everyone else knew absolutely nothing. But she was a fine cook and kept the place tidy. Paul and she generally stayed out of each other's way.

"Doris," he said, "this is my niece, Caitlin. She's going to be staying here for a few days. She wants to take a shower, have something to eat. She'll stay in the guest room. I'd appreciate it if you'd look after her. I have to run back up to Marin County in about two minutes..."

"The old man didn't tell me about her," Doris replied. She despised Bud; she seemed to need people in life to hate.

Paul grinned. "Well, the old man didn't know. I don't tell him everything."

"I made enough for you and him to eat. If you're leaving for the evening, the girl will get yours."

Paul nodded. "Fair enough."

Caitlin stood alongside Paul, shooting him an anxious glance.

"Okay, young lady, let's get you settled in the guest room," Doris said, her voice full of its usual weary resignation.

"Thanks, Doris," Paul said as the two left the room. Needing a drink, he went into the refrigerator and helped himself to one of his father's beers, which he sipped in the living room. The room, like the rest of the house, was modern and new, a pleasing contrast to the old-fashioned, musty places in San Francisco. He had even had the house filled with new, stylish furniture: leather chairs, globular lamps, Danish tables. His father complained that the place "lacked character." A fat lot you know about character, Paul thought. He drank his beer slowly, wanting to procrastinate as long as possible on his next task, which awaited him upstairs. Minutes later, however, he hoisted himself up from the chair and traipsed up the stairs till he reached his father's closed door.

"Dad? Mind if I come in?"

"You'll come in anyway," came the reply.

Paul opened the door and found his father in his navy-blue track suit, exercising on his stationary bicycle, which had recently been repaired. His face was bathed in a light sweat.

ENTREPRENEUR

Modern medicine had given Bud Steeves a new life. When they had Bud's Good Eats and lived in the apartment above the deli, he refused to have the treatment he quite obviously needed. "Can't afford it," he snapped whenever the subject came up. But in the years since, Bud read the newspaper writeups of Paul's business triumphs, saw the fine new car and moved into the big new house. Then he allowed Paul to take him to the specialists, who put him in the hospital and fixed him up: phlebitis, cataracts, minor orthopedic procedures. Paul assured his father that these doctors all had gone to the best schools and charge dteh highest fees.

Bud had emerged from all this as a new man. Money, not doctors, had cured him. With his sight restored, he could now drive again, and Paul bought him his own Lincoln Town Car. Bud joined the San Francisco Men's Club, a social organization that would have laughed at him when he owned Bud's Good Eats but now admitted him happily as the father of Cherry Computer co-founder Paul Steeves, and around the club he was treated a something of a celebrity; was his handsome entrepreneurial son still unmarried? Would Paul like to meet a nice young woman—the daughter or niece of another member...?

Steeves, after visiting the men's club, sometimes went over to Brooks Brothers and bought piles of clothes which mostly hung in his closet. He had fine clothes but mismatched them horribly: browns and blacks together, vertical and horizontal stripes, socks that never matched shoes. But he seemed happy enough, and certainly more vital than he had been in years. Paul largely left him alone.

"Who's in the house?" he demanded. "I heard noises."

"Your granddaughter," Paul said. "Take a shower, get yourself spruced up and come meet her like a gentleman."

"No."

"Caitlin is here now and she's going to stay till I say otherwise. And we're all going to be helpful and supportive of her. Understand?"

"What will the boys at the club think?"

Paul laughed. "Well, they probably won't know unless you tell them."

Steeves thought for a moment and shook his head. "I won't permit it. I'll get a hotel till the kid leaves."

"If you do that, you better get one with yearly rates, because I won't have you back in here ever again." Paul looked at his watch. "I don't have time for this nonsense with you. Bayliss expects me back up in Marin."

He shut the door as his father pedaled and pouted.

Paul went down to the living room and called Dee to explain the situation and assure Dee that their father was being cooperative. "What now?"

"Put Caitlin on a plane down here whenever you can. Thanks, Paul."

"Hey," he said, "what are brothers for?"

Paul knew something was up when Bayliss personally answered the door. No servants in sight. Just you and me, kid. Bayliss dressed much like Paul's father: expensively but without taste or style. His home was like Lido Grandinetti's: big and grand, beautiful as a museum. Please don't touch anything, and do take off your shoes.

"Glad you could make it," Bayliss said.

"Yessir. I think I'm a little late."

"But you're here. Come." Bayliss led the way, a rich old man who looked and acted the part. Taken out of the game, no longer the boss. An unlikely pair, walking into the library:

the short, fattish old man who had sold his soul, and the tall, skinny young man who bought it.

"Have a seat, Paul," he said when they were in the library.

"Yessir."

Bayliss paced a bit in front of Paul, who knew instantly that this was a big deal, and not a good deal. Something was really troubling the old man.

"I wanted you to come over to discuss a personal matter, Paul. My wife and Suzi are out for the evening, gone their separate ways towards their own amusements. We will have no interruptions."

Paul nodded. Good God. Was he dying of cancer? Was he going to try to have Paul booted out of the company? Get to it, old man.

"Paul," he said finally, "I am deeply disappointed."

"Why?" Couldn't be professional. Cherry was doing great. Had to be something else. His stomach burned with dread.

"As an executive, you have the highest standards, and I respect that enormously. I am just disappointed that your private standards falter. In business, you have always come to me with matters that involved me. But in your personal life, you have lately taken the low road."

"In what way," Paul asked, leaning forward, "have our *personal* lives crossed?"

Bayliss looked down at her, stony. "I am talking about your relationship with Suzi. My daughter."

"What?"

"Don't play stupid or shocked, Paul. You've been stringing her along, treating her like a plaything." Bayliss' face tensed, like a courtroom lawyer grilling a witness.

"Mr. Bayliss, this is bullshit!"

"The hell it is. She talks to us. We know what's going on. She is deeply in love with you. She wants to move down to San Francisco, to get a job and be closer to you."

Paul burst out laughing. "Oh, Christ—"

"I beg your pardon?" The Baylisses were deeply religious.

"I'm terribly sorry. But Suzi and I have absolutely, positively no relationship of any kind, unless you call conversation more than just talk."

"She sits up there in her bedroom and strums her guitar. She sings songs about you. She draws sketches of you. You are about the only thing on her mind, day and night."

Paul pictured Suzi up there in her bedroom, strumming and singing. She had sung and played when Paul came over once a month for dinner, and he had to admit that she had some musical talent. What she needed was to get away from Mom and Dad, pay her dues and become her own woman.

"So," Bayliss was saying, "we have an issue here. How will we resolve it?"

Paul sat back. "You tell me, Mr. Bayliss."

He knew that if he and Bayliss had a dispute over some colossal matter that no arrangement could fix, Bayliss could conceivably make trouble for Paul. Engineer his ouster from the company, or at least strip him of his prized authority. The matter creating all the tension would have to be personal, since in business Paul was flexible and crafty, always ready to placate Bayliss and make him think he was getting his own way.

That selfish, weird, spoiled brat Suzi Bayliss!

Bayliss said what Paul expected to hear. "Marry her, Paul. Don't be a fool. Do this for me and, when I die...You think you're rich now? You'll have all *my* assets, too. If Cherry Computer becomes the enduring phenomenon you've predicted, you will be one of the world's richest men." He now spoke softly, conspiratorially. "If I may speak very, very candidly, you're a nice-looking man, but you're not getting any younger and you're still unmarried. It might be better for everyone involved if you tied the knot fairly quickly."

"Well," Paul resented some of what he'd just heard. "This aging bachelor is not going to become Mr. Suzi Bayliss anytime soon. Really, I had no idea about her..."

"Oh, come on." Bayliss waved his hand. "The way she moons over you when you come for dinner? Hangs on your every word? And you, a business professional, are one of the smartest, shrewdest people I've met. Can't you even see the advantages, the practical financial benefits in marrying her?"

Paul arched his eyebrows. He wasn't having any of that crap. "Mr. Bayliss, let's wait here till she gets home and I can ask her, right to her face, just when and where and how I have led her on. If she says I have, I will call her a liar and walk out the door. You can keep your Cherry shares and marry your girl off to a nice, store-bought little prince with dollar signs in his eyes." Then, "If you want the God's honest truth, I am deeply in love with someone else and we're making plans together."

"Someone else?" Bayliss looked puzzled. "Anyone I've met?"

Paul nodded. "You met her at the grand opening of the Cherry factory. The photographer. Black hair. Big blue eyes. Funny accent."

Bayliss thought for a moment. "Marie?"

"Marni."

Bayliss poured himself a stiff drink, then another one.

"I try to keep an open mind about things, Paul. I didn't know that about you, but I should have guessed. You're entitled to your own happiness, I suppose. I don't know what it is with Suzi. She has no friends, she has no great interests besides you, and if she doesn't get her own way she throws a temper tantrum. My wife thinks we've spoiled her, expected nothing and let her become a lazy bum who thinks our money will get her whatever she wants. I honestly thought I could buy you as a husband for her, Paul. Please go now so I can figure out where to go from here."

They stood up and walked to the door together.

"Mr. Bayliss, for what it's worth, I know exactly what Suzi needs."

"What's that?" Bayliss asked wearily.

"To go to San Francisco and try her luck with music and have some independence."

"Thanks for sharing," Bayliss muttered as Paul walked out the door.

When he drove back to South Bay, Paul looked forward to telling Caitlin that she would be moving back in with her mother in Los Angeles soon. That might make the girl's stay with him a little easier. And it would certainly make Paul's life easier, not having to keep some distance between the troubled girl and the cranky old man who lived there.

Paul slipped the key into the lock and felt exhausted as he walked slowly through the hallway. He could definitely hear his father's voice in the kitchen, but it seemed odd, somehow; subdued and quiet.

He reached the doorway, still out of sight, and stopped to listen for a moment.

"If there's one thing I can't stand, it's a young lady who's got no meat on her," Bud Steeves said, his voice as honeyed as any radio announcer's. "It's unhealthy. I'm glad to see you've got sense enough to eat a healthy meal. That's why you're so nice and tall."

The girl just giggled.

Well, as I live and breathe, Paul thought.

"Another thing we value in this house are good manners. I'm glad to see you've got them. My son Paul has wonderful manners, too. And he's tall, like you. Guess you got your height from my side of the family."

"Actually, my dad's tall, too. Everyone says I look like him." Caitlin giggled again.

"Is that so? Well, I've never even met the man. Haven't seen your mom in the longest time, either. Maybe she's mad at us for something. Sad to say, sometimes those things happen in families."

Paul walked in. Caitlin was at the near end of the table, Steeves at the far end, just far enough to give the girl her space. Caitlin was bathed and seated, with a blue terrycloth robe, her hair a sparkling, shampooed golden blonde, smiling as she forked food into her mouth. Doris, standing at the stove, looked less exasperated than usual. Paul's father was nattily attired in a well-matched burgundy slacks, beige shirt and dark-brown cardigan.

"Is everything to your satisfaction?" Paul asked the girl. "Are they being nice to you?"

"The food is yummy," said Caitlin, apparently now completely over the trauma of her bad experience at Heavenly and her emotional lunch with Uncle Paul.

"I hope you like cheesecake," Doris said. "That's dessert."

"My fave," said Caitlin.

"Paul, don't you want something to eat?" Steeves asked.

"No, thanks, not hungry." He felt completely worn out, in no mood for food, talk or anything else.

"Well, time for this old man to retire." Steeves got up and walked past his granddaughter.

"Got a kiss for the old man?"

"Yes, sir," said the young girl.

"Grandpa," he said.

She chuckled, pecking him on the cheek. "Grandpa."

He smiled and walked past Paul, shooting him a snarl that said, And you didn't think I had it in me to be a gentleman!

Chapter 4

Dee read a book on grieving and overcoming the sudden death of a husband. The book instructed her to make herself some promises. She wrote them down on index cards and read them to herself every morning. Here is what she wrote:

I will never look outside after dark at the spectacle of Los Angeles at night that inspired Jackson so much. That was his thing, not mine.

I will not wear black. I will not advertise to the world that I am mourning my husband.

I will not spill my guts in reply to those who send sympathy cards with notes about how extraordinary and irreplaceable my husband was. I will send them notes thanking them for concern, but that is all.

I will not get emotional and fall apart in front of Caitlin.

I will politely refuse social invitations from Jackson's friends who pity me for my tragedy and who think they are doing me a favor by keeping me company.

When an issue comes up where I would have called out, "Jackson, what should I do?" I will deal with it myself. Jackson is no longer here.

I will not call Jackson's editors in New York City and dictate to them how to put the finishing touches on his final book.

ENTREPRENEUR

I will stay completely private about Jackson's death. I will not go public about any aspect of him, even if well-meaning people suggest I make a career of sorts out of being "the man's widow."

I will forget Jackson's birthday, our wedding anniversary, our first lovemaking session and all other dates and occasions I swore I would never forget. I will forgive myself for remembering them after promising myself I would forget them.

I will refuse to participate in any event honoring Jackson Worthy—famous writers reading his books, famous recording artists singing his praises—and, if asked, will not comment.

I will, when seeing planes fly overhead or Oldsmobiles drive by, try not to think of Jackson and our travels.

I will not drink or take pills anymore. I will get through this without drugs, period.

I will clear out Jackson's den and throw out all his unfinished work. The many people who have requested every scrap of these works-in-progress will not get them.

I will put only one small picture of Jackson in our living room and put the others in storage. I will try not to look at it every time I pass by it.

I will tell myself, at dinnertime, that I am grateful not to have to cook the awful soul food that Jackson craved and insisted on having twice a week.

I will be calm and even-handed with my daughter when she has her first boyfriends and gets dumped for the first time. I will give her lots of space and insist that she give me mine, even if I do not especially want it. Whenever she is invited to go out with friends, I will insist that she go, even if she wants to stay at home with me.

I will tell myself, as often as it takes to learn, that I am only her mother and that she must be with others her own age in order to grow. Let the child grow.

I will think about sex, and will forgive myself for doing so.

I will laugh at Tommy when he calls, drunk, telling me perhaps it was best that Jackson was killed because "interracial marriages don't work anyway" and maybe we should get back together for our daughter's sake...?

I will do all the things I usually did and will not avoid doing them just because many of them remind me of Jackson. I will be the best mother, not father, I can to my daughter. I will not cling to her, no matter how desperately I want to. I will be very reasonable when Caitlin asks me to let her go up to see "sweet old Grandpa" in South Bay, who has invited her for the upcoming summer.

I will not avoid anyone or anything, and will try to keep a full and busy life. More accurately, I will try to get a life. Is there a book that tells me how to do this?

Chapter 5

The wind and rain out at sea suited Jamey just fine. He had always liked the outdoors, period, and enjoyed the ups and downs of the ship as it plunged through the Pacific Ocean. When it was dark the vessel just seemed to go on and on through the vast darkness, and then miraculously end up somewhere.

The ship flew the Philippines flag, but they hadn't gone there yet, just to Guam. That man at the Commodore Hotel in Long Beach, Butch, had really come through for him: Jamey, getting off Greyhound after the six-hour ride through the Mojave Desert, went to the hotel and said only, "Wasserman sent me." Butch nodded and took care of the rest, even getting him clothes appropriate for his new life as a merchant seaman. Butch was a big, grizzled, middle-aged guy who sensed right away that this kid Steeves was in big trouble and that Wasserman was doing Jamey a favor. Butch offered to act as room service to Jamey, who gratefully accepted, knowing nobody in Long Beach and afraid that if he went outside there would be someone with a gun waiting for him. Butch had gotten Jamey onboard the *Joni Tavis*, which sailed to Guam, the P.I. and Hawaii.

The ship sailed at dawn. Butch personally drove him there and watched him board. Jamey thought that his new life wouldn't be half as much fun as his former one, but beggars couldn't be choosers.

The ship was ten thousand tons, built during World War Two. It had been all over the Pacific, a real wreck that no one cared enough about to maintain properly. The only thing that mattered was that it got from Long Beach to Honolulu to Guam and the P.I. and back again. The crew seemed to be guys liked Jamet: losers and throwaways unable to get better jobs. He paid little attention to them and the ship itself. He said little and made himself useful. He hadn't gotten drunk or laid in a while and felt better than he had in a long, long time.

He heard a voice behind him and turned around.

"Gonna be a sh-sh-shaky night, this one." It was Everett, a young black guy from the Bronx who stuttered when he got nervous.

Jamey said nothing. He did not even look at Everett, who paid him no mind anyway and went on talking, as always. "This storm better not be r-r-rough, 'cause the old tin can isn't getting younger and seas can easy break 'em in h-h-half, especially when we're this l-l-loaded. This your first time aboard?"

"No. Second."

"Well, bright side is it can only g-g-get better." Everett had signed on in San Diego. "Thing is, I got my third mate's papers, so I'm at the bottom on American ships I would be an old man before I got any higher, but here there's so much turnover that I can get ahead f-f-fast enough. You goin' for papers here, too?"

"Dunno." Jamey just stared out at sea, listening closely but pretending not to.

"Well, start thinking about it. When we get back I might even go for second mate's papers. A guy can make a career on these third-rate tubs, and a man without a career isn't much of a man. Know what I mean?"

ENTREPRENEUR

Jamey turned and looked at Everett. The two men were dressed about the same: pea jacket, navy-blue sweater. Everett wasn't a big man and in his clothes looked like a smooth-faced boy trying his hardest to look like a man. He had a cracking, adolescent voice and something desperate, pleading in his eyes. He looked like every black boy in Mississippi or Alabama the white cops loved harassing. Jamey wondered why such a young, earnest kid signed up for such an experience as this. Especially with that stutter; how could this motley crew on the high seas resist picking on him, and what could Everett do about it?

"If you're so ambitious and all," he asked Everett, "how come you can't do any better than this sorry bunch?"

"Because I've got flat feet," Everett said. "People think I'm retarded because I have this stutter. The American ships don't want me because I'm black. You can just tell when they meet me and see my face, all their enthusiasm is gone. Only way I can get ahead is by going to the only place that will have me." He looked closely at Jamey. "I figured you for the one guy here who doesn't hold things against me because I'm black and I stutter. So I like to come by and talk to you once in a while."

He turned around and left. Jamey returned to staring out at nothing at all. Mate's papers. A career on the high seas. Maybe Everett had the right idea. And Jamey didn't have race or stutter holding him back, just a death threat from some very dangerous people. Maybe I can have some respectable job as merchant marine brass. Jamey smiled for the first time in a while, resolving to ask Everett about getting the papers the next time they spoke.

They were in the middle of the South Pacific when the weather deteriorated further. Jamey and Everett were in the gun crew's quarters, although of course there were no longer any guns mounted on the ship. The two men were at the table, reading materials on navigation: sextant, star chart reading, all the things that were required knowledge for a career on the high seas. And that career was something Jamey increasingly sought. He pondered his future constantly, even in his dreams, seeing himself as a high-ranking officer on board one of these ships. He looked forward to this future because he looked at the slobs he worked with and saw them as proof that nothing but Jamey himself stood between this dirty, difficult life and a better one. He could graduate to a respectable life if he relied on Everett for help. He smiled as he contemplated the benefits of first mate's papers and then...who knew?

Everett had an amazing memory and seemed to have a basic understanding of the engine room. He had to explain engineering problems several times before Jamey understood them, but eventually Jamey caught on. Everett was from Mississippi and had spent little time around the water but had gone to the library and gobbled up whatever books he could find on ships. Jamey had a mechanical bent and gradually came around to follow what Everett was talking about.

Everett was careful not to inquire about Jamey's past and whatever events had led him to the *Joni Tavis*, and Jamey was relieved that Everett was minding his own business. Jamey, despite himself, was beginning to grow genuinely fond of the younger man.

"If we both get lucky," Everett said at the table after a session of maps and statistics, "we'll each have our own sh-sh-ship. That's how these things work; America gets into a war again of some kind—and it's gonna be before too long, 'cause there's always someone out there we gotta fight—the guys with the good jobs get killed and they need new guys, so they promote us. Who says war doesn't s-s-solve anything?"

They both chuckled and started poring over the charts again.

When they reached Honolulu, their plans changed a tiny bit. Jamey got an idea. It was around midnight and the *Joni Tavis* was due to lift anchor at about six; as long as they were back by then, there would be no problem. They ate dinner and walked around, and ended up in a bar where the music blared and the prostitutes efficiently hit on all the men. Jamey wouldn't have minded a roll in the hay, but this was Hawaii and the whores in the bar weren't up to his standards. He could wait till later. Jamey had some more to drink and got to feeling pleasantly light-headed, then the two left the bar and walked the short distance to the harbor where all the boats, including the *Joni Tavis*, were docked.

"I got an idea."

"W-w-what?"

"A great idea."

"T-tell..."

Jamey smirked. "Let's jump ship."

Everett's eyes grew wide with horror. "Uh, we can't *do* that, Jamey."

"Who says?"

"Simple common sense. We got jobs, you know. Serious problems if we b-b-bail out..."

"Bullshit." Jamey guffawed. He pointed at their ship, as ugly at night as in daylight. "That old tub goes from here to the P.I. and Guam, then back to here on its way. Right? We hop onboard again when it gets back here and tell them we went on a drunk and missed the boat and we're awful damn sorry. Think they'll forgive us? That boat is so shorthanded that they'll probably kiss us both hello when they see us again."

Everett frowned.

"Look, we rent a boat and you teach me what you know. And you know a lot, right?"

"I know it out of a b-b-book. Not the same thing."

"Close enough. I'm gonna stay here in Honolulu and sail on a boat. You're invited; if you say no"—he stuck his hand out for the other man to shake and offered him an icy smile—"it was nice knowin' ya."

Everett blew out a loud breath. "Damn, Jamey, you're making me put my whole f-f-future on the line. But, hell...if you're staying, I guess I am, too. Just hope you know what you're d-d-doing."

His stay in Hawaii wasn't as good as it could have been, mainly because he had Everett there and not some young Polynesian lovely, but it still beat spending his days and nights among a bunch of vulgarians and losers and eating crap three times a day.

They found a small, cheap hotel in downtown Honolulu and spent their days swimming and admiring the palm trees, the blazing blue of the sky and the brisk breezes, the Mai Tais and the mangoes and the pineapples. Most of all, he could get drunk as he pleased and not have to worry about dealing with that crabby Wasserman.

They rented a small sailboat and Jamey grinned like an idiot as Everett took over and sailed the craft about. The young man from Mississippi certainly did know how to handle himself on the water. Jamey made mental notes and helped in every way he could.

"Honolulu seems like a real popular place to sail," he said to Everett. "Every rich guy in the world probably comes by here at least a few times. All this wealth and we got none of it."

Jamey sometimes found life around Everett exhausting, mainly because the guy stuttered. He wandered into a Honolulu Radio Shack and bought a Walkman. He loved to sit under a palm tree and listen to whatever came over the airwaves; Everett took this as his cue to leave him in peace for a while. If Everett ever asked about what Jamey was listening to, his friend simply said, "Buy your own and tune in." Often as not, Everett contented himself with long swims in the ocean. On one afternoon Everett swam and Jamey listened to the radio. He tuned into a talk station where the guest was apparently a writer of some kind— or merely an entrepreneur who had gotten rich and written a book on his experiences. The guest owned a boat, a sixty-footer with five cabins. "It's not the newest of boats, the *Gwen*," he told the interviewer, "but I sail it all over the world. I'm the captain and I charter it. I sort of inherited the boat. The owner died and left it to me since I was the only one he knew who wasn't hitting him up for favors right and left. Of course, that's just pure luck, requiring no entrepreneurial shrewdness."

Jamey listened, watching the boats and yachts far off in the distance, wondering if one of those was the *Gwen*. "I have the perfect life. Don't have to break my back as a merchant seaman, just show my people a nice time. It's as much fun for me as it is for my clients."

The radio host seemed as interested in the topic as Jamey. "How much would it cost for someone today to live the way you do? How much would the boat cost?"

"Twenty thousand dollars, at least, for something decent. Depends on how badly the owner wants to be rid of it, of course. To do what I did, you'd have to buy a ship from around here, a military vessel, and you would have to do the refitting yourself rather than pay the crooks around here to do it for you."

That next morning, they boarded the *Joni Tavis* with heavy hearts. If they had boarded half an hour later and a few hundred feet further off, they would have seen Jamey's brother Paul with a pretty brunette and a backbreaking amount of brand-new designer luggage.

They headed straight to the waiting limousine that took them to the Waikiki Grand Hotel. Paul had made it clear that he wouldn't drive at all for two weeks or do much of anything else that wasn't fun and easy. After all, honeymoons were supposed to be fun and easy. The bellman showed them up to their ludicrously expensive penthouse suite, Paul gave him a lavish tip and took Marni out onto the balcony for a long sunlit kiss.

Paul and Marni had finally married, and it was a minor miracle. Their disagreements about having a wedding were difficult to resolve. Suzi Bayliss also complicated matters. Fred Bayliss urged her to move to San Francisco to pursue a career of some sort, but Paul swore her career choice was to be a lonely spoiled girl unable to control her obsession for a man obsessed with another woman. Paul spent as much time as possible at his Nob Hill apartment so he wouldn't be near Bud Steeves, but Suzi was always nearby, with a big smile and an excuse that she was just out "getting some fresh air." She called often and left messages on his machine; changing his number would have resolved nothing, for she could get his new one quickly enough. So he simply said hello to Suzi and asked about her father and wished her goodnight before disappearing up the steps. He was grateful that the young woman still lacked the nerve to solicit an invitation up to his suite.

Marni continued to keep her own schedule and not invite Paul to her place. When Paul told her about Suzi, she laughed. "Well, you're an attractive man. You should have admirers. Maybe give her a try, and if you're dissatisfied, come back to me." When they walked to Paul's from a nearby restaurant and saw Suzi just across the street, Marni said, "Oh, is that her? Let's invite him upstairs for a nice hot *menage a trois*. I've never been with another woman. Might be fun." Only when she saw the sweat break out on Paul's forehead did she say she was kidding.

Paul slept poorly and dreaded the drive down to South Bay each morning and evening. He was grateful that the company was doing so well and things were taking care of themselves, because he wasn't doing well in taking care of himself and his creative energies were drained.

"I curse the day," he told Marni, "that you came into my life and captivated my soul."

He called her again and again and again, with no answer. He thought: Her cell phone is turned on, but she isn't answering, maybe because she knows it's me and she's punishing me. I will try once more. If that Canuck bitch doesn't answer, I will go downstairs to see if Suzi Bayliss is there. I will bring Suzi up here and turn on my Camcorder and fuck her till my cock explodes, then upload the naughty little video on the Internet for all the world's perverts to watch.

Eventually Marni answered the phone.

"Where have you been?" Paul asked.

"Oh, you know. Here and there."

"Without your phone?" He didn't like how whiny and desperate he sounded.

"No, with it."

"Then why didn't you answer before now?"

"I had it on vibrator. I guess I didn't feel it. Or maybe I *did* feel it, and that's why I left it alone." She chuckled.

Don't mock me. "Well, let's meet. OK?"

"When?"

"Now," he said.

"Come over."

"Really?" He couldn't believe she would invite him over.

"Sure."

Paul went where he was told, to a charming Telegraph Hill apartment. Inside, he was met by the roommate, a brown-haired girl who said, "She's in her bedroom."

In the bedroom Marni was putting on her makeup. Paul didn't notice that, or much of anything else either. What he did notice was the blowup of him and Marni that was big enough to cover the entire wall over which it had been meticulously taped.

Paul said, "It looks like you've made your choice."

Marni peered into the mirror. "You're so perceptive."

They had dinner and talked about their future. They continued talking and got so mad at each other that they were both tempted to break up right then and there.

"I won't have a wedding," Marni said. "I don't believe in them."

"I want us to be official, to present ourselves to the world as a couple and make a commitment in front of our families forever."

Marni smiled. "How nice. Seriously, let's keep this a secret. That's what I say."

"I have a father and two siblings. What'll they think?"

"They'll probably think we're a couple of assholes. Besides which, I have a family of my own up in Canada and I came to the States to get away from them. We make a clean break from our families and go it alone—just us, our careers and our friends. What *are* families? Just people who put you on guilt trips that suck out all your emotional energy. Haven't you learned that by now?"

Paul found it hard to argue. Dee couldn't have herself a grand old time at such a wedding with Jackson in his grave only a few months, Jamey was missing and presumed dead, his father might get into a snit and boycott the ceremony at the last moment...But he had to tell Josh Hawkins, Fred Bayliss and Hank to stay on good terms with them, if he wanted to leave immediately with Marni.

"Go ahead," Marni said, "but just them, and make sure they don't tell anyone else."

Bayliss was deeply disappointed. "Away for a whole month? You work in is high-tech. A month is like a year. But I can see your mind is made up." He looked downcast. "Aw, Paul. If only you'd agreed to go along with my plan to marry Suzi." He sighed. "You're as greedy as I am. You could have had my mountain of Cherry stock in addition to your own holdings just by marrying Suzi. You could have kept going on the side with this photographer gal, if you had been discreet. Simple as that."

Paul laughed at the notion of marrying crazy Suzi Bayliss for her daddy's mountain of assets. Marrying and cohabitating with Suzi while carrying on discreetly with Marni. Simple as that, huh? Oh, yeah, Marni would have loved that.

Finally they decided to marry at City Hall and fly to Honolulu. Hank promised to call Bud Steeves once they were airborne and tell him the happy news.

Paul was relieved when they set out for San Francisco International Airport with only the bare necessities. Neither of them was what one might call a clothes-obsessed fashionplate. Paul, who for so long had worked so hard to save money, felt happy Marni was not a spendthrift. All of his wealth was in Cherry Computer stock; if things went bad quickly for the company and stayed that way for a while, he would be in a financially pinched position. American business was full of stories of people who had won and lost fortunes. He asked himself if Marni would still love him if he lost his wealth. He decided not to answer the question.

ENTREPRENEUR

Hawaii was wonderful. They stayed near the beach and under the sun. Although Paul got sunburned if he stayed out too long, Marni got a lovely all-over tan he envied. Their hotel was a deluxe establishment with every sort of amenity; Marni bought them tennis outfits and rackets and Paul taught her to play. Soon, she could hit the ball like a pro time and played to win, shaking her head in disgust whenever Paul couldn't return a serve or made some other error. Marni could dive into the hotel's vast swimming pool and glide underwater its entire length. They took surfing lessons and even their instructor was impressed by how quickly she caught on.

They played more and more tennis. Paul one day beat her by one brutally fought-for point. Marni got so enraged that she threw her racket at Paul, who ducked and laughed.

Against his bride's wishes, had brought along his Cherry laptop and checked his emails. He sent Fred Bayliss a message that they were having a wonderful time and hoped Bayliss was enjoying life too.

He visited Cherry's Website, then the IBM site. Cherry used the operating system that Hank had developed, and all the other computer makers used a different one. For the umpteenth time, Paul regretted having not entered into some sort of arrangement with Big Blue to use compatible operating systems. Maybe they would, someday. He still thought Cherry's was better—in fact, he knew it was. But his honeymoon wasn't for thinking about business. He shut off his laptop and put it aside.

They rented a car and spent a day cruising through Oahu. At one point they passed a gorgeous home with a vast front yard in one of the city's most exclusive neighborhoods.

"I'll buy you that," Paul said.

"Or *I'll* buy it for *you*," Marni retorted.

Paul cocked an eyebrow. "On a photographer's salary?"

"Well, that's just my hobby. My family owns a logging company in B.C. and their land is just filled with big fine trees the Americans want."

He asked her the name of the company and whistled at her reply.

"Yeah, I've heard of them. That's a big logging outfit."

"I could buy myself quite a position in Cherry Computer, if I wanted," Marni said. "But I'm not sure if it's that well managed. Must investigate the situation further."

Paul laughed and they drove quietly back to the hotel. When they arrived Marni took a shower and Paul covertly switched on his laptop to check his email.

"Come home immediately. Your father is very ill. Dr. doesn't know if he'll make it through the week." The message was from Hank.

He showed Marni the message. She picked up the room's phone. "I'll call the concierge and see if there's a plane out tonight."

Paul shook his head. "No, we'll wait till tomorrow. My father wouldn't dream of missing out on the satisfaction of having some final words to say to me. I don't think he's quite done yet with laying guilt trips on me."

Chapter 6

When he and Everett got back on board the *Joni Tavis* on its return trip to Long Beach, Jamey had a bad feeling about things. He knew there wouldn't be the same crew from the last trip. But what he didn't expect was Lofgren, a tall, burly bully with a head of thinning blond hair and a Fu Manchu mustache. An ex-con who'd been sent away for manslaughter, he expected to have things his own way and always got what he wanted. Jamey watched as he slapped faces and threw elbows randomly until greater force was needed, which he was more than happy to apply. If Lofgren wanted to sit at the table and there were others already there, he would simply have to walk up to them, scowl, and watch as the others gave him the entire table. If Lofgren wanted to eat at the table alone, the other men would sit on the floor or eat standing up. If they didn't like it, too bad. Speaking up about the matter could get a man beaten to a pulp.

Lofgren had pretty much avoided Jamey, though the bully was much bigger than Jamey or Mike Tyson or any other man Jamey had met. Still, there was an aura of street-guerrilla aggressiveness about Jamey that made Lofgren reluctant to hassle him, especially when there were so many other men who clearly feared the big Swede and who were therefore easy targets.

But once they were on the high seas and dinner was over and the men were sitting around playing cards, Jamey and Everett came in. Lofgren looked up and said to Everett, "Hey, b-b-boy, h-h-how you d-d-doin'?"

Jamey could see Everett practically shake with fear.

"Hey, fellas," Lofgren continued, "you know another word for cocoon? It's n-nigger."

There were gales of forced laughter, because if someone didn't laugh, Lofgren was apt to slap him. "Chocolate and vanilla are my favorite flavors," he said. "Had lots of vanilla, but it looks like I got a few days to sample me some chocolate."

Jamey took the one seat left and pretended to read the paper. He could nearly see Everett's eyes burning through the newsprint, wide and terrified. But Jamey wasn't about to start punching it out with Lofgren until there was no alternative.

"Hey, c'mon, Everett," Lofgren was saying, "I wanna know. Are you spooks hung like I heard you was?"

Everett got up and bolted out of the room. Lofgren thumped the table and roared. "Aw, do ya think I hurt his feelings?"

Jamey stared at his newspaper, which concealed his face. He was sweating bullets. But he wasn't going to call out the bully until the guy hassled him personally.

He didn't have to wait long.

"You." Lofgren leaned over and slapped Jamey's newspaper. "Fuck off. I don't like no nigger lovers in here."

Hell, Jamey thought. Just fuckin' hell. He got up and walked slowly past Lofgren, who was still sitting, then yanked the man's stringy blond hair and said, "You ever call my friend that again, I'll knock you cold."

"Nigger, nigger, nigger—"

"Let's go, scumbag."

"Just what I been waitin' for," Lofgren said, scowling.

Jamey strode out onto the deck. It was roughly the size of a boxing ring. Good. Perfect.

He knew a lot about fighting, of course, and could see that the big fat Swede, with his paunch and labored breathing, had brute strength but little else. No stamina; Jamey could probably take him in a fight in two minutes, and so could many of the other men here, though everyone seemed too afraid even to try. So Jamey would kick Lofgren's ass; what then? Someone would probably recognize him as a former boxer and claim it was an unfair fight. These guys, as ignorant as they were, probably loved to watch boxing and maybe had even seen Jamey in the ring with Mike Tyson. If that happened, maybe it would get back to the goons who wanted to kill him.

Jamey stared at his hands, disgusted. I'm still at it. Still fighting, still punching it out.

Lofgren ambled out onto the deck. Jamey wanted him riled and wild, enraged and unthinking. The big guy could probably hurt him badly in a wrestling match, so it was important to keep this a boxing match. Punch the hell out of that gut and tire him till he can't fight any longer.

"Hey, fatboy, I'm over here," Jamey said. "Come kiss my ass. I know you want to."

Lofgren said nothing but charged after Jamey, who stepped aside and delivered a series of his hardest jabs to the man's giant paunch. Lofgren was instantly winded and grabbed his stomach with both hands. Jamey reared back and smashed him in the head with both hands. "You leave my friend alone or I'll punch you out some more."

Just then Lofgren reached down to his ankle and came up with a gun, a .22. He pointed it at Jamey and pulled the trigger. The bullet missed Jamey's cheek by and inch and he karate-chopped Lofgren's hand, who howled and dropped the weapon. Then Jamey, infuriated, kicked the gun overboard and pulverized Lofgren. There was an awful *snap!* as Lofgren's nose broke and he tumbled to the ground.

Christ, he thought. Wish I coulda done *that* to Tyson when I had the chance.

At that moment Everett appeared and Jamey said, "He's out cold."

Everett looked at Jamey closely. "What h-h-happened? You're sure shakin'..."

He shook his head and smiled, exhilarated. "Goddamn. I never had so much fun since I was a kid at the movies, picking fights with Marines."

Everett scratched his head. "Huh?"

It was a dreary, overcast late morning in Long Beach when Jamey and Everett left the *Joni Tavis* forever and joined the bustle of southern California once more. No one said a word to either of them. Everyone had given him the cold shoulder and even shot him some dirty looks. All because of Lofgren.

Jamey could never figure people. Here he was, in the middle of the ocean, standing up to the guy who had been terrorizing everyone. When Lofgren woke up after their fight, he had an awful mess of a face and his nose was crooked. He avoided Jamey but kept calling Everett names under his breath and threatening to kill him. But he kept his hands to himself.

It was those gambling sessions that finished the big guy, Jamey figured. Each night, the men on the ship would play poker. Lofgren loved cards, loved cash and bragged that by the time they docked, he would have everyone's money in his own pocket. He thought himself a clever poker player who didn't need to cheat to win. He bet with non-repayable "loans" he'd demanded from other crewmen, but when he played fairly and lost hand after hand. As his pile of "borrowed" greenbacks dwindled, he resorted to pulling face cards from his sleeve and magically won back all his money.

After Jamey roughed him up, he warned Lofgren never again to cheat or use anyone else's money. A compulsive gambler, Lofgren couldn't resist the poker games and began coming to the table nightly with his own cash. Jamey also changed the seating arrangement, so that Lofgren was bookended by himself and Everett. Incapacitated by sitting next to a black man, Lofgren couldn't concentrate on the cards and the others, mostly Jamey, cleaned him out in just a few evenings. "I'm broke," he muttered as the last of his cash went to another player with a superior hand.

"Then you're through," Jamey said, sliding out so that Lofgren could be excused. The big guy lumbered out of the room all hangdog and the men resumed their game.

Nobody was quite sure as to exactly when Lofgren threw himself overboard. The man on watch claimed not so see him, and it was only till the others retired that they noticed his empty bunk. They searched the ship, found nothing, and the captain wrote a report. Then they promptly forgot about the big man and his reign of terror.

Really, the only time after he beat up Lofgren that anyone spoke to him was the last night at sea, when a guy named Harris said to him, "After seeing you stand up to him and kick his ass, I wondered where I'd seen you without the beard. You fought Tyson in Atlantic City last year. You went the distance." He grinned.

Jamey shook his head. "Not *me*, guy."

Harris pointed at Jamey's broad, brawny shoulders and tapered waistline. "Yeah, it was you. No one gets those kinda fuckin' muscles by being a merchant seaman. I was surprised, him hassling you like he did when you look like a trained fighter." He shook his head and

ENTREPRENEUR

whistled. "Whew, you went from Tyson in Atlantic City to the *Tavisora* in just a year? You got some shitty luck."

"I told you, I never boxed and I never met Tyson—"

"Whatever you say, 'Dynamite Hands.'" And the guy walked off, cackling.

Jamey and Everett took the Greyhound up to Los Angeles. Honey and their kid still lived there, and probably well, too, from all the Tyson fight money Jamey had sent them. Well, he didn't care much about Honey anymore, but he was dying to see his son.

They got into a taxi and Everett was let out where he always stayed while in Los Angeles—at the Pacific Paradise Hotel, a downtown flophouse where nobody made fun of his stutter or called him the N-word. Jamey remembered his days living in this city, and his job at the Wilshire Men's Club.

"You gonna c-c-all me, right?" Everett handed him the hotel's business card. "When you get all settled in?"

"Yeah, sure." He didn't feel just then like hearing Everett's many questions about his plans. The taxi took him back to the Greyhound station, where he boarded the next schedule right back down to Long Beach, hoping that this little zigzagging journey might throw off anyone following him.

Back in Long Beach, he headed straight for the Commodore Hotel, where he had stowed away his things with Butch. The hotel proprietor regarded him with a poker face as he checked him in and handed over the totebag containing the valuables. Jamey silently walked through the hot, musty, narrow lobby and entered the elevator. He went into his room, opened his totebag and smiled at the sight of his cell phone and Rolex. His two most prized possessions. He still had over a year left on his phone plan.

Minutes later he answered a knock at the door.

"Welcome back," Butch muttered.

"Anyone come by lookin' for me?" Jamey's heart beat faster as he started contemplating these serious domestic matters. Punching out bullies on the high seas, he could live with. Bad men with big loaded guns coming after him? No, thanks. No way.

"Yeah. Young guy. Said he was your brother. Tall guy with dark hair, good-lookin'. Shiny shoes."

Jamey let out a huge sigh. "Fuckin' Paul." Figures. God only knows how the jerk got to know I stay here. Probably got a private dick. "He ask for me by name?"

"Yessir. Said he needed to talk to you. Seemed to think he was pretty high and mighty, that one. If you don't mind my saying."

"Been that way all his life, Butch," Jamey said.

"Look," Butch said, "I think it's a real dumb idea for you to come back here. Guess I'm gonna have to provide you with room service till I can find you another ship. You can't go outside. Some dangerous people want you dead. Go down the hall to use the shower and toilet, but otherwise stay in this room. I'll bring you booze or beer so the time will pass better. Understand?"

Jamey nodded. "OK."

He got drunk in his room and spent that evening reliving the *Joni Tavis* and Lofgren. He had gone too far with the Swede; seeking to teach the creep a lesson, he had forgotten the difference between teaching humility and humiliation. He'd been dumb to force the brute to sit between himself and Everett; he'd had no right to enter Lofgren's environment and disgrace him in front of his peers. I'm as bad as he was, Jamey thought through his alcoholic haze. Maybe even worse.

ENTREPRENEUR

By now he knew all about his brother's success with Cherry Computer. He thought back to them as kids, Paul's contemptuous, condescending looks in his direction. Maybe he saw my true colors even back then. Wonder what he thought when he came here to the Commodore and saw that this was my_new home. Probably laughed his ass off and drove back home_in his solid-gold Beemer.

He dozed off, a tear running down his cheek.

Knock, knock.

Jamey awoke and opened the door.

Butch looked grim.

"Just got off the horn with Wasserman. Says you were dumb to come here. He told you to fuck off forever and he meant it. Kid, I gotta get you back out to sea before the boxing goons splatter your brains all over these walls." He paused. "Say, downstairs they were going on and on about you killing that big jailbird Lofgren on the *Tavisora*. That the truth?"

"No comment."

Butch grinned. "I better get you a whore or two, I guess, to curb your violent impulses."

Jamey stayed in the room for several days, drunk, eating the Big Macs and Whoppers Butch brought him and washing them down with Coors and Bud, then working off the empty calories with the vacuous, tanned girls the old man brought up for him to enjoy. Jamey had given his wallet to Butch for safekeeping. Most of the money he'd spent for the room, the food and drink and the whores, had come from his winnings on the *Joni Tavis* after making Lofgren stop cheating. The brute had always bet tens and twenties, most of which had ended up in Jamey or Everett's pocket. Jamey was just as glad to hand over the big bastard's cash in payment to Butch.

The walls closed in on him. He'd recharged his cell phone and at times felt the overwhelming temptation to call someone, but who?

Butch concurred: the Commodore's walls are made of Kleenex and spit. Shut up and listen to your Walkman until I can get you out of here and onto the high seas again. Whenever that happens.

At about ten in the morning Butch knocked. "That tall guy is back. Want to see him?"

Jamey nodded. "Yes. Send him up." He closed the door and waited. Then there was another knock. He opened the door.

"Hey, Paul," he said. "Come in." He extended his hand.

"Well, Jamey, I'm glad to see you're looking so well. Thing is, we've got serious family business to deal with right now. That's why I'm here. I have a taxi waiting outside, and a chartered plane at the airport. Dad wants to see you and Dee before he dies. We need to go now."

Jamey quickly threw his few possessions into the bag and the two quickly went downstairs. He retrieved his wallet from Butch and gave him the room key.

At the airport, Paul paid the driver and the two brothers marched out onto the tarmac. Jamey stretched his legs as he walked, feeling like Superman as he and his rich sibling climbed the steps of the double-engine plane. From a musty fleabag hotel to a private plane in just over an hour. Life, he concluded, was just so damn full of nice surprises.

The plane took off immediately. Once they were at cruising altitude, Paul mentioned that he had met the love of his life. He showed Jamey a picture of himself with Marni.

Jamey grinned at the picture. "What a babe."

He fell asleep quickly and didn't wake up till they landed at San Jose International Airport. A taxi took them to Stanford Medical Center. They went to their father's room but the nurse said, "Your father died about fifteen minutes ago."

"Dad said to me at the very end, 'We never did track down your mother, did we?'" Dee shook her head.

"He was in total denial about her suicide," Jamey said. "Well, at least he spoke to *you*. He was big enough to overcome his grudges." Then, "Geez, Paul, I would have thought you'd have grander digs than this, seeing as you're the Cherry Computer hotshot and all. Har, har."

They were sitting in the living room of the South Bay mansion Paul and their father had shared for the final years of his life.

"Don't you like it? Aw, shucks."

Caitlin was asleep in the guest room and Doris was crying her eyes out over the demise of the curmudgeon who had given her someone to look after and fight with. Caitlin had wanted to see her grandfather one final time, and Dee had agreed. If Dee had been apprehensive about seeing the father who'd rejected her years earlier, she needn't have been. The old man had clutched her and wept uncontrollably for minutes.

Paul promptly made funeral arrangements. They needed to make some fuss over Bud Steeves. He had been going to church and Reverend Totsno had agreed to perform the eulogy. Marni, on assignment in Seattle, said she was busy as hell but would fly down for the funeral.

She had been crabby and morose at the conclusion of their honeymoon, and she didn't like Paul's South Bay mansion. At the moment, with his sister and brother in his company and his father newly deceased, Paul was relieved that Marni wasn't there.

"I hope his funeral will be nice and quiet. No reporters wanting comments on Dad's death," Dee said.

"The reporters won't care," Paul said. "Because it wasn't the important Steeves who died."

"You're so humble, Mr. CEO," Jamey said. They all laughed.

"You seem different somehow, Jamey," Paul said.

"Really? How?"

"Less obnoxious, I guess."

"Gee, thanks."

"I meant that as a compliment."

"Like I said, thanks." After a pause he got up. "Well, I'm beat. Gonna call it a night."

He went upstairs, to the bedroom where his father had slept. No one else wanted to use that bed, so Jamey helped himself to it. He wasn't really tired; he had slept well on the private plane up the coast. But he wanted to get away from Paul. He couldn't stand his brother. He wasn't sure why, but he just couldn't stand him.

Jamey slid into his father's bed and thought, This sure beats the Commodore Hotel.

At the funeral, Lido Grandinetti was handsome and respectful in his mourning suit. Many people were present, and the San Francisco *Times* had run quite a flattering obituary:

ENTREPRENEUR

Buford James "Bud" Steeves, longtime proprietor of popular Western Hills eatery Bud's Good Eats, member of prominent local clubs, father of Cherry Computer co-founder Paul Steeves.

As Reverend Totsno spoke effusively, Paul smiled. I hope Dad is somewhere here among us, hearing his horn being tooted long and loud.

The preacher did not know when to shut up. He carried on and on. Paul looked over at Dee, then at Jamey. Neither seemed to be paying much attention to the hyperbole about Saint Buford.

In the cemetery, everyone stood in silence under the sun. Paul thought that nice afternoons were not for burying loved ones. Dressed respectfully in black, Paul, Dee, Caitlin and Jamey stood side by side as they watched the coffin being lowered into the ground.

As they walked away, Lido Grandinetti came up to them.

"I just wanted you to know I feel for you. I know your father had a difficult life. It's really such a shame he didn't live longer, to enjoy his family more and savor everyone's success."

"We appreciate your kind thoughts, Lido," Paul said.

Grandinetti looked much as he had years ago. Easy living had kept him young. Paul grinned at the sight of the chocolate baron humbling himself in front of the remaining members of the Steeves family of modest Western Hills.

"This young lady must be your daughter, Deirdre," Grandinetti said, looking at Caitlin.

"Caitlin, this is Mr. Grandinetti. We knew each other years ago."

Grandinetti shook the girl's hand and smiled.

Caitlin offered her hand and a small, distracted smile.

"I don't think we've met," the candy baron said, turning to Jamey and shaking his hand. "Lido Grandinetti."

"Jamey Steeves." You fucked my sister, guy. I tried to firebomb your mansion.

Grandinetti turned back to Paul. "Seeing as how Cherry Computer and Grandinetti Chocolate are so close to each other and we're now practically neighbors, we should make a point of having lunch at least once every other month. What do you say?"

"Lido, I would love to, but business is crazy."

Grandinetti chuckled. "Oh, yes. Still trying to persuade the world to buy your ten-thousand-dollar Suzi. Well, good luck. Deirdre, are you available for a free meal anytime soon?"

She shook her head. "We're going back to Los Angeles."

Grandinetti nodded. "Then I'll see you when I see you." He walked off, rebuffed again by this family.

In the limousine ride back to Paul's estate, Dee thought about Lido Grandinetti and how he had captivated her years earlier. She did not think much about her father. He had been an angry, disillusioned, vegetable cutter and sandwich maker in Western Hills when they parted, and a frail old frightened man at the end who just wanted to forgive and be forgiven. He meant little to her. But she thought back with amusement and pleasure of her time with overhung Grandinetti with his mansion, car and superhuman sexual stamina, pinning her to the bed and driving into her till she nearly screamed. Thank you, Lido, but I'll have no more of you.

The limousine pulled up to Paul's mansion. They all got out and headed inside. Caitlin headed straight for the Nintendo game upstairs. The adults all congregated in the kitchen for a drink.

"Gotta take this off," said Jamey, tugging at his tie. "God, I hate getting all dressed up, even when it's just for a few hours."

"Well, you look nice, brother," Dee said, admiring his muscular physique. "Sorry I missed seeing your championship bout with Tyson, but boxing is just not my thing."

Jamey smirked. "It's not mine either anymore."

"Paul, what will *you* do now?" Dee asked.

"Nothing. Stay put. Business as usual. I really like the idea of living here so close to the factory." He turned to Jamey. "Did you like Dad's room? If you're in no hurry to go, stay here."

"And do what?"

Paul shrugged. "Remember, this is the Bay Area. The local economy is booming. I'm sure you'll find something you like."

"Maybe I'll just go back down south will Dee and Caitlin. Stop in and see my kid along the way. Bug the shit out of Butch to find me another ship. South Bay isn't for me."

"Too close to me and Cherry Computer?" Paul asked.

Jamey shook his head. "Too close to Grandinetti Chocolate."

"What do you mean?"

"I was surprised as hell that he introduced himself to me and shook my hand. Boy, that's forgiveness."

"What *are* you talking about?" Dee asked.

Jamey took a deep breath. "Forgiveness for the night I tossed a Molotov cocktail into his living room."

Dee looked shocked. "That was *you*?"

"Yes, ma'am. Me and my boy Bubba. They had the window open, and it was foggy, and the Molotov just sailed in, landed on the sofa and went out."

"Why would you *do* such a thing?" Dee asked.

"Because I could, and because I was angry at a rich guy who was balling my sister and I had an accomplice who thought it sounded like an amusing Bicentennial stunt."

Dee frowned. "How did the cops find out?"

"Bubba. He busted his arm falling off his bike on the trip home. He panicked, told his daddy and the next thing you know, the cops are telling Dad about me and I'm exiled to Sacramento. So now you know."

"Thanks for sharing," Dee said.

Jamey smiled. "My pleasure."

"God only knows what other stunts you pulled back then," Dee said.

"God only knows," he said, thinking of the Franciscan Theatre and a Marine with his girl who just happened to have the misfortune of meeting Jamey Steeves. He got up and lightly touched Dee's arm. "Gotta go get my Nintendo fix. Caitlin said she'd teach me to beat everyone." He strode out of the room.

Dee looked at Paul. "You don't like him, do you?"

"I don't understand him."

"He's no worse than us." Adding, "We treated him like shit."

"We learned that from Mom and Dad," Paul said. "We're lucky we're not both bitter, struggling people like them."

"You've had enough good fortune for the three of us."

"Really?"

Dee rolled her eyes. "Yes, really. You were Mom and Dad's favorite. You were Grandinetti's new pal after he learned I didn't want him. You could go to People's University and meet Hank and build the Cherry computer. Jamey's life was almost normal till he saw me parading around nude in Lido's house, and in his resentment he tried to burn the mansion. I married Jackson because he was as far from being Lido and Tommy as you could get. Lido determined my attitude towards men, yours towards careers and Jamey's towards everything else."

"You are giving Lido Grandinetti entirely too much credit," Paul said.

Dee chuckled. "You shouldn't bad-mouth your mentor."

"He wasn't my mentor."

"No? He had you over to his place and showed you so much wealth and opulence that you nearly pissed your pants. I'm surprised he didn't adopt you."

"Guess I wasn't his type. You were."

"Too much so."

Paul said, "Let's talk about *you*. How did Grandinetti influence you?"

"He made me into a vain and corrupt bitch. Tommy was no good for me. Then Jackson tried to reform me."

"What will you do now?"

Dee shrugged.

"Don't mourn Jackson forever," Paul said.

"I won't. I'm going to school and see if I can become a doctor."

"Going to give people rhinoplasties now instead of becoming an actress?"

"Maybe. But I'll be doing something useful."

Paul sighed. "I spend my days trying to get people to spend ten grand to buy a computer named for an idiot stalker named Suzi."

"Is the Suzi selling that badly?"

"Worse. Everyone still wants the Cherry II. Or they're buying PCs. Makes me want to trade places with Jamey upstairs. At least he doesn't have to face the world every day and deal with snotty shareholders and the press."

Doris came in and announced that lunch was ready. Jamey and Caitlin came down. They all ate in silence. Then Dee said, "I think our flight goes soon. Paul, will you drive us to the airport?"

"Sure. Jamey, you want to come along for the ride?"

"Yeah, you might as well drop me off at Greyhound on the way back. I'll get my stuff."

They drove to the airport and unloaded Dee and Caitlin's things with little ceremony, and then it was just Paul and Jamey in the trip down to the San Jose Greyhound, the closest one to South Bay and the airport.

"Sure you didn't want to fly down to Los Angeles with the girls? Would have been more comfortable, you know."

Jamey shrugged. "I don't mind the bus."

Paul pointed to the garish purple-and-pink neon sign saying BAR right next to the bus station entrance. "Let's have a drink. I need to talk to you."

Inside were woeful-looking men and women waiting for their departures. Jamey and Paul sat down and ordered. Jamey sat back. "Well?"

"You remember when you gave me all that money that Mom used to bail you out?"

"Sure do." Jamey smirked. "Will it be enough for a master's degree if Cherry Computer collapses and you have to go back to school?"

"Joke. You told me where to put it, as I recall."

"I hope you didn't. You would've gotten hemorrhoids."

"Well, I bought a pile of Cherry Computer stock in the name of one Buford James Steeves, Junior. The shares have really skyrocketed because of our success."

"What's it worth now?"

"Well over a million dollars."

Jamey swallowed hard. "What? I have a million?"

"Yes. Leave it alone and it'll go higher..."

"How do I sell it for cold cash?"

Paul shook his head. "Don't do it."

Jamey's eyes bore into him. "You didn't answer my question. Come on, I wanna know."

He reluctantly took out his business card and wrote a number on it. "Call Josh Hawkins and tell him who you are and that you'd like to sell your Cherry position. That's how."

Jamey reached into his pocket and removed his cell phone. He entered Josh's number, then pushed some more buttons. "Excuse me a sec." He got up and left the bar.

Outside, he dialed another number.

"Pacific Paradise Hotel," said the weary voice at the other end.

"Everett Moore's room, please." Well, he thought, for such a dumpy hotel, it was nice that they had a phone in each room.

"Hello?"

Jamey smiled at the sound of Everett's high, boyish voice. "It's me."

"Jamey! Where are you?"

"Everett, we're gonna hop a flight back to Honolulu as soon as we can."

"What, no more working aboard the *Joni Tavis*?"

"No more of that bullshit. Get your bags packed and wait for further instructions from me."

"Yeah, sure."

Click.

Jamey hung up and smiled. It was becoming a very interesting couple of days. And the next days were going to be even more so.

PART FOUR

Chapter 1

1994

Steering her new Miata up her driveway, Dee was relieved to get out of the heavy rain that beat down upon her. The travel agents sure didn't tell the tourists about these relentless downpours. This kind of weather eroded the coastline and sent million-dollar Santa Barbara and Malibu homes sliding into the Pacific Ocean.

She was glad that tomorrow's classes were online. She liked attending school from her den. On other days, she attended classes at UCLA, finishing up her master's degree in biology. School was now a hobby; she didn't believe the graduate degree would lead anywhere.

She opened a wine cooler and checked her mail. Jackson had been dead for quite some time, but only occasionally could she get through the day without obsessing over him. Two years earlier, she'd stood on her balcony with its breathtaking view of the city and watched in horror as, far below and miles away, the fires from the Rodney King riots glowed orange-red and sent billows of smoke into the early evening sky. She would have turned to Jackson then, to have him tell her what it all meant. Actually, the news media would have been calling him for interpretations and analyses.

His insights were something she sorely missed; only recently had she started to realize she would have to provide her own insights. She would have to do her own thinking from then on.

Jackson's ex had made claims to his house, but Paul had stepped in and made that trouble go away. Dee now owned the house she and Jackson had shared. She went to school full time and drove a new sportscar.

Caitlin had gone to San Diego for the weekend with some friends, and Dee found it spooky, being all alone. She sliced open one envelope after another: a few bills, some flyers and a small padded mailer. She smiled. Inside the mailer was a microcassette. Paul. He had bought himself and Dee one of those minuscule Panasonic tape recorders and was like a little kid on Christmas morning. Somewhere along the line he had learned it was more fun to talk than write, so in America he picked up the phone and overseas he spoke into his new gadget, dropped it into a mailer and sent it away. He also liked the fact that speaking into the toy meant that he could talk without interruption and not have to answer the other person's dumb questions.

"Hi, Dee," said the unmistakable voice as the microcassette played. "Having fun with your tape recorder? I like mine so much that I even brought it up in a Cherry meeting and pondered whether my gang could do a better one, or at least different. They said no.

"As you know, I am in Europe, ostensibly to urge computer salespeople here to push Cherry hardware over IBM. Marni is here, of course, amusing herself in many ways, since she has been here any number of times. Frankly, I'm doing the bare minimum, mostly shaking hands and talking the talk. The rest of the time, I'm taking it nice and easy. Paris, Venice, Rome, London...one of these days, I'll let Marni take me here and show me around."

Dee smiled. Paul had brought her over a souped-up Suzi computer and installed it in her den as a "thanks for being you" gift. Dee would much rather have had an IBM or one of its clones, but owning a Suzi, the world's most expensive home computer, *was* kind of nice in its own way. Paul, for all his business acumen, didn't seem to understand that his high prices were turning consumers away from the Suzi in particular and Cherry products in general.

But she was damned if she'd say such a thing to Boss Paul.

"Dee, I have discovered that I have the capacity to be a lazy son of a bitch." Nice for you, she thought. "That grind a few years back of People's University, Amazement and then Cherry? It sure as hell wore me out. I am happy now to go through Europe with my darling Canadian wife who has been here many times and understands European culture far better than I ever will. She takes many pictures and speaks to everybody...how many languages she knows!

"We stay in fancy places, sort of because we're expected to do so, but we lose ourselves each day, just wandering around. Marni swore off books and newspapers and the news media in general some time ago, so she's happily ignorant of what's going on outside her own little world. I'm sort of doing the same thing. Bill Clinton's the president, right? He's the horny guy with the gray hair, as I recall. They tell he wants to meet me for a photo opportunity. I guess he doesn't know that I voted against him.

"At some point during her youth, Caitlin must come here and experience Europe..."

Dee stopped the tape for a moment because the phone was ringing. It was Marcia Goldberg, the acclaimed film editor who had won an Oscar the previous year for cutting *Underground Man,* a dark and sordid tale about a man driven to a murderous rage by inner-city decay. The top critics agreed that it was Marcia's editing that gave the film its sharp edge, and she had been an ardent admirer of Jackson. Dee liked her a great deal and enjoyed hearing from her at least once a week.

"A top director just had his picture in the can. Want to see the approval print?"

"Thanks, no, Marcia. I've got someone coming over."

"Okay. You enjoying our California liquid sunshine?"

"Haven't paid much attention to the weather. Been busy just now listening to news from Paul."

"Where is he?"

"All over Europe, trashing Big Blue."

"Good luck. *Computer Age* magazine says the Suzi is a real rip-off. Well, Dee, have fun with your studies and your company this evening and don't gloat too much in my face when you get your medical degree."

Dee laughed. "Thanks. I'll try to respect your dignity." She knew that Marcia, married for years to a medical malpractice lawyer, had little faith in doctors and believed that Dee's energies would be far better off directed in other areas. Such as film editing.

Marcia was quite a woman. Filmmaking was not a boys' club, she said. She had admired Jackson's books much more than his screenwriting ability, and insisted that Dee had the greater talent.

Marcia had been a true friend and a persistent one. Each time they spoke, Marcia reminded Dee that the film industry was still open to good women. And each time Dee began to wonder about her choice to pursue a medical career: Was it right for her? Was she right for it? Medicine was so esoteric; her premed classmates absorbed all the arcane information that Dee found baffling. Also, she knew that if she actually survived the training and became a physician, the field changed rapidly; she'd always be going full throttle simply to keep up with new drugs and developments. Was that *really* what she wanted?

The phone calls from Marcia always brought up these issues, and just thinking about such things fatigued her. She went back to the sofa and turned the tape recorder back on to listen some more to brother Paul, who had spent most of his adult life thus far trying to take over the world. Talk on, guy.

"I'm hearing from South Bay that Hank and Bayliss, among others, want me to wrap up my business here and get my ass back home. They seem to think that what I'm currently doing is some sort of vacation. Well, they're right. The thought of going back to South Bay and sitting through product and marketing meetings makes me get a big rubbery one. Starting up Cherry Computer was fun; running it, sweating over its ups and downs, is a huge hassle.

"I need to get my priorities straight. I have changed the world as much as I can. From this point on, the changes will be refinements and improvements only.

"Marni has just come in and I must ask her about her day. Have you heard from Jamey lately? He's reluctant to call me or contact me in any way. Give him my best."

Dee turned off the recorder, smiling at her brother's remark about the "big rubbery ones" at Cherry. Still, she liked to sit back and listen while he talked about what he thought and felt.

She also found him easier to take when they weren't face to face. Paul, several inches taller than her, looked down at her, literally, and made sneering, condescending faces when Dee said disagreeable things. Fortunately, Paul was starting to see the necessity, or at least the desirability, of mellowing out a bit. Life was about more than just making things and spending money.

What about Jamey? Dee didn't often hear from her brother, which she took as a good omen. The guy obviously was too busy with the *Maria* to bother with contacting her. He called whenever he felt obligated to do so. He spoke of business rather than personal issues. Which Dee took to mean that Jamey had no personal life at the moment. "Well, Paul, at least you and he have careers, instead of being over-the-hill students," she muttered to herself, sighing in the large, empty living room.

At that moment she heard Alejandro Sanchez's ancient Beetle struggle up her driveway. He loved the car and serviced it himself, scrounging around for parts—"I don't trust those greedy bastards at the repair shops; they're very corrupt," he'd told Dee.

She heard the doorbell and answered it promptly. "Come in out of the rain, you crazy macho bastard."

"A little rain doesn't hurt." He smiled, speaking in his lyrical Spanish accent. "It's the earthquakes, floods and race riots that you have to be careful of."

"The forest fires and lawyers are our other hazards."

He shrugged. "The forest fires don't scare me."

They both laughed. He was wearing a secondhand USC varsity jacket, which looked very strange when he walked around the campus of archrival UCLA. If he wasn't so big and tall, and hadn't walked with such swagger, he might have faced harassment by other students as he wore that jacket. But he wasn't the type to give a damn what anyone thought of him or his clothes.

Alex, as he liked to be called, seemed to be indigent, another super-bright student who somehow got by on a scholarship or stipend. He seemed proud of his Sally Ann and Wal-Mart clothes. He was tall and broad-shouldered, the same size as Jackson, so she offered him the many clothes her late fashionplate husband had acquired. Dee was more than happy to give it all to him. She would rather see Jackson's stylish, timeless things on Alex's back than on anyone else's. But he refused: "I won't have a murdered man's clothes on my back. He'll haunt me."

Alex, much younger than Dee, was finishing up his master's degree in kinesiology. He had a quick, absorptive mind and learned things seemingly without effort. They had a couple of classes together and he impressed Dee as the charming Spanish man who sat back, took it easy and had all the answers. They had conversations and became acquainted. There were other women in the classes who eyed him with interest, but he made a habit of spending time with Dee, even suggesting, because it was clear that she found some of the coursework nearly incomprehensible, that the two of them spend some time studying together. So once a week he drove up to her Hollywood Hills home and she fed him a modest dinner. Then they studied. Next stop for him was medical school, he said, and she said he would thrive there. As for herself, she didn't know. The more time she spent with Alex, the more she became convinced that he had the right stuff for medicine and she didn't.

She cooked burgers and fries for them both and they sat down to eat. "Where's Katie?" he asked. He meant Caitlin. Alex seemed fond of her. Too fond of her, Dee occasionally thought, but then silently chastised herself. She should be flattered.

"Away with friends in San Diego."

"Hope the weather's better down there than here."

They ate and chatted. Dee felt grateful for his company. He was a quiet, patient listener who was apparently genuinely interested in what she had to say. He was unimpressed by her big house in the hills and her new Miata; he already knew about her brother Paul, which explained why she had the leisure to stay in school and not work. He had sat at her computer and gone online to visit Websites he thought might help her in her studies.

"I feel lazy tonight," she said. "Wanna just watch a video or some HBO?"

"No, *amiga*. We'll study till your eyes bleed." He said this with a smile, but his time was valuable; he wouldn't waste an evening watching whatever garbage on was TV or video.

She sighed and they settled in to study. The material, which dealt in great detail with DNA, was easy for him; he couldn't understand why she hadn't mastered it yet.

"You need to pay attention, Dee. You need discipline. Do sloppy work and you'll flunk out."

She sat back and sighed. "You know, Alex, I'm a lot older than you..."

"So what?"

She clenched her teeth. "I'm not what you would call academically gifted."

"You're patronizing me." His eyes were cold. "I don't necessarily have a superior brain or inborn academic gift. I've worked my ass off and will continue to do so. And I don't care about your brother who started his little computer company in the back office of a sleazy video arcade. Frankly, the whole computer world is laughing at him over that ten-thousand-dollar piece of shit Suzi that's sitting in your den." He stood up. "This isn't doing either of us any good. I'm going home. I need to use the bathroom first, though."

He disappeared. Dee stood at the table and thought about what she had just said to him. I'm getting old and feeling useless. Those around me are somewhere, headed to some specific and desirable destination. That's why I said those things. It's not his fault.

He came out and ran a hand through his thick black hair. He was lithe and handsome, with coffee-colored skin and deep-set, dark eyes, smooth skin, pale lips.

"Alex," she said, "don't go away angry."

"I'm not angry," he said.

She moved forward, tentatively, and grasped his wrist. She took him into the gentlest embrace, and they kissed. She felt his strong hands slide all over her body and thought, Well, time for me to become a human being again. Alex tried to pull her towards the bedroom but she resisted. She would not have another man in Jackson's bed.

He undressed her quickly, then removed his own clothes in a matter of moments. They writhed together on her floor, and it was over so fast that she could hardly believe it had happened at all. What was it she had heard about Latin lovers? Alex must be the exception.

Alex got up slowly and dressed. "Happy now?" he asked. "Your first men were white, then you married a black, now you've been with me. Find an Iroquois, an Arab and an Oriental and you'll have covered the entire rainbow. Thank you for your wealthy Caucasian hospitality." He slipped out the door and was gone.

She got up, still naked, and dressed. Then she did the dishes and looked briefly at the maddeningly abstruse textbook Alex had tried to decipher for her. It's totally hopeless, she thought. I wasn't meant to go that path.

She slept long and well that night. Late the next morning, she called Marcia Goldberg at home and said she had made a very important career decision.

Chapter 2

Jason Duggan Steeves, son of Paul and Marni, was born early in the morning in St. Luke's Hospital in downtown San Francisco, delivered by one of the city's most prominent obstetricians. Paul, partly at Marni's request, was absent when she went into labor. He was at home in South Bay, or at the factory, or somewhere in between, caught up in the brutal world of American business.

Paul was exhausted as he left the hospital after a brief visit. Marni was groggy and Jason was sleeping. He was about to get into his car when he heard a voice.

"She's fat."

Suzi Bayliss emerged from a canary-yellow Mustang convertible parked near Paul's car. He could have sworn she owned a Thunderbird, which perhaps she did. Maybe she traded in her car every other week. Over the course of a year, she would drive every kind of car imaginable. A person had to find ways of coping with the chronic ennui of being young and rich.

"Those short, big-titted women get fat after pregnancy. Didn't you know that, Paul?"

Suzi's manner was matter-of-fact, as if she considered it perfectly natural to be there with him at that moment. He looked at her, his heart thundering in his ears. He had more in common with Jamey than he thought: no man alive could scare him, but women...

Suzi smiled.

"What are you doing here?" Paul asked.

"What's the matter? Don't you want me to congratulate you?"

"No. Go home, Suzi."

"I've been keeping an eye on you and Marni. As soon as the kid popped out, I knew."

"Why?" His head was spinning.

Her eyes narrowed. "Because she had *my* fucking baby. Wrong womb, boyfriend. Your .44 Magnum misfired."

Paul groaned. "Oh, God. Just go home. OK? This is irrational. I could call the cops. If your father found out about this..."

"He couldn't care less. Besides, he hates you already. You took over his company, rejected his daughter and took up with that Canadian bitch."

"Look, Suzi, get yourself a guy, get married and have your own kid."

"Well, maybe I want *yours*. You married the wrong woman, big boy. We can resolve that quickly enough." With a malicious glint in her eye, she added, "I can make a phone call and have Marni disappear permanently under highly ambiguous circumstances. Then we could be together."

Paul's mouth dropped open.

Suzi tossed back her long red hair. "Paul, I can make so much trouble for you. I have a private eye, tons of money. But you already know that, right?"

Paul thought he would vomit. His stomach convulsed and he felt sweat running down his back. He said nothing more to her. He just got into his car and slowly backed out, miraculously not slamming into a post or another vehicle. He drove off, panicked. He almost forgot where he lived.

Suzi tailgated him. Only when he reached his home did she pass and disappear into the darkness. *She knows me. She knows where I live. Of course she does. She knows everything about me. Probably knows when and where we conceived the child.* Paul parked the car and traipsed into his living room, carefully locking the door behind him.

At the Valley View Country Club, Paul always made a point of finishing up early so that he could have a few minutes to himself at the bar. Everyone else was out on the golf course or the tennis courts and would soon join him in the bar. It got too crowded much too quickly for him. These minutes alone were precious. Marni, all slimmed down, nearly beat him at tennis, playing with characteristic ferocity. She nearly made an obscene finger gesture as he smashed the ball past her to win their final set. Paul enjoyed getting a vigorous workout, and badly needed it. He was back at Cherry, running things, working well into the night and generally neglecting his physical well being.

Afterwards, they went into the bar.

"A Beck's, Mr. Steeves?" asked the bartender.

The first member to join him was Hank, who was wearing apple-green slacks.

"Those are some badass ugly pants," Paul said.

"Fuck you very much." Hank smiled. "Saw Marni out there. A tighter ass never walked the earth."

"Damn straight." He liked it when Hank spoke of his wife that way. "It's her Canadian blood, you know. Reaches all the right places." After a pause, he said, "Thanks for that birthday present for the kid."

Hank had set up a college fund for Jason. "Well, why not? We went to People's University. Hope in eighteen years little Jason's at Stanford. At least then he'll be *entitled* to look down his nose at people." Hank occasionally mentioned selling his Cherry shares, getting a master's degree at Stanford, then teaching design engineering. Paul thought Hank would be a better instructor than a business manager.

Soon they were joined by Greg Raines, manager of the country club. Greg wanted to buy the surrounding property and make the club the best one around, or at least the biggest one.

"We could add a second golf course," he said.

"Why?" Paul asked. "In America, does bigger always mean better?"

"Yes," Raines said.

"Give me some time to think it over," Paul said.

"I love this guy," Hank said, clapping Paul on the back. "Paul needs time to 'think it over' even when he needs to take a crap. It's cost him a fortune in underwear."

"Well, Paul," Raines said, "if you guys put your support behind it, we'd have it made. This establishment would be right up there with Pebble Beach."

Like hell, Paul felt like saying. "I will think about it. I promise."

With that, Raines went off to the showers. "Later."

Hank ordered another Beck's. "Paul, why does everyone here in South Bay kiss your ass?"

"Because I'm King Shit. I imagine Gates gets the same brownnosing up in Seattle. Of course, he could buy and sell both of us."

"Where you going once you leave Cherry?"

Paul frowned. "I'm not quitting Cherry, Hank. Why do you ask such a question?"

"Well, I hear things..."

"From whom?"

Hank sighed. "Suzi Bayliss. We've been dating."

"Suzi Bayliss," Paul muttered. The beautiful stalker, issuer of death threats, would-be seducer of new fathers in hospital parking lots. He couldn't see Suzi with Hank. Of course, maybe Hank was just weird enough for her. Well, better Hank than me, he thought.

"What else have you and Suzi talked about?"

"Her talent for fellatio. Our combined net worth. The usual. She assures me that she loves me. Truth is, we're gonna get hitched."

Paul's eyes narrowed. "Mind if I ask why?"

"Because I'm nearing forty and have been banging everything in a skirt for too long. I'm getting bored. Besides, everyone's getting married now, and I would hate to be the only one still single."

"Hank," Paul said. He told his friend about Suzi and her obsession with him, her stalking, their encounter in the hospital parking lot. Hank listened—he always gave his complete attention when something interested him, and zoned out when he got bored. But Paul spoke his piece, Hank said nothing and they let the matter drop.

Just then Marni came up and joined them. They all drank some more and Hank went off to the showers, a rich middle-aged boy who, Paul felt, never really grew up. Not long after, Paul and Marni Steeves received an invitation in the mail to the wedding of Suzi Bayliss and Paul Hankowsky.

Paul couldn't tell who was feeling what when Fred Bayliss walked Suzi down the aisle. Bayliss, if anything, looked relieved; Suzi, beautiful in a long white wedding gown, betrayed no emotion. Hank stood sweating and beaming with Josh Hawkins beside him as best man, the two men handsome in identical charcoal-gray chalkstripe suits. Paul stood in the front row with Marni. Many probably wondered why he wasn't Hank's best man. Paul was relieved he wasn't.

You're actually doing it, Paul thought. You're actually marrying her. You were a genius-hick from Reno and I made you rich. And now you're marrying that crazy bitch for all her father's money. Too bad for you, pal.

They had their reception at the Valley Country Club, a lavish spread outdoors under a large tent. The bride and groom danced well, even though Hank was stocky and did not seem to possess much grace. Paul kissed Suzi and she flashed him the same smile she flashed everyone else. Maybe the nightmare is over, he thought. Maybe Hank can help her get her shit together.

Marni wanted to dance with him. "But how can you dance in the middle of the day, in this heat?"

"It's a wedding, sweetie. Regardless of the heat, you dance. C'mon."

On the floor, she whispered, "Did you tell Hank about Suzi?"

He nodded.

She looked surprised. "He went ahead with it anyway?"

"Oh, I think it turned him on. Weirdness does that to him, you know."

Marni frowned. "And just think: you could have had all her family's money instead of spending your life with little old me."

"Yeah, I think I'll dump you tomorrow and urge the new Mrs. Hankowsky to do the same. Don't know what I was thinking of."

He wanted to slip away to the bar across the street for an icy Beck's, Heineken or even Budweiser, but Hank's wedding was dry. No alcohol, just a mild fruit punch.

"Come on," Paul told Marni, "let's go to the bar. I'm dying of thirst."

They went over and had a glass of fruit punch with Hank's father, who had flown in from Reno. A tall, thin, graying man in a dark suit, he looked more like a casino pit boss than a miner.

"I've followed your career closely, Paul," Hankowsky was saying. "The media have gone on and on about your youth and success. My boy is a little in awe of you. He went to that People's University, just like you, but I guess he didn't get as much out of it. So you boys built that computer and look what happened! Wish I would've thought of it. Well, I guess you guys are a lot smarter than I am."

Hank and Suzi came by and Hank's father danced with the bride, while Hank danced with Marni. Then Josh ambled by.

"Cheer up, Paul."

"What? It's a beautiful day, Hank just got married, I'm a new father. Everything is just peachy."

"Peachy or the pits?" Paul thought Josh would have made a good psychiatrist. Josh could smell your bullshit from the moment it left your mouth.

"Josh, we're both sober. Now is not the time to talk about serious things."

Dick Hartnell approached them. South Bay's former mayor, Hartnell was a dapper, smooth-talking man, Hartnell had run things at South Bay for many years until, as he put it, he started explore other opportunities. Wildly ambitious, he wanted to become a senator or even the president. At the moment, he was a lawyer with a very exclusive practice, a Republican with conservative values.

"Hello, Paul!" Hartnell said. "How's life for the soon-to-be retired computer king?"

"Retired? Where did you hear that?" Fred Bayliss and his big mouth.

"From a reliable source."

"No comment."

"I'll take that as confirmation of your impending retirement. May I speak frankly to you? I seriously think you should give politics a try."

"Not interested," Paul said.

"Politics interests everyone who's ever been in a position of power." He looked Paul up and down. "You're perfect for the game, too. Tall, good-looking, a successful entrepreneur. Now you have a gorgeous wife, a cute kid, the whole works." He nodded. "Yes, you would be irresistible to countless voters."

"And I guess you think I would make a good Republican. Just like Dick Nixon?"

"Joke," said Hartnell. "Of course, if you're going to enter politics, you must start locally. No United States Senate for you just yet. Mayor of South Bay is a good way to go. And like I said: you're quite a star around here. Everyone in South Bay loves Paul Steeves. Ain't that so?"

Josh pointed at Paul. "You the man!"

Paul chuckled.

"Besides, you have a reputation for actually having a conscience," said Hartnell.

"Truth is, I'm more concerned with my ten Mercedes and my four mansions," Paul said.

"Funny," Hartnell replied.

"Look, you don't even know my political orientation. I'm a closet Libertarian."

"Don't say that too loudly," said Hartnell.

"In fact, I may take out an ad in the *Register* coming out with my true political feelings."

"The *Register*," Hartnell muttered. "If I had the money, I would buy that rag and turn it into another innocuous entertainment tabloid."

"If only you had the money," Paul said.

"You're no Libertarian," Hartnell was saying. "Those guys are tax resisters who live on barter. Libertarians don't make millions by starting up high-tech companies."

Paul laughed and clapped the man on the back. "You've found me out. Seriously, I do want to speak to you about politics. I am definitely interested in going that route. But today is a wedding and not the place to talk."

"You're right. But place I have in mind for you is South Bay City Hall. That's the first step for you, and I can facilitate it. Then there's the senate. Senator Steeves from California. You like?"

Paul smiled. "I like. I'll send you a postcard from Capitol Hill. But now, I want to go dance with Suzi."

He went off towards the bride. He didn't especially want to dance with her, but if he didn't, Bayliss would get mad.

Suzi stood with her new husband at the other end of the tent. Paul said, "Hank, may I borrow your bride?"

Hank chuckled.

Paul gave Suzi a tiny, courtly bow. "May I?"

She nodded. "I thought you had forgotten me."

I wish. He led her onto the dance floor, feeling her hand dry and cool on his, her gaze somehow a tiny bit playful. She moved smoothly on the floor.

"They're all watching us, so we better dance well," he said.

"They *should* watch. We're the stars, sweetie." She smiled. "Power, money, looks. We have it all. They envy us."

"I think you made an excellent choice. Hank is a good guy. He'll make you a happy woman, Suzi."

"And if he doesn't, I'll kidnap you and make you my love slave."

"No, Suzi." He could feel her hips grinding ever so gently against his own. He finished their dance as quickly as he could and walked her back to her groom. It's all my fault, he thought distinctly. Crazy Suzi Bayliss wants to make me her love slave and it's all my own fucking fault.

Paul told Marni he wanted a few minutes to be by himself, to sit and sulk under the tent. She joined the others to throw rice as the couple went off under a shower of white grains.

Paul sat for a few moments, and Fred Bayliss sat down, too. They stayed silent for a while. Then Bayliss spoke.

"This wedding was something, huh? I've been thinking about those two. He wants to succeed you as CEO. I don't like Hank and I don't trust him. He's a slob, he smells, he drinks too much and he chases everything in a skirt. Plus, he doesn't know squat about running a company."

"Scalia from marketing should be the new CEO."

Bayliss nodded. "Yes. Swarthy guy. Worked on the Cherry Two, didn't he?"

"Yep. Scalia's an MIT grad we lured away from Xerox. Fantastic computer guy. Kind of like Bill Gates: half technologist, half executive. One of the best. He would make a very competent CEO."

"Fair enough. We'll make the announcement tomorrow."

"You better do it alone, Fred," Paul said. "You're the chairman of the board, the patriarch of the company. It would look better coming from you. I'm too close to Hank to break his heart myself."

Fred Bayliss made the announcement the following day. Nobody seemed surprised that Paul was resigning after all those years of developing Cherry into a lucrative company. But many industry observers raised their eyebrows when Bayliss gave the promotion to the cerebral, low-profile Anthony Scalia.

Hank took the news well, publicly congratulated Scalia and said nothing more. But one month later, he, too, resigned. He announced that he was returning to Reno to assume control of his family's mining operation. He made arrangements to sell all his Cherry stock, despite its temporarily low price. After he and Suzi moved into a beautiful in Reno, he called Paul and said he was thinking of producing a Woodstock-style, three-day rock-music extravaganza north of Los Angeles. He would book the biggest stars in the world. He told Paul he was happy to be back in the Silver State, running a company that he'd known all his life and understood well. He hoped Scalia would succeed as head of Cherry.

Paul listened with patience and empathy, careful not to say that Hank would probably screw up his father's mining company, too.

Jamey wiped his hands on his jeans. His sweated-through T-shirt was plastered against his back; wood polish covered his fingers. The sun beat down on him, even with his sunglasses and 49ers football cap. Well, it was better to have the cap, glasses and shirt than to have heatstroke and sunburn. He had lost weight, too; he was no longer the enormous, rippled heavyweight boxer he had been; now he looked like just another well-muscled young man.

He heard the voices of Oz and Everett from down in the engine room, giving everything a close look. Oz was one of the best engineers around; he was looking after the *Princess,* one of the harbor's most expensive yachts. Trouble was, there rarely was anything that needed doing aboard the *Princess,* so he made himself quite available to Jamey and Everett. As a favor he had been taking a look at the *Maria's* engine, to make sure it wouldn't have any problems once things got busy.

Jamey couldn't resist smiling whenever he looked at or thought of the *Maria.* When he bought it, he changed its name to the Maria, in honor of his first real love. Everett didn't bother to ask about the name change. Jamey felt compelled to name it for a woman he had known intimately, and he sure wasn't about to call it the *Honey.*

The ship was a find; a Saudi oil sheikh had sold it for an excellent price, apparently just not wanting to have it any longer and not especially minding taking a loss on the deal. The problem was that the *Maria* was 102 feet long, much more boat than Jamey needed or even wanted. But its sheer size thrilled him and clients loved all the walking-around room. He found out soon enough that the boat's size was the probable reason the Arab had sold it. Jamey and Everett spent most of their time keeping it shiny and tidy. They had had a couple of viable seasons and would certainly have more. They made do, financially, but not much more. Oh, well. Jamey didn't care as long as he was happy, and he was. He had never imagined that the simple life on the sea, wandering about and cleaning, polishing and whatnot, could bring him such delight. The kitchen was clean, the flags and charts and other odds and ends were always in order and the boat sparkled. It all made him beam like a new father.

ENTREPRENEUR

In town, he had gone into Neiman Marcus and put some wear on his American Express card. He bought a variety of heavy, fancy cocktail glasses and a bartender's guide two inches thick. He learned to mix any number of drinks and some of his guests swore that they came aboard just to see what kind of exotic potion he would serve them next.

He couldn't speak any foreign languages and neither could Everett. It made them both glad that they were still in America and not operating out of some foreign country where they would both be stressed out over the simple matter of communication. Dee laughed about this when he told her about it in a letter. She marveled at the picture of the *Maria* he had enclosed, saying it looked as big as the *Queen Mary*. She assured him that she and Caitlin were healthy and happy, and that while she had totally abandoned all plans for medical school, she was now deeply involved in writing movies and was getting much more gratification from it than she'd ever gotten from school or science textbooks. Jamey knew little about the movie business but thought she was continuing Jackson's career. He was pleased that Dee had promised to come out to Honolulu sometime soon with Caitlin and sail with him.

He got homesick occasionally for Market Street movie theaters, amusement parlors and certain girlfriends, and he wrote to Dee sometimes. He didn't ask her about his son, but he resolved to go back to Los Angeles at some point and visit the boy.

He no longer drank or fought. He dreamed often of Lofgren and deeply regretted humiliating the brute into suicide. He also thought about Leonard "Forever" Young and their fight in the parking lot that ended Young's career and, according to his fight manager Wasserman, made Jamey a marked man in the minds of Young's underworld financial backers. Was Jamey still in danger? He tried not to think about such things but couldn't help himself. When you were in Hawaii on board your own yacht, there were certainly better thoughts to have.

"The boat looks great, Jamey. Perfectly sound," said Oz, emerging from the engine room. He shook his head at Jamey's good fortune.

Jamey smiled. "Great to hear. Everett and I can handle little things, but if there was anything wrong with that engine—"

Oz waved him off. "Not to fear. You've lots of knots ahead of you even before you need routine maintenance." He looked around for a moment and chuckled. "Christ, Jamey, you've the biggest bloody boat around. A hundred feet—"

"A hundred two."

Oz shrugged. "Whatever. Probably some of the people here think you've got something too big on the water to compensate for having something too small between the legs."

Jamey smiled. "My ex would agree."

Oz laughed. "You've got clients coming soon, right?"

Jamey nodded.

"Then why don't we cruise a bit just to make sure this behemoth is up to the challenge?"

"Sounds good to me."

They did all the usual things: Jamey started the two engines, Everett handled the anchor with Oz's help and they slowly moved out of the harbor. Jamey had gotten used to steering the big boat and only under adverse conditions did he need to let Everett take over. Jamey smiled at the engine gauges. No problems, just as Oz said. The *Maria* was still fairly new and they could expect worry-free sailing for some time. They moved slowly out into the water and into the expanse of ocean between the islands.

Oz was a rowdy Australian with gold hair and a perpetually sunburned face. He drank too much and became belligerent when drunk, which was problematic because he was big and powerful and knew how to throw a punch. Around Hawaii's boat circles people were ambivalent at best about him and his boss, the owner of the *Princess,* had fired him many times before rehiring him hours later; Oz was so expert with boats of all sizes that he was nearly indispensable. And he knew it. He helped Jamey and Everett with the *Maria* because they put up with him and his drinking and he appreciated the hard work and luck that were involved in two ordinary guys making a go of running a charter with a 102-foot yacht. "That's the first time I've ever seen two guys survive that way. I admire you. I'll help you keep the boat in good condition," he had said.

At their first meetings Oz noticed the size of Jamey's muscles and guessed that the American had been a boxer. Oz seldom watched television and missed the B.J. Steeves title fight but listened raptly as Jamey spoke of it. Oz exclaimed, "Oh, so *you're* the white bloke who went the distance with the great black bloke! Wow!"

"I didn't actually *fight* him. I danced around him for twelve rounds." He sounded a tiny bit embarrassed.

"But still!" Oz shook his head and ordered them more beers. "You couldn't get *me* into a ring with that monster unless you put an Uzi in my hands first."

Jamey also told him about the parking lot fight with Young. "You beat him without throwing a punch?" Oz enthused, loving it. Then Jamey spoke of his hasty trip on board the *Joni Tavis.* But he had sense enough to stay quiet about the big Swede.

"They say fighting doesn't resolve anything," Oz said. "But, Christ, it's always made *me* feel better."

Oz became a Jekyll-and-Hyde whenever he drank. One night he saw Jamey in the bar and said loudly, "That man fought Tyson. If I caught him in a dark alley, I would kick his ass." Then he went over and bought his friend a drink.

One night on Bath Street, Jamey and Everett, starved for entertainment, wandered into a bar and overheard Oz addressing a group of Samoans. He was telling them some unpleasant things about themselves, their color and their culture. Oz, in his worldwide travels, often made a point of going into a local watering hole, getting drunk and flagrantly criticizing the locals, their customs and cultures. The Samoans were getting fed up, and Jamey took it upon himself to placate them.

"Gentlemen, this Aussie is my friend. He is also an alcoholic and a fool. Please pay him no attention. He is not worth the trouble." Oz sneered at Jamey, who added, "The drinks are on me." And all was well.

Later on, Oz came by when he was sober. He looked sheepish. "Thanks, Jamey. When I get drunk I become terribly obnoxious. I think that because I'm drunk people won't hit me. That's not the case. What would you have done if there had been trouble?"

"I would have stood there and let you get your face beaten in."

"Thanks. I'll remember that if I ever see you in a similar situation."

"That won't happen. I gave up that sort of thing a long time ago. Wasn't worth the price."

"Well, no matter. You're living right, far as I'm concerned. Especially with this boat. It's ready for the charters. You guys are just having too much fun."

"Well, to tell the truth, we've got trouble in paradise. We've lost our cook, that Polynesian guy."

"What happened?"

"I saw him slipping a .32 into his waistband. 'What's that for?' I asked. And he just smiled and said, 'Intimidation.'"

"Lovely," said Oz.

Jamey fired him immediately. "Now I'm without help. Know of anyone immediately available?"

"Sure. Would work out well, I think."

"Is he available immediately?"

"She."

Jamey shook his head. "Can't see a woman doing this. It's a man's job."

Oz smirked. "Don't be so sure till you've met her. I think she'll make quite an impression. She works as a cook at the Denny's in Waikiki. I've been in there many times after a bender, and if she can make Denny's food taste good, imagine what she can do for your clients."

He explained to a skeptical Jamey that Bernadette Rudeloff, a Scot, had been working in Honolulu but was sick of her job. Oz knew where to contact her and brought her by one evening. Jamey watched them walk towards the boat together. Bernadette was certainly no cover girl. She was a tall, sturdy-looking woman with shoulder-length blonde hair. She and Oz walked up the gangplank and she introduced herself to Jamey, shaking his hand firmly. She was from Glasgow and spoke with a prominent brogue. She said she could cook, serve, clean, do laundry—"but my shorthand is a bit rusty." She explained that she was American by birth, which was why she was able to work in the States. "Fat lot of good it's done me, though. Working at Denny's, which I hate. Putting up with drunks and punks and people running out without paying their checks. And working all night! Ugh! I'm really eager to get another job...something like this."

"Gee, Bernadette, and all this time I thought you'd found your true calling at Denny's," Oz said.

She made a face. "Look, Jamey, I'm the best candidate you're likely to find, especially since—if you don't mind my saying so—your wages aren't all that high. I can do many things, and I like the *Maria*. It's a nice big boat, not one of those dinky little things where everyone is always tripping over everyone else. I can't imagine anyone on board will be trying to pinch my ass or give me hell because they're drunk or hung over or crabby."

"On the *Maria,* we have snobs instead of slobs," Jamey said, laughing.

"Snobs I can handle," Bernadette said. "In fact, it's about dinnertime. As part of this interview, let me fix your dinner. If you don't like it, say so and that will be that. If you like it, I promise I can start immediately and do a few thousand more of them. Well?"

"OK. Everett is down there right now with some mahi-mahi. Maybe you should go down there right now and help him."

"Good enough." She nodded and went into the kitchen, inspected the fish and told Everett he obviously didn't know how to buy mahi-mahi. Then she told him to get out of her way and wait till she was done. He might, in fact, make himself useful by going into town and buying a few things like French bread and cheese, plus a bottle or two of wine. "Like Napa Valley white. Think you can manage that, Everett?"

They sat outside and ate on the deck as the Hawaiian sun turned cobalt and magenta. Bernadette had fried the mahi-mahi lightly breaded and added asparagus, garlic bread and rice, among other touches. The men had all had a couple of margaritas by then and were pleasantly buzzed and hungry. They had showered and shaved and put on fresh clothes.

Jamey poured the white wine, which had been chilling in a bucket of ice, then sat down before the steaming plate of food Bernadette had set before him. He took a large bite, chewed and smiled.

"This is wonderful." Turning to Everett, he said, "You're fired as cook. Stay out of the kitchen." To Bernadette he said, "You are hired. Go back to Honolulu, get your stuff, say goodbye to your roommates and get back here as soon as you can."

She beamed. "Aye, aye, sir."

Jamey lifted his glass, not quite believing how good the meal had been and how lucky they were to have Bernadette aboard. No more of Everett's dubious attempts at cooking. "A toast. To our newest crewmember. And, ideally, our last."

"Hear, hear," said Everett and Oz in unison.

After dinner Bernadette cleaned up and worked in the kitchen while the men happily dozed on deck. Jamey sat back in a deck chair and looked up at the warm, darkening sky. "Everett," he said, "*this* is the place to be."

"I hear you, Jamey," Everett said, lifting his face to see the same stars and chuckling at his own great fortune.

Jamey and Bernadette took a taxi into Waikiki to Denny's so she could tell the manager she wouldn't be back. She seemed hesitant to go in there and give the boss only a day's notice, but Jamey assured her not to worry; at places like Denny's, they were ready to deal with sudden departures, especially considering the low wages they paid.

Jamey waited outside till Bernadette came back out with her final paycheck and a big, relieved smile. Then they returned to the *Maria* and Bernadette loaded her things into her cabin while Everett moved in with Jamey. Well, Jamey thought as he settled in for the night, that was a productive day.

The Lovejoys came out to Honolulu every winter. An elderly couple, they would stay nowhere but on the *Maria*. Mr. Lovejoy had done well in advertising. His agency had offices in all the most important cities. He had grown tired of "the game" and his wife insisted that they spend the rest of their days having fun. He put up little resistance.

Mr. Lovejoy reminded Jamey a great deal of former president Ronald Reagan: tall and thin, with dark hair and a ruddy complexion. Just as Jamey almost laughed at how Reagan went through those years as president without aging at all, so Mr. Lovejoy seemed to have emerged from the dog-eat-dog world of advertising without any medical problems. "The trick to staying healthy through many years in advertising," Lovejoy explained to Jamey, "is to pay other people to do the worrying for you."

Mrs. Lovejoy was as healthy as her husband, with a svelte figure and tastefully frosted short hair. They had chartered the *Maria* the year before and promised Jamey they would be back. And here they were.

The Lovejoys wanted to trouble Jamey and his crew as little as possible. They came aboard with their food already prepared by their favorite deli; Bernadette simply had to present it as attractively as she could, which she did with a big smile. They also brought on board the most expensive liquors, and in the early afternoon they were ready for Jamey to serve them their first drink of the day, usually a Manhattan or martini. Everett would spread the awning and the Lovejoys would devour their deli spread. Bernadette also had a special talent for making robust, piping-hot coffee, which impressed Jamey and Everett.

"This," said Mr. Lovejoy, his comment including both the coffee and the charming Scot who made and served it, "sure beats the hell out of Starbuck's."

Sometimes the Lovejoys would disappear into one of the cabins. Jamey, hearing their subdued grunts and moans, marveled that after many years of marriage, they still had sex. In fact, they didn't just have sex; they *made love*. Jamey knew all about the former but very little about the latter. The Lovejoys treated each other and everyone else with grace and dignity. Jamey and Honey's relationship had been a travesty compared to the Lovejoys' marriage. He resolved that if he ever remarried, he would remind himself daily of the Lovejoys and do his best to follow their example of what a marriage could be.

The Lovejoys' stay on board the *Maria* was wonderfully lazy and thoroughly enjoyable. They would reappear at four in the afternoon and go for a swim. They invited the Maria crew to swim with them. The trouble was that Everett, who Jamey thought would be a masteful swimmer, could manage only the clumsiest of strokes and everyone in the water feared for his safety. Everyone felt relieved when Everett finally got back on board.

Afterwards the Lovejoys got dressed and Mr. Lovejoy asked for a drink. "A scotch and soda would be nice."

"Coming up," said Jamey. He had become quite good at mixing drinks. As they sat and sipped, Mr. Lovejoy said, "Skipper, do you mind if I ask you a question?"

"Not at all."

"A personal question?"

"Go right ahead."

"Are you related to Paul Steeves of Cherry Computer?"

Jamey nodded. "He's my older brother."

"Ah. Thought so. A little bit of resemblance, though he's got dark hair and is kind of skinny, while you look like you could punch your way out of any barroom brawl."

Jamey smiled. "Well, I had my days of brawling while Paul was in college. He had the brains in the family."

"Oh? Do you think so? You cruise around on a yacht all day while he works like hell sixteen hours a day. I founded an ad agency that grew and grew—but it's only now that I'm really enjoying the lifestyle I could have afforded many years ago. You're the one with the brains, far as I'm concerned."

Mrs. Lovejoy joined them presently and Jamey, without having to be told, went off to fix her a drink. She always drank with her husband, and he always drank. But neither ever seemed to get drunk.

The Lovejoys paid two thousand dollars a day for the charter, and at the end he gave Jamey a thousand-dollar bonus. All the while, he and Mrs. Lovejoy kept a deluxe suite at the Hawaiian Paradise Hotel, famous for being one of the world's most expensive places to stay. "He goes absolutely first-class and pays huge bills without sweating it," said Everett. "And it's all because he got rich through advertising. TV, radio, billboards—it's all propaganda." Everett was convinced that all lawyers, ad executives and Wall Street types were filthy rich and totally corrupt.

Jamey didn't necessarily agree but he did feel that rich people considered themselves superior to all others, and that whatever politeness they showed was just a gentle form of condescension. But then he met the Lovejoys and changed his mind.

He regretted seeing the Lovejoys go. The *Maria*'s next guests would likely be demanding, sarcastic, whiny people who tested Jamey, Everett and Bernadette's patience.

With a heavy heart, Jamey spent the last day on board with the Lovejoys. Mr. Lovejoy liked it best when they sailed out into the Kauai Channel and dropped anchor when no trace of land was visible; he liked to pretend they were floating around in the middle of nowhere. They sailed around in the distance, with both Oahu and Kauai well out of sight, but soon the wind began picking up. Whitecaps were suddenly everywhere and the *Maria*, big and heavy as she was, swayed. Jamey and Everett agreed to head back to Oahua and say goodbye to the Lovejoys. Both the Lovejoys, drunk and still in their swimsuits, got a bit surly at having their fun end over a touch of inclement weather. The Maria swayed and the wind blew hard. Mr. Lovejoy smiled and laughed. Jamey questioned his client's sanity.

Jamey called out, "I better go tell Everett to turn back toward Oahu before this weather gets any worse."

He turned but Mr. Lovejoy grabbed his arm. "No. I like it. Some adventure is good for the soul. We can ease our way back, but make sure we can't see land."

Jamey automatically thought of *The Poseidon Adventure* and *Titanic.* Still, he said, "Yessir. I'll tell Everett go return slowly."

He went into the pilot house. Everett was doing all he could to turn the *Maria* around. Bernadette watched him with alarm.

"I'm taking her back as fast as I can," Everett said. "Can you believe this weather?"

Jamey shook his head. "Go slowly."

"Why?"

"Because Lovejoy likes it out here."

Everett rolled his eyes. "Damn, Jamey. This is their last day and we got a hundred things to do before our next charter comes on board. Well, you're the boss, so we'll do it your way."

"Ease us back towards the harbor. They'll get sunburned and wanna go back to shore after a few minutes. Trust me."

"Yeah." Everett looked through the window and said, "Look at him. He wants another drink!"

Jamey looked down at the deck and saw Lovejoy smiling drunkenly and motioning for another scotch for himself and his wife.

"Better hop to it," Everett said. "And get them into life jackets right away, in case they stagger overboard." He furrowed his brow.

Jamey went into the salon and mixed the drinks. He brought them out to the Lovejoys on deck, who were soaked by the spray but seemed to be having fun. "I'll be back in a moment," he said, pleased to see that both of them were wearing swimsuits. He came back momentarily with two fluorescent-orange life jackets, with one on himself. "We'll need these," he said.

Mr. Lovejoy smiled as Jamey put the life jackets on them, as if they were putting on costumes to play a special game. "There's no getting a boat out here, you know," Jamey said. "I'm afraid we'll have to go into port."

"Then do that." Lovejoy stuck out his chest with boozy bravado. "But the wife and I are taking our chances with swimming in. But get us in closer."

Jamey scowled. "It's way too dangerous for that!"

"For you, maybe. We've gone into waters much worse than this. We'll send for our things later, Skipper. Just get us in a little bit closer and we'll do the rest." He pointed to his lifejacket. "I don't really need this thing."

Jamey rolled his eyeballs. "As you wish." He carefully made his way back into the pilot house and said to Everett and Bernadette, "They're gonna try to swim in."

"They might not make it, even with the lifejackets," said Everett.

Jamey shrugged. "Well, they're drunk enough to try, and I can't stop them." Then, "Bernadette, put on your swimsuit. Now." He was wearing his, along with a T-shirt.

She went below deck and came back shortly in her sensible one-piece black nylon swimsuit.

Jamey said, "Everett, as soon as you see us swimming towards shore, you should head to port. I don't want this boat damaged. When we reach shore, we'll walk or take a bus back to shore."

The Lovejoys were ready to go, drunk and old but fit. Their life jackets fit snugly, so Jamey didn't have to worry about that. "Well," said Lovejoy, "we'll see you folks back on Oahu."

"Nope." Jamey smiled. "It's such a pleasant evening that Bernadette and I thought we would join you two for the swim back to shore."

"Suit yourselves." With that, Lovejoy and his wife plunged into the water, followed by Jamey and Bernadette. The water was warm but choppy, even worse than Jamey expected. But the current seemed to be going their way, and as he watched Mrs. Lovejoy struggle, he grabbed her and kicked furiously and the two gradually made their way to shore. Bernadette was having similar success with her charge. Jamey couldn't believe how much this labor exhausted him. It was as difficult physically as any pugilistic training he had done. The thought flashed through his mind that if he had stayed a boxer, he wouldn't be doing this right now.

They made it onto the beach. Jamey and the others stayed there, resting, for what seemed like hours. Jamey's heart pounded with a violence he had never before experienced.

Then they marched up the beach. The Lovejoys disappeared into their hotel as Jamey and Bernadette went into the health club and toweled off. Minutes later the Lovejoys reappeared and the old man said, "My car is waiting for you. I know you have to wait for the *Maria* and clean her up. But I'll come on board for a farewell drink and we'll settle up. All right?" He smiled, a young boy of seventysomething who had been naughty today and felt quite pleased with himself.

"Yessir," said Jamey. The car delivered him and Bernadette to port, where they would wait till Everett could bring in the yacht. The two had on only their swimsuits and towels they'd used to dry off and both shivered in the car, partly from being chilled and also from the adventure they'd just shared and the work that lay ahead of them.

The night was balmy as they waited for the *Maria*. When it came in, they boarded, changed into dry clothes and drank several cups of coffee before setting out to scrape all the salt off the yacht. "What a mess. What an unnecessary mess," said Everett. Jamey knew Everett blamed this ordeal on the Lovejoys and their rich-man's insistence on having everything their own way.

Jamey sat on deck, tired but content, waiting for Lovejoy to arrive and pay his bill. Bernadette and Everett had gone into Honolulu to do some laundry, and they'd just eaten the last of the premium food the Lovejoys had brought along. That was another thing he needed to thank the Lovejoys for.

The sun had nearly set when Jamey saw the headlights of Lovejoy's car. The vehicle stopped and Lovejoy got out and headed up the gangplank. He was dressed in a seersucker suit now, with gleaming black shoes. In city clothes he lacked the agility and exuberance he had when in a swimsuit. Jamey guessed the old man would rather have been a yachtsman than King Shit of some huge ad agency. A lifetime of kissing clients' asses and making commercials and billboards? Who needed it? Certainly not Jamey Steeves.

"Good evening, sir," Jamey said. "Something to drink?"

Lovejoy nodded. "A Bud this time, Skipper."

"Yessir." Jamey headed up into the cabin and retrieved two icy bottles of Bud. He returned with the beers and the two men sat together on deck chairs. "Mrs. Lovejoy's had her excitement for the evening, so I don't imagine you'll be seeing her again till next year. But she sends her best. She said this was the best trip yet."

Jamey smiled.

Lovejoy chuckled and drank down his beer. "Mind if I have another one?"

"Will you need another lifejacket?" Jamey got up and went to get Lovejoy another beer. When he returned, Lovejoy examined the bill. "I was just thinking," the old man said, "that we don't spend enough time on this cruise. Next year, let's make it a full month. What do you say?"

Jamey grinned. "If you like."

"You know, this is the most fun I've had in a very long time," Lovejoy said. "And I have had every kind of expensive fun imaginable. You three here are so earthy and unspoiled. Maybe the missus and I will take along one or another of our grandchildren for next year." Lovejoy looked at Jamey. "Where shall we go, Skipper?"

Jamey shrugged. "You tell me, sir."

"Where have you been?"

"Everywhere, just about."

"With a month, where would you take us?"

"Probably down to Australia, with that amount of time. Have you been there?"

Lovejoy shook his head. "Haven't been many places but the office. That's why I retired." He eyed Jamey. "You spend your life taking people to all these fun places and they pay you for it?"

"Not as well as you pay," Jamey said. "You and your wife seem concerned with our comfort as much as we do with yours. That's highly unusual. Sometimes clients are difficult."

"Well, that's nice of you to say. In fact, why don't we make a commitment right here and now to spend six weeks on the *Maria* next year? We can go to Australia and then to Alaska. Hell, we can go all over the whole damned world!"

"You're the boss." Jamey said.

They sat in silence and drank. Then Lovejoy said, "People must have a low opinion of us, being a couple of spoiled old folks with all this money to throw around and whatnot. Sometimes it bothers me."

"It's probably envy, because you live so well."

Lovejoy frowned. "You've lived hard, I've lived easy."

"Not so hard. And when it *has* been hard, I made it that way."

"Your hard life has made you a big, tough guy. I envy you that." Lovejoy glanced at Jamey's thick, muscular arms. "And I admire your positive attitude towards life even though you haven't had nearly the advantages of some young men I know."

"Optimism," Jamey said, "takes work." He was glad that Lovejoy didn't know about his fights in and out of the boxing ring, his clashes with those around him and everything else he'd done. Overcoming his past had taken effort.

"Old age is an awful thing." Lovejoy's voice deepened in anger. "All the money in the world can't buy you back your youth and your zest for living." He sighed, finished his beer and said, "Well, I must be going." He stood up and shook Jamey's hand. "I'll leave you with one bit of advice."

"Yes?"

"Don't ever get old. You hear me? I mean it. Promise me you'll never get old."

Jamey nodded.

Bernadette and Everett came back after doing their errands in Honolulu. Jamey told them Lovejoy had come by, paid and left with the news that he and his wife would return the following year.

Everett's girl had contacted him and said that she had gone to the Commodore Hotel and they told her Butch was dead. Jamey thought she was brave to go to the Commodore. So Butch was dead, probably murdered. His customers were shady characters and he told lies to protect them from even shadier characters. Butch probably knew some shady character was going to kill him.

The crew retired early, because they were exhausted and planned to set out for Manila at dawn with South African clients. Jamey and Bernadette shared the master cabin that night because it was only the three of them, and Bernadette insisted on having one good lovemaking session before it was business as usual the next morning. She wasn't Jamey's idea of the physically perfect woman but she was an enthusiastic and considerate lover. Afterwards they cuddled for the longest time. Jamey said he was pleased to be with her in Hawaii. He was glad that Oz said it was a good idea to have a woman on board. Bernadette said she was glad for everything, period.

"Everett said when you bought this boat it wasn't named the *Maria*, it was something else. What's so special about that name?"

"Maria was special," Jamey told her. "I knew her long ago. She loved me. She taught me to love myself.

The trip to Manila was uneventful, and nobody seemed especially interested in the Philippines. It was just somewhere warm to go. Jamey's clients this time were two garrulous South African diamond bigshots and a couple of broads they'd apparently picked up in Paris. The men stayed drunk most of the time and ogled their two female companions. Jamey sighed and thought, Oh, well, they'll play grabass for a while and get drunk. As long as they left Bernadette alone—which they would, since she clearly wasn't their type—he would just sail along as instructed and keep his mouth shut.

The two Parisian women liked to walk around completely nude and smeared with suntan oil. Bernadette glowered at Jamey, but he just shrugged. He certainly didn't want to alienate their new clients and spoil the possibility of a good tip. So they cruised around for four days and then the South Africans flew to New York to meet up with their wives and the Parisians flew back to Europe. Jamey was quite happy as Everett steered the *Maria* back to Honolulu. The clients had given him a one-hundred-dollar tip, which wasn't bad but wasn't great, either. The next charter was a long one two weeks, and once again Jamey and Bernadette enjoyed the master cabin for a night. "I'm glad those Parisian tramps are gone," Bernadette said. "You were horny! Admit it!"

"They were clients." Jamey laughed. And indeed he *was* horny, much to Bernadette's delight. Afterwards they lay quietly together for a while and then drifted off to sleep.

Everett steered the *Maria* so that Jamey and Bernadette could sleep late and wake when they were rested and ready. In Honolulu, two letters waited for them. The first was from Paul.

"Dear Jamey," the letter said, "I finally got an update on you, and from the least likely source: Roald Lovejoy, the retired Madison Avenue ad president who cruised with you a short time ago. His firm handles Cherry Computer, and he personally called to invite me and Marni over for a drink. From the picture he painted, you and yours on the *Maria* (is that the name?) really are having yourselves one hell of a good time. Sounds like you made a good choice, selling your stock and buying that yacht. Well, more power to you. My pal Josh Hawkins is getting married soon and may be booking with you for their honeymoon. Hope you don't mind the referral. Wish Marni and I could drop everything and come sail with you guys."

The other letter was from Hawkins, asking about the availability of the *Maria* for a certain date. Hawkins said he wanted only to sail around Hawaii for a couple of weeks, with no particular destination in mind. Just a couple of weeks for himself and his wife in the waters between the islands. This guy can afford it, Jamey thought. He knew that Hawkins, one of Paul's best friends, was the financial wizard who'd helped Paul and Hank start Cherry Computer. But the Hawkins who wrote the letter sounded like the easiest-to-please guy on earth. The truth, Jamey guessed, was somewhere in between.

Jamey sent Hawkins a note saying the suggested date would be perfect. He mentioned to Bernadette that Paul had practically talked Hawkins into booking with them, and she said, "Then write Paul a thank-you!" As he did so, he remembered that Paul had said, "If there's anything I can do for you..."

You sure can, Paul. "There's a guy named Wasserman in L.A. I introduced you and Dee to him that night. I want to know if my trouble has gone away, and he would know. Also, he might have some contact info concerning my son. Please check into these matters."

Chapter 3

Paul was astonished by how easily he could track people down. When he got Jamey's note asking about retired boxing manager Sol Wasserman, he called *Boxing Today* magazine; if that didn't know Wass, he would simply call a private detective and let *him* worry about it. But the magazine had a current address for Wass, and Paul almost wished they had withheld it as he walked up the concrete steps of the Joseph Hotel. He'd read a newspaper article recently about the Joseph, a large rooming house some bleeding-heart agency had had renovated for needy people. The hotel, on Stanford Street, sat in the middle of skid row. Paul took a taxi there.

Straight-backed and dapper, he pressed the buzzer on the door of the rehabilitated building in the unrehabilitated neighborhood full of decrepit old people and hopeless young ones.

A sorry-looking old man with a reddish-blue nose opened the lobby door and squinted in the autumnal brightness. He smelled of death. If Paul hadn't been here on urgent personal business to help Jamey, he would have turned around, gotten back into the first taxi he could find and sped off.

"Is Mr. Wasserman here?" he asked.

"Room three-oh-two," the old man said. "He expectin' to see ya?"

"Yeah, I think so." Paul stepped inside, stepped past the old man and climbed the stairs at the back of the lobby. The entire building smelled of death. The House of Usher, Paul thought. Poe would have been inspired by this place.

Music and voices were audible from inside the rooms. Paul reached room 302 and found it open. On the bed sat Wasserman, dozing, bald except for wisps of gray hair. He wore a yellow T-shirt and ill-fitting jeans. Paul remembered being introduced around the night he saw Jamey fight, but nobody looked like the old wretch sitting before him.

"Are you Mr. Wasserman?"

The old man looked up vacantly. "Who wants to know?"

"I'm Paul Steeves." He offered to shake hands.

Wasserman looked at Paul's proffered hand as if it were covered with leprosy. "Steeves? I remember a B.J. Steeves. What the hell you want?"

Paul smirked. Well, old man, your memory's all right, at least as far as grudges are concerned. Only Jamey could get someone that pissed. He took out a hundred dollars and dropped the money on the bed beside Wasserman. "B.J. says he owes you this."

Wasserman looked at the money. "He owes me more."
He stuffed the bills into his pocket without getting up. "How's ol' B.J. these days?"

"Surviving."

"Too bad. I hoped he was keeping Jimmy Hoffa company."

"Look, sir, I just came by to ask you one question. B.J. wants to know if there's still trouble here for him."

Wasserman sighed. "No trouble, no nothing. After he got done with 'Forever' Young, my luck went downhill. Young lost his edge and left boxing. I never found another guy who could have taken Tyson. And now here I am. All because of B.J. 'Dynamite Hands' Steeves. What a joke."

"Thanks, Mr. Wasserman. Also, I wanted to ask—"

"I thought you said one question. But while you're here, go ahead."

"It's his wife. Where is she?"

Wasserman nodded. "Honey. Got picked up for prostitution. Public drunkenness, too. Made her name as a stripper while her old man was in the ring. Got old and fat and turned to the world's oldest profession. Couldn't happen to a nicer guy."

Paul figured he had enough information, so he said, "Thanks for your help, Mr. Wasserman. I got to be going."

Wasserman cocked an eyebrow. "What's the hurry? Could use a little more conversation. No entertainment in here. Got no cable."

"Honest, sir, I got to shove off." Paul bounded down the steps, hurried through the lobby and went out the door, immediately noticing the nearby Los Angeles River. The river, by comparison, actually looked good to him. At least it didn't look or smell like death.

Jamey felt himself being shaken awake and looked up to see the smiling face of a pretty flight attendant. Over the Pacific Ocean, he'd gobbled up his bland microwaved chicken-and-vegetables airline meal and, out of boredom, had a couple of scotches over ice. Then he'd sunk into a deep sleep and still felt muzzy as he trailed the other passengers off the airliner and into the terminal of Los Angeles International Airport. Paul was waiting for him.

He collected his bag and shook Paul's hand as they struggled past the countless people coming or going. "Airport's really crowded, huh?"

Paul shrugged. "About the usual."

Jamey looked around. "All these people. Unreal. Second-largest city in America now. I don't know what they see in it."

"You can wait here and I'll go get the car," Paul said as they left the building.

"Naw, I'll walk with you. My legs are cramped from all that sitting."

"Suit yourself."

As they walked, Jamey said, "You do that little favor for me?"

"Yeah. We'll talk in the car."

Outside, Jamey looked up into the haze. "Nice shit-colored sky." He was already sweating into his light blue T-shirt. He saw some palm trees in the distance that looked near death. "I haven't been back here in years and I'm already looking forward to going back to Honolulu. But I have things to do here first."

They got to Paul's rented Cadillac in the parking lot and Jamey tossed his bags into the backseat. "So? What's the good word?" Jamey asked as Paul drove.

Paul sighed. "Well, I found Wasserman. He says nobody here knows or cares anymore about B.J. Steeves."

"Okay. And Honey and my son?"

"Well, that's a bit more complicated. I got my private eye on that one. Honey was picked up twice for prostitution and public indecency, and Buford—apparently he goes by Ford—is in a military school. Don't know who arranged that."

"Well, at least the kid has a fighting chance." Jamey grinned at his own pun. "Say, with her legal problems, wouldn't that make it easier for me to get custody of him?"

"Probably. You want to go see my lawyer about that?"

"Yeah, you should. I want to get my kid, take him back to Hawaii and forget all about Los Angeles. Just do my thing and raise my kid in my new home."

"I'll set up the meeting with the lawyer," Paul said. "But I need to head back to South Bay to look after things. You can use the car and the apartment here."

"Sounds good. The car and apartment, I mean. Till I can get my divorce, my kid and head back to Hawaii."

They drove on in silence. A traffic sign said Long Beach next exit. "Want to go to Long Beach?" Paul teased. "All those boats docked there. It'll make you homesick."

"The only thing Long Beach would do for me would be to make me praise God that my *Maria* is back in Honolulu."

"Speaking of the *Maria,*" Paul said, "Josh Hawkins can't stop talking about how much he and his wife loved sailing with you. So, what did you think of him?"

"Josh? Smart guy. Then, "Say, are you *really* gonna run for mayor of South Bay?"

"Yes. Don't you approve?"

"I think politics is a dirty business, filled with corrupt, self-serving bastards."

"Well, maybe there's room in the world for a good one."

"I seriously doubt it."

They went the rest of the way in silence. They reached the condominium complex where Paul and Marni kept a suite. The place was a pastel-and-stucco development, like a hundred others in L.A. Jamey was expected something much bigger and fancier.

Paul unlocked the big iron gate at the entrance and the two men walked up to the second floor. Inside, the place was done in a fashionable Western motif, complete with cowboy paintings covering the walls. The air conditioning was on full blast, making Jamey feel nice and cool after the oppressive heat outside. "Nice, real nice," he said, looking around at the brown leather sofa and Western-style furniture. "Didn't know you liked this Wild West stuff."

"Not me. Marni. It's all *her* idea. Not that she sees any of it that often. She's pregnant again and stays up in South Bay mostly. I'm being pulled in every direction, too." After a pause, he said, "Well, Jamey, tell you the truth, I came down here just to show you where the apartment is. Gotta head back home right away. You have a home here as long as you want and a car too. If you want to order in, there's a pizza-and-chicken place not far where I keep a tab. If you need anything..."

"Go," Jamey said with a smile. "I'll be fine. Just wanna see that lawyer, get my kid and off I go. You do your thing and I'll do mine."

Jamey took a shower, drank a cold beer, put on fresh clothes and walked around the neighborhood. West Los Angeles. He remembered it fairly well from when he lived and fought here. He ate an artichoke salad at an outdoor place and wandered around all evening. He enjoyed himself but didn't feel nostalgic for any of it. He especially enjoyed the good news Paul relayed from Wass, that it was safe for him now to come back and collect his kid. He had to get his brother and a private eye to look around and ask questions to make sure he could set foot on California soil again. How had he managed to make so much trouble for himself and others?

He closed his eyes for a moment and shook his head. Christ, what a life.

Mulholland Military Academy, up in the hills, surrounded by trees, was named for the city engineer who, decades earlier, had brought water to Los Angeles and changed the place forever. Mulholland-this or –that wherever you go, Jamey thought. Bring them water, dig them oil or make them enough money and they'll name the whole damn place in your honor.

The great iron gates swung open and he drove slowly through. He saw boys in uniform doing drills of some sort. Half the place seemed to be grass, with the boys on some sort of activity or another. Jamey didn't see his son there at all, but guessed he was somewhere. He parked and went up the stone steps, and into the front hall. He saw no one guarding anything. But he followed a sign directing him to the administration office and soon found a woman working at a computer. She looked up. "Yes?"

"Hello, I'm here to see my son."

"What is his name?"

"Buford James Steeves the third."

The woman looked at him as if he'd just slapped her in the face. "Just one moment, please. I'll get the head man."

Jamey sat down and wondered at the expression on her face. He looked around and saw how orderly and immaculate everything was. Well, maybe Honey had the right idea after all. A military school might be just the thing the boy needed. Maybe there was something like that in Hawaii. He would have to look into it.

"Mr. Steeves? I'm Colonel Haverford. Please come in."

Jamey stood up and went into the office with the man. He had all kinds of military things and such all over his office. A career man, probably, from Vietnam. "Have a seat," he said.

Jamey sat and said. "Look, I don't want to take up too much of your time. But is my son available right now?"

"Mr. Steeves, you weren't the person I was expecting to see. In the application it indicated you were deceased."

Fuck you, Honey. Fuck you in the heart. "Probably just wishful thinking on my ex-wife's part."

Haverford chuckled. "I see. Maybe we just misunderstood. I've never actually met her. She just covered Buford's expenses, and sent him here. At any rate, we don't consider your marital issues any of our business, so we'll pass on that part of this visit. I'm glad you're here, Mr. Steeves. Not a moment too soon."

Jamey raised his eyebrows. "Relieved? Why?"

"It's Buford..."

"Yes?"

"He's an insufferable bully." Haverford looked at Jamey closely. "If you don't mind my saying so, sir, you're quite a big man, physically. I would think twice about tangling with you, and I'm a career soldier. Well, Buford is a big guy like you, and he has a vicious temper. He'll punch first and ask questions later. He has everyone afraid of him, and he seems to thrive on intimidating others."

Jamey blew out a big breath. "Well, isn't physical aggressiveness a desirable quality in a military cadet?"

"This level of aggression? No, sir. Getting along with others is paramount. Around here it seems to all of us that Buford Steeves has singlehandedly declared war on the Mulholland Military Academy."

"Then your problem is mine," Jamey said.

Haverford offered him a small smile. "I'm glad you see it that way."

"As of this moment, you can consider Buford James Steeves the third a *former* cadet."

Haverford frowned. "I don't think it's that simple, Mr. Steeves. I've never met you before now, and he's a minor. I can't just let him go into your custody."

Jamey calmly reached into his jacket pocket and took out the documents provided by the private eye. They were about Honey. He practically flung them across the desk to the colonel, who seemed reluctant to touch them.

Haverford studied them for a moment. "Harriet Steeves. Soliciting, public indecency." He shook his head, not knowing exactly what to say. "Nasty stuff."

"Tell me about it," Jamey said. "So, you still want my boy around here?"

Haverford handed back the papers. "I'll have him sent right away."

Jamey nodded, putting the papers back into his pocket.

Within half an hour Ford and Jamey were in the Cadillac, on their way out of Mulholland Military Academy, Ford's trunk stowed in the backseat, the boy sullen and edgy but tanned and handsome and prodigiously broad-shouldered. Jamey looked at his son with ambivalence, admiring the boy's good looks and brawny physique but worrying that Ford was going to turn into a troublemaker.

"We'll get you some changes of clothes tomorrow and then I'll tell you what's going on. You're leaving California for a good long while. You'll like where I'm taking you. But no more fighting. Ever. Understand?"

"Understood," Ford said, staring out the window.

"Good," Jamey muttered, driving past the great iron gates of the institution.

Chapter 4

1996

Dee had honestly believed that she would not live to see her fortieth birthday. She was so wrapped up in her new screenplay that she had forgotten to get depressed over this personal milestone.

She wrote scenes, got better ideas and rewrote them. Each time, they got tighter and better focused. Many disliked the drudgery and loneliness of screenwriting, but she thrived on it. It could be fun and fulfilling, conjuring these movies in your head and writing down what you saw.

This was her third screenplay. Her first two had been produced and received moderate critical acclaim. Moviegoers seemed a bit indifferent to her work.

Her screenplay was set in Los Angeles and would be filmed there. All her work was set in the two places that had been home for her—the City of Angels and San Francisco. She had never lived in New York City and felt she couldn't convincingly write about such a place. It was nice that her work was virtually guaranteed to be produced—the director of her first two efforts, Douglas Kaplo, was also her lover.

When she wasn't writing, she carried on the political activities that had kept her sane since Jackson's murder. She went to political rallies to protest American military involvement in Central America. She did many things to try to keep busy, sometimes going places with Marcia Goldberg.

Douglas's new film was in the early stages. Dee had written its screenplay and was serving as an editor of sorts as well; she went in to watch the dailies and gave her opinion as to whether the dialogue worked.

In this case she had a special chore. The rushes featured a key scene between Jon Pinoli, a celebrated stage actor making his film debut, and a new actress named Diane McKee. The scene was nothing like what she had written; Pinoli, a dramatist and master improvisor, had forgotten his lines and simply winged it; McKee played along, and the scene was purely spontaneous. "Douglas, why didn't you just say 'Cut!' when it was clear Pinoli had forgotten his lines?"

Kaplo shrugged. "Well, he *is* a great improv actor. I just wanted to see what he could do."

"He didn't do much this time. His improv is boring."

"Well, the improv stays in the picture."

Dee shrugged. Why did she write dialog when the actors were just going to be too lazy to memorize them and then just say whatever came into their heads? Still, it was better not to push it. Douglas Kaplo would have his own way and that was that.

He put on his coat and said to her, "By the way, are you free for a birthday dinner?"

She shook her head. "My brother's flying down to pick me up and take me to his place up in South Bay. Sorry."

"Flying you up there just for the weekend. Jesus, rich people." With that, he added, "Did you see that *American Business* story?"

"Yes." The magazine had run a piece called The Man to Watch. Paul and Marni at home, beaming at the camera. The magazine called the mayor of South Bay "an imaginative high-tech innovator and a no-nonsense elected official." A humble, hardworking San Franciscan who had attended People's University and changed the world.

Blah, blah, blah, Dee thought. What about Josh Hawkins, Paul Hankowsky and Fred Bayliss? Paul now ran South Bay, a place that ran itself. Good publicity for him, though.

Douglas swung out the door and into the Los Angeles night.

"I always like him better when he's about to leave," Marcia said. Dee laughed.

Paul came in at around dinnertime. He sat back and listened while Dee had Marcia rewind the Pinoli improvisation scene.

Afterwards, Paul, said, "No offense, Dee, but if that's the best dialogue you can write, maybe you better to go to film school and take a few courses."

"I hear ya." She got up and put on her coat. "Be seeing you, Marcy." With that, she blew out the door.

Paul and Dee said little to each other on the ride to LAX. Nor did they speak much when they boarded the Learjet to head up the coast.

"So," she finally said, "how's stuff?"

Paul laughed.

"Seriously, Paul, that article on you was a bit too promotional, don't you think?"

"It was a big hand job. But, in the words of my favorite porn star, 'A hand job can be a very nice thing to receive.'"

Dee considered this for a moment as she saw the flight attendant come by for their drink orders. She was on a Learjet on her fortieth birthday, courtesy of her brother, the zillionaire high-technology entrepreneur. If the magazine's hand-jobbing article was a good thing in *his* opinion, so be it.

"Wish I had gone home first and put on some fresh clothes or had my hair done or something."

"You look fine."

"Well, I don't feel fine. I feel middle-aged, unwanted and used up." She turned to her brother. "Did you know my current boyfriend is banging at least two other women?"

"I read that in the *Times* this morning," he replied.

"Funny. Let's change the subject. How's Marni?"

Marni had suffered a miscarriage and become taciturn and moody. She had been sober for some time but started smoking marijuana, which she seemed to think was an improvement over booze. Paul hated the smell of the burning weed and insisted that she smoke outside.

The flight attendant came by with their drinks. Paul reached into his travel bag and took out a square case. He handed it to Dee. "Happy birthday, sis."

She smiled and unwrapped the gift. It was a gold Rolex, encrusted with diamonds. She leaned over, said "Thanks," and kissed his cheek. Thinking: I must not cry. I must face this day with dignity.

"What else did you get?"

She pointed at the watch. "This is it."

"Did Caitlin at least call?"

"Nope. Maybe she's too busy up there at the university," Dee said.

Paul frowned. "She couldn't be too busy to pick up the phone and call her mother to say happy birthday."

"You don't know my kid as well as I do."

"Your kid doesn't like me too much, I'm afraid."

"She's ambivalent about *me,* too."

Caitlin, upon graduating from a public high school in Los Angeles, announced she wanted to attend Yale. But she'd essentially traipsed through school, wasting time and barely passing. Sometimes she actually flunked and had to go to summer school. Dee called Paul and asked, frankly, if Caitlin stood any chance of getting into Yale. Paul said that the Ivy League schools were prestigious for a reason—they were fiercely competitive. If Caitlin had her heart set on Yale, she should have studied harder and done better.

So Caitlin ultimately decided to stay on the West Coast and attend People's University. She chose her uncle's alma mater because of its pretty campus and comfortable distance from her mother. Plus, her Uncle Paul ensured her admission.

As a student, she was making do and enjoying life on her own. But she seldom called her mother, and when the two did speak, she was terse and unenthusiastic. Caitlin, in Dee's opinion, could go for months without speaking to her mother.

"My daughter's mad at me," she told Paul.

"Why?"

"Because of my relationship with Douglas."

"You have your own life, right? She's old enough to respect that."

"Tell *her.* She's met him once or twice and practically sneered at him. She thinks he's an overrated jackass who's gotten very lucky."

"Is he?"

She smiled in spite of herself.

"Has he asked you to marry him?"

"No. He's on too much of an ego trip right now. Besides, we probably thinks he can do better than marry a 40-year-old widow with a snotty kid."

"Does he love you?"

"Yes, and I love *him*. More often than not." They both laughed.

When they entered the South Bay mansion, Paul and Dee heard the awful racket of things being smashed. In the living room, they discovered Marni swinging Paul's old aluminum softball bat, tossing up pieces of photographic equipment and shattering them. "Grand slam!"

Paul stepped cautiously towards her. Christ, he thought. She's fucked up again. "Marni!"

"Better stand back, dude," she said, her eyes glittering. "I'm batting a thousand."

"What are you doing?" he asked, his arms outspread.

"Hizzoner wants me to explain myself, so I'll tell him. I'm taking batting practice."

"Batting practice is over." He snatched the bat from her.

Marni plopped onto the sofa. "Fuck."

"Do you know how much shit you just destroyed?" Paul used the bat as a pointer, poking it in the air at all the debris strewn about.

"Well, what of it? You can always buy me more. You're good at buying things, people, political offices..."

Paul glowered.

She rubbed her nose and looked over at Dee. "Have you read any of the crap they're writing about Paul? He wants to be president but maybe he won't get there because he is married to a foreign national. That would be me. A mixed marriage in the White House!

And you, sister of Hizzoner, widow of Jackson Worthy, *you* know a lot about mixed marriages, eh?" She winked.

"Well, I think I'll just go on up to the guest bedroom," Dee said. "Goodnight." She hurried up the stairs and locked her bedroom door.

In the morning, nobody spoke of the night before. Someone had cleaned up the smashed photographic equipment. Dee, Paul and Marni were driving up to Marin County to pick up Caitlin. Dee felt grateful that her reunion with her daughter would occur in the company of Paul. Caitlin could be moody and difficult, and if it was just mother and daughter, Dee would be terribly uncomfortable. They drove pleasantly up the freeway and enjoyed the view. Then Marni announced she needed to use the ladies' room and as soon as Paul pulled into a gas station she got out.

"Paul," Dee said as they sat alone in the car, "let's all go on the wagon in support of Marni."

"Why?"

"Because she's a drunk."

"Nobody's perfect."

Dee made a face.

Just then Marni got back into the car. Dee's cell phone rang. Caitlin. "You're on your way up, Mom?" she asked. "That's nice." Ever since moving up north and starting classes at People's University, she had been terse and cool with her mother, and Dee longed for the old days when Caitlin had been a sweet little kid who loved her momma.

"Look," Caitlin was saying over the phone, "I know I promised lunch, but I have a softball game today and they count on me to pitch. Maybe we can hook up another time..." Her voice trailed off.

"Well, we're in the car, on our way over, so while Uncle Paul and Aunt Marni have lunch, I'll see you. I'll just come to your game and watch you. Maybe I'll boo the other team." Dee laughed but Caitlin didn't.

Dee joined Paul and Marni for lunch and then took the car while Paul and Marni wandered around downtown South Bay. She had an easy time finding People's University and was impressed all over again by its beauty, with its redwoods and beautiful lawns, so far removed from the urban oppression of a big city. If the college did a questionable job of preparing students for life in the real world—Dee always felt that Paul had succeeded *despite* higher education—this place certainly was a nice hangout for four years or so.

This was Saturday, so few people were around. Past the buildings was a large green field with some activity. Dee walked over and found the coed softball game in progress. Caitlin stood on the mound, dressed in faded cutoffs and a white baseball shirt with blue three-quarter sleeves. Her blonde hair was bound up into a floppy ponytail that hung down her back. She also wore dark sunglasses in the painful glare. Dee's quickly put on her own dark glasses.

Dee watched Caitlin's windup. Long and lithe, with narrow shoulders and plump breasts. Her smooth, tanned legs were bathed in sweat. The spectators were mostly young men and women unable to take their eyes off the pitcher. Although her naturally pink lips were upcurved into an eternal smile, Caitlin showed no mercy, pitching everyone hard, high and inside. One at a time, her opponents stepped into the batter's box and soon were called out; the boys, angered at this smiling cutie's intimidating pitches, took vicious hacks at the ball but hit mainly fly balls that the outfielders easily caught. Caitlin laughed at the frustrated hitters.

Dee, full of admiration, watched Caitlin retire the side. *My little girl has the face of an angel and the instincts of a killer.*

Caitlin reached her mother, said, "Hi, Mom," and offered her a peck on the cheek.

"Surprised to see me?"

"No, I knew you'd find your way here." Caitlin said to the others, "I'll be gone for a few minutes," and started walking away with Dee, who said, "So, where shall we go?"

"Let's just walk around the campus a little bit. Didn't Paul and Marni come? I thought he might have liked to see the school again."

Dee always cringed a bit when Caitlin called her uncle and aunt Paul and Marni, which the girl did even to their faces. "You know, your Uncle Paul says he's invited you over lots of times, but you never visit them. You're just minutes away."

"I guess I'm just not very good about visiting people," Caitlin said.

"You should see them. After all, everything we have, all our advantages—"

"Courtesy of Paul Steeves, from his Cherry Computer fortune." Caitlin nodded. "Tell him I'm grateful for whatever strings he pulled to get me here into good old People's U., even if it isn't quite Yale."

"Tell him yourself," Dee said. "And leave out the Yale part."

"Mom, it's a sunny day." Caitlin smiled at her. "We really don't see each other all that often. So let's not get an attitude, okay?"

"Was your boyfriend one of those guys you just struck out?" Dee said, changing the subject. Caitlin had mentioned dating a chemical engineering major.

Caitlin laughed. "No, he's on our side. Maybe I'll introduce you later on. Anyway, he's just this guy I've been seeing. His parents don't like me. They think I'm just a stuck-up Steeves."

Are you just a stuck-up Steeves? "I really don't know you anymore. Is there anyone you approve of?"

The girl nodded. "Immanuel Kant. Jean-Paul Sartre. Buckminster Fuller. And how's that other philosophical giant, Douglas Kaplo? Working hard or hardly working?"

"Douglas is fine, thanks for asking." Dee wanted to smack her daughter when she talked like that. "Do you get down to Los Angeles often?"

Caitlin shrugged. "Now and again."

"Well, next time, let me know beforehand and we can make some plans together. Bring your guy along."

"As I said, he's nothing much."

"Oh, I'm sure he's very nice." Dee paused. "So, how's school?"

Caitlin gave a small shrug. "Okay."

"Just okay?"

"Yeah, really."

"Paul says you're on academic probation."

Caitlin took off her sunglasses and glowered. "How the fuck would *he* know?"

Dee took off *her* sunglasses and glowered back. "Are you serious? I'm surprised they haven't renamed this place Steeves University, after all he's done for it. He keeps an eye on you."

"God," Caitlin said, "being mayor of South Bay must be a lame job if he's got nothing better to do than spy on me."

"What would you do if they threw you out?"

"Go somewhere and make a difference. Join an armed settlement on the West Bank. Maybe the Peace Corps. It would be a hell of a lot more interesting and meaningful than life here at People's U. I'm just biding my time, you know."

Dee knew she wasn't kidding. Beautiful, blonde, bored Caitlin Wilhite, of the Steeves family, reeking of new millions, or perhaps even billions, would do just that—impulsively join some radical group and go overseas, seeking excitement and danger. To hell with what Mother thought.

"You know"—Dee tried not to sound condescending—"you don't have to go all the way to the West Bank to make a positive change in the world. You can do that from *here*, can't you? Demonstrations, protests, getting involved in the political end of things..."

Caitlin laughed. "Join a bunch of zealots who march and shout? They're just in love with the sounds of their own voices. They did that in Washington, D.C. back in the Vietnam days and Johnson just ignored them. They did that at Kent State, too, and the National Guard shot them."

"Caitlin," Dee asked, "do you consider anything meaningful?"

The girl paused. "No. If People's University has taught me anything, it's nihilism. If I flunk out of here, too bad for me. If you disapprove of me and what I've become here, too bad for *you*. I'm a grown, independent woman now. I have my own mind and can make my own decisions." She put her sunglasses back on. "I'm going back to my softball game. Tell Paul and Marni I said hi."

Caitlin hurried back to the playing field. Her teammates waved for her to hurry. She broke into a run and didn't look back. Dee headed back to Paul's car. She stayed for dinner, then flew back to Los Angeles that night. She still worked hard at thinking about absolutely nothing.

Chapter 5

1997

Paul peeked out the Learjet's window, saw nothing new and stretched his long legs as the small, powerful plane soared over the Mojave Desert to Las Vegas. Next to him, Josh Hawkins sorted through printouts. Paul reviewed documents, too. As mayor of South Bay, he had to submit a budget, which he hated. Paul saw himself as a world-changing entrepreneur and philosopher, a visionary and technological wizard, not a number-crunching, paper-pushing bureaucrat. He stared for a moment at the paperwork in his lap. Did Clint Eastwood, when mayor of Carmel-by-the-Sea, have to put up with this shit? Paul bet he didn't. The mundane facts of municipal life. Ugh.

Josh Hawkins was also looking at numbers and dollar signs, and those belonged to himself and Paul. They had invested in Paul Hankowsky's Nevada mining company. Hank had relocated his operations from Reno to Las Vegas following the death of his father; Paul and Josh were flying out there to confront him about the vast amounts of money Hank had been spending in Indonesia. The press releases he had disseminated boasted of the discovery of "millions of troy ounces of gold" that his company was about to extract and ship to Nevada.

Josh Hawkins said to Paul, "I smell bullshit."

Paul admonished him to say nothing further until they got to Las Vegas. Paul just couldn't believe that Hank would fabricate press releases, especially considering how much money he had made over the years. Plus his marriage to Suzi Bayliss, who had plenty of greenbacks in case Hank ever managed to piss away his own.

When the flight landed, a charming Mexican woman said, "Hello, I'm Mr. Hankowsky's assistant. I will deliver you to the Versailles Hotel and Casino." The Versailles, newly opened, was considered the world's most expensive gaming resort. The woman escorted Paul and Josh to a waiting limousine which took them to the Strip. The hotel was just a few miles from the airport, but bumper-to-bumper traffic kept them in the big car for nearly half an hour. Paul and Josh shivered from the air conditioning as they sat looking out the window. One gargantuan resort after another shimmering in the desert heat.

The Palace of Versailles was a cross between Parisian whorehouse tacky and Las Vegas glitz. Hank had rented them a huge room with a majestic view. A huge bar occupied an entire corner of the lavish suite.

"Mr. Hankowsky will be by soon as he can," said the assistant. "Please make yourselves at home." Then she slipped out the door.

"We've come to find out if he's broke and he's put us up at the most expensive hotel in the world. How's that for irony?" Josh said, shaking his head.

"Well, I'm gonna make some phone calls." Paul disappeared into one of the two spacious, opulent bedrooms and took out his cell phone. In a moment he had Marni on the line from South Bay. She had stopped drinking, for the time being. He made at least a couple of calls per day out of concern for both her and their child. She had discovered TV talk shows and watched them for hours at a time. "How's Vegas?" she asked, cheerful and apparently sober.

"Hotter than hell."

"We're a bit fogged in here," Marni said. "Will you be there long, Paul?"

"I really hope not."

"Me too."

He hadn't told her the purpose of the trip, and she hadn't asked. Good. They spoke for a few more minutes, then he called his secretary at South Bay City Hall.

"I've been trying to reach you," she said. "We have problems over at People's U. that the police chief wants to check out with you."

"I'm on it." Paul hung up and looked in the mirror for a moment. He looked far beyond his years. Gone was the fresh-faced boy from Western Hills, replaced by a young old man who had started a world-changing high-tech company and now, for an encore, to show off for the world, was the mayor of South Bay, California. Shit, he needed a vacation. He needed his Marni back, needed her sweet and sober the way she was when they fell in love. He wondered how much longer he could go before he had a coronary, stroke or nervous breakdown. When it happened, would there be someone ready to do his job? Of course. People were eager to take shit if there was money or glory in it.

He pressed a button on his phone and within moments had Police Chief Lee on the line. "We have trouble at People's, Mayor. A large number of young people are occupying Central Quad. They say they're protesting the greed and corruption of corporate America."

I guess they're protesting me. Paul took a deep breath, wishing he could just hang up, fly back to South Bay and cuddle Marni on the sofa for a few months. "Okay, Chief, here's what to do. Call Day and tell him you've spoken to me and that I have authorized you to give the students an ultimatum: they have twenty-four hours to vacate the campus or they will be bodily removed."

He hung up. Paul wandered back into the living room. Josh was in his undershirt, sitting at the coffee table, frowning at the Hankowsky paperwork. He looked up. "Paul, I'm afraid Hank has fucked us right up the ass."

"Maybe that's why my hemorrhoids are bleeding." Paul opened the refrigerator and took out a can of Budwesier.

There were other calls he needed to make, and he stood at the window deciding which person to call next when his cell phone rang. Dee. Paul was still angry at her for calling Marni a drunk.

"Got a minute?" she was asking. "I know you're down in Vegas on urgent business. But I need to talk to you. It's really important."

"Where are you?"

"At home in L.A. Did you know that Caitlin's been expelled from People's?"

"No." Well, he knew Caitlin wasn't college material. She had been all hot to attend Yale, but they said no and even Paul couldn't help her with that. He wondered if she was one of those agitators "occupying" Central Quad at that moment.

"And did you know that she's been *shacking up* with some guy in Oakland now!"

Paul laughed. A twenty-year-old girl shacking up with some guy? Whoo, bad stuff, man.

"Paul, I'm serious. She's likely to end up in one of those freaky cults. Christ, this is California! We've had Charles Manson, the SLA, the Moonies, the Hell's Angels..."

"Aren't you overreacting? She's a grown woman and can make up her own mind about things once her situation stabilizes a little bit." After a pause, he said, "What exactly can I do for you, Dee?"

"You can use whatever influence that you might have to give her some direction in life so she doesn't go off and join some bullshit weirdo cult."

Paul rolled his eyes. His sister at forty was still naïve in so many ways. She probably never would figure out how the world worked and would be calling upon Brother Paul even from the grave. She also kept forgetting that her daughter was now a legal adult who didn't have to take orders from Mommy anymore. Against his better judgment, Paul said, "Dee, I'm not really sure what I can do to help in this matter—"

"Well, *I* do," she snapped. "Cherry is now a worldwide company. I'm sure there's *somewhere* you can put her. Overseas, on the moon, wherever. If you really give a damn about her."

Paul heard the phone slam down and gently slipped his cell phone into his breast pocket. Nice to hear from you, too. After thinking for a moment, he took out his phone again and punched Dee's number. "Relax. I'll do whatever I have to. I'll look out for her. I'll kidnap her if necessary, have her sent up to the Aleutians."

Dee laughed. "Paul, you've always been there for me."

Hank arrived at the Palace of Versailles suite around dinnertime. He looked sunburned and harried; he had lost weight. He was wearing a tan linen jacket and matching slacks, with a red T-shirt underneath, like Sonny Crockett from TV's *Miami Vice*. Paul half expected to see a fake gold Rolex on the guy's wrist.

"Sorry I couldn't come sooner." Hank went to the bar and twisted open a plastic bottle of chilled spring water. He took a swig and smiled. "I don't drink anymore, you know. Down here, the alcohol dehydrates you. Want to do some sightseeing? I can take you around. Vegas is going through some huge changes. An exciting time, let me tell you. It's a shame Suzi couldn't join me, but her dad's sick. Well, I'm sure he'll get better." He shrugged and drank more water.

"Hank." Paul sighed. "We know why Suzi's not here, so please cut the crap." Bayliss had contacted Paul confidentially with the news that Suzi had left Hank because her husband had gotten involved with an actress and was apparently pretending to be a latter-day William Randolph Hearst, flying between Las Vegas and Los Angeles every other day, using his resources and influence to promote his girlfriend's career. Paul grew concerned and called Josh.

"Paul," Hank was saying, "I won't deny it. Suzi and I have had our problems, but we're working things out and my personal life hasn't affected my professional life."

"It's all over," Paul said. "We have to find out what's going on with you and our money, Hank."

Hank shrugged. "You get statements."

Paul laughed.

"Well, look. That thing in Indonesia has been more complicated than we would have thought. But they assure me the gold is there. Damn, if we mined the stuff, the money we could make..."

"Hank," Josh said, "we've been doing our math, and it seems you've lost three million dollars of our money."

Hank frowned.

But when Paul and Josh just stared at him, Hank plopped onto the sofa and said, "OK, you win. No more bullshit. Let me tell you boys the long, sad story of my life after Cherry Computer."

He told them about Gillian Huberty, the striking, Julliard-trained, Los Angeles-based young actress who was getting great reviews in the trade magazines. "She was being compared to Meryl Streep, for Christ's sake. Do you understand that? She'll probably win some Oscars. I met her at this party, and she was like no other woman I had ever met. And I've been married to crazy Suzi, so you can imagine how wonderful Gillian was in comparison. So Gillian, she wants a man of means, of course. Well, pretty soon I'm flashing my platinum American Express card all over Rodeo Drive. Jesus, I bought her a fanciest Mercedes convertible you ever saw."

Since Hank had shown bad timing in unloading his Cherry stock at its lowest point, he had less cash than the others. He got a lead on a gold mine in Indonesia. "I run a mining company. We got a tip that there was a huge gold mine overseas. We started digging, costing more money. Those officials wanted big bribes, and I was too proud to call it a loss and pull out, so I just basically began doctoring the statements and putting out false press releases. What can I say?"

"I'll tell you what you can say," Paul muttered. "Fraud, pure and simple. You'll do time for this."

"You guys wouldn't press charges," Hank said.

"Yes we would," Paul told him.

Hank gasped. "With all the money you have? I'm broke but you're not."

"That's not the issue, Hank," Josh said.

"And after all I've done for you?" Hank looked hurt and angry. "Don't forget that I practically *invented* that damn personal computer the world can't live without now. Remember all those tricky engineering problems I overcame? The fucking disk drive I singlehandedly built? I'm the only reason you guys are stinking rich."

Josh Hawkins thought for a moment. "Do you have any assets, any money?"

Hank nodded. "Sure. Anyone will lend me as much as I want. If you mean cash on hand, I have just under a million stashed away."

"Wait here. I want to talk to Paul," Josh said. The two men stepped into the hallway. Josh looked feverish. "Paul, I don't want to get into some nasty, prolonged financial issue with that fool. And I don't want to get into the legal aspects of this matter right here and now, but if he can reimburse us for some of our losses, I would just as soon split his cash on hand with you right now. That's the best deal we can hope for."

Paul's eyes narrowed. "Is that legal?"

"He's not in bankruptcy yet, so I'm sure it would be technically legal. Otherwise, every shareholder gets a piece of what little he has left."

"Good old Josh. Always the pragmatist. Nope. We'll do it by the book. Keep it all absolutely and completely legal."

Josh grimaced. "Uncle! Uncle! You win!"

They went back inside.

"We've decided, Hank," Josh said, "that we're going to collect whatever capital you have tomorrow morning. Is it all in the same bank? We'll throw it into the pot and put you into bankruptcy. The authorities will claim everything of value that you have. If you've got a Rolex somewhere, hide it well."

"Is this really necessary?" Hank asked. "Can't we work something out? The amount of money we're talking about is chump change for guys like you."

"It's necessary," said Paul. Whatever sense of brotherhood or friendship he had felt for Hank was now gone. He despised the man, was disgusted by his friend's lack of personal responsibility. Normally nonviolent, he wanted to hit Hank, pound him in the face. "Just come back here at nine tomorrow morning."

"Whatever you say." Hank shrugged and left the suite.

Paul woke up at dawn the next day. He had weird dreams all night about friends, lovers, drunks and lies. He decided to call South Bay in a couple of hours, and he assumed that everything was all right back home. Hank knocked on his hotel room door at about eight, and looked as if he had spent the entire night running a marathon. He had brought a handful of safety deposit keys from banks in Las Vegas.

Paul, Josh and Hank went to see a lawyer Josh knew, and the attorney drew up the appropriate forms for Josh to act as Paul's legal representative. Josh agreed to remain in Las Vegas to sort through Hank's mess. They went to all of Hank's banks and emptied his safe deposit boxes. They counted the money and signed receipts saying that they had received these sums from Paul Hankwosky. Ultimately the money would end up in a newly created account in both Paul and Josh's names. The total from all the boxes was just under nine hundred thousand dollars. Paul and Josh didn't ask him how he had gotten the money. They just knew it was theirs for the time being.

The business with Hank had used up much of the morning. Paul had made arrangements to fly from Las Vegas to Washington, D.C. to meet with Senator Kay Roth about passing some laws that would benefit Cherry. He'd told her how much he enjoyed her speech at People's University; now, because of who he was, and what he had accomplished, and the fact that he had accomplished it in her state, he could get in to see her whenever he needed her help. So he would stay at one of the big hotels and go to see Senator Roth, ostensibly as one public servant conferring with another. But he would talk to her about what she could do to make life just a little bit easier and better for Cherry Computer.

On the flight from Las Vegas to Washington, Paul asked himself why he hadn't simply sent Josh Hawkins down to Las Vegas to sort out matters with Hank. Josh was Hank's friend and had been his best man, but the two had never had the same rapport that Paul and Hank did. Ironically, their confrontation in Las Vegas had been more painful for Hank because of Paul's presence. Certainly, Paul simply could have called Josh and sent him down alone, and Josh would have been resolved the matter with characteristic efficiency. So why didn't Paul let Josh handle it alone? Because Paul would have considered himself a wimp for doing such a thing, and he couldn't stand the thought of wimping out.

After the mess with Hank was over, Paul thought he might put Hank to work, pay him, give him some sort of pension that nobody else needed to know about. Enough to keep him going indefinitely. Would Hank accept the help from Paul, after all the bad blood that had passed between them? Did he have a choice?

The captain announced that they were about to descend into Washington. Paul put away his paperwork and buckled his seat belt. One crisis resolved; what about the next one, and the one after that?

When he entered the hotel's lobby, he remembered his cell phone was off, so he switched it back on. He tried to call his office in South Bay. Busy. He did not especially want to talk to anyone there, he just wanted to stay in Washington for a day, see Senator Roth and give her some very specific advice about how she and the other senators could help Cherry sell products in the United States. He also wanted her to know how the senators could make it harder for Japanese companies like Sony and Panasonic to sell their products in America. Had Senator Roth ever heard of "chip dumping"? Well, the Japs were doing it to the Yanks, and that wasn't cool. After his meeting with Roth, he wanted to fly back to South Bay deal with whatever awaited him there.

He tried South Bay once more and his secretary answered.

"I've been trying to reach you, Mr. Mayor. You've got to come back here immediately. The occupiers have set up tents and they say they're prepared to stay there indefinitely. Then they started marching over to your home and holding a demonstration there. Mrs. Steeves has been quite shaken up by it."

"I'm on my way back. You can give me the details when I get there."

Click. Paul's meeting with Senator Roth would have to happen another time.

Kennedy was paunchy, old and asthmatic. A longtime police officer, he didn't look able to bust a jaywalker. He was closing in on retirement age and worked as Mayor Steeves' driver. Paul looked forward to Kennedy's retirement, whenever that happened.

"Worst thing in this world," Kennedy was saying between labored breaths, "is to be a cop in a college town where they have everything: whites, coloreds, Jews, Arabs, queers, dykes. All those smartassed kids who think they're being discriminated against. Nothing but trouble."

"Quiet," Paul muttered. He didn't like to have his employees use offensive language, and he didn't like how slowly Kennedy drove.

"I'm just tellin' you how it is. Segregation was a good thing. They never should have put the races together, especially a bunch of young people. Kids got no respect for anyone in the first place, not even the police. You know, you can get on the horn to the governor and get the National Guard. Those guys know how to handle troublemakers."

"Maybe."

"I'm serious, sir. This is an occupation we have here on campus. Civil disobedience. They're just getting started. Better get the Guard in here so they can take care of business."

"Remember Kent State?" Paul asked.

"Well, those little snots had it coming. You gotta use a little muscle to keep these college kids in line. You gotta show them who's boss. If you had been at your home last night, you would understand where I'm coming from."

"I heard about it."

"Well, it was worse than you heard. They all know where you live, and a bunch of them went to your home and started calling you every filthy name they could think of. Boys and girls, you understand. And the girls were dirtier than the boys. Then your missus opened the door."

"Why did she do that?" Paul asked.

"They were yelling things at your home and your wife opened the door to tell them to go away. They said, 'Tell that cocksucker to come out. We want to talk to him.' So she yelled back at them."

"I guess they didn't take her altogether seriously."

"No, sir. Especially when she was drunk and naked."

Paul said nothing. He just stared straight ahead.

"Another thing, sir. I guess you know this, because of your high-tech success and all, but everyone now has a Camcorder or whatever the hell you want to call it. Lots of those kids were recording the events of last night, and plenty of them got footage of Mrs. Steeves in her birthday suit. I'm afraid it's all over the Internet now."

When Kennedy and Paul arrived at People's University, Central Quad was so lit up with emergency floodlights that Paul had to shield his eyes. He saw a handful of police officers standing around as if wondering what to do. South Bay, a small city, had a small police force. Paul wanted to hire more cops but his aides told him there was no money for that.

He found Ed Lee, South Bay's police chief.

"Troubled times, Paul," the chief said. "You may want to handle this aggressively. As you can see, they've set up camp." Then, "Those punks were out of line," the chief muttered. "I guess you know all about their visit to your home. The troublemakers saw this occupation here and got their nerve up to go to your place."

Paul sighed. "Naked and drunk."

The chief shrugged. "We finally got there and chased them off. Made a few arrests. But not before they did what they wanted to do."

As he became more visible in the people occupying Central Quad, Paul heard laughter and turned around to see some students in university sweatshirts pointing at him. King Shit had arrived.

"I knew you were on your way, so I waited till you had a chance to see what was going on before we actually did anything," said Chief Lee. "If you want, I can call in the National Guard and have those kids out by midnight."

Paul ignored him. "You take them out yourself. Call the CHP if you need help. I won't have any tent cities on my campus." The sight of his naked, drunken wife acting out on computer screens worldwide played in his mind's eye like an obscene waking nightmare.

"You want us to use force?"

"Yes. Handcuff them and put them in wagons. Before this shit ends up on the news."

"I'll need an order straight from you," said Lee.

"I just gave you one."

"A *written* order, sir."

"Give me a piece of paper."

Chief Lee handed him a small notebook, and Paul scribbled an order. Lee pocketed it and spoke into his radio. His men began to drag the squatters away as others loudly protested but did not physically resist them.

It ended soon. All ended up in patrol vehicles that took them to the city jail. Just then another car arrived and from it emerged Robert Brett, president of the college.

"What happened here?" He looked at the trampled-upon grass and dismantled tents. He went up to Paul. "Is this your doing?"

Paul nodded.

The president shook his head. "Why did you have them forcibly removed?" Then, "You've been a huge disappointment as mayor. You're away on personal business as often as not. I'm going to suggest a recall tomorrow publicly. Read all about it." He glared at Paul. "Get out of here."

"I'll drive you home," said Kennedy.

Paul got into the car. His only words during the drive to his South Bay mansion were barely audible: "I hate this freakin' job."

Chapter 6

2000

He was back at Los Angeles International Airport, but this time without Paul to meet him. He didn't call Dee because he knew she and Paul both had enough on their minds and he didn't want them worrying about him and his shaky extremities. The same with Bernadette and Ford; he'd hidden his problems well, so far, keeping his back to them both most of the time.

The tremors had gotten worse, and it embarrassed him when his hands shook, though they didn't shake badly. He got a cab to a hotel and then went to see the doctor.

On board the *Maria* he had noticed the tremors, and a local doctor had given him the bad news: Parkinson's, just like Muhammad Ali. The pugilist's syndrome. He had contacted Mr. Lovejoy and asked for the name of a neurologist. He had an appointment with the doctor and when he went in the man said, "You'll need brain surgery. Sounds much worse than it is. Just a simple procedure." Jamey went into the hospital and soon afterwards was discharged. He was okay for now. He went back to his hotel and called Dee, who still lived in the house she had shared with Jackson.

"Hey, sis!" he said on the phone.

"Jamey?" She sounded more shocked than surprised. "Are you calling from Honolulu?"

"Nope. I'm here in Los Angeles. Mind if I come see you?"

She laughed with delight. "Get over here! Do you know the way? Should I come get you?"

"Naw. I'll get a cab."

He went outside and hailed a taxi. He arrived at Dee's place and she was standing outside in the driveway, smiling and waving. She was wearing a white blouse, denim skirt and pumps, like a Gap model.

"God, Jamey, it's been forever!" She took him into her arms. Then she released him and looked him up and down. "You sure you're okay?"

He shrugged. "Take me inside, give me a Bud and I'll tell you all about it."

Inside, she fetched two cans of beer and joined her brother on the sofa. "So...?"

"I've been here for several days. I got Parkinson's. Brain surgery. Lost the ability to speak in complete sentences."

She laughed. "Well, as long as the surgery made everything all right. You sure have lost weight."

"I'll gain it all back, I promise." Then he said, if only to change the subject, "Where's Caitlin? You said she was out of school, living with some guy..."

"Oh, Paul fixed that. He got her a job as the entertainment reporter at some English-language magazine in Paris. After all her bluster about rejecting everything in life, she's happy. Hope she stays busy for a while."

"Was she going to the West Bank?"

"Yes. Just a lot of noise, I guess." Dee paused. "Paul resigned as mayor of South Bay."

Jamey nodded. "Yeah, they had some kind of occupation and he ended it by having the cops take everyone away."

"Everyone around him was trying to talk him into running for the senate or even president."

Jamey raised an eyebrow. "But no more?"

"No more. He's in semi-retirement for now. They sold that mansion in South Bay and got a cute little place in San Francisco. Marni is still trying to get her shit together."

"Well," Jamey said, "I need a huge favor from him when he isn't reeling from his personal issues. I need a speedy divorce from Honey. See, Bernadette—the woman I live with—is pregnant and I want to get all this legal stuff with Honey resolved before the baby comes along."

"You don't need Paul for that. We all use the same private eye here, and he's quite good at fixing things. I can take care of that stuff for you. I'll have him call Honey and talk to her about this matter."

They left it at that. Later that week, Dee called Jamey and said, "Good news. Honey is in Las Vegas now and has agreed fully with your terms."

"How the hell did *that* happen?"

"Money talks, brother," Dee said.

"Hope you didn't bribe her too generously."

"Just enough."

Dee had given such instructions to their lawyer, who contacted Honey in Los Angeles and asked her how much it would take to get her to grant Jamey his divorce. Honey had asked for "some of those Cherry millions" until the lawyer assured her that they were Paul's millions, not Jamey's, and that Jamey was just a humble cruise operator. Honey received a cash payment, enough to cover a decade and a Las Vegas condo. Reluctantly she agreed, mainly because the lawyer assured her that Jamey wanted the divorce but didn't need it, and if her demands were outrageous she wouldn't get a damned thing from anyone named Steeves.

"That's terrific. Just incredible," Jamey was saying to Dee over the phone. "Bernadette and I can get married and everything's gonna work out. Look, why don't you come to our Honolulu wedding in June? Paul and Marni, too. We can have a reunion."

"I would love it. I'll check and see if Paul and Marni can make it."

They hung up and Jamey sat there for the longest time, smiling like a fool.

The mayor of Honolulu performed the wedding on board the *Maria*. Jamey and Bernadette were dressed in nautical blue, he in a dazzling blue suit with a crisp white shirt and burgundy tie, she in a silk dress. Behind him, Ford was dressed the same as his father. Paul and Marni sat with Larry, who seemed quite uninterested in the goings on. Everyone was brown from weeks of being lazy under the South Pacific sun.

Dee was there alone, regal and magnificent in her white dress, tanned like the others, slim and voluptuous, her pulled-back blonde hair slowly turning gray. Paul looked at her with admiration. Middle age becomes you.

The mayor read the ceremony with a delightful Polynesian accent. Paul thought back to his recently ended days as mayor of South Bay. *He* hadn't married anyone and was suddenly envious of this mayor who was doing exactly that. Did this mayor have to look after a computer company on the side or deal with squatters on college campuses?

At first, Paul, who had married Marni mainly for her physical beauty, felt disappointed in Bernadette, who despite wide blue eyes and blonde hair somehow had a Plain Jane quality that turned him off. But after seeing the devotion she had for Jamey and Ford, Paul was ashamed of himself for thinking so little of her and told Jamey he had made an excellent choice.

After the ceremony they ate and toasted each other. Paul reminded himself that the last wedding he had attended was Paul Hankowsky's. He had danced with Suzi Bayliss and felt her grind against him. She had threatened to make him her love slave. This time, there was no dancing.

They spent the rest of the trip on board the *Maria*. The plan was to sail around the Pacific, the way Jamey and Bernadette preferred. But Everett and Ford wouldn't let the couple go anywhere near the controls, they just sat on deck and enjoyed the day.

Within minutes of leaving the harbor they were away from land and surrounded by deep blue water and a priceless South Pacific sky. "What an unbelievable place," Paul said.

Jamey nodded. "Beats the hell out of Western Hills."

Paul and Dee sat on deck chairs on the *Maria,* gazing out into the blueness everywhere. They both sipped bottled water and shivered a bit in the brisk breeze. "Now admit it," Dee said. "It was a great idea, coming here."

Paul nodded and smiled. "There has to be more to life than computers and politics. And we're all here, too. Not really a reunion, but still..."

"And because of Jamey, who swore us off for life all those years ago."

"Did you notice at the wedding," Paul said, "the love everyone has for him? By the way, how's Caitlin?"

Dee sighed. "Caitlin's no happier overseas than she was here. She laughs at everyone there and makes no effort to get along. She practically brags about the losers she takes home and the dope she smokes. When I visited her in Paris, she went on about Douglas and me. 'You're as pathetic as I am. You're a middle-aged fading beauty. You had one good man and your Establishment couldn't cope with him, so they killed him. So you fuck up your life and then go to the shrink so he'll give you meds and make everything okay. Until you own up to the hypocrite that you are, we don't have anything to say to each other.'

"She wants to change her name to Steeves so she can forget about being Tommy Wilhite's daughter. She really pisses me off sometimes."

"Welcome to the world of parenting. I guess my kid will call me things worse than that when he gets old enough." He couldn't help then looking at big, handsome Ford, hair blowing and steering the ship like an expert. "You never know how they'll turn out. Jamey's kid was raised by that goddamn Honey, with a pug for a papa. Gets into military school and beats up everyone till Jamey pulls him out of there and puts him on board the *Maria,* among a worse bunch of characters than you'll find in the boxing clubs. Lives with his father and the pregnant girlfriend. So what happens? The kid becomes a gentleman. Go figure.

"You think Jamey's got a bottle of something stashed on board? It's cocktail hour, you know."

"I thought you said the rehab counselors told Marni she can't drink."

"She's Marni. I'm Paul, you're Dee. She's asleep, we're awake. I'll ask the kid."

He went into the cabin and said to Ford, "Your dad got a bottle around here? We're getting cold on deck and need something nice and warm."

The boy shrugged. "Have to ask Everett."

Paul went over to where Everett and Bernadette stood. "Jamey got any booze?"

"I thought Marni couldn't drink," Bernadette said.

"Well, she can't and she won't. But Dee and I will."

Bernadette shot him a dirty look, then reached up into one of the cupboards and withdrew a bottle of vodka. "There's some orange juice in the refrigerator, too. Cheers."

"Thanks." He grabbed the plastic container of orange juice and the bottle of vodka and quickly mixed the drinks. He brought them out to Dee.

She took hers and sipped. "Screwdriver. Yuck."

Paul laughed. "Oh, well. At least if Marni gets up, she'll think we're drinking straight juice."

"This is what Douglas likes to drink."

"How you two gettin' on?"

"Like an old married couple. He and Caitlin hated each other, so things have been quieter lately. But I'm an old bag of forty now, so I try to be happy with what I have."

Just then Marni appeared, in jeans cutoffs and a red T-shirt. She came over to Paul and pecked him on the cheek. "Screwdrivers? And you didn't invite me?"

Paul made a face. So much for being sneaky. "Do you want a sip?"

Marni shook her head.

"I'm glad," he said.

Everett came out and set the table for dinner, as quick and deft as a four-star restaurant buser. They always did things up nice and fancy, Paul observed. Jamey and his little crew here had a very stylish life, with their suntans and windblown hair and trim bodies. It had taken Paul time and trouble to get to the gym often enough to reduce his love handles, and he still was not nearly as tight as these people.

Just then there was an awful thump that made the *Maria* jump a bit. "No!" Ford shouted. "We hit something!"

Everett rushed to the wheel. "Yeah, we did. Not sure what. Coulda been anything, even a whale."

In a moment Jamey and Ford were also at the wheel. Ford said, "Sorry, Dad, I shoulda looked closer—"

Jamey patted his son on the back. "Forget it, son. Things happen. Look, let's just make sure everything's okay and head on back to Honolulu. Check the gauges and everything else."

So they did and announced that the *Maria,* no doubt partly because of her size, was largely unhurt and they cruised on back to Hawaii.

"Sorry, all, but our wanderings through the Pacific are over. Gonna cruise back home and do some looking down below to see what the problem is. Probably need some repair work done."

"Awww," Marni said. "Going back to Honolulu. What's there to amuse a girl back there?"

Jamey smirked. "Oh, I'm sure you'll think of something. Anyway, let's eat. Crises always whet my appetite."

By the time the *Maria* fairly struggled back into port, Honolulu was dark. No one cared about the big hobbled yacht except Jamey, Ford and Everett, who knew the damage was much worse than they had let on.

Jamey couldn't figure out what was making that awful noise. A flock of birds, maybe? In the darkness he could feel Bernadette's arms around him but that chirping and calling making him sweat.

He got up and put on his robe. What the hell were parrots and macaws, or whatever they were, doing outside the *Maria?*

But no. Oz stood there. He used such vocal signals whenever he needed to get someone's attention discreetly. Jamey tiptoed out of the cabin and scratched his head, thinking, This had better be awful damned important.

"Jamey," Oz whispered, his voice hoarse. "Bad news, bloke. You know where Paul's old lady is right now?"

"Marni? In bed with her old man."

Oz shook his head with vehemence. "Wrong. I just got back from Bath Street. She's there, and pissed out of her skull."

Jamey nearly laughed at how drunk Oz was too. "Shit, man, you're hallucinating. You wouldn't know her if she staggered into you on the street."

"Like fuck. She's a cutie, right? Black hair, big blue eyes, great knockers? I seen her at your wedding. Better pay attention to what I'm saying."

Bath Street. The one part of Honolulu that was filled with guys even meaner than Jamey had met back in Western Hills.

Oz nodded. "Drunk at a place called Aloha Bobby's. I wanted to take her back here but she told me, verbatim, to fuck off."

Jamey sighed. "Guess I better go get her, then, in time for her to wake up with her hubby."

Oz shook his head. "There's more to it than that, mate. She's talking a lot about your family, that she's Marni Steeves, that her old man's Paul Steeves, the rich computer guy. She even said her brother-in-law is B.J. Steeves, who fought Tyson."

Jamey muttered to himself.

"Oh, it gets worse than that. There's a guy with her in a tan linen suit. His name is Mako, or they call him that because he has a shark tattoo on his arm. He's a professional goon.

He got really interested in her when she mentioned you. Could be the wiseguys back in Vegas are still looking for you and he knows they've put a price on your head."

Jamey sighed. "Bath Street, here I come. Later, Oz."

"Don't you want any help? You know what that part of town is like, especially at night." Oz's voice suggested he would just as soon take a rain check on this one.

Jamey struck a boxing stance. "I went the distance with Mike Tyson, fella. I think I can deal with those drunken losers on Bath Street."

"Tyson was ages ago, Jamey. Long ago and far away. You're soft now. You've got a business, married with kids, a peace-loving man. You've lost your fighter's edge. Even made a gentleman of your son."

"I better get dressed and go to Bath Street."

"Sure you don't need some help?"

"No. You go to bed. I'll manage."

Oz shrugged and made his way unsteadily towards his own ship. Jamey looked up. It was a slightly cool evening, the kind he especially liked, and the sky was filled with sparkling stars. A huge white moon hung just above the harbor's water line. He would much rather have just enjoyed the evening for a few moments by himself and crawled back into bed with his wife. Let Marni take her chances with Mako. But no. Instead he went back into his cabin and gently woke Bernadette. "There's trouble. It's Marni. She's drunk on Bath Street."

Bernadette wiped the sleep from her eyes. "Take Paul with you."

"No. He fights like a girl." He kissed her forehead. "See you soon."

Jamey got a taxi on Ala Koa Boulevard, two blocks from the dock. "Take me to four-oh-five Bath Street."

"Bath Street? What for?" the driver asked.

"Just do it."

Only on Bath Street could Honolulu look ugly, Jamey thought as he paid the driver and stepped out of the taxi. The bars and hotels were as smelly and foul as anything in San Francisco or Los Angeles. Plenty of servicemen arrived to drink and get laid, and all kinds of other lowlife were here, too. Aloha Bobby's was the largest and seediest of the Bath Street hangouts, so it relieved Jamey just a bit when he entered the place and saw that Marni wasn't there.

Jamey ordered a Coors and said to the bartender, "I'm looking for a woman who was here earlier tonight. Medium height, black hair, big boobs..."

"Lots of people fit that description."

Jamey took out a fifty-dollar bill, folded it neatly and slipped it into the pocket of the man's gaudy aloha shirt. "Well...?"

The bartender leaned in closely, his voice not much above a whisper. "That lady has a big mouth. When the band took its break and it was quiet in here, she started blabbing that she's married to the Cherry Computer guy and how his brother was a boxer who now owns the *Maria*. Wanted to buy drinks for everyone for the rest for the rest of the night, but she had no money. Mako took her across the street, to the Love Affair."

Jamey rolled his eyes. "Thanks." He finished his beer quickly and headed across the street, to the Love Affair, which was no worse than Aloha Bobby's, just noisier.

Very few people were on the dance floor as the music played. Jamey saw the usual assortment of whores and hustlers. He went up to the bartender, handed him a fifty and simply asked, "Where's Mako?"

"With the drunk woman. In the back room."

Jamey headed in that direction, his heart pounding. He heard the sound of a woman screaming. He tried the back room's door but it was locked, so he kicked it open.

"Jamey! Help me!" Marni screamed. Either meeting Mako had sobered her up or Oz had exaggerated her drunkenness. She tried to free herself but Mako simply tightened his grip around her neck.

"What you looking at, Joe?" said Mako, a powerfully built man with a dark, pockmarked face.

"She's mine," said Jamey. "I've come to take her home."

"Fuck you Joe, she's mine tonight." Mako squeezed Marni's breast. Outside, the music started up again. Happy people were dancing.

Jamey walked slowly over to Mako. "Just give her up. She's mine. I'm taking her home."

"You want her, Joe? Then try to take her. I dare you." Next to Mako was a workbench. He reached down and came up with looked like a crowbar.

Fuck, Jamey thought. Here I go again.

"Help me, Jamey." Marni was whimpering.

"Leave now, Joe, or you're both dead," Mako said. He stepped towards Jamey and brandished the crowbar.

Jamey knew one thing: he had to make sure the crowbar didn't strike him on the head. If it did, it would be so long, Jamey. He took a step back, threw up his hands and said, "You win. I lose. I don't want any trouble." Then he charged at Mako, wrapping his arms around Mako's legs as the crowbar swung. It hit Jamey in the shoulder as he butted Mako in the groin. Jamey took him down in a football tackle, and Mako offered no resistance. Maybe he's out cold, Jamey thought. He looked up and saw Mako swing the crowbar again.

Jamey caught him by the wrist and, with his free hand, punched Mako in the face again and again. Mako loosened his grip on the crowbar and it slid away, and Jamey retrieved it. In a moment, both men had regained their footing, although Jamey's legs felt weaker than he could ever remember them being, and the whole left side of his body felt dead.

Jamey's head was full of noise. He could hear the music in the nightclub, his own heartbeat and Marni's screams. Or maybe they were his own screams.

Mako grinned at the sight of Jamey's crippled leg. Mako came at him and threw a roundhouse punch. Jamey raised the crowbar just in time to block the punch. Mako howled in pain and shook his hand in the air, trying to reduce the sting. Jamey reared back and threw his best right cross, catching Mako flush on the chin. Mako crumpled to his knees and Jamey crawled onto his chest. Jamey beat his torso and arms with the crowbar until Mako just lay there, limp. die, but let someone else do the honors.

"Let me live! Oh, please, don't kill me!" Mako's voice sounded like a child's squeal. Sweat streamed from his face.

This is your lucky day, pal, Jamey thought. If you had won this fight, what would have happened? You would have killed me, then raped and kidnapped Marni and extorted millions from Paul in return for her dead body. You wouldn't have given a shit about the lives you had ended or ruined. You deserve to die, and I hope someday soon someone will kill your worthless ass, but it ain't gonna be me.

Jamey put aside the crowbar and reared back, smashing Mako in the right eye with a punch so hard that it split the man's eye socket and induced instant unconsciousness.

"Marni!" Jamey called out. "Come here. I need help. I can't get up."

Marni, huddling in a corner with her hands holding up her torn dress, gave the smallest of nods and rose. She crept over to Jamey and, with much effort, hoisted him to his feet.

Both of his legs were wracked with pain, and he winced as he managed to step away from the damp, prostrate body of his opponent.

He felt worse than he had in a very long time. He had won the most important fight of his life, but there was no exhilaration or jubilation, just an awful dizziness and a desperate feeling to get back to the *Maria* and into Bernadette's arms. Marni helped him out into the nightclub, much as a trainer would assist an injured athlete off the playing field. Behind them, Mako lay motionless, his eyes already badly bruised, closed tightly and shining.

They walked past the dancers and cocktail waitresses, who paid them no attention. Jamey felt relieved when they made it out onto Bath Street and saw taxis lined up.

"Let's get in," he said. They both struggled into a cab. Marni huddled in a corner and bawled into her hands. Jamey felt sick and dizzy. He told the driver where to take them. His eyelids felt heavy, so he closed them for a moment. When he opened them, they were back at the port. Marni helped him out of the taxi and over to the *Maria.*

They took their time boarding the boat, but they made it.

"Go in there with your old man," Jamey said.

She squeezed his hand and said, "That's the last time I'll ever drink. I promise."

Yeah, right, he thought. "Sleep well."

Marni scampered off towards her cabin. Jamey grimaced as he took baby steps towards his own. The lights were on and Bernadette sat on the bed. She gasped at the sight of him.

Jamey shushed her.

She raised her eyebrows, as if requesting an explanation.

"The other guy's a bit banged up, too. I got her out of there, just barely." Gingerly, he sat down beside her. "Get me a doc. I'm hurt real bad."

Jamey woke up to the sounds of Everett and Ford hard at work. At first he wanted to go out there and help them, but it hurt just to breathe, so he stayed put and stared at the ceiling for a few minutes. As much as Jamey ached, the doctor said he had no broken bones and mostly just needed to take it easy and let his body heal. So he lay there, listening to the kitchen noises as Bernadette made breakfast, and he thought back to other fights, and other opponents, and other mornings full of aches, pains, bumps and bruises. Even Tyson hadn't worked him over this badly, Jamey thought. He sighed and began the ordeal of getting dressed. He moved slowly and grimaced often, and made a point of not looking at his battered body. But he knew he needed to comb his hair, so when he looked in the mirror, his face, swollen and bluish as it was, did not shock him so much. He had been punched out before. He only hoped the others wouldn't make such a big deal out of it, and that little Jason wouldn't freak out when he saw Uncle Jamey's puffy lips and nose.

Deeming himself presentable, he made his way into the kitchen and said to Bernadette, "Good morning, sunshine." After the doctor had checked him out and essentially told her that the beating looked worse than it actually was, Bernadette settled down and was now back to her usual, calm self. Before going to sleep, Jamey told her, in much detail, what had happened. He saw the disgust on her face each time he said Marni's name. Despite her good manners, Bernadette was not by nature a forgiving person, and would be frosty towards Marni for a very long time.

Bernadette smiled at him the way a nurse might smile at a patient.

"I guess nobody knows anything yet," he said.

"I'm sure you're right."

"I would like to tell everyone that I had a relapse," he said. "I want to tell them that I got drunk, went to Bath Street and got into a fight. But," he added, "I have a feeling that no one would believe me."

"Ford and Everett have been underwater for most of this morning," she said. "They've been checking on the damage to the yacht. They aren't really saying anything, but I have a feeling it's quite bad."

Jamey nodded. "Yeah, she's pretty banged up, too. Several days to a couple of weeks."

They went over to the breakfast table with the coffee and orange juice. Everett and Ford were already there. Everett said, "Damn, Jamey, what the hell happened to you? She beatin' up on you already?" Ford just said, "Dad!"

"I guess you folks want a few questions answered," Jamey said. "Let's wait till everyone is here and I'll tell you what's going on."

Paul emerged, holding Jason by the hand. Jamey could tell by the grave look on his brother's face that Marni had told him, more or less, what had happened. Jason looked up at him and said, "Uncle Jim, you don't look so good today."

Jamey smiled and patted him on the head. "I've had better days, little man."

"Marni's not feeling so great, either," Paul said, sounding sheepish. "So she'll be up when she feels like it. I'll bring her some orange juice and coffee once breakfast is over."

They took their seats, and finally Dee appeared. She frowed at Jamey and said, "Jamey, you look the way you did when you were a kid looking for trouble. You wanna talk about this, guy?"

Jamey chuckled in spite of himself and said, "Yes, I'm prepared to talk about it." Then he went into some bullshit story about waiting till Bernadette was asleep, then sneaking out to Bath Street and picking a fight. "We were both so drunk that we didn't feel the punches we were throwing at each other. I'll bet he's having a hard time this morning, too."

There, he thought. Boom. Done. If you don't believe a word of what I've just told you, good. But that's my story and I'm sticking to it.

"Well." Dee sighed and looked around. "I'm hungry. 'I Got Drunk on My Wedding Night and Started a Fight' stories always whet my appetite. Let's dig in."

"Let's," Bernadette said, and they all ate.

Paul and Jamey were alone together in the rear of the Maria. Bernadette and Dee had gone to do some shopping and taken Jason with them. Everett and Ford were again under water, trying to figure out how to repair the boat by themselves.

"Thank you, Jamey," Paul said. "I don't know what else I can say. Marni told me what happened."

"You're welcome." Jamey shrugged, wishing his brother would shut up about it. But Paul had plenty to say and had no one to say it to but Jamey.

"Her drinking." Paul shook his head in disgust. "It just gets worse, and our lifestyle. Is there anyone alive named Steeves who doesn't abuse alcohol? So she told me that, as a photographer, she is always looking for new places to shoot, and Bath Street looked like the ideal place, so why not go out there at midnight and have a look around? Can you believe how naïve she is?"

"She was fucking *drunk*, brother. That's why she did that. She is an alcoholic. She has a bad problem."

"Oh, I know she does—"

"*Do* you? Do you honestly know that?"

Paul waved him off. At that moment was not interested in being lectured by Jamey about how Marni needed to be back in a treatment program immediately. "Look, here's what she told me about last night. She was checking things out on Bath Street when this nice foreign guy in a fancy suit says he's a photographer, too, and he can show her the best places in Bath Street. Whenever she's ready to come back here, he will drive her himself."

"A nice foreign guy in a fancy suit," Jamey said. He thought of Mako, who would surely have killed Jamey and made a whore of Marni or kidnaped her. Mako would recover from his beating and go back to being a nice foreign guy who befriended women on Bath Street.

"I can't imagine what possessed her to do those things last night. I can't imagine any of it," Paul said.

"It's ancient history," Jamey said. "It's better just to forget about it."

Paul snarled. "Don't patronize me, Jamey. Why didn't you wake me up when you decided to go down there? I'm her husband. It was my business, too. More than yours."

"Paul"—Jamey paused and tried to think of the right words to say—"she was at a strip joint on Bath Street in the middle of the night. Rough characters, you know? The kind of people I've been around for most of my life. You're a thinker and a businessman, not a fighter. That Mako guy was bad news. He nearly kicked *my* ass." Then, "Like I said, it's over with and we have to face today's challenges right now. Let's find out if Everett and Ford can fix this yacht." Jamey walked away, expecting Paul to follow him but not especially caring whether he did or not.

He sat on the *Maria* and gazed out into the darkening sky. Bernadette was off somewhere, and the others had all gone to investigate the island of Oahu. They were still assessing the damage the *Maria* had sustained and Jamey knew that the replacement parts would take a little while to arrive and some more time to install, but he was content to just take it easy indefinitely, mostly because he still didn't feel well enough to take on a new charter and look after paying customers properly. Marni was slinking around, ashamed of herself. Dee took her shopping each day to the Louis Vuitton or Versace boutique, where she could always find something nice that would make her smile for a few minutes. They naturally invited Jamey along on their sightseeing day, but he declined. He insisted that they take Everett and Ford, who had listened to his Bath Street story with dubious frowns and probably already were collaborating on some harebrained scheme to confront Mako. Well, he thought, to hell with that nonsense. He looked forward to when Paul, Marni, Jason and Dee left and that whole ugly business with Mako started to fade away.

All around him, things were quiet and dark. The air was warm and Jamey's body had started to heal. He was in great physical condition, which would make him heal that much faster. He hadn't made love to Bernadette since his fight with Mako, but he was starting to feel like a man again, and that old romantic nip stirring down below made him smile. He would make Bernadette smile, too, in a night or two.

Jamey was thinking about his wife and sex when he saw the sleek dark car driving along the harbor. It stopped and three men got out. He thought he recognized one. Mako. He had a large bandage over his left eye.

Jamey stood there, considering his options. He didn't have many. He could dive into the water, but they would just come on board and shoot up the *Maria*, then find Bernadette and shoot her, too. There was nothing for him to do but stand there and see what happened.

"Are you Jamey Steeves?" one of them asked.

"Who wants to know?" he answered.

Then everything went dark.

Jamey woke up once. He tried to focus his eyes and mouth a few words. Then he gave up and closed his eyes. Paul called South Bay and arranged to have a top neurologist fly to Hawaii to check on Jamey. But while the doctor was on the flight to the island, the patient died. There had been too much trauma to the head and body, the doctor explained.

Paul moved Dee, Marni and Jason to a Waikiki hotel. Dee's job was to keep a suicide watch on Marni. Paul had contacted the police and told them everything he knew. They tried to question Marni, but she just kept bursting into tears and so they finally gave up. They questioned Mako, too, but couldn't hold him for longer than twenty-four hours and no one would be willing to testify against him.

Paul and Dee had Jamey cremated in Honolulu and personally collected his ashes. Then they took a taxi to the harbor, where Bernadette, Ford and Everett awaited them. Marni was at the hotel. She told Paul she couldn't face Bernadette, couldn't stand by the woman's side on the *Maria*. Paul agreed. Marni would probably stay drunk in the hotel room for the entire day.

In the taxi, Paul explained everything to Dee. He answered all of her questions about why Jamey had gone to Bath Street to rescue Marni.

"Jamey," Dee said as the taxi inched its way to the yacht. "He was the only one of us who found himself."

"And look what happened to him."

"Don't blame yourself for this. He chose to get involved."

They both stayed silent until they arrived at the *Maria*. Bernadette, Everett and Ford were already there. Bernadette seemed mournful but dry-eyed, stoical. Everett and Ford both wiped at tears streaming from their faces. Paul came on board carrying the small box containing his brother's ashes and Dee trailed him. Everett started the engine, Ford removed the gangplank, threw off the stern lines and hopped over to help Bernadette.

Paul watched them, thinking that they all did their jobs so automatically and effortlessly. Jamey had trained them well.

The gleaming yacht made its way out into the open water. Everyone remained silent, for there was nothing to say and the five people on board had decided in advance what they wanted to do. They went out just far enough for the coastline to disappear, so that they would have the illusion of being in the middle of nowhere.

Everett cut the engine and there was silence. Nobody could hear the lapping of waves. Everett took the box and gave it to Ford, who opened it and stood at the front of the boat. Paul took a handful of ashes, dumped it into the water and stepped aside. Dee did the same thing, as did Bernadette and Everett. Ford got the last handful and watched the remains of his father dissolve into the blue water. Ford then went into the pilot house and revved up the engine to begin the brief trip back to port.

Bernadette blew her husband a final kiss and disappeared into the cabin. She passed by Paul and Dee, who stood silent and ashen faced.

Everett stood in the bow, feeling the gentle breeze on his face. He looked up at the marvelous blue sky. *The closest thing to paradise*, Jamey had said.

ABOUT THE AUTHOR

George Onstot was born in San Francisco but has lived near Vancouver for a number of years. After working at many pointless occupations while writing on weekends and evenings, he decided to stop toiling for a living and start writing full time. His previously published novels are *Bullies on Juice* and *Macho Fellows*, both of which are set in the world of Canadian sports.

www.ingramcontent.com/pod-product-compliance
Lightning Source LLC
Chambersburg PA
CBHW080722020726
47503CB00010B/2750